Joshua Spiller writes prose fiction and comic books.
He can currently be reached at joshua.spiller@gmail.com.
The 8th Emotion is his first novel.

"Not fantasy so much as post-science Science Fiction, not a
game of thrones so much as a game of misunderstood antique
recliners, Josh Spiller's striking debut shows us Utopia dwindled
to an underfunded sink estate and threatened by the discovery of
a devastating new colour in the spectrum of the heart. *The 8th
Emotion* marks the emergence of a fascinating fresh voice in the
field, and I urge you to feel it as soon as is possible."

Alan Moore

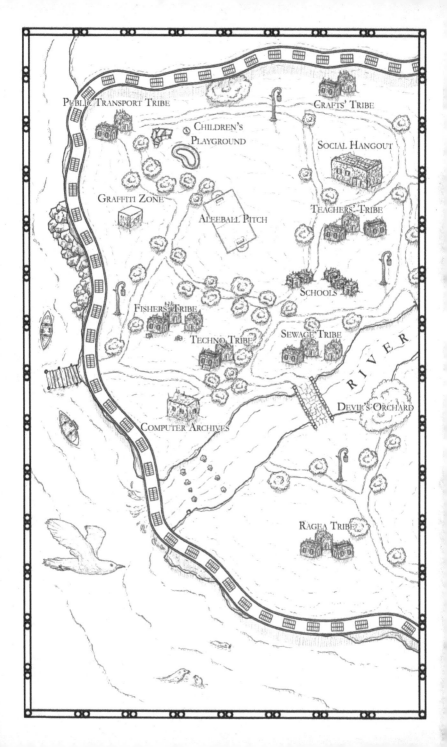

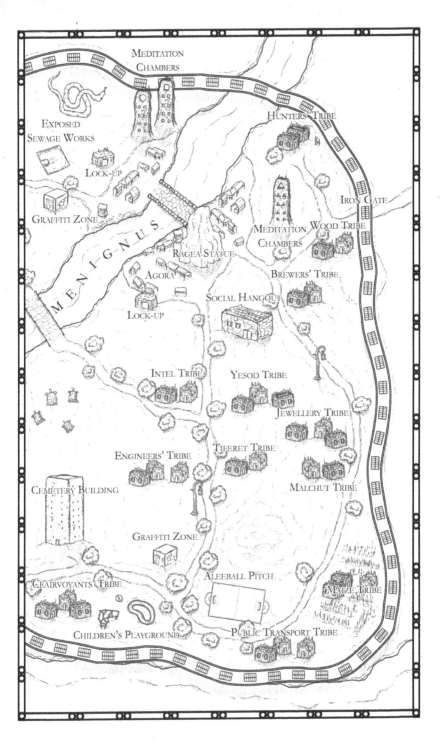

JOSHUA SPILLER

THE 8TH EMOTION

SPLENDOUR PUBLISHING

A CIP catalogue record for this title is available
from the British Library

ISBN 978-1-999-63440-7

Typeset in Minion 10.5 pt by
Daniel Knight, Born Group, Pentonville Road, London
Cover design by Niámh Keenan, Joe Tabrizi, and Born Group
Splendour Publishing logo design by Joe Tabrizi
Printed and bound in Great Britain by
Clays Ltd, Elcograf S.p.A

Emotion (n.): origin, 16th century – "a (social) moving, stirring, agitation"

Act I

Chapter 1

Within the Wall was a World...

A World where, as they played amongst its disorganised sprawl of tribes, the laughter of Karthalian children filled the air.

Where the River Menignus, which divided that World in two like a wavy, watery spine, gurgled peacefully.

A World surrounded on one side by sparkling sea, and on the other by dead inland.

Within the Wall, there lay a utopia, where joy reigned supreme. At least, that's what most of its people thought.

Hauled by twenty-five muscle-bound horses, a strasmag travelled down a wide dirt road.

Sunlight filtered through the carriage's shell of curving stained glass, becoming diffused along the vehicle's wooden base and flooding its interior with dim shades of every colour of the rainbow.

But on its journey, the light also passed through various glycons: symbolic images, one fashioned upon each pane of glass, each representing a particular tribe in Karthalia. Collected together like this on Karthalia's main form of transport, they were meant to reflect that land's general sense of unity.

Sat near the back of the strasmag was Martin, his head drooping forward as if it were too heavy for his neck, his eyes barely able to stay open. He'd just finished playing a game of aleeball in the afternoon heat, and he felt exhausted.

Nonetheless, a sense of duty nagged at him. And so one of his pupils' Permaculture textbooks lay open on his lap, as he tried to review her work for that week. But the series of horizontal, dark green strips of light, which rolled rhythmically down the book's pages as the strasmag rolled down an avenue of trees, only lulled him further towards sleep.

Determinedly, he blinked his eyes open.

Concentrate, he told himself. *Focus.*

On the first page, near the top-left corner, the pupil had jotted down – presumably for her own pleasure – her location in the universe, starting from a local point of view and moving up through to the cosmic. The ink-marks read:

Karthalia
Exanthus
Earth
The solar system
The Unive—

Oh, I can't be bothered, Martin thought, his sense of duty having puttered out after only seven-and-a-half words. He closed the textbook and, with tired arms, returned it to his woollen satchel, which he tucked back under the bench he was sat on.

Beneath his sandy-coloured shorts, which were covered with fresh mud and grass stains, his legs ached. Sighing, he wriggled into a more comfortable position, then let his head loll to one side, welcoming the sweet sense of relaxation.

But through his half-drooping eyelids, he couldn't help peering at the man who sat next to him. Jak's posture was erect and stiffly upright, like a child sitting to attention in a classroom. His unusually pale white face – long, thin, and with high pronounced cheekbones that almost made him look gaunt – was set in a serious, thoughtful expression. Through narrowed eyes, he was studying the sights that lay beyond the strasmag's coloured glass, scrutinising them like a man memorising the pieces of a puzzle.

What's wrong with him now? Martin wondered, as his own thoughts began to blur and drift towards sleep.

For the last month or so, his friend had regularly been in dark moods, withdrawing into himself and muttering his concern about the direction Karthalia was heading in. The Ragea tribe – he'd said, cryptically and solemnly – were a danger to society. Martin had told him that was nonsense, but his words didn't seem to dent Jak's rigid, mysterious belief.

The fact was, the Ragea were just like any other tribe in Karthalia. Jak had simply developed some sort of weird vendetta against them, probably because his sister's boyfriend – who he didn't like – was working for them. Like Martin had said: it was nonsense.

Yet all of that had been bubbling away for a while. But today, Jak had been in a particularly abstracted and solemn mood. And Martin had noticed that the skin beneath his friend's eyes was dark and baggy, as if he'd spent most of last night awake with some sort of worry.

So much stress, Martin thought sleepily, *all based on nothing. I need to do something to snap him out of it...*

But for now, that could wait. Turning his gaze away from Jak, Martin looked blearily ahead down the strasmag. Then slowly, so that the passengers, the benches, and the strasmag's prism of rainbow lights all melted into each other, Martin let his eyes fall shut.

From within his new private darkness, he heard the familiar sounds of strasmag chatter... felt the Mediterranean heat pressing in upon his face... and a moment later, a gentle lurch as the strasmag came to a stop, followed by the rhythmic, soothing noise of donkey hooves crossing the road ahead...

"Hey!"

Martin eyes snapped open, and he froze in momentary panic. That shout – so loud and furious – had come from right beside him. Then there was a *bang bang banging* noise, and another shout:

"Stop them!"

Martin looked to his right. Jak was on his feet, hammering his fist against the window.

"Stop them!"

For a split-second, Martin was terrified that Jak had gone mad – that all of his stress had somehow exploded outwards in an unexpected and horrifying way. But then he noticed, through a large teardrop-shaped pane of dark blue glass, what Jak was staring at...

Another strasmag had pulled up beside theirs at a fork in the road, its body angled down the opposite path. Both vehicles had been brought to a halt by the herd of crossing donkeys. But at first, Martin couldn't see anything wrong. All he noticed was that, within its shadows and dim rainbow light, the other strasmag was only half full, its passengers scattered sparsely across its various benches.

Then he realised that all those people were frozen still, their bodies twisted round to look at something, something near the back of the strasmag—

And then he spotted what it was.

In the vehicle's rear, standing in its central aisle, was a circle of roughly seven shadowy female figures, gathered close together. Although they were basically silhouettes, Martin could tell that they were all wearing balaclavas by the way that their faces were pitch-black against the shadows around them, and the way that any long hair they had, if it was visible, emerged suddenly at neck level, as though until then it had been pressed tightly against their skin. Judging by their figures, they were a group of teenage girls, probably around fourteen years old. And two of them, facing the rest of the strasmag, had in their hands the dull silver glint of knives, pointed as if they were holding the rest of the passengers at bay.

The other teenage girls were all focused on whatever was in the middle of their circle. Over the benches of the opposite strasmag, Martin could only see the upper parts of their bodies, where their arms and torsos kept jerking and twisting in strange, sharp, spasmodic movements. Any sounds that might have helped him work out what was going on were swallowed by the thick glass walls of the two strasmags. But it quickly became obvious what they were doing. They were kicking, viciously, whatever lay in their midst.

With a growing sense of horror, Martin bent forward in his seat, and pushing down his head so that it was near floor level, he squinted through the two intervening walls of coloured glass, peering beneath the benches of the other strasmag – between any legs that were in his way – towards the back of the vehicle.

There, he glimpsed the vague outline of a shadow curled up in pain, its body convulsing with the rhythm of the kicks... and a slender feminine arm futilely covering its face.

By now, the carriage he was on was roaring with the noise of people on their feet, banging their fists against the glass like Jak, and shouting and screaming for the passengers on the other carriage to *do something. To help that girl.* Everything about him felt mad and confused. And amongst this frenzy of noise, Martin pushed his head down towards his knees. Then, pressing his palms against the side of his head to block his ears, he tried desperately to make sense of what was happening.

On the other strasmag, those attacking girls were outnumbered by at least twice as many other passengers. And most of those passengers were adults. Together, they could definitely overpower those vicious girls. So why weren't they doing anything? Surely, even if getting involved was dangerous, they couldn't just sit and watch a young girl get battered to death?

And what about that strasmag's driver? Why weren't they intervening? But maybe they hadn't seen what was happening. Maybe the thick noise-cancelling glass, and the way their vehicle was angled away from the panicked and urgent faces on Martin's strasmag, meant they were still oblivious to it. Was that even possible? And Jak's hammering fist seemed to be growing louder and louder, and the imagery of those kicks kept playing over and over in Martin's head, and it felt harder and harder to think.

And then it hit him, sudden and loud like the roar of a thundercrash. He knew what he had to do.

Springing to his feet, he raced towards the strasmag's exit, the pounding adrenaline in his heart barely allowing him to gasp for breath. If the people on the other strasmag weren't going to save that girl, then he'd have to do it.

For a terrifying moment, his panicked, shaking hands fumbled with the handle of the strasmag's wooden door. But then, fingers clasping it, he threw back the door and dashed outside.

He ran as fast as he could, his leather sandals pounding against the dusty road. His adrenalised legs, aching moments ago, now felt like they had the energy to run for miles. The exit on his strasmag had faced away from the girls' one, so he had to get round to the other side of his vehicle.

Come on...

Behind him, he heard a small stampede of runners following in his wake, other people who had had the same idea as him. The rapid drumming of their feet only heightened the sense of urgency and desperation coursing through his veins.

Come on...

He careened around one corner to the front of his strasmag, then around the final corner, just in time to witness plumes of trailing dust. He ground to a halt.

The other strasmag was speeding away, moving too fast for him to catch up with. And as he watched it go, one thought, filled with a sense of loss, resounded throughout his mind. *He'd failed her. He'd failed her, and there was nothing he could do about it.*

A few moments later, Martin stood at the tail end of a queue of sombre people who were reboarding his strasmag.

"Hey. Chou sar?" the driver called, standing up in his perch. He was addressing everyone in the queue, and his face wore a mixture of confusion and concern.

Martin didn't even look up. He didn't have the heart to explain what had just happened. He felt stupefied and numb, as if he were half drunk on arak. And in his mind, he kept imagining himself, later that day, hearing news of the girl's death.

Back inside the strasmag, a solemn hush filled the air, punctuated with a smattering of whispered, horrified conversations. Martin walked through them, back towards his seat.

As he approached it, Jak turned from the window to look at him. The expression on his friend's ashen face was frightening. With a look of barely restrained rage, Jak was almost snarling, his top lip curled up and twitching, while his green eyes burned with a dark look of scorn and fury. But it didn't feel like his anger was directed at Martin. Instead, it felt like his friend was glaring with hatred at the universe and its unfairness. Then Jak turned away, and went back to staring out the window.

But in that brief glance at Martin, Jak's eyes had also had another quality... as if, behind the fury, he were wrapped up in deep, agitated thought.

The strasmag set off, its colourful lights rippling on and off once more as it passed down another avenue of trees. Almost as if they'd never stopped. As if the assault had never happened. But in Martin's mind, those horrific moments were playing over and over again, in vivid and raw detail.

He thought of how his Mum had died giving birth to him, and how his emotions – whenever he thought about losing her – resembled what he was feeling right now. It was the painful revelation that, fundamentally, the World was a dark, cruel, and capricious place. The good things in life were just flimsy decoration, easily ripped away in the space of the briefest moment, to reveal the darkness that lay beneath.

That realisation, experienced again with full force, felt almost like a betrayal... as if he'd managed to put his trust in the World again, only for it to use that trust to hurt him all the more deeply.

"How could the people on that strasmag not help her?" he muttered, turning to Jak. He needed to talk about what had happened, to vent, to get some perspective on it. "There were more of them. They could've stopped those girls, and they just..."

He paused, trying to find the right words.

"Is that... is that how little people care about each other? That they'll actually *watch* a girl get beaten to death, as long as it means they don't get hurt themselves?"

Jak had shifted his gaze away from the window, but he wasn't looking at Martin. Instead, he was staring down at the floor. Martin waited for his response, for Jak to offer him some sort of help.

Still gazing downwards, Jak replied, his voice flat and emotionally detached: "It's not their fault. Violence is so rare these days, most people go through their whole lives without ever really experiencing it. So you can't blame them for being terrified when they finally do.

"No, the thing that has to be dealt with here is the Ragea. They're the ones who did this."

Martin stared at Jak, dumbstruck. He knew his friend was obsessive, but this...

"Jak – *wake up*," Martin said. "There's nothing wrong with the Ragea. This is all in your—"

"*Fine*," Jak cut in dismissively. "Don't believe me."

There was the half-beat of a pause. Then Jak spoke again, but this time much more quietly.

"The point is," he said, "I recently found something out..."

Then, leaning in to Martin's ear, he whispered:

"A way we can end *all* violence forever."

Chapter 2

With a steady rhythm, the chisel shattered off pieces of stone, its noise resounding through the gloom:

Clang. Clang.

As he worked away at the gigantic block of limestone, sweat slid down Amik's aquiline nose, to be soaked up in the black hair of his thick, bristly beard.

Clang. Clang.

A nearby solar light illuminated the bulging veins in his massive, muscly arms. The elation of eight hours' sustained hard labour coursed through him. At times like this, he knew the truth with crystal clarity: this was what he was made for.

Clang.

But now, his arms felt like dead weights, the build-up of lactic acid having transformed his blood into something like lead. Breathing heavily, he dropped them to his side, then laid his chisel and hammer upon the wooden platform on which he stood.

What time was it? Having been lost in the rhythms of his work, he had no idea. Squinting upwards, he gazed at the small circle of light that hung just a few metres above him, the only proper opening in the immense, forty-foot curtains that concealed his massive project. Judging by the shade of the light, it must already be evening. Time was passing quickly.

Soon, this statue – the largest in Karthalia's history – would be unveiled to the World.

From below him, he heard the labour of his fellow engineers, the ringing metallic cacophony of chisels and stone rising up to his ears. Of the several tiers of construction, Amik was alone at the top. The carving of the statue's face was his personal project. And he was devoting himself to it, utterly, to make sure it was the crowning achievement of his life.

But he needed a brief rest, a break from that gloom and its reek of sweat. Pulling back a flap of the heavy curtain, which had grown dirtier and dirtier over the last few weeks, Amik stepped out onto the external section of the scaffolding. As the curtain fell shut, the noise of clanging tools and workers' shouts faded dramatically, as if it had somehow raced away into the distance.

Standing in the grey light of a cloudy evening, Amik ran his fingers through his black, slicked-back hair, clearing out the chalky dust in it and revealing the large and prominent forehead beneath. The delicate evening breeze cooled his warm skin.

From far below, he could hear the faint commotion and clamour of people milling about the agora, as they inspected the various wooden stalls, checking what goods and services were available today. This was Karthalia's hub, the noisy centre of its bartering, money-free economy. It was also where the Ragea had chosen to site their incredibly expensive statue.

When completed, the statue would loom over the agora's market stalls, which were arranged in a neat crescent, with the River Menignus flowing by in a perfect curve just behind their backs. Feeling a sense of pleasure, Amik imagined that each stall would look like a kneeling worshipper at his statue's feet.

After the Cemetery Building and the three Meditation Chambers, this project would be – by far – the tallest edifice in Karthalia, towering over the bungalows that made up most of Karthalia's building work. And strangely, it was going to be a dead man who gazed over the World; a man who had died seven months ago: Sanif Ragea.

Sanif had been a member of the Ragea Tribe, back when they'd had their old name, before they'd rechristened themselves in his honour. That the Ragea had chosen Amik to head up this almost sacred project, essentially putting him in charge of his own clan, the Engineers' Tribe, was a fact his pride still continued to savour.

Then at that moment, he spotted something that improved his mood even more.

From amongst the hubbub of people strolling across the agora's paving stones, or sat on the edges of its ornate meditation-fountains, Amik's keen eyes picked out someone he recognised: a tall, thin, pale man, with a smaller and slightly stockier friend walking at his side.

The smaller man had acne-ridden cheeks (visible even at this distance), and a bizarre, long haircut with intricate patterns shaved across his head. Amik had met this person only once, a few months ago, but his razor-sharp memory immediately recalled that the man's name was Martin. Both he and Jak walked in silence, neither man looking at the other.

Quietly, Amik smirked to himself. He knew that Jak disliked him; Jak had made that perfectly clear. So Amik saw any chance to rile him up as fair game. Considering how uptight and highly-strung Jak was, like some sort of walking raw nerve... how could Amik resist?

Leaning across the platform's wooden rail, Amik cupped his hands over his mouth and shouted:

"'Riah!"

Jak froze mid-step, and he and his friend looked up at Amik. Their expressions, by their intensity, surprised Amik. Jak looked stern and angry, while Martin – startled out of his reverie – appeared confused and almost vulnerable. Amik wondered what had happened between them.

The two men stood within the scaffolding's shadow.

"Chou? What d'you want?" Jak shouted back, instantly snapping at Amik.

Almost imperceptibly, Amik's large, powerful hands clenched the railing he was holding. He felt a thrill of rage shoot through him. How dare *anyone* talk to him like that? He'd always hated rudeness, especially when it was unprovoked. He'd barely even said anything to Jak yet.

Fortunately, he had the perfect ready-made response:

"Just thought I'd let you know," Amik said, "next dimanche, me and Laura are celebrating the completion of this statue. Don't know if she mentioned it, but we're holding the party at yours."

The expression on Jak's face instantly darkened.

"Hope that's alright," Amik added. Then, as the coup de grâce to prevent Jak's protests: "I know it's short notice, but Laura is looking forward to it."

Amik let a smirk creep openly across his face, just to annoy Jak all the more. He felt like an eagle taunting its grounded prey.

"Is everything alright?" a sweet, familiar voice suddenly interjected, coming from nearby.

Amik turned to his left. Laura was standing a few feet away from him, a look of concern and worry on her face.

Amik had already known she was on-site: she'd spent her lunch with him, before going off to chat with his fellow engineers, and give them some slices of the lemon cake she'd baked with her mum (truth be told, it wasn't the tastiest thing in the World. But Amik knew the other engineers liked her too much to do anything other than smile and compliment her on it). The scaffolding's main ladder lay on the other side of the circular platform that Amik was stood on, behind the statue's concealed head. Laura must have only just climbed up it, and caught the tail end of his conversation with Jak.

One look at her expression, and Amik knew what she was thinking: were he and Jak antagonising each other again, even after she'd pleaded with both of them, separately, to try and get along? Would she have to live with this conflict between her brother and her boyfriend for the rest of her life?

Not wanting to distress her, Amik quickly and smoothly erased the mocking smirk from his face.

"Hi honey," he smiled, walking over and giving her a quick kiss on the cheek.

Unlike Jak's strangely pale skin, hers was olive, the usual colour in Karthalia. And her thick, beachy hair – dark, but streaked with blonde highlights from sun exposure – was worn in a style Amik had never seen on anyone else. Stretching back diagonally over each shoulder, her parted shoulder-length hair – a tangled mess of loose waves – hovered in mid-air, as if swept back and stiffened by the sea breeze. It was cute, arty, and unique. Just like her.

Gazing into her light green eyes and wearing a look of heartfelt honesty, Amik replied to her question: "Of course. Everything's fine."

He glanced down, and raising his voice so that her brother could hear as well, he said:

"I was just telling Jak about our party this dimanche."

Those words were like a magic spell. Suddenly, Laura's worry vanished, and her usual happy smile lit up her face. Leaning over the railing with an endearing, almost childlike excitement, she shouted:

"Oh yeah! Is that alright? Sorry, I meant to ask, it's just that it's such a special occasion and—"

"It's *fine*," Jak interrupted. Although he was trying to be civil, Amik could still hear the sharp edge of frustration in Jak's voice. But apparently, in Laura's happy World, such dark emotions didn't make it through...

"Great! Thanks!" she called back. "Oh, and don't worry. I'll make sure you enjoy this one, I promise."

She beamed at Amik with a look of success. In that fleeting, everyday moment, it struck Amik again how sweet, how innocent and radiant her smile was. It reminded him how much he loved her.

So what if Jak doesn't like me because I'm working for the Ragea? he thought. *I don't care about that. What matters to me is Laura. It's just a pity that Jak happens to be her brother.*

"Oh wait," Laura shouted to Jak. "Are you going home now?"

"Yeah," Jak said, his voice still flat, heavy, and tinged with annoyance.

"Perfect. I'll come with you."

Laura turned to face Amik: "Right, I'd better head off. I wanted to start writing a new song this evening, so I might as well do that now before you come round."

"Sure," Amik said with a small smile. Laura's lifestyle seemed so simple, so full of goodness, that he somehow found it amusing. "Love you," he said.

"Love you too."

They hugged and kissed, and then Laura hurried round to the ladder on the scaffolding's opposite side. Glancing over her shoulder at him, she smiled one last time before disappearing out of sight.

She's so wonderful, he thought. *I am lucky to be with her.*

Then, looking down, he noticed Jak again, and imagined how much simpler things would be without him. If only life were like a piece of stone, from which he could chip away certain parts, and leave only the bits he liked. If only.

Far below, he saw Laura join Jak and Martin. She gave him a happy, enthusiastic wave goodbye, before the three of them set off for the stone bridge, stepping out of the scaffolding's shadow and leaving it behind.

To Amik, what lay within the curtains and scaffolding was something glorious waiting to hatch. But to Jak, he knew it was something... repulsive, seeded at the heart of Karthalia. Just one of the many differences that separated them...

With Laura gone, Amik turned his attention back to the grey sky. He sensed rain approaching, and pictured its patient, millennial task of erosional crafting, shaping Nature's cliffs and mountains into new forms, leaving a legacy that could last for aeons. It was a great, epic sculptor – a force he needed to channel and emulate.

Disappearing back behind the curtain, he rejoined the orchestra of clanging tools, every strike dragging the Ragea's statue design further out of idea space, and deeper into reality.

Chapter 3

With dead, expressionless eyes, Martin stared over the wall of the bridge.

He stared at the eel as it held its position there in the dark river, twisting its head from side to side, seemingly without purpose. He stared at its mindless, beady eyes. Its idiotically slack-jawed mouth. There wasn't even a glimmer of intelligence in that creature's face... no hint of meaning in its existence...

And in Martin's mind, that strasmag kept speeding away from him, disappearing behind its plumes of dust... and destroying any chance he had of helping that girl. The grim hopelessness of that memory was eating away at him.

What if humans are just like this eel? he thought. *Repeating the same mindless patterns of behaviour over and over, except our patterns are violent ones. We see the behaviour of animals for what it is: basically stupid, and almost totally predetermined by genetics... but maybe we're blind to seeing these same traits in ourselves.*

If that were true, civilisation was an insubstantial thing. Everything in it could fall away, as so much of it had done in the past.

Take the agora they'd just come from: Martin couldn't imagine life without its noisy bartering, and its pungent aroma of fresh seafood, sweet fruits, and raw meat. But centuries ago, people had felt the same about paper money, and about police forces. Both had seemed like essential elements of life.

And both were gone in the blink of History's eye: the first, after 1500 years; the second after a mere 300. There was no reason why all the good in Karthalia – all its accomplishments, and all its progress towards a better humanity – couldn't be swept away just like them.

Sickened by his depression, Martin tore his gaze away from that dismal eel, along with the other eels, bass, and mullet that were swimming around it, and trudged apathetically after Jak and Laura.

After crossing the bridge, the three of them walked in silence, through the half of the agora that lay on the opposite side of the river. And still without speaking, they headed down one of the pedestrianised dirt paths that lay beyond it.

Finally, and from an obvious sense of discomfort, Laura broke the silence:

"Are you two alright?" she asked in a cautious, tactful voice. "You haven't had an argument, have you?"

"No," Martin replied sullenly.

"Then what's happened? Come on, tell me. Maybe I can help."

But Martin didn't want to talk. He wanted to stay withdrawn, to converse only with his own thoughts. Glancing at Jak, he urged his friend to answer the question for him. For a moment, there was a look of resistance in Jak's eyes. Then his stern and grave expression gave way somewhat, and he turned to face Laura:

"Alright," he said. "I'll explain."

As they carried on walking, Jak told Laura what they'd witnessed on their journey home. Martin tuned their conversation out. He didn't want to hear that story again.

Instead, he gazed idly at the flowerbeds that flanked their path. They contained a variety of bright, colourful flowers, but one predominated over all others: the vibrant Karthalian violet. It was a flower that this land had been famous for, long before Karthalia existed.

Martin watched the violets and other flowers shift their bodies with excruciating slowness, so slow their movements were barely visible. Some were twining their stems around each other; others peeling back or furling their delicate buds; others simply repositioning their leaves at different angles. It all amounted to the same thing: they were *talking* to each other. Speaking in the strange, sluggish, and basic corporovisual language they'd only developed in the past hundred years.

Martin felt a scant sense of consolation. There, at least – unlike with the braindead eel – was some form of progress.

"That's horrible," Laura said, after Jak had finished recounting what had happened. "Do you think her tribe will catch them?"

"Hnaravor e," Jak replied. "But even if they do, the problem is bigger than that. Karthalia was founded to be a place where everyone would be equal. That was the *whole point* of it. No more hierarchies, no more violence. Capitalism was dead, so this was the next step forward.

"And for three hundred years, *it's worked.* But can't you feel it changing? Look at this attack – that never would have happened in the past. Look at the Ragea. They're building that huge statue to themselves, which your *boyfriend* is helping with. It goes against everything Karthalia was mea—"

"Jak," Laura butted in. "*Please.* Can we not have this argument again? What happened to that girl on the strasmag was terrible. But this thing you have against the Ragea – it's ridiculous. I don't know *anyone* else who has a problem with the statue. So please, for my sake... can you just let it go?"

Jak looked away from her, deliberately avoiding her gaze.

Even them, Martin thought. *I don't know anyone closer than those two, and yet even their love can turn into bitterness and resentment. Nothing good is permanent.*

"Fine," Jak finally muttered.

"Thank you," Laura said. "Sorry. I just... I don't want to go over all that again."

She gave him a small but loving smile, as if trying to lift his spirits. Then, with a teasing look in her eye, she said:

"Y'know, sometimes I think there's a different reason why you don't like the Ragea. That really, you only make them out to be the villains... because you never grew out of wanting to play the hero."

She grinned at him cheekily, daring him to rise to the bait.

But Jak simply stared at her, then bowed his head and shook it. "La," he muttered. "It's not that."

The three of them were coming up to a small building, which lay on the grass just off to the left of the path. The building was only big enough to contain one small room, but it had no doors or windows, just an exterior of solid stone. It was one of Karthalia's "art walls".

Images had been spray-painted all over it, mostly in monochrome grey. They bled in and out of each other, the older work gradually being buried beneath the newer work that was applied on top of it. The only contrast in this art wall's general drabness were several tiny golden ovals, also spray-painted on, which looked like a shower of heavenly manna tumbling from black and invisible clouds. Instead, they were a romantic depiction of antibiotics, the life-saving miracle which had been lost to humanity for centuries.

But it wasn't that gilded image, or any of the other spray paintings, that stopped Martin in his tracks...

"Hey – what's that?" he called, bringing Jak and Laura to a halt ahead of him. Both looked round at him quizzically, and in that moment of seeing their heads side by side, he was struck by their physical resemblance – something in the bone structure of their faces. It was only a trivial insight, but it hit Martin with a strange, sudden clarity.

Brushing it out of his mind, he pointed towards the nearest side of the art wall.

Over part of someone's bleak, morbid spray paintings of extinct species – creatures that had been half-based on fact, and half mythically reimagined – had been pasted several identical posters. Each poster showed a sketch of a man with glasses, who had a small round head that tapered sharply into a narrow chin, and a prominent forehead that seemed to take up a third of that small head, and which was creased by years of deep stress-lines.

Printed above the drawing, in large, thin letters, were four words: WANTED BY THE RAGEA. And directly beneath the image, it read: REWARD: TWO WEEKS OF MEAT. There was more information towards the bottom of the page, but it was in smaller type, and Martin was too far away to read it.

Along with him, Laura and Jak stared at it.

After a short pause, Laura replied to Martin's question: "I don't know," she said, sounding uninterested. Then, obviously realising what the involvement of the 'Ragea' might set off, she tensed up: "If you say one word..." she said to Jak.

But Jak didn't respond. He seemed distant. Then finally he spoke, addressing Martin: "No. For a moment, I thought I recognised the guy. But I've got no idea."

Jak sniffed, wrinkling his nose in disgust.

"Urgh," he said. "What's that?"

He looked around. Nearby, some underground irrigation works were being repaired. A large, square area of earth had been dug out from the ground, exposing a subterranean tunnel which was leaking the stench of excrement, urine, and waste into the air.

"C'mon. Let's go," Jak said, and he began to walk off. Laura followed him, and hesitating, Martin did the same.

It was like he used that smell as a distraction, Martin thought, *to stop us talking about those posters.* Concern pricked him. He'd known Jak long enough to sense when his friend was hiding something. He decided to ask about it again later, when the two of them were alone.

During the rest of the walk, Martin considered Jak's hope of ending all violence. It seemed impossible. Martin's Dad taught Civil Brutality classes, which involved a great deal of history on warfare and societal violence in general. Thus, growing up, Martin had learnt all about humanity's masochistic love for its own destruction: had discovered that its packs of hunting animals, and its weapons, and ultimately its global wars, represented merely an evolution of ever-larger sacrifices upon its sacred altar of violence.

But Karthalia was meant to be the first real utopia; a post-civilisation where all those evil tendencies reached their historical end point. In fact, in his twenty-four years of being alive – and in all he knew of Karthalia's three-hundred-year-old history – Martin had never heard of any Karthalian resorting to physical violence to solve a problem. It was simply too taboo, its people indoctrinated at too young an age into a peaceful mindset of co-existence.

Clearly though, those darker instincts were creeping back in.

If it's in the eel's nature to be stupid, then maybe it's in humanity's nature to be violent, Martin thought. *Maybe we're chained to it by our genetics. And what can Jak know that will stop that?*

Suddenly, the cloudy grey heavens split apart, and a heavy rainfall plummeted into the World, drenching everything in sight.

"Come on!" Laura shrieked, covering the top of her head with her hands and laughing. "Let's run!"

Within a minute, the three of them were hurrying through the line of currant bushes that sketched out the border of the Teachers' Tribe. Dashing down his tribe's central lane, Martin saw parents hastily ushering their children indoors, into the trib-dwells which, with their rectilinear shapes completely covered with vertical gardens of grass and flowers, seemed to have sprouted naturally from the soil. Like the three of them, everyone else had been caught out by the rain while wearing their usual garb of T-shirts, shorts, and sandals.

Trailing behind Jak and Laura, Martin charged into the tribd-well that those two shared, into the rectangular gloom of its open front door.

Chapter 4

In a tribdwell situated in Karthalia, but beyond the boundary of any tribe – like some exiled building – Pavneet worked frantically.

Night-time candles glowed on his desk, while a cooking fire burned in the corner of his tribdwell's main room. The smell of acidic chemicals singed the warm air, emanating from the beaker of green liquid that sat on his desk.

Taking yet another sheet of paper, Pavneet scrawled more notes, his eyes – behind his brass-rimmed glasses – in a trance-like state. He wore a long, stained jacket which he used as a makeshift lab coat. Above his greying temples, his craggily lined forehead was furrowed in intense concentration. His World had contracted to the sheet of paper that lay before him, so much so that he hadn't noticed that Bastian, his sandy-coloured dog, was barking in agitation and fear.

Two strident door-knocks resounded through the room. Cowering, Bastian fell silent, before leaning forward and barking with even more aggression.

Pavneet, frozen still, stared over the rim of his glasses, at the front door that lay directly ahead of him. No one had knocked on that door in years. Cautiously, he rose from his wooden chair, and started to shuffle around his desk.

Then with frightening suddenness, something shattered loudly. Pavneet instinctively ducked, snapping his gaze in the direction of the noise. Any last dregs of his trance state were gone. The real World had come roaring in, flooding his alert mind with intense, vivid impressions. From beneath Bastian's deafening barking, he heard, with acute sensitivity, a dull and solid thud strike the floor-boards somewhere nearby. Then he saw that the single window in the left-hand wall was smashed open. And framed within its new jags of glass, which were like a jaw of predatory, vitreous teeth, a balaclavaed face stared back at Pavneet.

"Shut that dog up!" the balaclavaed man hissed. Then, with menacing slowness, he raised a lit candle into view. "Or we'll blaze this place to the ground."

In a state of shock, Pavneet whispered: *"Sh-shush boy. Shush."* Bastian fell silent.

"Good," the balaclavaed man said, and Pavneet could practically hear the smirk in his voice. "Now – open the door."

An enormous fear gripped Pavneet, rattling his heart in its gigantic grip. *Please*, he thought. *Oh please, don't let them hurt me...*

With a trembling hand, he unlocked the door, and pulled it towards him.

Two imposing men, balaclavaed like the one at the window, stood before him. One held a knife, its sharp point only an inch away from Pavneet's gut.

"Get inside," the man with the blade said. Within the holes of the man's balaclava, Pavneet saw tiny, gloating, vicious eyes. Silently, just enough to prod the flesh without cutting it, the man jabbed the knife into Pavneet's stomach.

"W-what do you want?" Pavneet mumbled, fearfully stepping backwards towards his desk. He couldn't believe a stranger was attacking him. Such a thing had been known to happen in other lands, in other times, but never in Karthalia. It was a peaceful place. "P-please. I'll give you anything."

"We already know that," the man carrying the blade said, speaking with a twisted and gleeful sense of power.

He forced Pavneet back into the chair by the desk. Half-collapsing into it, Pavneet rubbed Bastian's neck with trembling hands, as if he were trying to soothe his beloved companion, when it must have been obvious that it was simply a nervous expression of his own terror. Bastian growled, baring his teeth.

"E-easy, boy," Pavneet whispered. "*Shhh.*"

The other two intruders seemed subservient to the man with the blade. Both were now searching Pavneet's tribdwell, one rifling through the sheaves of pamphlets and notepaper which Pavneet, to get them out of his way, had piled up around the edges of the room; the other, taller one standing nearby, inspecting the notes in the drawers of Pavneet's desk. It was obvious that neither was finding what they were looking for.

The man carrying the blade spoke, still holding the knife just in front of Pavneet's chest: "You're not a liar, are you Pavneet?"

"N-no."

"So this is true?" 'Blade' withdrew from his pocket a scrunched-up piece of paper. He flattened it out on the top of the desk, before showing it to Pavneet. With a gut-wrenching sense of horror, Pavneet recognised it at once. The page had been ripped out from the last scientific pamphlet he'd written, published only a week ago.

The chain of reasoning Pavneet had expounded in the pamphlet flashed into his mind, fierce and white-hot like burning magnesium:

1. Single-celled organisms don't experience emotions, or if they do, they experience very little.
2. Humans evolved from single-celled organisms.
3. Humans experience emotions.

4. Thus, humans must have evolved emotions.

Then came the main part of Pavneet's article. He'd claimed that he knew how to unlock humanity's next emotion, so that it could become a permanent part of anyone who wanted it. What's more, he'd said that when everyone possessed it, it would end all human conflict, equalising everyone profoundly, and ushering in a true paradise.

For now, though – he'd ended his article – he needed to do more testing, to check that what he'd discovered was safe. But in the next pamphlet he released, he would explain how people could tap into this emotion for themselves.

This memory of what he'd written hit Pavneet with the force of a tempest, and then, following close behind, realisation stabbed through him: these men were searching for proof that he really could unlock this next emotion. Why? He had no idea. But if they found it, he knew they'd have no reason to keep him alive.

"I lied," Pavneet blurted. "I just did it to sell the next issue. I'm alone, my income, it's all through trading these pamph—"

Out of nowhere, Blade's knife-gripping fist smashed into Pavneet's cheek, knocking him into his desk and rattling the container of chemicals that sat on top of it. Bastian barked ferociously, but Pavneet retained his terrified, white-knuckled grip on the dog's collar. As he gasped from the blow, Pavneet could almost feel Blade grinning at him sadistically from behind his balaclava.

"Give me a reason to do that again," Blade said.

Then one of the other men came over to Blade, pointing at something on a piece of paper.

They've got it, Pavneet thought, a cold thrill of terror running though him, shifting the hyper-real present into even sharper focus. He felt upon his back the heat from the cooking fire in the corner. Saw the fire's light gleaming upon the knife, as if the blade

29

shone with its own golden, vicious soul. An inchoate, instinctual plan was forming in his mind.

With regret, he remembered how – on the day of his break-through – he had told himself that he would never again inflict any type of injury on another human being. A sort of premonitory sympathy pain shot through him: he understood the agony these men might be about to suffer. And there was something still worse...

He looked at Bastian with sorrow.

Blade stared at the piece of paper, his eyes widening in a look of quiet awe. All humour had dropped out of his voice: "So you really can do it."

And with that, Pavneet's decision was made.

With his right hand, he shoved Bastian forward and released the dog's collar. "Go!" he shouted, and Bastian leapt upon Blade, slobbering fangs barking and snapping. Spinning round, Pavneet snatched up the container of chemicals and threw it at the cooking fire. A blaze exploded upwards, blasting a wave of searing heat over Pavneet's face. Everything became confusion and clamour. Fire-tongues gobbled ravenously at floorboards and terracotta walls, vomiting black smoke. Pavneet bolted across the room, past the indistinct shapes of his attackers, through a haze of barking, swearing, and shouts. Leaping, he hauled himself up to the smashed-in window, his adrenaline making him oblivious to the jags of glass that were slicing open his forearms.

Then, through the whirlwind of smoke and shouts, there cut a sharp, canine yelp. For a moment, Pavneet froze. Tears brimmed in his eyes. Blood poured out of his arms. He wanted to look back, but he couldn't bring himself to do it. Struggling over the knives of glass that jutted up below him, he toppled out the window's other side, landing with a thump on the soil and vegetables below.

Gasping for breath, he hauled himself to his feet, and ran, tramp-ling vegetables, fruit, and grass, sprinting alongside the winding

River Menignus. The reek of sulphur burned in his nostrils, beneath a clear, starry sky.

Who were those men? Why were they after him? He didn't know. And that meant he couldn't trust anyone.

Still running, he tried to ignore his screaming desire to go back, even as tears ran down his cheeks. *Bastian...* It was Pavneet's fault. And it was too late for him to do anything about it.

And as he ran, Pavneet also imagined that gang of men, amongst the fiery confusion, enduring an emotion they'd never felt before... enduring Oceanos, as the flames ate through the scientific specimens stored in his bedroom, and released their psychotropic vapours into the air.

The door was locked, the curtains drawn. Two candles illuminated Jak's bedroom, one on the small bookcase, one on the reading desk next to his bed.

"... and yesterday morning," Jak said to Martin, "they found Pavneet's tribdwell burnt to the ground."

Jak had told Martin everything he knew: had told him about the pamphlet on Oceanos, and how this emotion was meant to deliver complete and everlasting peace, and how, shortly after the pamphlet was published, Pavneet had disappeared, his tribdwell destroyed. But that was all he knew. To him, most of what had happened to Pavneet on that fateful night was a mystery.

Still, today, he'd found out something important. After a short pause, he said:

"It was Pavneet's face on that 'Wanted' poster."

Chapter 5

Martin sat on the rumpled coverlet of Jak's single-bed. Gilt arabesques – meditation aids painted on the room's gloomily lit, terracotta walls – flickered in the candlelight, while the faint, sour scent of smoke curled through the air.

His skin still wet, he hugged himself in the dry clothes that Jak had given him to wear. They were too long and a bit too tight for him, and like many of Jak's clothes, they had holes in them, signs that Jak should have replaced them long ago. Still, they helped Martin to warm up.

But inside, he felt a chill. Jak – as he told Pavneet's story – had stood almost rooted to the spot, staring down at Martin and gesturing like some fervent orator, but with eyes that were remote and intense. As if, mentally, he was in some other place altogether.

"How did you find out about all of this?" Martin asked, his voice initially croaking because he'd been silent for so long.

"Tessalli told me," Jak replied, having also changed into dry clothes. "She thinks the theories in Pavneet's pamphlets aren't true. That they're crackpot ideas, sold only to those still interested in science."

"And are they?"

"Probably most of the time. But yesterday, I read twelve of Pavneet's pamphlets, all the ones that I could find. And the most recent one feels different to the rest. It feels true.

"The Ragea must have thought the same."

Something in the look of Jak's green eyes shifted, darkening slightly. He was back in the present, back in this room with Martin.

"For months," he said, "I've heard rumours of them behaving violently towards others: stealing people's goods; secretly growing their own power. But I haven't been able to prove it.

"But this... this is obvious. The Ragea were the ones who burnt down Pavneet's tribdwell, and that's why"—he pushed on, before Martin could object—"they've now put out such a large reward for him. They're *after* him. Because if Oceanos is real, and it will end all violence, then any power they've accumulated will be destroyed.

"Don't you see? *It all makes sense.*"

Jak's words and conviction hung in the air. Martin stared at his friend, someone he'd known for seventeen years. He didn't know what to say.

"I'll bet that group of girls on the strasmag today were from the Ragea," Jak continued, as if trying to reinforce his argument. "Just look at how their kids have been growing more violent in our classrooms. Hitting other children, getting into fights more often."

"So? Jak, some kids are just like that. It's *normal.*"

"No. This is different. It's as if, in the last few months, something's changed their whole tribe. But I don't know what."

A realisation slowly dawned on Martin: "So this is why you've been so moody lately. You've been thinking about all of this."

Jak behaved as if Martin hadn't said anything, his eyes focused intensely on the room's wooden floor.

"Stealing from others," he continued, "also explains how they can afford their statue. Otherwise, the sacrifices from their monthly budget would have to be huge. Would any tribe really make them, without some other source of valuables?"

"So have you told Laura about this? Et Amik alors? He's helping them build the statue. Do you think he knows what's going on?"

Jak looked away from Martin. "I haven't really told her anything. I've hinted that the Ragea are connected with some... dark things, but it's not something she wants to hear. You saw how she reacted earlier, when I brought up the statue – she doesn't want to talk about anything that might reflect badly on Amik. I wanted to wait until I had some proof she couldn't deny.

"And also, this could be dangerous information. I don't know how far the Ragea will go to keep what they're doing a secret. So I thought the less she knew, the better."

Oh great, Martin thought. *Don't worry about me then. Give me all the dangerous information you've got.*

In agitation, Jak began to pace across the room.

"Yesterday," he said, his voice filled with a stronger sense of purpose, "I learned about an emotion that can end violence. *Today*, we see an assault that shows how much that emotion is needed. And more than that, I'm already connected to Pavneet. When I was ten, he and my dad worked on a study of some plants together."

He stopped, turning to face Martin.

"*All of these things centre around me.* It's too much to be a coincidence." The shadows pooled across his gaunt pale face made him look almost sinister. A dangerous, revolutionary gleam blazed in his green eyes. "I'm meant to do something about this. *We're* meant to. It's destiny."

The silence returned, with Jak awaiting a response. Only the patter of rain could be heard.

Martin didn't know if what Jak believed was true, but he was unnerved. He knew Jak, knew that when his friend was in a zealous mood, nothing would dissuade him from his beliefs. And Martin realised he didn't have a choice.

Best to go along with it, he thought. *Keep Jak onside, and make sure he's alright.*

"Okay," Martin said. "I'll help."

The stern, expectant look on Jak's face broke into a small, sincere smile. Behind him, the still flame of the desk candle glowed, providing a small spot of resistance in a room filled with darkness.

"So," Martin said, half-sighing, "what do you want to do now? Denounce a whole tribe? That's a massive thing to do."

Jak's expression changed again, but this time into a look of tired frustration. "No. We don't have enough proof. So we have to find Pavneet. If he can show us how Oceanos works, we can cut their violence off at the source.

"But that's why I need your help. I can't figure out how to contact him."

Chapter 6

Pavneet hurried east, his body rustling through a large, golden field of wheat. The tip of the sun had just dawned above the Wall that circled Karthalia, its rays igniting the field into a large swathe of blazing yellow, with Pavneet's darker, more shadowy form forging its way through it.

His lab coat, dark blue trousers, and face were caked with dried mud, mostly on one side of him, from where he'd lain through the night in the poor cover of a shallow ditch. Terrified, he'd barely slept, if at all. But at least he'd formed a plan.

Come on, he thought. *Just let this turn out okay...*

As he strode clumsily through the tall stalks of wheat, the thought of the Maize Tribe's summer ritual flashed into his head. He pictured the way they would take a life-sized carving of their deity and, mimicking the cutting of healthy stalks at harvest, scythe off the deity's head. Another morbid image, to add to those that had preyed on his addled mind throughout his sleepless night.

It's all part of science's decline here, he thought with a sense of fatalism and depression. *Everyone thinks there's no more progress to be made. That we've already reached utopia. And so, as science has fallen, superstitions have risen up to take its place.*

Emerging from the dense field of wheat, he followed the curve of the Wall from a distance – the Wall that had been made to cut

Karthalia off from all outsiders, and shield the community that lay within. The Wall that was over one hundred feet tall, made of solid stone, and almost impregnable. The Wall that he was about to try and escape.

The dew-wet grass beneath his feet started to rise up into a hill. What he saw at the top of it could mean freedom, securing him the rest of his life. Exertion, anticipation, and anxiety heated his body, as he staggered upwards through the warming dawn air.

Just before the summit, he paused, and crouched down.

Take every precaution, he repeated to himself. *Don't let them catch you again.*

Slowly, through his glasses, he peered over the ridge.

He'd come for the only exit in Karthalia's Wall: the large, centuries-old Iron Gate, with its horizontal and vertical bars forming a tight latticework of rusting black metal, while the top of each vertical bar was fashioned into a curving and sinister arrowhead, meant to warn outsiders away.

As soon as Pavneet peered over the ridge, all his hope dissolved in the acid of what he saw.

Crimson hands of sunlight bathed the gate's dark, veiny iron in morning blood. And in front of this gory light stood two guards. Just from the look of them, Pavneet knew they were part of the same group that had assaulted him in his home. They had similarly intimidating physiques. And there was no other reason for them to be there, other than to stop him from escaping. Worse still, to be at the gate this early, they had to have been guarding it throughout the night.

Like the men in the balaclavas had been, they were also dressed completely in black. But it was daylight now, so they couldn't be wearing it for camouflage.

They're from the Ragea Tribe, Pavneet realised. *But why? Why are they after me?*

He ducked back beneath the crest of the hill, his heart hammering in his chest. There was no way out. Karthalia had become his prison.

He felt like the mouse he'd read about in an experiment when he was young. The mouse had been positioned at the centre of a maze, and at each of several exits had been placed a snake. Exposed to predatory hisses, the mouse scrambled for an escape, while the ring of serpents slowly, inexorably converged upon it.

Pavneet pictured the flailing mouse bloodily skewered on a snake fang. He'd long ago forgotten the point of the experiment, but never its grim conclusion.

Chapter 7

Jak growled: "Aargh! This is driving me mad!"

He and Martin were lying in a grove known as Devil's Orchard. Afternoon sunlight cascaded down between the overhanging boughs of the trees. The River Menignus wound silently nearby, and buzzing insects carved secret animal patterns through the warm air.

Despite its name, Devil's Orchard was a small forest. Maybe it had been an orchard at first, but that must have been a long time ago.

Jak glanced at Martin, who sat beside him.

"Right," Jak said firmly, trying to re-energise their conversation. "Let's go over it again."

He lowered his voice back into the tone they'd been using for most of their discussion – a hushed whisper: "Okay. Firstly, *she* is never at home. Secondly, no one knows where *she* is. And thirdly, I can't leave a message for *her*, in case someone *else* might see it."

Some of the 'else' stood nearby. They all wore black trousers and long-sleeved black tops, making it obvious what tribe they were from. The Ragea had started wearing these clothes several months ago, as their new "religious dress". They had never worn any sort of uniform before.

Their new religion also meant there were several of the Ragea in Devil's Orchard at any one time. But today, there seemed more of them than usual. Maybe it was something to do with Pavneet. *Stick to the plan,* Jak had whispered to Martin, reassuring him. As long as the two of them spoke in their pre-prepared and, admittedly, fairly ridiculous code, they should still be fine.

But they'd been there forty minutes, and they hadn't got one step closer to working out how to contact Pavneet...

Putting his hands to his face, Jak groaned, and flopped back onto the grass in defeat: "I just can't figure it out. Maybe it is impossible."

He pulled his hands away from his eyes, and stared up at the leaves as they gently wavered in the shimmering canopy above. A sense of disappointment filled him. He'd been thinking obsessively about this problem for two days, and failed to come up with an answer. It had been too much to expect Martin to just pluck a solution out of thin air.

Jak looked to his side. With an expression of calm and quiet thoughtfulness, Martin was absent-mindedly playing with a lilaxe, twisting its stem – with its dark green and purple leaves – around his forefinger. It was one of the only non-sentient plants in Karthalia. A couple of Ragea nearby were eyeing him suspiciously.

"They really piss me off," Jak muttered, nodding subtly towards the Ragea. "So what if the lilaxe is suddenly their "sacred plant"? That doesn't mean it's only theirs. And I don't see why worshipping it meant they had to start wearing long-sleeved clothe—"

"Wait a sec!" Martin said in a hushed voice. He paused, thinking something through. Then his face broke into a big smile. "You are going to love me for this," he said.

He beckoned, and Jak shuffled closer.

"You know what you said," Martin whispered, "about your dad and Pavneet doing a study together on plant language, right?"

Jak nodded eagerly. "Yeah."

"*So*. That's *it*. Pavneet knows plant language. That's a really rare thing. So if we look up that language, and write our message in it round Karthalia, I bet the Ragea won't understand it. They'll think it's just some pretty flower drawings. But Pavneet *will*."

After taking a second to process this, Jak grabbed Martin round the shoulders. It wasn't just the insects that were buzzing. "Yes! That's brilliant! We can graffiti it on buildings throughout Karthalia."

"Yea—" Martin's smile died mid-word. "Wait. What? Jak, I don't want to deface other people's homes."

"Well if you don't do it, I will," Jak said, his face alive with an irrepressible, almost maniacally confident grin. "Look, you know what's at stake here. And it's not like anyone's going to get hurt. Come on."

For a drawn-out moment, Martin hesitated, staring back into Jak's eyes. Jak held his gaze.

"Oh alright," Martin muttered. "But we've got to be *very* careful."

"We will be. Don't worry. This evening, we'll go to the Computer Archives, and look up the plant alphabet. Then we can start spreading the message tomorrow."

"Sure," Martin said. Then, after a pause: "Sure."

Glancing up at the sun's position, he added glumly: "We probably better head back now."

The two of them walked off to teach their afternoon classes.

Chapter 8

In the Ragea Tribe, within his tribdwell, Leo swallowed the last of his lilaxe, discarding its stem onto the floor. Then he walked towards his bedroom mirror, to watch the transformation of his flesh.

Framed by the ringlets of his shaggy, shoulder-length hair, his beady pale blue eyes stared back at him. He had a square, heavy-set face, and his nose – having obviously been broken at some point – was crooked to his left.

Standing topless, he scrutinised the small, pinkish scar that marked his tanned midriff, a cold fascination burning in his eyes. He could feel his heartbeat accelerating, feel the rush of adrenaline surging out from his chest and round his body, as the colours in his vision began to pulse, acquiring an almost psychedelic intensity.

Heightened alertness; fight or flight – this was the state his body was entering.

The scar on his midriff now lay caught within a web of veins that were bulging against his skin, like a map of intersecting rivers. They were visible all over his muscular torso, as if he'd been snared in some pale blue net that lay beneath his skin.

He closed his eyes, and inhaled.

He felt his muscles growing bigger and stronger, felt a sense of indomitable, physical power rising up within him. An instinctual, animal aggression flared up in his mind, turning his thoughts red and predatory. And finally, and most sweetly, he had the growing awareness that he was the universe's centre. The very reason for its existence.

He clenched his hands into fists.

So much power... he wanted to exert it on something, or someone... anyone...

But now wasn't the time. He put on a lighter and much cooler top, to replace the long-sleeved one he'd been wearing in public all day to hide his bulging blue veins. Then he made for the door.

But before he left, he glanced at the lilaxe stem that lay on the floor, now devoid of its leaves. *All that power*, he thought, *from one tiny plant found almost solely in Devil's Orchard... who could imagine it would be so important?*

Then, as he had done so often before, Leo headed towards the man who had inflicted his scar upon him, and who had broken his nose into its current crooked shape.

He crossed the Ragea Tribe, towards a tribdwell four times larger than those around it. Entering the building, he strolled down a long corridor, and knocked on the door at the far end. He had heard a voice speaking from the room inside.

"Yes," a second, more familiar voice shouted. It was a curt order for Leo to enter. He opened the door.

The room that appeared in front of Leo was nearly half the size of most people's entire homes. It was a bedroom of decadence. Beneath a marble mantlepiece, the luxury of a fireplace lay unlit in the room's corner. A new wooden floor, exquisitely smooth and polished, was gleaming to within an inch of perfection. And a small wooden plate, of fresh fruit and half-eaten baklava, sat on the bedside table.

But more than anything, the room was dominated by the counter-pane that lay draped across the grand double-bed: it was a gorgeous sultry flood of purple, the most expensive dye in Karthalia. To make it, murex molluscs had to be caught off Karthalia's coast, their shells smashed and the molluscs dried out, before salt water was added to their corpses to produce the colour purple. It was an incredibly time-consuming process, with only a tiny amount of dye procured from each shell. Leo could only imagine the hours and hours of toil that that counterpane represented.

The room's opulence was unlike any other room in Karthalia. Proof of the Ragea's ascendancy.

And amongst all of this exorbitantly expensive finery, hanging on a wall, was the Ragea's glycon, the image the tribe had chosen to symbolise itself. In stained glass, the glycon depicted a shadowed person of indeterminate sex lying prostrate on the ground, a sunray gashing open their back, as from the wound grew a lilaxe, its leaves on one side a poisoned purple colour, while the leaves on its other side were a dark, lush green. The image, its starkness, its solar-yellow glass at interplay with the rest of the piece's seductive darkness, exuded its own minor magnificence and potent magic.

The room's owner sat on the edge of the purple counterpane: a scrawny runt of a man, his thin shoulders hunched, his shaven head rocking in an intense, agitated fashion. His manner was like that of a caged animal.

Leo – with his towering height and broad, muscular frame – looked like he could have easily picked the scrawny man off the ground, and crushed the man's throat in his fist if he'd wanted to. Instead, he walked towards him, and bowed with the utmost deference.

Then he took a step back, so that he stood in line with Francis, the man he had initially heard from beyond the room's door. Looking at the intense, unblinking, and almost predatory eyes of both these other men, it was clear that they were dosed up on the lilaxe as well.

Suddenly, Leo started coughing, a dry hacking noise coming from the back of his throat. Burying his mouth in his fist, he choked the cough into silence, before clasping his hands behind him once more and regaining his composure. He could taste a thick, tarry smoke residue clogging up the back of his throat. A lingering leftover from two nights ago.

The mean, calculating eyes of the man perched on the edge of the bed studied Leo, dissecting him with the scalpels of his dark pupils. Then after a long, uncomfortable moment, Corin finally spoke, his voice toneless, emotionless, and cold: "So?"

Leo could still feel the lilaxe-blood throbbing through his temples. His voice came out stern and authoritative.

"There doesn't seem to be any danger. No one's seen Pavneet near Devil's Orchard. And it doesn't look like he's sent anyone on his behalf, either. We also checked out the Fishers' Tribe. They said they hadn't seen him, and I reckon they were telling the truth. Everyone still seems to hate him there. Even his ex-wife."

Corin had fixed his gaze upon the wooden floor, like a chess master staring with relentless eyes at a problem on the board. Clearly, he still thought this was a serious situation.

For his part, Leo just hadn't expected Oceanos to be real.

He remembered how the tide of that alien, overwhelming emotion had suddenly swept over him, almost drowning him in its madness. Oceanos... it had felt...

He clenched his jaw, trying not to let the unnaturally vivid memory of the experience affect him in front of his tribesmen. The worst part had been the shame and self-loathing he'd felt after he'd come back to his senses, at how he'd allowed his mind to be invaded, and at how quickly he'd surrendered his most important beliefs...

He focused on the blood pulsing in his temples, on that inner, martial drumbeat. The lilaxe: that was where his power lay, where his sense of self was strongest and most acute. He had to cling to that.

Vengefully, he imagined beating Pavneet to death for unleashing Oceanos upon him. Imagined breaking that man's bones with the force of his punches, snapping them one by one. With the strength the lilaxe endowed him with, that's exactly what he could do.

Corin was still staring at the floor with his obsessive, trance-like gaze, when Francis spoke up: "Ne t'en fais pas à propos de Pavneet. He's just one man. He doesn't threaten us."

Without lifting his head, Corin's agitated eyes flicked up in their sockets to fix upon Francis. Suddenly, Leo could hear the noise of Corin's breathing: it was shallow-sounding, with a steady, tightly controlled rhythm, like the snorting of some wild beast. For a long moment, Corin kept his gaze locked upon Francis.

(Out of the corner of his eye, Leo could see Francis almost squirming with regret over what he'd said.)

Then slowly, measuredly, Corin stood up, took a step to his left, and picked the glycon off the wall. He looked at it for just a second. Then he span round to face Francis, and smashed the glycon over his own bare skull. There was a brief spray of multicoloured glass, and a prolonged rattling noise as the shards rained down upon the gleaming floor.

"Does this look like a joke to you?" Corin screamed, his face contorted with a look of insanity. "Does it?!"

He was holding a large and sharp blade of stained glass in his hand, brandishing it violently. Blood trickled down his scalp and forehead in dark rivulets, like some sort of gory crown.

He strode purposefully towards Francis, who was frozen to the spot, his eyes wide with fear – strode so close that their bodies were almost touching. Craning back his head and leaning in to Francis' ear, Corin hissed: "Pavneet could cost us *everything*."

He gestured towards the opulent room, breathing his hot breath onto Francis' face. Of the two men, Francis was taller, stronger. He could have hit Corin. Instead, even while dosed up on the lilaxe, he just stood there and took Corin's cruelty.

"And don't you forget it," Corin said.

He leaned back from Francis' ear. "Haskatsar?"

"Yes," Francis replied, quickly and firmly.

"De gna... *durs korir!*"

Corin spoke as if he were straining not to rip the flesh from Francis' face. Spinning round, Francis half-marched and half-dashed out of the room.

Leo smirked. He'd had a small grin on his face throughout the whole dramatic scene. He wasn't scared. Being Corin's right-hand man, he'd seen him behave like this before. And more than that, he knew how to physically handle himself.

In fact, very little scared Leo. But Oceanos... that had frightened him to his core.

"You too," Corin snarled at Leo.

Leo turned to leave, Corin clearly having forgotten about whatever he'd requested him for.

"Wait," Corin said, when Leo was halfway to the door. "The girls on that strasmag. Were they punished?"

"Yes. And they're banned from using the lilaxe for a year. Maybe then they'll learn some self-control."

But, as he felt the power and hunger of the lilaxe surging within him, Leo could understand how those girls had succumbed to it.

He left.

After Leo left the room, several long seconds passed before there was the sound of the tribdwell's outer door being shut. Then Corin's shoulders sagged into a more relaxed position. He let out a sigh.

Due to the lilaxe he'd eaten, his heart was still thudding rapidly against his chest. Otherwise, everything else about him became noticeably calmer. He was alone. He could drop the fierce pretence, remove the costume of hunched, bestial posture and frenzied, paranoid eyes. There were no longer any Ragea present for him to intimidate.

He wiped his finger against one of the dark rivulets that had trickled down his forehead. The cost of his dramatic performance. Nonetheless, such outbursts were necessary. They kept his subordinates afraid of him, kept them doing what he wanted. And with the lilaxe boosting the strength, self-confidence, and lust for power of the Ragea, he needed that fear to keep them in check.

Rooting through his closely cropped brown hair, he began to pluck out the glass shrapnel embedded in his scalp.

Interlude

18th Jan, 2--- A.D.

THE WEB

Keeping All Karthalia's Tribes
Connected

By TESSALLI EKUNDAYO

Yesterday afternoon, Yesod tribeswoman Tiffany Burroughs, 15, was travelling on a strasmag, when she was savagely attacked by four girls about the same age as her.

Tiffany sustained heavy bruising & deep lacerations to her face, as well as severe injuries to the rest of her body.

After the assailants fled the vehicle in their balaclavas, passengers came forward to tend the victim's wounds. She later regained consciousness, and they delivered her back to her tribe.

To date, neither Tiffany nor the other passengers on the strasmag have been able to identify the assailants. The Yesod Tribe are currently making what efforts they can to track the culprits down.

On a personal note, this reporter hopes they succeed, and that their justice is swift and merciless.

Notice:

In only five days' time, the Ragea's statue will finally be unveiled.

It is being built in honour of Sanif, a Ragea member highly regarded by his tribal brethren, who died earlier this year. He is said to have been crucial to the Ragea adopting the lilaxe a year and a half ago as their spiritual symbol.

There are rumours that the forthcoming statue will feature the lilaxe in some form.

Chapter 9

Laura shrieked.

The people before her in the dense, tightly packed crowd watched her. Those closest, their faces illuminated by the large chimney-fire in the room's corner, stood far enough back to give her a small rectangle of space. They gazed at her strong fingers thrashing against the strings of her acoustic guitar, listened attentively to her ragged screeching lyrics and half-formed cries. Her song, like much of Karthalian music, was loud, heartfelt, and had the air of being half finished.

A minute later, a wave of applause washed over the audience. From the other, more shadowy end of the long room, Jak saw his firelit sister take off her guitar, and raise her hand in a humble 'thank you' to her audience. Then she disappeared from the performance area, and a philosopher-rapper took her place.

Jak looked away, and took another swig of his drink. The harsh sounds of Laura's song had captured his mood.

Already, three days had passed since he'd been told this party would be happening. Now, his tribdwell was filled with Laura's friends from the Teachers' Tribe, and Amik's friends from the Engineers' Tribe. All of them celebrating the completion of the Ragea's statue.

But beyond the room's safe and bohemian candlelit gloom, beyond its open windows, the night was humid and restless. And Jak felt that same restlessness echoed in his own mind.

Slouched drunkenly in the room's corner, his thoughts wandered aimlessly over the throng of people who were dancing around him, or else nodding their head to the music's beat. Then a word from a nearby conversation caught his attention.

"... graffiti someone's been spraying on all the buildings?" one man said, shouting to be heard over the music.

"The one with the flowers?" another man replied.

"Yeah."

"Yeah I've seen it. Lurj em asum. Ruining all those people's homes. What stupid person does a thing like that?"

The other man laughed. "Je sais. Must be someone who's gone a bit mad. Thinks they're making the place look more pretty or something."

This time, they both laughed, the noise of it resounding through Jak's mind.

Swaying slightly, he leaned in to Martin's ear, and whispered so that no one else would overhear him. His words were half slurred. "They're laughing at us."

Martin turned round to look at him, recoiling. "Urgh, Jak, your breath stinks. Are you alright?"

"*I'm fine.*"

Like everyone else at the party, Martin's face had a painted design on it. Beneath the shaven swirl patterns in his hair, a string of dark blue diamonds had been limned on his roundish face, trailing down from the left side of his forehead to perch above his left eyebrow. A big, clownish, dark blue smile surrounded his lips.

"Anyway, who?" Martin said. "Who's laughing at us?"

"Henne." Jak nodded in the direction of the two men. "They're talking about the graffiti. Why hasn't Pavneet responded? He *must* have seen it by now."

Through his blurry vision, Jak saw all of Martin's sympathy evaporate. "Then maybe he doesn't want to see us. Perhaps it would be best if we dropped it."

In revulsion, Jak pulled away from Martin, and stared at his friend with a scornful look. Tonight, he could sense the black hostility of the World bubbling up all around him. Perhaps it was always there, undetected. But now, it was out to get him.

"Don't say that," he said to Martin. "Don't back out on me."

"Okay okay," Martin said, raising his hands in a show of apology. "I won't. I didn't mean to upset you."

But all Jak could see was the laughing, dark blue smile on his friend's face.

He staggered away, taking another gulp of aniseed from the small wooden cup he held in his right hand.

Jak didn't normally drink. He liked to stay mentally sharp. And the alcohol had hit his senses hard. The faint smell of jasmine from the room's scented candles repulsed him. The coloured crystals of necklaces and bracelets, hung as decoration upon the walls, glinted irritatingly in the firelight, threatening him with a painful headache. The warm press of people frustrated and angered him.

He looked at the room with nothing but disgust.

He wished all these happy people would get out of his home, and stop celebrating the statue that he hated. They were celebrating a cancer in Karthalia: they just didn't know it.

And how could Laura have said that he'd never grown up, that he just wanted to play at being a hero? How could she patronise him like that? But maybe there was nothing he could do. Maybe he wasn't meant to save Karthalia after all. Anyway, who was he to think he could bring true, everlasting peace to the World? Many great people in history had attempted it. All had failed. What made him any different?

Then someone appeared by his side, like a demon rising up out of his gloomy thoughts.

"Hello," Amik said.

Laura slipped out of the performance area, and back into the throng of people.

Like after most performances, the World swam by her in a sort of pleasant, dazed trance. She was riding a post-performance euphoria, the upswing to her pre-performance jitters. She was also feeling a little tipsy from the couple of drinks she'd had earlier to steady her nerves.

In her happy, almost delirious thoughts, it struck her how strange music was. How did vibrations of sound, floating through the air, trigger emotions inside people? There was no intellectual content to the chords she played, nothing specific that they said. And yet they seemed to commune directly with the emotional part of the brain. It was a kind of magic.

"Hayete, well done! That was fantastic!"

Out of nowhere, Laura had stumbled across a group consisting of her parents and their friends. It took her a moment to recognise the speaker through their paint-mask of vermilion spirals on their cheeks, and a green tear sliding down their nose.

"Oh, thanks Mum," Laura replied.

"Yes, good work, dear," her Dad added, smiling with that glowing, merry smile he only had when he was tipsy. Using the hand that wasn't holding his drink, he stepped forward and gave Laura a brief hug.

The four other people standing with her parents all belonged to the Teachers' Tribe, and were squashed uncomfortably close to one another by the crowd. Laura smiled politely at them, not knowing what to say to a group of people nearly twice her age. Then, just when the silence was on the verge of tripping into awkwardness, her Mum stepped in with a piece of gossip she'd heard. The general conversation resumed, before one of the men in the group – Tobias – leaned in towards Laura's ear.

"Laura? Is it alright if I have a quick word?"

"Um, yeah. Of course." Laura looked at Martin's dad, wondering what he wanted. She'd never really spoken to him one-to-one before.

Tobias nodded to a quieter corner of the room, and led her there through the dense maze of bodies. Physically, for a man in his fifties, he was in good shape. But his face had a permanent sadness about it, and his eyes looked tired and baggy, as they had done as long as Laura had known him. She'd heard from her Dad in passing how different Tobias had once looked.

Having half-escaped the room's crush of people, Tobias turned to face Laura.

"Sorry about this," he said. "Uh, it's a bit odd, but there's just something I wanted to check. I've heard there's a lot of friction between Jak and Amik. Est-ce que c'est vrai?"

"Yeah," Laura said, half warily. Where was this conversation going?

"Why?" Tobias asked, talking loudly to be heard over the noise. "What's the problem between them?"

"Well, basically, Jak doesn't like the Ragea. Don't ask me why. He says their statue's creating some sort of inequality. I don't even really know what he's talking about. Anyway, he doesn't like Amik because he's helping to build it.

"I do hate it, though. I feel like I'm being torn between the two of them. I've tried to make them get along, but they're both too stubborn."

Tobias nodded. "Do you ever think about marrying Amik?"

Laura couldn't help a startled expression from crossing her face. "Of course. We're talking about getting married next year.

That's when I'll move in with him. I want us to have our first kid when I'm twenty-five. Then another one about a year and a half after that."

"Wow. Sounds like you've got everything planned out."

"Yeah." Laura grinned cheekily. "But don't let Amik know about all this. It'll only freak him out."

In fact, Laura knew that Amik wasn't afraid of commitment in the slightest. But she enjoyed making this joke, and she knew that people found it funny.

Beneath his white, wispy hair that was combed to the side, Tobias smiled. It was a lingering, thoughtful smile, as if in approval of Laura's life.

"Well, I just wanted to say..." Tobias put his left hand on Laura's shoulder. "If you were holding back your relationship with Amik because of Jak, don't. You know I didn't get very long with my wife. And when she passed away, what hurt the most was the future I'd taken for granted. All those happy moments I'd imagined us having together, but which we didn't get time for. So all I'm saying is, don't slow down your relationship with Amik for anyone. Make the most of it now. You don't want to be left with the memories of what you could've had."

Laura slowly nodded, with a look of deep appreciation.

"Thanks. A few thoughts have been playing on my mind recently, and that's helped me see things more clearly."

Amik: "Enjoying the celebrations?"

Jak's muscles tensed. He glared at Amik.

"No, sorry," Amik said. "I'm being callous. I know this must be hard for you. And I appreciate the effort you've made."

Amik's sharply intelligent, deep brown eyes gazed at Jak. His face, with its black slicked-back hair, stern alpha-male features, and thick, well-groomed beard, somehow looked like a face of

Judgement, staring down at Jak. Then Amik smiled reassuringly at him.

"But there is one thing you have to realise," Amik said.

He put a big, heavy hand on Jak's shoulder, and pointed through the crowd at Laura. She was off to the side of the room, talking to Tobias.

"I know," Amik said, "that you've said things to your sister, to try and persuade her to break up with me. But it hasn't worked. We're stronger than what you can do to us. In fact, we're talking about getting married next year."

Jak twisted his face round, and stared at Amik.

"So there's no point being mad at me, Jak." He leaned in to Jak's ear, and hissed: *"You've already lost."*

Jak took in Amik's looming, intimidating physique and his gloating face. His last hazy thought, before all the chaos and commotion broke out, was how satisfying it would be to punch him.

Chapter 10

A sharp, deep cry tore through the room, and as it died away, so too did the room's conversations. Laura recognised the voice.

Rushing over to its source, she saw Amik and Jak standing together, with Amik doubled over in pain.

"What's happened?" she shouted.

Out of fear and uncertainty, the groups of people nearest Amik and Jak had backed away from them. There was now a wide, open hole in the crowd, and Laura, her boyfriend, and her brother were isolated within it. No noise came from the performance area. A dead silence filled the room. And most uncomfortable of all, Laura sensed all eyes turning upon her, the stifling weight of their combined gaze growing heavier with each moment.

She saw what many of those eyes saw: Amik clutching his nose, his short beard dark and wet with blood.

"Amik!" she shouted, bolting to his side. She turned to face Jak: "Did you *punch* him?"

A group of four burly men burst from the edge of the crowd. They immediately formed a defensive blockade in front of Amik, and stood with their arms up, ready for a fight if Jak tried to attack Amik again. Laura recognised these men. They belonged to Amik's tribe of engineers.

"Get back!" one of them shouted at Jak.

From behind the wall of men, Laura saw Jak glance at each of Amik's saviours, then at her, then at the silent audience of the crowd, whose eyes were fixed upon him. He stood motionless, except for the rising and falling of his chest as he panted with slow, even breaths.

"Look," said the same man in the defensive wall. His voice was sharp and forceful, like a succession of hammer blows. "Come any closer, and we'll knock you ou—"

"*Shut up,*" Jak shouted, spit flying from his mouth in his rage. Then he turned his gaze away from the man with a look of disgust, although Laura couldn't work out if the disgust was for the engineer or for himself. "I'm not going to do anything else."

So complete was the general silence, that Jak's words had been audible throughout the whole room. He turned to face the tense, frightened crowd that surrounded him, and raised his hands dramatically like an orator.

"What are you celebrating?" he shouted, his voice fuelled by a righteous anger.

For the first time that night, Laura was afraid *for* her brother. He sounded like he'd lost his mind.

Jak began to pace around the edge of the circle, slurring his words:

"Wake up! All tha's 'appening is the Ragea are growing in power. Karthalia's s'posed to be different. To be *equal*. But look. We're becoming like everywhere else there's ever been. Why don't you *do* something about it?"

With dumbstruck expressions, the audience stared at Jak. They didn't look as if they were absorbing his message. Instead, they looked as if they were witnessing a mental collapse.

"Jak," Martin half-gasped. Laura glanced at him. He looked aghast, but not as if he couldn't believe Jak was saying this; but as if he'd heard it before, and couldn't believe Jak was saying it in front of everyone.

"Tha' statue," Jak continued, "is a symbol of their power. And they've put it in the agora, where you'll walk beneath its gaze every day. Don't you think that'll do something to your mind? That you'll start looking up to them?"

He paused, swaying, and looked at his audience as if judging them.

"They've built that statue on fear and violence. And d'you know why? Why the people they've assaulted haven't spoken out? I's not just intimidation. I's 'cause they can't imagine this "utopia" being ruined. Can't imagine their existence ever really being different from what it is now."

Laura noticed one of the men guarding Amik disengage himself from the blockade. It was the one who had warned Jak not to come any closer. Slowly, he walked over to her brother, then said something to Jak in a hushed voice, too quiet for Laura to catch the words. But his tone was firm and measured, as if he was trying to calm her brother down by reasoning with him.

Then suddenly, Jak lifted up his right hand sharply and aggressively, as though the man was about to do something, and Jak was stopping him. Jak whispered a couple of sentences. The man frowned and stood still, as if suspended in a moment of indecision. Then Jak strode towards Laura, and the man – although he watched Jak warily – let him go. Seeing this, the wall of engineers parted, and Jak stepped through it.

As he marched towards Laura, Jak yanked from his pocket something small and crumpled. Then he stopped before his sister, and stood over her. She was half-crouched beside Amik with tears in her eyes.

"Just visit her," Jak said, staring fiercely at Laura, a mute desperation in his eyes. "She can show you."

Grabbing his sister's hand, he shoved the crumpled thing into it. And even as Laura backed away, she instinctively took the object. Jak looked at her: "Stop living in ignorance."

Laura stared back at him, feeling disorientated. Why was he insulting her? All her words had fled, leaving her stranded in dumb silence. She could only watch as Jak stormed away, hearing the muffled commotion as he forged a path through the closely packed crowd.

She looked down at the crumpled object in her hand. It was a piece of brown card. Unfolding it, she saw that printed on it, in a simple font, were four words:

Tessalli Ekundayo
Intel Tribe

Laura knew Tessalli was a friend of Jak's, but that was all she knew about her. Why had he given her this card? What was the point? In her confused state, nothing quite made sense.

Stuffing the card into her pocket, she forced the thought of it from her mind. Right now, Amik was what needed her attention.

At the end of the room, she heard the door slam shut. Jak was gone.

Chapter 11

The night's violence and drama had sobered Laura, squeezing her dry of any intoxication, and leaving her physically and mentally exhausted. Having washed off her paint-mask and dumped the last of the dirty wooden cups in the kitchen sink, she headed down the corridor of her tribdwell, a deep anxiety weighing on her heart. Before letting her go to bed, that anxiety pulled her towards another door in her home, one whose room didn't belong to her. She stood sombrely before it, then pushed the door back.

It creaked open, revealing a dark, empty bedroom – Jak's. He still hadn't come home.

For a moment, Laura just stared into the room, letting it intensify her feelings of sadness and regret at what had happened. Then, only when she'd tasted enough of these emotions, did she decide to close the door. She blew out the last candle in the corridor and entered her room, which lay next to Jak's.

Amik sat on the edge of her bed, his broad, alpha-male profile illuminated by a bedside candle, the only light in an otherwise dark room. His eyes were fixed intently upon the sheaf of papers he held in his lap, and Laura could hear the soft scratching of his pencil. He was writing in his diary, something he did every night; the ritual of a minor obsession. As he wrote now, doubtless about the events of the party, he smiled with a deep and private pleasure, even under his newly crooked nose.

A moment after Laura entered the room, Amik either finished his diary, or terminated it abruptly. Fastening the papers shut with two pins, he stowed them under the bed.

By now, Laura was also sat on the bed, a short distance away from Amik. As usual, he had quickly got over any turbulence in their lives. In contrast, her posture was slumped, and she stared with obvious sadness at her amber bracelet, fiddling morosely with its crystals. She wanted her boyfriend to see her, to come and comfort her.

Amik didn't miss a beat. He shuffled down the bed towards her till their legs touched. Then gently, he laid his big, strong hands on her shoulders, and began to slowly massage them. Laura tilted back her head, and closed her eyes. Waves of soft pleasure rippled out of Amik's powerful hands, and down through her body. She felt some of her tension evaporate.

He's always so good at this, she thought. Having his broad, muscular frame so close to her... and his protective arms half-enveloping her... it made her feel so safe.

Amik spoke, his voice calm and soothing, in harmony with the sensual movement of his fingers: "Don't worry about him."

Laura mumbled: "Who?"

"Jak. He'll be fine."

"Oh, it's not him. Well, not really." She turned to face Amik. With the glow of the bedside candle behind him and to his left, half his bearded face was softly lit, while the other half was steeped in shadow. "What if... I don't know. What if he's right? What if the Ragea are having a bad effect on Karthalia?"

"But they're not. Jak's just—"

"But what if they *are*?" She hesitated. "Then we'd be partly responsible."

The sensual movement of Amik's fingers stopped. He gazed at her, with a mixture of puzzlement and a faint trace of amusement. "Is that what you really think?"

Laura briefly held his gaze, then looked away, embarrassed. "Maybe. No. Oh, I don't know. It's just since Jak shouted about it, I can't get it out of my head."

Amik sighed, but there was a sort of kindness in the sound. He touched Laura's cheek with the rough, calloused fingers of his right hand, and turned her face towards him.

"Look," he said, "we both love Jak."

Laura frowned, her face a mixture of surprise and scepticism.

"Quoi?" Amik said. "Honestly, I do. He's your family, and I love you. So of course I love him. Even if we do bicker a bit, it doesn't *mean* anything. Not even this."

He pointed at his newly crooked nose with a small, playful smile. Then he continued:

"But you've seen him recently. He's looked exhausted. Didn't you say that, for the past few nights, he hasn't come home till very late?"

Laura gave a tiny, reluctant nod. "Yeah. The other night, I don't think I heard him come home till about three in the morning."

"Precisely. So that's all this is. He's tired and stressed. And you know what that can do." She felt him caress her cheek with the back of his fingers. "It can make you see problems where there aren't any."

Laura felt the faintest hint of a smile on her face. "Yeah. I suppose you're right."

"I am. Trust me. When Jak gets some proper rest, this delusion of his will slip away, and he'll see how silly it was. I mean, forget about what he said, and look at what's *actually* going on. One tribe wants to commemorate someone who died, because they loved him so much. That's not immoral, is it?"

"No."

"And you've been with me every step of the way that I've been building this statue. Has it felt unethical *at any point*?"

Laura shook her head: "No."

She'd felt lost in the mist of her anxiety. But now, Amik's words were burning that mist away like the rays of the morning sun. Suddenly, everything seemed clearer.

"Of course it hasn't. So ignore Jak's drunken ramblings, and focus on *that...*" He tapped her chest, over her heart. "... because that's what you know is real."

He squeezed her hand reassuringly. "And don't let Jak make you worry about Karthalia, or whatever he was saying. Tonight, someone got drunk at a party, and said some things they shouldn't have. Sounds like everything's pretty normal to me."

Laura giggled, mostly from relief, and her usual smile spread across her face once more. Then she stared at her boyfriend with a sort of muted awe, and thought how he always, always knew how to make her feel better. Her smile spreading further across her lips, she playfully pushed him down onto the bed's coarse linen, and sprang on top of him. She bent her face close to his.

"It's gonna be so good," she whispered, "when the statue's done." Tobias' advice flashed through her mind. "Then we can move in with each other. Either your tribe can adopt me, or mine'll adopt you. I know most of the teachers would be happy to do it."

"Perfect. And hopefully by then, people will have realised what a genius I am."

"'Genius'? Uh, you're not being at all arrogant, are you?"

"Not in the slightest." Amik grinned, as if nothing in the World could shake his self-belief. Then his voice became softer, more introspective. "I'm going to get rid of this World's bland, uniform tribdwells, and replace them with something beautiful. I'm going to leave behind a real legacy." He leaned upwards, bringing his lips towards hers. "And I want to do it all with you."

They kissed.

A sweet and tender silence followed, so eloquent that all speech felt redundant. Looking directly down at him, Laura studied his shadowed face. She glimpsed some tiny, dark spots of blood just beneath his nose. Saw the rich browns of his eyes, and stared down into their pools of deep calm, into their soulful depths.

"It'll all turn out for the best," he said.

He took her slender hand in his (the one on which she wore the amber bracelet) and rubbed it soothingly, so that the calloused fingers of both their hands brushed against one another. Each set of callouses spoke of their owner's individual life: Laura's were the marks from years of guitar playing; Amik's came from his manual labour, where the heavy tools he wielded chafed against his hands. United by this similarity, their hands appeared like the feminine and masculine halves of the same whole. A perfect match.

"Yeah," Laura smiled, picturing what the rest of their lives together was going to be like. "We're gonna be fine."

Then she heard a soft, distant noise. The front door had clicked shut. Laura listened attentively. The sound of footsteps grew louder, as they headed down the tribdwell's corridor and towards Laura's room. They passed by her door, grew fainter for a couple of seconds, before stopping altogether. The door next to Laura's quietly creaked open, and with that, Laura felt the last traces of her anxiety disappear.

Jak was home. Even though Laura didn't regard herself as superstitious, she viewed his return as a sign that harmony in her life had been restored.

Later, when Amik had gone to the washroom, she looked again at the card Jak had given her. Dismissing it with a shake of her head, she stuffed it into her bedside drawer. Then she got into bed, tired and ready for sleep.

*

The next morning, Amik visited his employers.

He spoke with a man as tall as him, but who had shaggy, shoulder-length hair. His name was Leo, and he would often call on Amik to see how the building work was progressing.

"There's a man," Amik said, "called Jak Marcy, who lives in the Teachers' Tribe. He's trying to derail the building of this statue. If I were you, I'd keep an eye on him."

Chapter 12

He wanted to scream. Wanted to cry. But for his own safety, all he could do was remain silent, bottling up all that painful emotion within himself.

Immersed up to his chest, Pavneet was washing himself in the cold water of the River Menignus. He could barely see what he was doing. Everything was almost pitch-black, except for the faint and pallid glow in the east. The sun wouldn't rise for another couple of hours. And in this nocturnal World, his only company was the high-pitched cries of distant birds, and the silhouettes of turtles as they crawled along the shore.

There was no one to understand his muttered cussing to himself, or his occasional sobs.

But if the night was dismal and lonely, it still had one factor that outweighed those downsides: it was relatively safe. With everyone presumably asleep, there should be no one to spot him – no one greedy for the Ragea's reward...

Yesterday, he'd seen the 'Wanted' posters with his face on for the first time. As an exile from his tribe, he was already shunned by most people. Now, those posters had obliterated any last trust he had left in his fellow Karthalians. He had no friends. Hadn't for years. And thanks to that reward, everyone was now a potential threat. Danger towered all around him.

He stood in the current for a few more moments, breathing slowly and trying to pull himself together. Then he waded out onto the grassy shore and dried himself with a towel, including his grizzly beard, which was already growing thick and scraggly after his six days of being on the run.

He'd stolen the towel in the dead of night, pilfering it from a washing line in the Crafter's Tribe. Lately, he'd stolen a lot of things...

The first time had been the hardest. His knotted, famished stomach had felt like it was gnawing at itself with its own corrosive acids. So he'd stolen a cucumber from the allotment of a tribd-well, and in a deserted spot, far from any public walkway or dirt road, he'd sat on a patch of muddy grass and devoured his food. Cucumber juice helped wash away the dry, sickly taste that had accumulated in his throat during the previous torturous, sleep-starved night. It tasted wonderful.

And felt like the most bestial thing he had ever done.

He had never stolen before. Even as a child, he'd felt it was beneath his dignity. But the hunger... the hunger had eaten that principle.

And as he'd sat gnawing that cucumber, a food he'd never even liked, he felt the Pavneet Hansraj he'd been for thirty-eight years fading into the past, as a new and warped identity ascended into its place. An identity that only grew stronger with each meagre necessity he'd had to thieve...

Still, a vestige of his old, scientific self remained: brooding, thinking, formulating a plan.

He'd deposited his ill-gotten spoils in the new home he'd eked out for himself, which lay to the north-west of Karthalia, in a small wood with its green back pressed against the immense grey of the stone Wall. This location had two main appeals: it provided camouflage for him to hide in, and it was right on the outskirts of Karthalia, with little reason for anyone to visit or pass through it.

However, there was one drawback: the wood was infested with snakes. And it was hard to sleep in a wood infested with snakes. Especially since they reminded him of that grim experiment...

He picked up his sandals, not putting them on. Of all the bad luck, the sole of the right one was coming off from wear and tear. It made a slapping noise with each step, meaning Pavneet had to walk slowly and cautiously to suppress the sound. So he only put the sandals on when he crossed the forest floor, where the twigs and tree roots could be painfully rough against his feet.

Now, barefoot, he traipsed back towards his den. The intensity of his hunger pains had lessened, which, he thought morosely, must mean that his stomach had shrunk.

His nocturnal trips hadn't only included the river. Four times, the last one out of sheer boredom, he'd hazarded the long journey to gain a glimpse of the Iron Gate. Each time, it had been guarded by alert and intimidating Ragea.

Which meant he had no choice. He had to form an alternative plan of escape. So far, only one idea had come to mind: plunging into the River Menignus and letting it carry him along to its exit, a large rectangular opening at the base of the Wall, where the river waterfalled out into the sea.

But this plan did contain some undoubted snags. He might drown; or crack his head on the river's stone weir; or find it impossible to climb up the rugged cliff face and back onto land. In his heart, Pavneet cowered at the unknown blackness of death, too much to ever actively place himself in such mortal danger. He didn't have physical courage. He never had.

So he'd have to think of something else. At least the intellectual stimulation would help him kill the empty, slow, grinding hours that had now become his life.

As these drably familiar thoughts passed through his mind, he suddenly stopped in his tracks, and, like most nights, gazed at the collection of dark shapes to his left-hand side.

The buildings of the Fishers' Tribe stood before him. And as Pavneet stared at them, he remembered the community he'd left, and the bitter, loveless marriage which he'd abandoned, all those five years ago. For most of that time, any feelings he'd had for his old tribe had felt dead and buried. But recently, they'd been resurrected, as pangs of regret at being so long away from them, and a longing to be with them again.

He glanced at the simple, unadorned metal wedding ring on his finger. Just under two weeks ago – for the first time in years – he'd taken it out of his bedroom drawer, and put it on again. This was just after he'd experienced Oceanos for the first time... just after he'd drowned in that glowing, psychedelic, spinning, humbling, and enlightening mindscape...

Shaking away that vivid and emotion-drenched memory, Pavneet noted the red markings that had been sprayed on the side of one fisher's tribdwell, over the foliage of its vertical garden. In the dark, these graffiti markings were extremely dim, but Pavneet could recall what they looked like. During his treks across Karthalia, he'd seen replicas of them on several buildings.

The graffiti depicted a group of generic flowers, their sinuous stems all bending at different angles. Rendered in red spray paint, they almost seemed to be performing some sort of fire dance. But there was a secret code underpinning the image, one which Pavneet had identified almost immediately: it was the rudimentary corporo-visual language evolved by certain species of flora.

Though extremely limited due to its relative infancy, the language was nonetheless intricate, with the pose adopted by each flower stem forming a crucial element in its visual "grammar". Together, written down as they were in the graffiti, the flowers became like a line of falling semiotic dominoes: the meaning of one stem having a knock-on effect upon the meaning of the next.

But despite the language's unique capabilities and potential, it was still primitive, and not built for human reference points. The writer of the graffiti had struggled to express themselves:

MAN ON RUN. MEET AT HIGHEST SUN-STONE. ELEVEN AT NIGHT.

However, with a little imaginative guesswork, Pavneet had figured out what they'd meant: *Fugitive. Meet me at Karthalia's northernmost sundial, at 11 p.m. tonight.*

This offer had seemingly been extended to Pavneet every night for the past few days. But who was the message from?

Pavneet had learnt the flower language years ago, during a botanical study he'd conducted with Kevin Marcy. Could it be from him? Unlikely. They hadn't exactly ended on the best of terms.

So who was his mysterious contact? And how was this connected – if at all – to the Ragea, and his discovery of Oceanos?

Part of Pavneet was desperate to find out, to meet whoever this message was from. Sensing his life was near its end, he wanted to feel some connection again with a living being before it was done. Wanted to plug the aching hole in his heart that, for years, Bastian had filled...

He remembered how he'd woken up that evening and believed – for a brief, dreamy moment – that Bastian was still alive. Then he'd felt a sickening lurch inside himself, as his mind sunk back into reality.

Of course, it was obvious why no name had been left to say who the graffiti message was from. A name couldn't be translated. There was no corresponding alphabet between the languages of humans and plants. In this case, Pavneet decided, that was a good thing. It was good because it made up his mind: he would not respond to the message.

Over the past fortnight, he'd lost so much. His dog. His home. His dignity. But he refused to lose his wits. Even with a name, the message could always have been an elaborate trap. But without any clue as to who wrote it, it definitely wasn't worth the risk.

Decisively, Pavneet turned away from the Fishers' Tribe and the graffiti, and headed back towards the relative safety of solitude and snakes.

Chapter 13

"So..." Jak said, standing in front of the classroom's blackboard.

Two days had passed since the party, and he was still trying to recover from the sense of self-loathing which he'd woken up with the morning after it. How had he allowed himself to lose his self-control like that? Thankfully, most of his tribe had the tact to pretend his outburst had never happened. He'd apologised to Laura for his behaviour and, grudgingly and in front of her, to Amik.

Worse still, he understood now that the graffiti had failed. He'd tried it one last time the previous night, without Martin. Still no response. Pavneet must have seen it by now, and decided against meeting him. The truth was as simple and as painful as that.

At least the class of ten infants sat before him weren't going to judge him, or remind him of his mistakes. They stared up at him, listening attentively.

Behind the kids, at an angle, was a small bookcase full of children's reading material. Amongst its fantastical moralistic stories and other items, there were several bound, printed digests on the Second-Age Chinese philosophy of harmony. This was a key component of the Gardening & Cultivation class that Jak was in the middle of. He was teaching the kids how the idea of harmony related to Karthalia's permacultured landscape, and how it shaped what methods Karthalians used to grow their food.

But there was a crucial subtext to the lesson. He was also trying to instil in the kids the need for harmony amongst people. With its various co-existing tribes, Karthalia was a delicate set-up. It would be the task of this next generation to ensure its future. Part of the teachers' job was to prime them for that role through a kind of benign brainwashing.

"Now," Jak said, in a sort of tired, formal voice. He'd done this a hundred times before. "I'd like you..."

The sunlight streaming through a window disappeared for a moment, as if blotted out by a passing object.

"... to get into pairs, and—"

The classroom door burst open, and a horde of dark figures charged into the room.

"Get back!" Jak shouted at the kids.

But the intruders, all balaclavaed, weren't going for them. They were coming towards him.

"Hey, there you are!" one of the men shouted at Jak. Apart from an undercurrent of menace, the man spoke in a friendly boisterous voice, as if he were Jak's mate and this was all part of some big laugh.

Instinctively – risibly – Jak snatched up a large wooden ruler from the blackboard's ledge, and faced the swarm of intruders.

"Who are you?" he shouted, but in his heart he knew.

"Yeah! We thought we'd never find you!" another one of them cried joyfully, as if Jak hadn't said anything.

One of the men crouched down before the frightened-looking kids, and spoke in the same half-happy, half-demented voice. "Don't worry," he said, stroking the head of the nearest boy. "Everything's going to be alright. This is just a game that grown-ups play."

"Get away from them!" Jak snapped. But then the group of invaders were beyond the kids, and almost upon him. Quivering, he swung the ruler violently at the face of the man who was at the head of the pack. With his forearm, the man blocked the attack, snapping the ruler and sending half of it tumbling to the floor.

Through the balaclava, Jak saw the man smile, as if he'd experienced no pain whatsoever. "C'mon Jak, don't be like that. We just want a quick word."

With Jak now weaponless, the mob of black figures converged upon him. The children, as though they'd always believed that adults were above danger, watched the scene in fear and confusion, uncertain what to make of it.

"Get *off!*" Jak shouted, as he was swallowed amongst the crush of black figures. A second later, he was spewed out into the air, his whole body suspended on a group of hands as if he were laid out on a bier. He writhed and struggled, like an eel out of water, but their grips were like manacles. His wrists and ankles burned, so tightly were they squeezed. He moaned in fear and helplessness, but the mob drowned out his cry with laughter and raucous, party-like shouts.

They bore Jak out of the classroom. Shutting the front door, they left the children behind.

As Jak lay supine, eyes squinting against the dazzling sun, he tried to scream for help. A half-second worth of noise escaped his lips, before a hand clamped down on his mouth, trapping the cry. His attackers had dropped the pretence of gaiety. Now, grimly silent, they were taking him somewhere.

A couple of moments later, and from above head height, Jak was dumped onto the grass. He hit the floor, a sharp pain shooting up his side.

Instinctively, even as he groaned in anguish, he glanced at his surroundings. A vertical wall of vegetation lay before him. The mob had taken him out of sight, round the back of the building where he'd been teaching.

Much of the sunlight suddenly vanished, and shadows engulfed Jak. He looked up. The black-garbed figures, which seemed to include both men and women, towered over him on all sides.

Then, all at once, he was caught in a vicious hailstorm of kicks. In terror, he shielded his face with his hands, barely hearing his own cries over the screaming agony of his flesh. His body jerked violently in the storm, as if it were suffering a seizure... his mind contracted, shutting down awareness, so it knew of nothing... not even the bruises and bloody cuts blooming all over his skin... nothing save the endless savagery of the kicks...

Each blow was more painful than he'd have imagined possible. It was if his attackers possessed superhuman strength. As if their legs were less like flesh and muscle, and more like heavy, powerful axes being swung into a tree of bones...

Finally, the storm passed. The blows ceased.

Jak lay on his side, his pale cheek slumped against the dirt and grass. All the kicks had been to his body, which now felt broken; a limp sack of flesh, swollen and seeping in infinite places. But his face... apart from one kick that had smashed across his mouth, they had left his face untouched.

Between fluttering, half-closed eyelids, a man crouched down into Jak's bleary vision. The man's face was hidden by his balaclava, but his husky voice practically hissed with venom.

"We've been warned about you, Jakariah. We've seen you graf-fitiing your message. And we know you're not trying to capture him."

He leaned forward, bending down to Jak's ear. Jak felt the warm pressure of his ragged, excited breathing. The man whispered:

"Stop interfering."

Then he sat back on his haunches. "And tell Martin the same thing. Or we'll have to repeat ourselves."

He rose to his feet. Belatedly, Jak became aware that the sunlight had returned. The mob had disappeared. And with it, his remaining strength. Surrendering to their own weight, his eyelids fell shut.

Chapter 14

"There he is!"

A panicked, familiar voice. One he recognised. A woman from the Teachers' Tribe.

Then other voices.

"Jak? Jak, wake up. Can you hear me?" This one was breathless with worry. Jak realised it was Kevin, his Dad. He groaned in response, forcing his eyelids to open.

"Oh – oh thank goodness," his Dad panted. "Jak, what happened? Who did this to you?"

Who had done this to him? And where was he? Then, in a brief and nasty revelation, Jak remembered. Grinding his teeth with the effort and pain, he tried to push himself off the floor: "Aaaaaarrrghh."

"Don't! Don't move. We'll help you up. Hayleigh," his Dad's voice was trembling, "give me a hand."

Two people gently hooked Jak's arms around their necks and over their shoulders, before slowly hoisting him into a standing position. His limp, injured legs dangled against the grass.

"Let's get you home," his Dad said. They set off. His head lolling with the rhythm of their movement, Jak glanced at his Dad through bleary eyes. He saw the anguish on the man's face. It was the look of a father who felt he'd failed his son.

The next thing Jak knew, he was being lowered onto the firm cushions of a wooden, upholstered bench. His reclining head looked up at a terracotta ceiling, and he recognised the odd bumps and faded, years-old stains in the plasterwork. He was home. But it didn't feel like a safe place anymore.

He heard someone enter the room.

"Jak! Oh yelean el seea, chou sarlak y ebni," his Mum swore. Rushing to his side, she began caressing his face with a quivering hand. He could see the tears in her eyes.

"Mum... I'm fine..."

But his voice was just a pained whisper.

Turning to the door, his Mum spoke in frantic bursts, thanking some people for their help. Then she asked them to leave her and her family in privacy, and Jak heard the door click shut.

Coming from the kitchen, his Dad handed his Mum a medical kit. She began applying some potassium permanganate to Jak's wounds as an antiseptic. As she did so, she vented her worry with a rapid series of questions at her son. Was he okay? Did he need anything? Who did this to him?

But Jak only answered one of them: "It... was the Ragea... They did this..."

His Mum's eyes widened. "What? Are you sure?"

But then, someone burst into the room.

Jak twisted his head in fear, flashbacks to what had happened in the classroom stabbing through him. But no... it wasn't the Ragea...

"Jak... no..." Laura gasped, freezing in her tracks as if she'd just suffered a catatonic shock. Then she raced over to Jak's side.

Through bleary eyes, Jak saw that her face was pale, and her body was shaking.

"Who did this? Who did this to him?" she asked, turning to their parents.

Their Dad answered, his low, even voice not quite masking his agitation. "He just told us it was the Ragea."

Laura snapped her gaze back on Jak, a look of disbelief and horror on her face. "No. That can't be right."

"He *said* it was them! Isn't that enough for you?!" their Mum shouted, even though – only a moment ago – she'd been the one doubting what Jak had said.

Jak flinched. He'd never seen his Mum lash out at Laura like that.

"Gemma! Calm down!" his Dad cut in. "Everyone here's upset. Jak thinks it was the Ragea. But he might not be in a fit state to tell."

For a second, his Mum looked fiercely at his Dad. Then she glanced with a mingled look of shame and hurt at the floor, as if she were coming back to her senses.

"I just meant..." Laura said softly, her voice trembling "... well, you were at the party last week. He doesn't like the Ragea. I just wanted to make sure he knew what he was saying."

Throughout this three-way conversation, Jak had kept out of it. Kept his eyes closed, as if he were too tired to listen. But now, he sensed a crucial opportunity.

"I think that's why they did it..." he said, opening his eyes again. "Because I insulted them... at the party..."

Best not to tell them about the graffiti and Pavneet, he told himself. *That would only complicate things.*

He added: "After... they attacked me... they even admitted... it was them."

Crouched beside his head, Laura gazed searchingly into Jak's eyes. Jak didn't flinch. Instead, he frowned at her sympathetically and whispered: "It's true."

There was a hesitation, a doubt in Laura's green eyes as she stared down at him from above. Then she reached over and, her hand still shaking, gently took hold of his.

"I believe you," she said. She looked at him as if his injuries proved his honesty. Then she turned to their parents.

"We need to tell everyone in the tribe what happened. Then tomorrow, we can go to the Ragea and—"

"No. Wait..." Jak said, "... I want to take care of this."

There was a brief, awkward silence.

"Don't be silly," his Mum said. "We'll deal with this. You need to rest."

"No," Jak groaned, his voice having more force than before. "Let me... do it." Though he tried not to show it, the terror he'd felt during the assault still haunted him. "This needs to be handled... in a certain way."

"But it'll be easier if—"

"I'm doing it," he repeated. "Tomorrow." The weakness in his voice gave it a strange authority, perhaps because his words were all the more precious. His family fell silent as he spoke. "If I can't manage it... I'll leave it to you. Alright?"

Jak saw his Mum, Dad, and sister glance at each other.

Finally, his Dad spoke, for all of them: "Okay."

Half an hour later, his Dad persuaded his Mum that it was time for them to leave. Other people were having to cover their classes, and anyway, Laura would be there to look after Jak. They both left, with his Mum still gazing worriedly at her son even as she closed the door behind her.

Alone in the quiet room with his sister, Jak felt calmer. Suddenly, it was more peaceful.

"Feels like ages... since we've been together. Y'know... just us two." He tried to do his best imitation of a normal smile, but it just came out weak and full of pain. More of a wince than anything.

"Yeah," Laura smiled back. She'd pulled up a chair, and was again holding his pale hand in her olive-skinned one. "It really does."

Beguiling the time, they talked, and a sweet, meandering conversation developed. Even during its lulls into silence, Jak felt content. It was like a deep bond with his sister was being restored.

But even as he spoke and listened, he was planning and dreaming. He would gather an audience, find some makeshift podium, and declare his injuries to the World. Then, like a burgeoning army, other victims of the Ragea would rally towards him. Trials would be held. The guilty would be exiled. The rest of the Ragea wouldn't be able to move for the weight of scrutiny upon them. And their plan, to slowly intimidate their way into greater and greater power, would implode...

"Do you remember that time," Laura said, clearly in a mood to reminisce about her life with Jak. "When you stopped Daniel Al-Bishi bullying me?"

Recalling the memory, Jak felt a twinge of shame. "Yeah. Mum and Dad were horrified."

"*I know.* I've never seen them so angry with you. And the other teachers..." She shook her head in disbelief. "I thought you were going to be exiled."

"Really?"

"Hey, come on. I *was* only eight."

"I guess." Remembering what he'd done, Jak's dream of saving Karthalia suddenly seemed flimsy and fraudulent. He wasn't a hero. That wasn't in his nature. "At least... he stopped bullying you..."

"Duh! I'm not surprised. When you'd finished beating him up, he could barely walk..."

As he walked along, Amik felt serene.

The day was warm, his work was on schedule – life was good. If he'd been the sort of person who smiled much, he would have smiled then. Instead, his face was set in its usual heavy and serious expression. Because of his good mood, he was heading over to

Laura's tribdwell, where she often spent her afternoon breaks. He wanted to surprise her so that they could have lunch together.

In Karthalia, no one had locks on their front doors. Without knocking, Amik pushed back the door of her and Jak's tribdwell, and stepped inside.

His mood immediately altered.

Inside, he was confronted with the sight of a wounded Jak lying on the living room's bench, with Laura tending to his injuries. In the split-second when Amik first saw this scene, no surprise or horror registered on his face. In his head there lay only a cold, rapid analysis of this unexpected and unsettling situation. He absorbed the sight of Jak's bruised and swollen body, and detected the deep sympathy that his injuries had won from Laura. The dynamics between the three of them had shifted, and not in Amik's favour.

Then the split-second passed, and before anyone had a chance to notice it, Amik's emotionless expression was gone, replaced by a mask of worry.

"Amik?" Laura said. "How come you're—"

"What the hell's happened to him?" Amik exclaimed, but his incisive mind was already coming to the right conclusion. He remembered warning his employers about Jak... he'd expected them to take corrective measures, but in his busy mind, these would be accomplished in some vague and tolerable way. Not like this. This changed things far beyond what he'd wanted.

"It was the Ragea," Laura said, her sweet voice full of pain. "They dragged him out of the classroom, and they did this. You can't work for people like that. You've got to quit working on the statue!"

"Whoa. Hold on," Amik said, raising his hands as a sign for her to slow down. "How do you know it was the Ragea?"

"Because they said it was them, after they attacked him."

Mentally, Amik cursed.

"But why?"

"Because of what he said at the party."

"But why would their reaction be this extreme? And why do it a couple of days *after* the party?"

"Look, I found it hard to believe as well. But Jak's *certain*. And it makes sense. Maybe they heard that he'd been insulting them. Why are you defending them?"

"I'm not," Amik said, trying to pacify her with a soothing tone. "It's just—"

"He said it was them. It's as simple as that. You *can't* work for them anymore."

Feeling more and more uncomfortable, Amik glanced at Jak. He was politely staring at the ceiling, as if oblivious to the argument that was growing further out of control.

Speaking to Laura, Amik said: "Can we talk about this in private?"

She rose defiantly to her feet. "*Are you going to quit?*"

Amik felt his neck muscles tightening, as the rage inside him boiled. "Laura..."

"*Yes... or no?*"

Then all of his repressed anger erupted into a roar. "Of course I can't! Are you stupid?! The statue's almost done!"

"Then get out!" Laura screamed. "Get! Out!"

Amik's voice went cold. "You're such a child. After all I've given you, after always trying to look after you, *this* is what I deserve?"

He glared at her with brutal spite. He wanted her to feel the full force of his rage, to shock her into realising how far she'd crossed the line. Then he saw the tears in her eyes.

"*Fuck. You,*" he snarled, then stormed out of the tribdwell.

He slammed the door shut behind him, and its bang was so loud that it hurt his ears. His relationship was dead, and that sharp noise was the axe blade landing with a thud after the head had been sliced off.

Chapter 15

The night of the same day, through a drizzle that fell diagonally with the wind, a silhouette approached the solitary light of a black, ornate lamppost. The surrounding area was deserted, and the figure clutched something to its chest, protecting it from the rain.

Stepping inside the lamppost's sphere of light, the figure sloughed off its silhouette to reveal the features of a man. He had glasses, small dark eyes, and a hunched back. Eagerly, he opened the newspaper that he'd brought with him to read.

Small in size, stapled down its spine, and only about ten pages long, the newspaper was really more of a pamphlet. Having become slightly wet in the rain, some of its ink had started bleeding blackly down the page. The front-page headline, printed in the newspaper's spidery and delicate font, announced:

RAGEA STATUE UNVEILED TODAY

The newspaper was delivered to people's homes at night, so the "today" in the headline hadn't quite arrived yet. Pavneet had taken the newspaper from where it lay half-pushed into someone's letterbox. Keeping abreast of news in Karthalia made him feel less like a bedraggled outcast, and more like a normal person.

Beneath the headline lay a black-and-white picture of the shrouded statue. Even hidden under its black sheets, it seemed to exude the aura of something alive, something waiting and expectant.

In disgust, Pavneet turned the page. While the Ragea were being elevated with a grand monument, his own home lay burnt to the ground, its charred wood mingled with the black ashes of his beloved companion.

He flicked through the paper, scanning its pages for an arresting headline. Then his movements halted, and his eyes narrowed with a look of intrigue.

The article he'd latched upon was brief:

```
MASKED GROUP ASSAULTS MAN

    by Tessalli Ekundayo

Yesterday, Jakariah Marcy, 24, was
assaulted within the province of his
own tribe.

Around 1 p.m., a balaclavaed group
dragged Jakariah from the classroom
where he'd been teaching, & viciously
set upon him. He now has major contu-
sions, lacerations, and swellings all
over his body. Unfortunately, no other
member of the Teachers' Tribe
witnessed the assault.

If you can offer any information
regarding these attackers, then please
visit the Intel Tribe.
```

> As we reported, a girl from the Yesod
> Tribe was also recently attacked, which
> worryingly makes this the second group
> assault in less than a fortnight.

Next to the article were two small pictures: one was a shot of Jakariah's face, which looked stern and determined, as if he were unwilling to let the beating damage him or his life in any way. The other was a picture of his swollen and bruised torso. Even if the photo's harsh black-and-white colour scheme made the injuries look worse than they really were, the assault must still have been brutal.

But "Marcy"? Where did Pavneet know that name from?

Then it struck him. Jakariah must be Kevin Marcy's son. Pavneet remembered the thin, pale little boy he'd seen at Kevin's house, back when the two of them had been working together... when they'd been analysing the strange and alien language system evolved by plants...

Suddenly, Pavneet's mind leapt forward, so fast it was as if he could barely keep up with it. The plants. The graffiti. It must have been Jakariah who was trying to contact him. That's why he'd been beaten up... the Ragea had found out...

Which meant the message hadn't been a trap.

Tearing off a fairly dry strip of newspaper, Pavneet pulled out a pencil, which he'd found in the pocket of his lab coat after he'd fled his home. He began to write.

Soon after, he was sneaking through the Teachers' Tribe, and yes, there it was, where it had been all those years ago: Kevin and Gemma's tribdwell. Karthalians almost never moved tribdwell, instead preferring to renovate what they had. And when any children left home, they tended to build their own accommodation close to their parents'. That's what Pavneet was banking on.

The night sky had brightened to a deep, velvety blue, and using the meagre light it provided, Pavneet squinted from close range at the wooden boards that were nailed next to each tribdwell's door. Situated amidst a vertical garden, the white, painted letters on each board were often obscured by overgrown plants, which Pavneet had to push aside. He would then see the name or names of the tribdwell's occupants. After not very long, he found the one he wanted:

JAKARIAH & LAURA
MARCY

He folded the strip of paper, slipped it quietly through their letterbox, then disappeared into the night.

Late the next morning, Jak hobbled into his living room. Despite his long sleep, he still felt terrible. Every movement he made with his aching body incurred some sort of pain. And mentally, after all the emotion of yesterday, he felt utterly spent.

The silent emptiness of the tribdwell didn't help. Laura had gone to do her teaching, while a number of Jak's colleagues had kindly offered to cover his classes.

But what did his new free time matter? He'd failed to contact Pavneet, and now that hope was crushed, he felt purposeless. Even the fact that it was the Day of Valus didn't cheer him up. He was too injured to join in with tonight's celebrations. Worse still, the Ragea were going to crown the festivities with the unveiling of their statue.

As he staggered groggily towards the living room bench, he suddenly paused and squinted at something. Then he limped over to the tribdwell's front door and, bending down, picked up the mysterious object.

It was a folded strip of paper, with the words "For Jakariah" pencilled on the front. Presumably, Laura had missed it when she left this morning. Suffering the aftermath of her row with Amik, she had probably been too distressed to notice it.

Jak opened the piece of paper, which he saw had been torn from a newspaper. In one of its margins someone had scrawled a message:

Valus, 7pm, Grid 3, in the glade.

P.

The messenger's identity was at once obvious and unbelievable. Why, after over a week of silence, would Pavneet want to meet now?

Still, Jak's instinct was to trust the note. Why would anyone else send it? And the message was plausible. Since Pavneet was in hiding, it made sense for him to arrange the meeting in the north-west of Karthalia, when nearly everyone else would be in the north-east, watching the statue be unveiled. It was a safe thing to do.

Suddenly, Jak's aches didn't feel so bad. His drowsiness had melted away, replaced by a keen sense of anticipation. He could feel his life moving forward again. With an air of exuberant triumph, he clutched the note tightly in his fist, and hurried to get ready for the day.

When Martin stepped out of his empty classroom, shortly after 5 p.m., he was confronted by two things.

The first was a gorgeous sunset, with radiant strips of colour: golden yellow melting into deep purple, then into a blazing crimson. A faultless horizon, almost unearthly in its splendour.

The second thing was all too earthly, half-hobbling and half-striding over the grass. Through the evening gloom, Jak was heading towards him. Martin had visited his wounded friend only last night, so why was Jak making the effort to come here now? And why, with his ugly split and swollen lip, was he grinning?

Jak took Martin aside, and as Martin absorbed his friend's animated words, he didn't know whether to be excited or afraid.

Chapter 16

It was evening, and great herds of Karthalians were pouring out from their separate tribes and converging upon the same destination, as if by some soundless call from an invisible master. The Day of Valus had arrived, a humorous holiday where everyone got together and celebrated their own achievements for that year. On this special occasion, friendliness and jollity were infectious.

But there were two dissenters who were immune to the merriment.

Jak and Martin threaded their way against a moving tide of bright and colourfully dressed people. The air was alive with buoyant dancing and carefree chanting, while amongst this, the two men awkwardly shuffled and bumped their way through the crowd. At one point, Martin had to dodge a tub of sloshing alcohol, which four men were carrying and from which anyone could take a free drink.

Eventually, and with a sigh of relief, he and Jak broke free of the crowd from its rear side.

"Man," Martin said, glancing over his shoulder. "It's a shame we're missing that."

Jak glanced at his friend, with a dry, quizzical look of disbelief.

"The Day of Valus comes every year," he said. "We're about to discover something unknown in all of human history."

The two men headed north-west, towards an area located in grid three on all Karthalian maps. From the people they passed, they seemed to attract no attention whatsoever. It was as if the merrymakers operated in a happier World, and to them, Jak and Martin almost didn't exist.

After a while, Martin spoke, trying to forget his own anxiety about what they were embarking upon. "I wonder what it'll look like."

"What?"

"The statue." Martin paused, hoping Jak would respond. All he got was a sharp, irritated look. "What? Just 'cause you don't like what it means, doesn't mean it won't look amazing."

Jak shook his head, as if Martin's words weren't worth responding to. "C'mon," he said, looking ahead once more. "We're almost there now."

They had arrived at the edge of a forest which skirted the interior of Karthalia's Wall. Even though he was still hobbling, Jak forged ahead without hesitation into its dense undergrowth, hellbent on finding the glade that Pavneet had chosen for their meeting. Presumably, to guard against confusion, there would only be one glade in the vicinity.

Martin cautiously followed Jak from some distance behind, weaving between cedar trees – some of which were over a hundred feet tall – and underneath their dense, needle-like leaves, keeping an eye out for any snakes or lizards that might be camouflaged in the greenery. To his anxious mind, the forest was not a chaotic wilderness. Instead, it was a subtle and complex trap – a trap constructed by Fate. And when it ensnared them, that would be it. Their lives would be changed forever.

He was itching to leave the forest, but he couldn't bear to walk away. Not when it meant being plagued with doubt over Jak's safety.

After a short while, through a tangle of underbrush, the glade came into view.

"Here it is," Jak said eagerly, stepping into the clearing.

"Yeah, but where's Pavneet?" Martin replied, with a tinge of apprehension in his tone. The glade was not only deserted, but devoid of any sign that another human had recently been there. To Martin, the forest air felt thick with an uncomfortable, claustrophobic silence.

"He'll be here," Jak said. His voice, like that of a zealous believer, was filled with absolute conviction.

The minutes crawled by as if they'd been crippled, and still, Pavneet didn't show. Even though it felt like a betrayal of his friend's trust, Martin hoped that Jak's faith in Pavneet was also being crippled. For his own part, Martin's anxiety was getting worse. The general silence had undergone a subtle mutation, and now felt like the prelude to some dark and menacing event.

"Right. That's enough," Martin said, letting his fear get the better of him. He had to put his foot down and take control of the situation. "He's not coming, so let's just go. We've still got time to join in with the celebrations."

To lend his words more authority, Martin started to stride away, heading back the way they'd come.

Then a noise broke the forest's silence. A rhythmic slapping sound, moving through the underbrush. Approaching them.

Martin spun round to see what was causing it, and saw – emerging into the clearing – a short man with a ragged black beard and mud-smeared clothes.

"Pavneet!" Jak exclaimed, as if his most profound beliefs – on the precipice of death – had been pulled back and saved.

"Jakariah!" Pavneet beamed ecstatically. Without stopping, he marched straight over to Jak and, clearly catching him by surprise, embraced Jak in a big hug.

"And who's this?" Pavneet added in a rush, quickly disengaging himself from Jak.

"Uh, this is Martin," Jak replied with an uncertain smile on his face. "You can trust him. I've known him since I was about six."

"Great. Fantastic," Pavneet said with a fervent grin, vigorously shaking Martin's hand. Gazing down at him, Martin saw that – behind the scratched, mud-flecked lenses of his spectacles – Pavneet's eyes were wide and alert, with a sort of manic energy in them.

"Sorry I didn't show myself at first," Pavneet said. "I was watching you, checking this wasn't a trap. But then I heard him freaking out *haha*!"—nodding at Martin, Pavneet emitted a burst of nervous laughter— "and I figured I'd probably be safe. *Ha ha.*" He tittered to himself, as if this were all some marvellous joke.

Trying to hide his discomfort, Martin looked at the forest floor.

"But enough about me," Pavneet continued, swinging his attention back to Jak. "How are you? Apart from the injuries, obviously. But it was them that let me know you could be trusted. And that it was you who was trying to contact me. Anyway, I haven't seen you since you were about *this* big. How's Kevin? And Gemma? Oh, and you had a sister! What was her name? Lisa? How's she?"

One trivial question after another flew from Pavneet's lips, so that Jak never had enough time to answer anything. Concerned for the sanity of this wild-eyed and dishevelled scientist, Martin merely watched on from the sidelines. They'd made a mistake coming here. He'd known it, and this only confirmed it.

"Okay!" Jak cut in, after Pavneet had fired yet another question at him. "It's nice of you to ask, but… we don't have the time for these questions."

Pavneet's mood visibly dropped. He bit his lip with an air of apology. "Yeah. Sorry. Of course." His voice had slowed down. "It's just… I haven't seen anyone for a long time."

Even though he wasn't in mid-sentence, there was the sense of his voice trailing off.

Jak shared a glance with Martin, a reluctant pity visible in his eyes. Then, obviously trying to make amends, he asked Pavneet: "How have you been surviving?"

"Stealing. Only coming out at night, when no one would see me." Pavneet wore a dismal look of shame as he said this.

"You won't have to do that anymore. We'll make sure of it," Jak said. Martin gave a slight start at being volunteered for something without his consent. But he quickly realised that, in the light of Pavneet's grim existence, any personal objections were mere selfishness.

"We'll bring you food, bedding, anything else you need."

"You-you'd do that?" The mixture of gratitude and disbelief in Pavneet's voice was almost heartbreaking.

"Of course." Jak gave Pavneet a warm, kindly smile. Martin thought Pavneet was going to cry.

"We can arrange a system later," Jak continued. "But right now, we need you to tell us how to access Oceanos."

Chapter 17

"Alright," Pavneet said, suddenly darting nervous glances into the forest.

There was a brief silence, as he readied himself to speak. And in that silence, Martin detected something strange.

From his point of view, all he could see of Jak and Pavneet were their profiles as they stood facing each other, only a few inches apart. Pavneet was the shorter of the two, with glasses, black hair going grey at the temples, and a ragged beard. Jak, with his tall body, had a long thin face, pronounced cheekbones, and black hair that had grown out in a very short, almost gauche fringe.

They looked almost nothing alike.

Yet for a split-second – and only for a split-second – Martin felt as if he had some supernatural insight into the true natures of the two men. Felt as if he actually glimpsed the intense spirit that lay within each of them, and those spirits were identical: the same pale blue fire burning in their hearts. It was like some initial essence had been halved and shared between them, and only the distortions of age and circumstance gave their minds a superficial difference.

Did that mean Pavneet, a dishevelled outcast, was somehow a premonition of what Jak would become? That this was where

Jak's dangerous path was taking him? Hopefully not. But Martin decided it would be his job to stop that from happening.

Then Pavneet spoke, and Martin's hallucinatory insight into the two men evaporated. He would never experience anything quite like it again for the rest of his life.

"To access Oceanos, you need to burn two things together." Pavneet's voice was hushed. "The first is crascitine. It's a chemical that's easy to get hold of, because it's present in nearly all plants. In fact, it's present in pretty much every plant *except* the other one you need for Oceanos..." He flicked his gaze between the two men. "The lilaxe."

Much earlier that day, in the crimson light of early dawn, Amik was stirring from his troubled sleep. He lay cramped up on the sofa of Laura and Jakariah's tribdwell. When his eyelids separated, the memory of the previous night hit him.

He had come to Laura's, desperate to speak with her and heal the rift between them. To his surprise, Jakariah had opened the door, although very slowly, as if afraid that the Ragea had come back to attack him. Then he'd seen it was Amik.

She doesn't want to see you, he'd said. Just let me speak with her, Amik had replied, sickened by the note of begging in his own voice. Maybe Jakariah had been too exhausted to say no, or maybe he'd taken pity on Amik. Either way, and amazingly, he'd let Amik inside.

But Laura had refused to see him, or even open her door. After a protracted spell of pleading with her, then abandoning the softness of diplomacy for a loud war of words, Amik had relented and stormed back into the empty living room. He was too stubborn to go home. He hadn't succeeded in what he'd come there to do. Fortunately, Jakariah had gone to bed a while beforehand, so there had been no one to stop Amik sleeping on the sofa. He'd decided:

he would talk to Laura face-to-face in the morning, when she left her room to get ready for work.

However, when he awoke early the next day, Amik felt bitter, tired, and hopeless. Any optimism he'd possessed about saving his relationship had drained away in the night. What had he been thinking? Laura wouldn't take him back if he harassed her soon after she woke up. Their relationship was dead, unless he abandoned the Ragea and didn't take his credit at the ceremony tonight. He couldn't do that. He'd been working towards this moment his whole life, it was the key to all his artistic commissions and successes in the future. He couldn't throw it away.

But what if he visited Laura a week after the ceremony? Might her anger have cooled? And by then, there would be no reason for him to remain allied to the Ragea.

So that was it. He would wait. At least that would give him some slim chance of getting everything he wanted.

With a brute determination to get on with his life, Amik hauled himself off the sofa. As he did so, he resented Jakariah for telling Laura that his injuries were the Ragea's fault. Not for blaming the Ragea exactly, but because his words had been calculated. He'd known the destructive effect they would have on Amik's relationship with Laura. What did it matter if he'd let Amik through the door last night? It was like granting the loser a token of pity, a magnanimous gesture made only so the winner could bolster their own sense of greatness.

Then, standing up and stretching his aching arms, Amik noticed something that sparked his curiosity. It lay by the foot of the door, a small white piece of folded paper. He went to pick it up.

A few minutes later, after memorising the information on the note, Amik refolded it. He placed it back roughly where he'd found it, and then, already dressed, he snuck quietly out of the tribdwell. The note looked as if it had never been disturbed.

When Laura and Jakariah later awoke, there was no sign that Amik had spent the night in the tribdwell. So there was no reason for Jakariah to suspect he wasn't the first to open the note. Or that Amik, in malicious hope, had snatched at this potential opportunity for revenge.

Or that later, as he stood in the forest talking to Pavneet, the Ragea were on their way.

Chapter 18

Not far from the expectant faces amassed before the shrouded statue, and beyond the agora's crescent perimeter of market stalls, a man stood under the shade of a large lemon tree. In the soft gloom of twilight, his every movement exuded calmness – a quality that, to his subordinates, would have seemed almost incompatible with the body it belonged to.

Soon, the statue would be unveiled. And in private, Corin was savouring the moments building towards it. Eyes narrowing with an intense, hungry gaze, he extended his hand up into the dark innards of the tree's boughs. His slender, bony fingers wrapped around the firm rind of a succulent lemon.

Having recently devoured the leaves of a lilaxe, all his senses felt acutely receptive. The lemon's sweet, juicy, and acidic fragrance filled his nostrils, rich and intoxicating like fine wine. It smelled exquisite.

It also reminded Corin of the delusion that clung, leech-like, upon the hearts of many Karthalians: that their World was perfect. To Corin's predatory instincts, this delusion registered like an irresistible scent. A signal that Karthalia was ripe for the plucking.

With a sharp twist, he yanked the lemon from the tree.

"Sanif?" a female voice called. This was Corin's title amongst the Ragea. It was given in honour of Sanif Ragea, who discovered the potency of the lilaxe, and whose position as leader of the Ragea Corin now possessed.

At this noise, Corin once more assumed the public pretence he used when amongst his tribe. He set his body trembling as with a jittery, unstable anger. Made his eyes darting and paranoid, almost feverishly so. And hunched his back into a more feral posture, as if he were about to spring and savage his prey at any moment. In short – he turned himself into a being to be feared.

Only then did he respond.

"Here," he growled.

A severe-looking woman with black, ringletted hair joined him beneath the tree. Being of average height, she was a bit taller than him.

"It's almost time for your speech," she said, in her usual confident voice.

Corin knew it was the lilaxe that gave her that confidence. But then, how did she perceive him? Because whenever he ingested the lilaxe, it suddenly felt like everyone was his servant; that by the law of nature, they could only assist him on his road to power, whether they knew it or not. If his subordinates entered that same mental state, was it even possible for them to be loyal to him? Or were they all secretly scheming against him?

These thoughts plagued Corin relentlessly. He had no way to be free of them. All he could do was suffocate any potential rebellious urges with terror, and hope they spasmed and died without resistance.

Staring at the woman with a hint of madness in his eyes, he gave a slow, wordless nod. Then he walked back with her towards the busy agora, dropping the lemon onto the soft bed of grass as he left.

Its ripe body lay there, as if waiting for someone to take it.

*

"It flourishes too easily for the Ragea to ever wipe it out," Pavneet continued.

"That must be why there's been so many of them at Devil's Orchard recently," Jak said. "They're guarding the lilaxes."

"Is that why they worship it?" Martin asked, slowly being sucked into the conversation. Pavneet was talking about the lilaxe in such clear, practical terms that, despite himself, Martin was starting to believe Oceanos was real. "Because they know it can let them experience Oceanos?"

"No," Pavneet said. "Ma betsawar hek. They only found out about Oceanos a fortnight ago. But they changed their glycon to that lilaxe image roughly a year before that."

"So why do they treat it like it's sacred?"

Pavneet gave a shrug of defeat. "I can't figure it out."

"But the Ragea know how to access Oceanos?" Jak asked.

"Yes. Sadly. They saw it in my notes."

"But they're scared of it, aren't they?" Martin said, trying to gain a clear perspective on this web of information. "If everyone's connected through their emotions, then you wouldn't hurt someone else, because you'd feel their pain." He glanced meaningfully at Jak. "So they wouldn't be able to intimidate people anymore."

"Correct," Pavneet said. "It would level everyone. And I guess that's not in their interests." Sardonicism dripped from that last sentence.

"Bayts..." Pavneet turned solemnly to face Jak. "Do you know if they've attacked others as well – besides us? I mean, how far their violence goes? Because I had no idea that this is what they're really like."

Jak gazed away dismally: "I know enough."

Then he looked back at Pavneet: "How did you discover it?"

As if he were drifting back into memory, the hint of a proud smile crept over Pavneet's face. "It was... odd. In my free time, I'd been studying the digital file of an ancient book. I doubt you've heard of it. It was written by a man called Tokugawa Ieyasu. He was a Japanese shogun, and to his mind, the entire spectrum of human emotions could be divided into seven distinct categories: joy, anger, anxiety, love, grief, fear, and hate."

From the way that Pavneet rattled off this list, it was clear that he'd committed it to memory, if only through repeated readings.

"I found it thought-provoking. At the same time, I was desperate. I have no tribe, so I live off trading my scientific journals for the things I need. And my last one had been over a month ago. I needed something – some interesting result from an experiment, something that people would *want* to read about. So I was putting lots of chemicals together, at random really. Just testing and hoping. And then…"

Slowly, he smiled, his face brightening as if with the deepest bliss. "It was amazing…"

He didn't even try to express in words how Oceanos had felt. Then his beatific look gently faded.

"It's strange though, isn't it?" he continued. "Reading about the spectrum of human emotions, and then – completely coincidentally – you find out you've added to it."

"As if it's meant to be," Jak said quietly, as though to himself.

Then he added: "In your pamphlet, you said that if people kept experiencing Oceanos, it would become a permanent part of their psyche. Is that right?"

"That's what every test I've done suggests. I'd almost be tempted to say it's an emotion that humans would develop anyway, and the lilaxe is just accelerating our evolution towards it. But obviously, I can't know if it will become permanent until someone tries it for a long period of time."

"What I don't get," Martin said, "is why didn't you print everything you knew about Oceanos in the pamphlet? Why didn't you tell people what they needed to do to experience it? It would have made the whole thing more believable straightaway."

"Well," Pavneet said, with a sort of regretful cynicism: "It's always good to give people a reason to buy the next issue.

"Besides, I'm not unethical. I still needed to do some long-term testing. We're talking about people's emotional make-up here – one of the most fundamental things about who they are. I couldn't take a chance with that. What if everyone had started trying Oceanos, and it turned out that it caused serious psychological damage? No no, it wasn't safe for me to release the details. Not then."

Martin nodded, trying to pacify Pavneet. It seemed like his last question had irritated him, although whether Pavneet was annoyed with himself or someone else, Martin couldn't tell. "Okay. Makes sense."

"And can it?" Jak asked Pavneet.

"Can it what?"

"Damage people's psyches?"

Pavneet never had time to answer. With an expression of sudden horror, Jak pointed at something behind Martin's back and shouted, "Run!" From that moment, as Martin spun round, everything became chaos.

Martin saw balaclavaed men charging through the underbrush towards them, saw the long knives gripped in their hands. He turned back, and began to scramble away. He didn't know where he was going. There were shouts, a stampede of feet, his pounding heart, all in a dizzying rush of sensation. Then a cry of pain cut through the air. Without stopping, Martin darted a look over his shoulder. Pavneet was on the forest floor. He'd collapsed. There was blood, lots of blood, and a knife in his thigh.

But Martin didn't stop. He was caught in a blind terror. What about Jak? Was he okay? Oh please let him be okay…

No matter how fast he ran, in Martin's head, the Ragea were always bearing down upon him.

He didn't look back. He just kept running.

Chapter 19

In the deepening twilight, Corin stood on a makeshift wooden podium, thousands of expectant eyes trained upon him. Most of Karthalia's population was present, their clothes creating a frozen sea of bright colours, mostly pinks, blues, turquoises, and lush verdant greens. The audience was so large that it spilled out beyond the agora's stone paving slabs, and onto the grass that surrounded them.

Beneath his own black clothing, Corin's posture had now become normal and relaxed. In public, he could be the self he was when he was alone. It was only amongst the Ragea that he had to pretend.

"... for him," Corin continued, "we changed our glycon into a beautiful flower growing from a dead shadow. In memory of him, we changed our tribal name to Ragea. And in honour of him, we have created this statue. I only hope it's worthy of him.

"To Sanif," Corin shouted.

And in one sharp uniform movement, the black sheets that covered the statue were pulled away.

The audience stared in open-mouthed amazement. Then, in wild admiration, the crowd began to stamp its feet and whoop loudly. Even Corin, who had known what the monument would look like, couldn't take his eyes off the final piece.

At four storeys high, the statue towered over its spectators. Although carved from rugged, dark grey rock, it exuded such uncompromising power that it seemed to have transcended into something unearthly.

Enthroned upon an austere stone chair, the figure of Sanif Ragea sat in a rigid, upright posture, one redolent of both authority and an inner nobility. Its heavy feet, planted upon the flagstones, were suggestive of a potent and immovable spirit. Its simple clothing was carved with elegant folds, ostentatious proof of exquisite craftsmanship.

Amongst these folds, sprouting from the statue's chest, was the grey stonework of a lilaxe in full bloom.

As for the arms, each was bare and sinewy down to the elbow, where the hard rock began to spiral like a miniature whirlpool, shifting into a more inhuman form. The left arm morphed into the twisted trunk and foliage of a stone tree. The right arm mimicked the shapes of water, its forearm topped with petrified wavelets, its fingers seeming to melt and trickle down the armrest.

The head possessed a strong, heroic jaw, but where a mouth or lips should have been, there lay only a blankness of rock. Set into the face as eyes were two red gems that, presumably catching some sort of torchlight, were glinting coralaciously against the night sky.

Well done, Sanif, Corin thought, staring up at the statue's face. *You did lay the way for me.*

As the cheering started to die away, Corin turned back to gaze at his audience. Intoxicated by the lilaxe, he almost believed that the cheering had been for him. He felt like a god, with his ignorant mass of worshippers spread out before him in the gloom.

"And now," Corin announced, "please welcome the man responsible for building this statue: Amik Vornier."

Reluctantly, Corin stepped down from the podium. At the back of the crowd, Laura waited for the appearance of the next speaker.

*

After an hour of indecision, Laura had decided to go to the ceremony. She had arrived just before it commenced.

"… the gems," Amik's voice continued, "will glow red when they catch the sunlight…"

For months, she'd been looking forward to this day. Now that it was here, all she felt was a dead and numbing weight, like the corpse of that past eagerness.

"… This is not a dead statue. It interacts with its environment…"

Amik didn't look upset. His strong voice didn't quaver with regret. He appeared content, as if he'd made the right decision with his life. As if, after one day, his "love" for Laura had been easily discarded. Her life plan with him now felt like a stupid dream.

"… this is, by far, the most technically complex construction in all of Karthalia…"

So that's all our relationship was worth, she thought, with tears in her eyes. It felt like a betrayal, as if Amik had stabbed a knife into her love for him. That emotional violence – it *physically hurt*. And it felt like Amik had opened up a black hole inside her, the darkness of which was eating away at her, poisoning her life, sucking it dry of all its meaning.

"… we have given him no mouth, because his actions…"

But what was all this pain – and the end of her relationship with Amik – really based on? Were the Ragea as vicious as Jak claimed? Was it really them who attacked him? Standing on tiptoe, Laura surveyed the nearby faces in the crowd. There must be some people who at least suspected the Ragea's true nature. However, everyone looked happy. Did that mean Jak was wrong? Or that those who knew pretended not to? Was there that much fear in Karthalia?

Laura had blamed the Ragea for her brother's assault. She'd let them be the root of her break-up with Amik. And yet, in the cold aftermath of these events, she realised she still knew nothing about them. Instead, she'd been dragged between other people's views. First Amik's, and now Jak's. Neither of them was satisfactory.

She withdrew something from her pocket. It was the card her brother had foisted upon her on the night of the party. She had to take control of the situation, and find out the truth for herself.

Walking away from the agora, she left Amik's self-satisfied voice behind.

There was a spot where Jak and Martin had arranged to reunite, if the meeting with Pavneet had been a trap. Using the Wall that loomed over the forest as a rough reference point, Jak found it. But when he got there, it was deserted.

Pausing, gasping for breath against the trunk of a tree, he glanced over his shoulder... in the deep twilight, made deeper beneath the canopy of trees, he saw no sign of the Ragea... heard nothing, save the fearful blood pounding in his temples.

He couldn't believe he'd made it, when for the last couple of days he'd been reduced to a hobbling wreck. But his adrenaline had kicked in, dulling all that pain, enabling him to run, if desperately and unstably. Now he was here. But where was Martin? And how long could he afford to wait for him?

Time crawled by with an agonising slowness, like a hamstrung person clawing their way across the ground. In the lonely silence, one question kept torturing Jak: could someone have betrayed him and Martin? But no. It didn't make sense. No one else knew. But then how could the Ragea have ambushed them...

A movement further down the forest edge startled him from his thoughts. Instinctively, he retreated slightly. Then he saw Martin, looking terrified, stagger out of the forest.

Jak waved surreptitiously, and Martin hurried towards him.

"Where's Pavneet?" Jak demanded in a low voice, when Martin was close enough to hear.

"Back there." Martin pointed into the forest, gasping his words. "He had a knife… in his leg…"

Jak grabbed Martin fiercely by his shoulders: "And you left him?"

"Of course I did!" Martin snapped, flinging Jak's hands off him. "What else could I do, they were everywhere!" He jabbed his finger accusingly at Jak. "This is *your* fault. You brought us here."

Silenced by a surge of guilt, Jak gazed back into the forest's darkness. His eyes glistened with a futile desperation.

Misreading the look, Martin's tone softened, and a new edge of fear entered his voice. "You can't go back in there," he warned, placing his hand on Jak's arm as if he might need to restrain him.

Jak grimaced. He had no way of finding Pavneet, no way of rescuing him. "I know."

Then he glanced at Martin, and saw the look in his friend's brown eyes. Saw Martin's fierce desire to protect him, even though Jak had nearly cost him his life. And suddenly, all Jak's guilt at endangering Martin, and all his shame at having failed Martin's trust, roared up inside him. A tight ache formed in his chest.

"Martin…" Jak's bottom lip quivered with guilt. "… we can't go back home. The Ragea'll find us there. For a while at least… we have to go underground."

Martin didn't say anything. He just stared at Jak in a heavy silence. Then slowly, he looked away towards the agora. Jak followed his gaze.

Colourful human specks were pouring out of the site. The ceremony must have finished. Above the agora, the crimson light of sunset blazed through a large opening in the clouds, like the glow of an inverted volcano breaking through the inky heavens.

Held fast by awe and sorrow, Jak stared at the scene. He had the strange and alien sensation that, as it huddled low there in the darkness, the agora had turned its back on him.

Chapter 20

Laura hesitated. She'd deliberately taken a long route to this door, trying to convince herself that she should come another day. Surely no one would be in, everyone having gone to the ceremony? But it had felt like if she didn't visit today, then she wouldn't visit at all.

Stepping forward, she knocked on the front door of the Intel Tribe's headquarters.

There was the sound of heavy footsteps from within, then the door swung back with the suddenness and force of a thunder-crack. Laura stiffened. A woman stood in the opening, with a large face and a wide mane of black, frizzy hair pulled back by an even blacker headband. She was scowling.

"What do you want?" she demanded. She had a naturally huge frame, a curving motherly shape, and although she was about Laura's height, Laura had the unsettling sense that the woman was towering over her.

"Um, do you..." Laura was still amazed that someone had opened the door. "... s-sorry if I disturbed you. But... do you know where Tessalli Ekundayo is?" She presented the card that Jak had given her. The woman glanced at it.

"That's me," she answered. Her voice was deep and strong, as though it would reverberate well in a room with good acoustics. She spoke curtly. "Who gave you that card?"

"Jakariah Marcy." Laura hoped she'd see a smile of recognition on Tessalli's face. "He's my brother."

Tessalli didn't smile. She just gave a slow, thoughtful nod. "Bari. Come in."

Laura followed her inside.

The building was a large bungalow, its gloomy interior lit only with solar-powered lights. Apart from Tessalli, it seemed to be deserted.

Not only was the first room dark, but somehow – despite its large size – almost claustrophobic. A heavy atmosphere of serious, humourless thinking pervaded it. Laura felt like she was stepping into Jak's World, or rather, the part that he'd always kept private from her.

"Sorry for being a bit sharp," Tessalli said, as she took Laura's coat and hung it among some others on a wooden stand. "I'm just a bit stressed, trying to get the next edition finished. But are you alright? You seem upset."

"What? No no, I'm fine." Laura thought she'd kept her emotion over Amik tightly bottled up inside her. She was stunned that Tessalli had detected it.

"Whatever you say," Tessalli replied. She ambled over to one of the room's many desks, and plumped her considerable weight onto its chair. She motioned to a nearby desk for Laura to do the same. "So what did he send you for?"

"Who? Oh no, Jak didn't send me here. Well, not exactly. He just gave me your card. He said you could show me…" Laura flinched away from the question she'd come to ask. All of a sudden, it sounded incredibly naive. Instead, fiddling nervously with the amber bracelet on her wrist, she opted for a euphemism. "… what the Ragea are really like."

Tessalli's expression hardened like granite, reminding Laura of the Ragea's statue. For a moment, there was only silence, save for the faint buzzing of the solar lights.

At last, Tessalli spoke, in a much graver tone. "Jakariah does like to exploit our friendship."

"Does he?" Laura said politely, even as she privately disagreed with Tessalli's comment. From her experience, and excluding the events of the party, she didn't know anyone who possessed more integrity than her brother. "He mentions you a lot. I'm amazed this is the first time we've met."

"Mm," Tessalli replied with a total lack of interest. She seemed wrapped up in her own thoughts. When she spoke, it was much more slowly than before: "If I show you this... it's a big risk for me, you understand that? If Jakariah hadn't sent you, we wouldn't be discussing it."

Laura nodded nervously. It felt like she was teetering on a precipice, willing herself to jump. "That's fine. It's what I'm here for."

Tessalli gave a tired, cynical laugh. She nodded, then rose to her feet. "Come on then."

She turned and headed deeper into the shadows of the building.

Down a narrow corridor, and then Tessalli turned left, into a small room. Its only illumination was the weak, red glow of a strip light.

Bathed in this radiance, a line of cord hung loosely across the room. Pegged along its length were freshly developed photos, each one offering a tantalising glimpse into a larger story.

"This is our dark room," Tessalli said, heading straight towards what looked like a small, mostly empty bookcase in the corner. Kneeling down, she groped in the dark at the back of one of its shelves. Then, using both hands, she withdrew something heavy, and solemnly walked back into the room's faintly disturbing glow.

Stopping beside Laura, she lowered a metal box onto a small table. Due to its weightiness, it landed with a slight thud. Tessalli looked over her shoulder at Laura: "Anything you see here, you keep to yourself."

Laura nodded obediently.

Snapping open the buckles on the box, Tessalli added: "These people came to me in confidence."

She opened the dull, tarnished silver of the box's lid, only to reveal another locked box, this one wooden and much lighter. Laura wondered what would need to be guarded with such extreme caution.

Then Tessalli pulled back the lid.

Inside the small box was a scattered collection of roughly ten photos. About half of these lay face-up, but they were too shadowed for Laura to make out their images.

Tessalli sighed: "Don't say I didn't warn you," and raised a photo into the light.

Like all photos in Karthalia, the image was in stark black and white. It captured the upper half of a young man who was standing, his body slumped as he faced the camera. He wore no shirt, and he stared down the camera's lens with blank, lifeless eyes, as if some trauma had hollowed out all of his emotions. In the mono-chrome photo, his grey body was heavily discoloured by swollen patches of black.

"The Ragea attacked him." Laura's tone fell somewhere between a question and a statement.

Tessalli nodded. Slowly, she pulled out another photo, then another and another, building in Laura's mind a collage of grue-some violence.

The total twelve photos were of three men, each one captured from four different angles. Beneath the strip light, the injured bodies glowed blood red.

Laura hadn't had a clue about any of this. And yet a tsunami of guilt crashed in upon her, so that at first, she could only mutter a few stifled words above its waves:

"Why didn't he tell me about this before?"

"I'm not sure. This stuff – it's dangerous to know about. Maybe he didn't think you were ready. Besides, they don't *prove* the Ragea did anything."

"But why haven't you shown these to anyone?! You're helping the Ragea!"

"*Don't* talk to me like that!" Tessalli turned savagely on Laura. "You don't know what they're like! I've got a husband and kids to protect!" Abruptly, she stopped speaking, as if restraining herself.

"You mean... they'd attack your children?"

"Yeah. Yeah, I think so."

A brief pause, only a few heartbeats long.

"The first of these men," Tessalli pointed at the photos, "came here eight months ago. We were going to print his assault in *The Web*. But later that same day, three of the Ragea paid us a visit.

"They brought gifts, luxuries. Then one of them took me aside. He knew I oversee things here."

Tessalli hesitated, as though remembering something painful.

"That man from the Ragea... he stood very close to my face. His eyes – they weren't blinking, and there was this scary intensity in them. He said to me, in a hissed whisper: *never print anything that damns the Ragea*. Otherwise, even if they had to wait, one of his tribe would come for someone I loved.

"So I told the man in the photo. Said that I couldn't mention the Ragea in his article. After I took that away, he didn't want his injuries publicised. Why would he? It was the same with the other two men that came after him. When they saw that we'd... backed down" – she almost spat those last two words – "all their conviction disappeared. It was like they thought, if we didn't speak for them, then they didn't have a voice."

Laura could see the tears in Tessalli's eyes.

"It isn't just me. Everyone else here knows what's going on, even if they don't talk about it. At least I took these photos, in case they could be used as evidence. And you know what? The Ragea wanted to keep giving us gifts in exchange for our silence, but *I* turned them down. *J'ai* dit non! We've got some self-respect.

"So we've stayed silent, to protect the people we love. Would you have risked their safety? Risked them suffering like Jakariah did?"

"Of course not," Laura said meekly. The powerful woman who she'd met at the front door had crumbled, but it wasn't like crumbling into dust. It was like a mountain beginning to crumble, threatening an avalanche on the people it scorned, even if that meant causing harm to itself. For her own good, Tessalli needed someone's support.

Laura added: "It's not your fault."

Tessalli took a deep breath, and seemed to bring her feelings under control. With a cautious voice, Laura dared to ask another question.

"Why did they attack these people?"

Tessalli replied with much more calm than before. "For getting in the Ragea's way, somehow or other. Did you notice where the bruises were on those men? All on the body. None on their arms or faces. That's so no one can see the injuries the Ragea have inflicted. It's that calculated. Right down to the very last kick."

Laura remembered her brother's wounds – just one stray kick to the face. They'd tried to do the same thing to him.

"There are probably a lot more victims," Tessalli said. "These are just the ones who have come to us."

Then she retreated into a thoughtful silence, as if she'd said enough. Meanwhile, those graphic images floated through Laura's mind. Karthalia being a fairly small community, she recognised those three men. But whenever she'd seen them, they'd appeared so normal; hardly worth a second glance. She'd never considered that there could be so much pain lying beneath the surface.

This fresh knowledge was darkening her previously unblemished view of Karthalia. Discolouring it like a bruise on innocent skin.

A slamming noise punctured the silence, jolting Laura out of her reverie. The sound had come from the tribdwell's front door, several rooms away. Laura looked at Tessalli for reassurance, but found none.

"Que diable! Qui est-ce?" Tessalli said. She hurried out of the room, and Laura followed in her wake. Remembering that they'd just been talking critically about the Ragea, Laura's heart began to pound. But how could they know what she and Tessalli had been saying? Was it even possible that the Ragea could have been spying on them?

They reached the building's large front room.

"Hey!" A sharp male voice shouted at them from the darkness. It came from the room's other end. "Who's there?"

Tessalli breathed a sigh of relief.

"It's *me*, Judas," she called back to the man. "What are you doing here so late?"

A scruffy man – with a face that looked like it had been worn down by years of late nights and stress – stepped into the light. He was panting, as if he'd run to the building. "You mean you don't know?"

"Know what?" Tessalli said with impatience.

"Oh man," Judas said, a large grin stretching across his face. "I haven't heard about a story this big in a loooong time."

With furtive glances, Jak and Martin strode through a deserted lane, carefully evading the dark puddles so as to make less noise. It was late at night, and all other Karthalians were presumably in bed. The few valiant stars left in the sky were overwhelmed by black clouds.

From a few feet behind Jak, Martin suddenly hissed: "Jak! Look at this."

Jak turned round. A piece of paper floated in a puddle, and Martin stared down at it, his face full of horror. A moment later, Jak read it and suffered a similar reaction.

The wet sheet of paper was a bulletin:

BY NOTICE OF THE RAGEA

THE 'WANTED MAN' PAVNEET HANSRAJ HAS BEEN APPREHENDED, BUT HE HAD TWO ACCOMPLICES WHO ESCAPED: JAKARIAH MARCY AND MARTIN FELLASH.

THEY ARE RESPONSIBLE FOR THE MURDER OF ONE OF OUR TRIBESMEN.

UNLESS THEY GIVE THEMSELVES UP BY MIDNIGHT TOMORROW (THE 12TH), PAVNEET HANSRAJ WILL BE EXECUTED.

Act II

Chapter 21

They'd needed somewhere to hide.

Then Jak had remembered the exposed sewage works, near where he'd first seen the 'Wanted' posters of Pavneet. He and Martin had fled there.

The following night, they'd seen the Ragea's bulletin. But by then, there was barely any time left. Its announcement was already over twenty-four hours old.

"Jak, we've got to stop arguing about this!" Martin shouted. "It's got to be eleven already! They're going to kill him in *less than one hour* unless we do something!"

The two of them stood at a point where several sewer tunnels converged, in a large human-made cavern. Martin glared at Jak, his face eerily lit by the flickering, improvised torches that the two of them had fixed to the dank walls of their subterranean den.

"We can't just hand ourselves over," Jak snapped back. "The Ragea are saying we've killed one of their tribesmen. We don't know what they'll do to us."

"But if we don't do *anything*, they'll *definitely* execute Pavneet."

Martin's voice was frantic. He was gesturing forcefully with his arms. Jak could practically feel the time slipping away from them.

"Jak," Martin said, fractionally softening his tone but retaining all its urgency. "This isn't a game anymore. The graffitiing was one thing, but we're talking about a *human life* now. I mean, look at you. They battered you. You could barely walk. We've let this go too far."

"*I know that*. But we *can't* go back now. The Ragea won't let us survive. Not as long as we know about Oceanos. And even if we do give ourselves up, we have no guarantee that they'll let Pavneet go."

"They've publicly said they would."

"So what? They've *said* one of their tribe is dead! They'll find a way to justify murdering him if they want to! Think about it. He's tribeless. It's not like anyone's going to defend him."

"Then I'll give myself up, and *you* stay here. That way you'll be safe whatever happens, and we might still be able to free him."

Martin started to storm away, but Jak snatched his sleeve, pulling him to a stop. "Are you crazy? Then they'll torture you to find me. Or they'll threaten to kill you unless I come forward, just like they've done with Pavneet. It won't work."

Martin yanked his sleeve free of Jak's grip, and said with a mixture of haughtiness and disdain: "They wouldn't torture me. They're not gonna risk inciting a whole tribe."

"Then how come they attacked me?"

The torchlight wavered over Martin's frozen, uncertain expression. In the silence, Jak could hear the soft gushing of the sewage water, and a brief skittering noise, like a fat, slimy rat scurrying through the darkness.

Suddenly, Martin lashed out: "So what do *you* suggest?"—he pointed behind him, as if Pavneet were within viewing distance— "Because he's going to die unless we do something right now! So come on! *What is it?*"

"Look. I know it's horrible. I know it's the worst thing ever." Jak's voice was cold, calculated, as though he were explaining something inevitable. "But we can't do anything."

Jak tried to suppress any emotion he felt, for Martin's sake. But inside, he experienced a sickening queasiness rising up, something unrelated to the sewer's stench of mingled shit and piss. He saw the sewage water surging away on its course, a patch of its murky green surface dimly illuminated by the torchlight. The sewage water was like time: rushing away; Time had been contaminated by a horrendous choice.

Jak could almost sense Pavneet's pleading spectre in the cavern with them. This sensation hurt all the more because Jak knew what had to be done.

The question racing through his mind wasn't whether he should turn himself in. Instead it was: how could he prevent Martin from leaving? If it came to it, he would knock his friend out, bashing Martin's head against the cavern's rock wall. The only imperative was that Martin couldn't escape. That would only endanger both their lives.

Jak watched the indecision on Martin's face: the urge to leave, the hesitation to risk betraying both himself and his best friend into mortal danger.

"Martin, we can't save Pavneet now. That's just an illusion." With these words, Jak was also trying to persuade himself. "The Ragea will kill him whatever we do. The only decision we have is whether we put ourselves in danger as well."

"No... no, there's got to be another way. We could somehow rescue him – sneak in and help him escape. Or we could gather people together, march against the Ragea and force them to let Pavneet go. We could..."

"No. We can't. We don't have enough time."

The sickening feeling inside Jak was getting worse. It felt like he was the one executing Pavneet.

"Then this is your decision!" Martin shouted. "This isn't me! If we don't go, then *you've* made that choice." Martin's voice was cracking, as if with the onset of tears. "*You* have to take responsibility!"

Jak was trying to tune out Martin's invocations of guilt, when suddenly he saw something he hadn't noticed before: a heavy grate in the ceiling. As if in a trance, he stepped towards it, and lifted it up. A small quantity of moonlight pierced the subterranean darkness.

To eyes that had spent a lifetime gazing at the sky to estimate the time, the revelation was obvious and immediate: the moon was at its apex, or just past it. Martin had been wrong about how long they'd had left. He and Jak had been arguing far longer than they'd realised.

The crisis minute had passed without them noticing.

His voice half croaking, Jak muttered: "We're too late."

"What?" Aghast, Martin walked over to Jak, and stared at the moon for himself. For a long time, neither of them spoke.

But was Pavneet really dead? Or had the Ragea reneged on their threat?

There was no way Jak and Martin could know. Yet the darkness around them was pervaded by the heavy sense that now, for both of them, there was no going back.

And an acute, unsettling feeling of loneliness invaded Jak: that he couldn't know if his decision, to abandon Pavneet, had been right.

Chapter 22

The Khamsin howled, a hot, dust-laden wind that chanced upon Karthalia roughly once a year. Thanks to Karthalia's Wall, its conveyance of sand grains swarmed above Karthalia like a dome constructed by a sand god, veiling some of the pale evening stars, and blotting out others. Far below it, on the ground, two shadowed figures forged a weary path through the night, searching for food.

Jak still hobbled, his whole body aching from his injuries. Martin looked equally exhausted. They were both sleep-deprived: traumatised by what might have happened to Pavneet and, on a more practical level, their body clocks were struggling to adjust to their new nocturnal way of life.

But Jak fought on. Having been an insomniac for years, he was probably coping with the strain better than Martin. And he needed to. Needed, as best he could, to be a pillar of strength for his friend.

"The Khamsin has to come *now*, of all times," Martin said miserably, half to himself. Jak looked at Martin's downcast eyes, and saw the depression and sense of everything being meaningless that lay within them.

"We can't allow Pavneet to have... for it to have happened in vain," Jak said, hearing the hollowness in his own words. Then, like the faint, pearly glow of dawn against the night's blackness, an idea came to him. A long shot, but maybe a way to restore meaning to what they were doing.

He said to Martin: "Follow me."

The two men picked their way through the darkness, through an almost silhouetted Karthalia. They passed the Word Tribe, the Solar-Salvagers Tribe, and others, against a backdrop of faint night calls from sea animals, which issued from the other side of the Wall.

At last, they reached their destination: an unassuming tribdwell; and one of the most useful resources in the intelligence network that Jak had created for himself.

Raising his hand, he knocked on its wooden front door.

For the second evening in two days, Laura was searching for Jak and Martin. It was the 13th, the day after the two of them were supposed to surrender themselves to the Ragea. Laura remembered her night at the Intel Tribe HQ, when Judas had brought the news. She'd become frantic, almost delirious with horror and panic. She'd raced straight to her parents, told them what was happening, and then, not knowing what else to do, the three of them had headed out into the evening to look for Jak.

The more time passed without finding him, the more it felt like reality and the horrible imaginings in the pit of Laura's stomach would soon be one and the same. Midnight passed. Tears were shed. But the dreaded news never came.

Now, Laura felt a cautious sense of relief. She hadn't heard anything to suggest that Jak and Martin were at the Ragea's mercy. She hoped that meant they were safe, although she tried to hide that hope even from herself, in case, by some nasty and contrarian law of the universe, it somehow made it more likely that Jak and Martin had already been captured and executed.

Garbed in a brown cloak, Laura had tucked her distinctive light and dark hair into its raised cowl. To all eyes, her cloak should – she thought – look as if it were being worn to protect her against the blustery downdrafts of the raging Khamsin above. But really, it was to protect her from something much more dangerous. Since the midnight ordained for Pavneet's execution had passed, packs of Ragea had started roaming the streets, bearing weapons. They were hunting for Jak and Martin. Even as family, she couldn't be seen to be helping them. All through her trek, she'd kept herself vigilant, but so far she hadn't encountered any Ragea that evening.

Far above, the Khamsin moaned incessantly like a banshee. It was one of the three extreme weather conditions that Karthalia endured, along with earthquakes and tsunamis. With Laura's World falling apart, it felt like an appropriate time for such a destructive elemental force to appear.

Most of the people she saw during her search were clearly in a state of agitation or fear. This was the first murder that anyone had heard of in over a century, and they were so horrified by the Ragea's declaration, that it never crossed their minds that it might not be true. The fact that Jak and Martin hadn't come forward only made them look even more guilty.

But Laura couldn't believe that either of them had intentionally killed a member of the Ragea. Maybe, somehow, they'd committed manslaughter, but even that seemed vastly improbable. Martin wouldn't hurt a fly, and Jak...

Laura remembered the way he'd viciously assaulted the boy who had been bullying her at school. Remembered the blood spilling everywhere, and the way Jak was still swinging his fists even as the teachers dragged him away...

Nonetheless, that beating was something different. It wasn't murder. He could never murder. Never.

But whatever else was true, this was almost certainly Jak's fault. He must have led Martin into this storm of a situation, where a fatal, monstrous wave could engulf both of them at any moment.

127

With a sense of sibling's guilt, she kept imagining Tobias distraught, barely able to sleep, looking more haggard than ever.

But Laura didn't care why Jak had done whatever he'd done. She only wanted find him and bring him home. As for how they'd resolve things with the Ragea... well, they'd cross that bridge when they got to it.

She was now passing through the quiet district of the Techno Tribe, where spare solar panels leaned idly against the vegetation of tribdwell walls, and where almost everyone seemed to have retreated indoors. It was the seventh or eighth tribe she'd investigated that evening, and still she'd had no luck finding her brother. Not even a sign of him. She was exhausted, physically and emotionally. And in her desperation, a longing that had grown horribly familiar gnawed at her mind once again: Amik.

No matter how much she hated him, she wanted him right now for comfort, for a sense of security. And the thought of him – and the conflict it stirred in her – was driving her mad, like an insect that had flown into her ear and was slowly, constantly picking away at her brain.

A memory surfaced...

Its imagery was soft and dreamy. Misty red light from the rising sun poured onto her tired, bleary-eyed face. Her limp body bobbed up and down, held in the embrace of Amik's strong arms. She had just begun to stir from her sleep, but instead of feeling alarmed at not knowing where she was, her calmness was barely disturbed. She was in Amik's arms, and that was enough to tell her she was safe.

They were ascending a flight of steps. Then suddenly, Laura felt her body fully bathed in sunlight: they had reached the top. Her eyes opened.

Seeing beneath her the flat expanse of a stone roof told her where they were. Only one building in Karthalia was made of exposed, unvegetated stone, and it was sacred to all tribes: the Cemetery

Building. Below her, thousands of urns – many acting as cenotaphs – were shelved within hundreds of cold, unfurnished rooms. Laura had been there many times before, to pay her respects to dead relatives or dead friends. In Karthalia, there were no antibiotics, and almost no one made it to adulthood without losing at least one loved one along the way.

But she'd never been on the building's roof. Never experienced its panoramic view, where Karthalia's tribdwells, its Wall, its open swathes of lush grass, and its river, were burnished red with the spectacular glow of sunrise.

Laying Laura upon the cold stone, Amik then spread out a blanket for the two of them to sit upon. He removed a wicker basket from the crook of his arm, opening it to reveal several of Laura's favourite pieces of food. In a state of quiet and contented love, they ate, watching the sun climb higher in the radiant sky. Then the two of them fell into an intimate embrace, making love atop that memorial to the dead, bathed in a light that was the colour of roses and blood.

The memory reaching a painful climax, Laura let go of it, dragging her mind away from that searing beauty and back to the comparable greyness and emotional safety of the present. Slowly, she breathed in, then out, trying once again to force Amik out of her mind, and her thoughts back to the present.

She'd stopped at a point where she could see between two tribdwells: in the distance, the statue towered, a symbol of the Ragea. Its immense weight was like a centre of gravity, dominating the landscape, and pulling her thoughts towards it. Staring at the memorial, it felt like the Ragea's eyes were everywhere. Like they were unstoppable, and whatever they wanted, they would get.

She looked away and down at the ground.

For the second day in a row, she had to concede the grim truth. She wouldn't find Jak or Martin tonight. For now, the best thing she could do was hope they remained safe, and go searching for them again tomorrow.

But she didn't dare return home. She'd tried that yesterday, only to find out the Ragea were surveilling the places Jak and Martin were most likely to visit, and perhaps the people they were closest to as well. She couldn't let herself fall into their clutches.

So she had headed somewhere else to sleep: somewhere she was confident the Ragea wouldn't look for her.

Once more, she knocked on its door.

"Ov e?" Tessalli called.

"Me," Laura replied.

"Come in." But Tessalli sounded almost hesitant. Maybe nervous? Laura's hand rested on the door handle, unsure whether to open the door. It could be a trap. Could be the Ragea, holding Tessalli under duress.

Cautiously, Laura pushed back the door, and peered inside.

The living room was empty. But – partly hidden behind a wall – Tessalli was sat at the kitchen table, as if facing someone Laura couldn't see. Quietly, Laura crept forward.

And saw that, sat beside Tessalli, were Jak and Martin.

Chapter 23

Laura's heart jumped. The World around her seemed to physically brighten.

"Jak!" she cried. She ran over and hugged him, squeezing tightly as if to make sure that he wasn't some ghost. Then she embraced Martin, and noticed that a moment passed before he weakly hugged her back. She glanced at his face. He looked like a pale shell of his former self. She gazed into his eyes, and through her tears of relief, gave him a reassuring smile.

The World was a wonderful place again. It seemed impossible that the depressed, washed-out life she'd been living before could – in a matter of seconds – transform into this.

The three of them caught up with each other, Laura saying through tears that she'd seen Tessalli's photos, Jak explaining where he and Martin had been hiding.

"But what are you going to do?" Tessalli asked. "The Ragea are *everywhere*."

Steam whistled from the metal pot that hung over the kitchen's cooking fire.

"I know," Jak muttered. "Finish making that coffee. There's something I need to ask you to do for me."

Four small wooden cups were filled with coffee. The kitchen

was warm with the fire's blaze. And decorating one of the room's walls was a carving of a red, serpentine dragon, its iridescent fish-like scales flickering in the firelight.

Taking her seat, Laura noticed that on the table was both an inkpot – no doubt for Tessalli's work – and a child's well-worn sock puppet. She stifled a sudden low-level sense of panic.

"Where are your kids?" she asked Tessalli. "Did they see them?" She pointed at Jak and Martin.

"No," Tessalli said curtly. "Eli's tucking them into bed now. But he saw them."

A slight pause.

"He'll stay out of the way while we talk in here."

Laura could hear the edge of anxiety in Tessalli's voice. Everyone in that tribdwell was in danger. They were either a fugitive, or in contact with fugitives. The atmosphere tingled with an electric frisson.

Jak broke the silence. His thin face was grimmer, more drawn, and even more pale than usual. "Have you... heard anything about Pavneet?"

"Not yet," Tessalli replied. "... Sorry."

Jak just nodded, like someone still in shock.

"I still can't work out how they found us," he said. "How could they have known where we were meeting him? Only me and Martin saw the note. There's not even anyone who could have betrayed us."

"There must have been someone," Laura said.

"Then who?"

Jak's only answer was silence. Laura glanced uncomfortably from him to Tessalli, and back again. The gloominess of the kitchen felt disquietingly appropriate for this new, darker World that she'd stepped into.

"So. Jakariah," Tessalli said, fiddling – as if in agitation – with the reading glasses that she now wore round her neck. "You had something to say?"

Starting at a slow, maybe even hesitant pace, Jak began. He told Laura about Oceanos: how it was like an untapped colour on the spectrum of human emotions; how it would fundamentally transform human behaviour; and how it appeared that humans would, ultimately and inevitably, acquire it through evolution.

Laura found her initial confusion drifting into a quiet, uncertain awe.

As he pressed onward, Jak's speech gathered in momentum and fluency. Laura was struck by the difference between now, and when he'd drunkenly declaimed his view of the Ragea at her party. Not only was he sober: he was eloquent, fired with belief in a noble cause. His speech, full of gravity, possessed a magnetic pull. He and Martin had been through a horrible ordeal, and it had changed them, of course. But privately, Laura was impressed. From the desperation of the situation, Jak had found a deeper, more focused strength.

But Tessalli was frowning. She appeared increasingly sceptical and concerned, as if she were watching a friend whose mind had been infected by the raving pronouncements of a nascent religion. Jak, turning his attention to her, clearly noticed her expression.

"Look," he said, his low voice full of conviction. "Pavneet believed Oceanos is real. And the Ragea obviously do as well. It's why they attacked him."

"I'm sure they do," Tessalli said. "Doesn't mean they're right."

"True," Jak said, the hint of a daring look emerging onto his face. "That's why we need to find out for ourselves."

He gave Martin a brief, meaningful glance, then carried on.

"We have to experience Oceanos. Find out if Pavneet knew what he was on about. To do that, we need a plant known as the lilaxe, which only grows in Devil's Orchard."

"And which the Ragea always have under constant guard," Tessalli cut in with a mutter, her mind leaping ahead.

"There's even more of them there now," Laura said. "Since they've been looking for you two."

"I'm sure," Jak said. He turned to Tessalli. "You're a reporter. That means you can go places others can't... without arousing suspicion."

Incredulously, beneath her mane of frizzy black hair, Tessalli's eyes opened a fraction wider. "You mean you want *me* to fetch you a lilaxe? And how am I supposed to smuggle it out of there?" She looked horrified. "No. I'm sorry Jakariah, but no. Not this time. I'm not risking my life for this, and I can't believe you'd ask me to."

"I'm not asking you to *smuggle* it out of there," Jak said, his tone shifting to the comforting, half-mocking one of an old friend. "Come on. I wouldn't put you in that sort of danger. And look, if they do suspect you, here's what you can say..."

Maintaining his low voice so as not to disturb the rest of the tribdwell, he outlined his idea. Tessalli listened, her features, full of concentration, gradually creasing once more into a look of worry. When Jak was done, she took a moment to think.

"But even if we do get rid of the Ragea," she said, "it won't change anything. I've spent years looking through old newspaper articles in the computer archive, and if there's one thing it's taught me, it's this: having hierarchies is human nature. One powerful group is deposed, another *will* take its place. You can even see it at a social level – there's no relationship, no friendship circle, where someone or some group doesn't have a greater share of control. That's just the way it is.

"Face it: Karthalia's three hundred years of peace and equality – that's just been a historical blip. A utopia that was *never* going to last. And now, things are reverting back to the natural order. And it's not worth us stupidly risking our lives to try and stop that happening. We'd be better off helping you hide or escape instead."

Defiantly, Tessalli stared at Jak.

"But things *don't* have to be that way," Jak said, leaning forward. And despite his thin frame, there was a weight and intensity to his movement. "That's the point. If everyone's emotions are connected through Oceanos, it'll be like they're all part of one body. No one would hurt each other, because it would be like biting your own flesh, or clawing at your own eyes. Everyone would feel the pain of it, including the person who inflicted it.

"And the greater good and the personal good will become one and the same thing, because each person will feel the pleasure that others experience. Acts of selfishness will disappear, and the benefits of the whole will always come first.

"That's what's at stake here. This isn't just about the Ragea. It's about all inequality, all violence, being wiped out forever..."

He clicked his fingers.

"... Just. Like. That. Your kids – your whole family – would be safe from the Ragea. But more than that – they would never grow up in a World where violent and powerful people ruled over them. That's what you could give them."

His gaze was unblinking.

"And on a more personal level, me and Martin need you to do this. This eighth emotion is our best chance of stopping the Ragea. Without it... the two of us will soon be dead."

By this time, the cup of coffee in Laura's hands had grown cold. She'd listened to Jak in silence, entranced. Now, she stared at Tessalli, awaiting a reaction. She could feel a tightness in her chest from the tension.

Finally, Tessalli looked up from the table.

"Fine," she sighed, with a grudging grimace and a small shake of her head, as if she couldn't believe what she was saying. "I'll do it."

She turned in her chair.

"Honey," she called to Eli, in an exasperated voice. "I'm just popping out."

Chapter 24

Tessalli walked nervously through Devil's Orchard. She could sense the pack of Ragea behind her, could sense their eyes following every step she took. Gathered in a loose group, there were roughly seven of them, each wearing the Ragea's typical black clothing and long-sleeved tops. At the same time, in the cloudless sky above, thousands of stars – the night's silver eyes – were gazing down on her. She felt like everyone, every*thing* was watching her.

So much for the night giving her a sense of camouflage.

Back at her tribdwell, Jakariah had described to her the appearance of the lilaxe. Now, she just had to pull off his plan...

Walking at a deliberately leisurely pace, she scanned the surrounding flora. From the earlier Khamsin wind, grains of sand speckled the flowers and grass, like the dewdrops of a barren, harsh World.

Because they flourished in Devil's Orchard, Tessalli quickly spotted what she sought: a patch of intermingling dark greens and purples. A cluster of lilaxes.

She strode over, her powerful, zaftig figure a moving shadow in the darkness. Then, quite openly, she crouched down in front of them. Bending her head close to the flowers, she caught a whiff of the lilaxe's perfume, which somehow smelled – faintly, and probably only to her – the way moonlight looked upon a Summer's evening.

By now, Tessalli felt the hostile, focused stare of the nearby Ragea boring into her. As far as she knew, there was no way to distract their attention from her. Nor could she smuggle a lilaxe past them.

With a slight quivering of her hand, which she hoped the Ragea were too far away to see, she reached forward and, after doing the same to a couple of other flowers, plucked a lilaxe.

A vicious shout cut through the air. Its source, a man in the Ragea, stormed over, followed by the other members of his tribe.

"What are you doing with that lilaxe?" the man snarled, grabbing Tessalli's arm so tightly that it hurt.

"Get off me! What do you think you're doing!" Tessalli struggled, reeling back and wearing the angry, horrified expression of someone suffering an unprovoked attack. "I'm just getting some flowers to remember him!"

Belatedly, as if slow to process this information, the Ragea man stopped fighting against her. His grip slackened, and a look of confused suspicion crawled across his face.

"Chou asdak?"

Tessalli wrenched her hand free of the man's grip. To better look the part of the injured, hapless victim, she soothingly rubbed her sore skin.

"My father died on this day, nine years ago," she said. "He used to come here all the time. I was just getting a few flowers, to make a wreath in his memory, and let it drift down the river."

Still playing the indignant victim, Tessalli didn't do what she wanted to and nervously look at the ground. She gazed directly into the faces of the various Ragea. Like a camouflaged animal, she couldn't flinch, or she might reveal herself.

The man's brow furrowed.

"Sorry," he said in his deep voice, sounding uncertain of himself. "But the lilaxe is sacred to us, and we thought... never mind. If you're putting it in the river as a memorial, that's fine."

"But here," one of the Ragea women chipped in, with a smile that Tessalli could tell was fake. "By way of apology, we'll help you."

With some of the Ragea leaving to stroll around the forest once more, the others helped Tessalli assemble her wreath. She was happy to let them do most of the work.

They're only helping to make sure I don't steal any lilaxes. They really are worried about this plant disappearing. Maybe Jakariah is right about Oceanos...

Then she and the Ragea with her stood at the grassy edge of Devil's Orchard, just before the curving dark blue of the River Menignus. The man who had grabbed Tessalli handed her the wreath, and with a muted sense of relief, she saw the dark green and purple leaves in its midst.

Crouching low, she respectfully laid the flowers in the river. The Ragea watched the wreath drift away, but Tessalli sensed the smugness lurking behind their solemnity.

In a sudden flash, a white dagger of lightning stabbed through the evening sky. For a second, the environment was starkly lit, including – on the far side of the river – the distant spectacle of the Ragea's towering, intimidating statue. The side of the floating wreath nearest Tessalli was also thrown into thick shadow.

The lightning must have been a natural event, caused by the humidity. Regardless of the wreath, of this first step that Jakariah had led her down a strange and blind path, that lightning strike was always going to happen.

But it felt like something more. Whether divine or demonic, it had struck like a supernatural omen.

Tessalli stayed another couple of minutes, to make her act of remembering her dad convincing. By the time she left, the wreath had long drifted out of sight.

*

A slim figure stood on the bank of the River Menignus, its face hidden by the cowl of a raincoat.

It gripped a long fishing net, stolen from the Fishers' Tribe, and held it upright like a spear.

On the water, a wreath drifted into view.

The figure fished the wreath out of the water, took the flowers out of the net, and walked away.

On her way back to Tessalli's, Laura saw posters with sketches of her own face. Now, alongside Jak and Martin, the Ragea also wanted people to report any sightings of her.

"So..."

"So that's it."

Not wanting to wake up Tessalli's family, Laura, Martin, Jak and Tessalli spoke in hushed voices. As if transfixed, they stared at it.

Like a commonplace home decoration, the still-wet lilaxe lay perched in a vase at the centre of the table. The low-crackling fire in the kitchen's corner, along with several candles dotted round the room, dimly illuminated its three waxy petals.

"Doesn't look like there's enough for four of us," Martin said.

"How do you mean?" Jak asked.

"Well, I'm just guessing based on our old Chemistry classes." He gestured at the lilaxe. "It's only got three petals. I mean, assuming they're fairly potent, then roughly one whole petal per person should be fine. But for four of us? The doses could easily be too weak to really do anything."

Tessalli nodded reluctantly. "Sounds about right. So someone has to miss out."

Slowly, everyone began glancing uncomfortably from one person to another. No one wanted to take the fall. Then, into the tense silence, one of them spoke:

"I'll miss out."

The three others, wearing concerned expressions, turned to face the speaker.

"It's fine," Laura said. "You three can do it."

"No, wait," Martin said apologetically. "It's alright. *I'll miss out.*"

Jak fired Martin an irritated glare. "Don't be stupid. You're the reason I wanted to do this in the first place. We just need to... think of something else."

"Well," Tessalli said, with so much reluctance it was almost painful. "Maybe I could give up my spot..."

Suddenly, an idea struck Laura. A glimpse of an opportunity. But for it to work, Tessalli would have to experience Oceanos.

"No. *No*," Laura cut in, taking control. "Jak: you're definitely doing this. This whole thing's your idea.

"Tessalli: you just took a major risk getting this lilaxe. And you need to find out if we actually can get rid of elites forever. So you're not missing out.

"And Martin: Jak's right. You don't have to give up your place for me. Seriously: to me, it doesn't matter so much. If you three say this Oceanos is real, and it works, then... I'll help you with whatever you think needs to happen next. You don't lose anything by leaving me out."

Grudgingly, the other three conferred with each other through uncertain glances. Finally, Jak spoke:

"Okay, Laura. Metel ma baddik." A small smile appeared on his face; gratitude from a brother who, only hours ago, she'd feared was dead. "And thanks."

"Perfect." Laura rose to her feet. "I'll leave you three to get on with it." Reaching the doorway, she looked back over her shoulder and whispered: "Good luck." Then she paused, before walking across to one of the room's sunbaked terracotta walls. Taking down the ornate carving of the serpentine dragon with the fish-like scales, she grinned at the group with a hint of cheekiness: "Don't want you having a bad trip."

Carving in hand, she left the kitchen. As she closed the door behind her, she heard Tessalli whisper to Jak: "So – d'you know if it's safe?"

Jak, sounding as if he were shrugging: "It was for Pavneet."

"Oh. *Great.*"

Laura lay down on the living room sofa, way too tense to close her eyes and go to sleep. Wriggling to get comfortable, she wished she were in her own bed...

... in her own home...

... with Amik...

She shook the thought out of her head. This wasn't the time to get caught up in that. She had to be alert for Jak, Tessalli, and Martin, in case anything went wrong.

And also, she had to think through the idea that had just come to her...

Chapter 25

"The smoke's not rising," Tessalli said, quizzically narrowing her dark brown eyes.

She showed Martin and Jak the vase, removing from its open top the earthenware plate which they'd used to trap the fumes and let them build. At the bottom of the vase, a small, struggling fire was eating away at both the lilaxe and another plant. Their mingled fumes were a striking jet black. But the smoke must have been unusually heavy: it wasn't ascending, just growing thicker at the bottom of the vase.

"We'll just have to turn it upside down," Jak said, "and almost drink the fumes."

Tessalli nodded. Lifting the vase to her mouth, she tipped it back, burying her nose and mouth into its open top. For a few moments, she held that pose, tendrils of thick, almost congealed smoke trickling out of the vase and seeming to crawl down her chin, like the limbs of a living being.

Then she passed the vase to Jak. Without hesitation, he took a deep draught of the fumes.

Then he passed it on to Martin. For safety, the three of them sat cross-legged on the floor, so that they wouldn't, while intoxicated, topple off their chairs.

Ever so slightly, Martin's hands trembled. He'd never done anything like this. What had Pavneet said, about Oceanos potentially ruining someone's delicate psychological make-up? Then he threw back his head, and it was done. To him, the fumes tasted of rotting vegetation.

"Doesn't seem to be doing much," Tessalli said, wrinkling her wide nose as if the smell were lingering unpleasantly in her nostrils. "Maybe the dose wasn't strong e—"

Her eyes shot wide open. Two seconds later, Jak's did the same, as if he were suddenly in thrall to an incredible sight.

Then, Martin felt what seemed like a previously untapped portion of his mind surge with activity, as if it were opening like a flower...

For Martin, the physical World faded into blackness. He should have panicked, but he felt too delirious to do anything other than accept what was happening.

Then, as if blown from the past, came a wave of cherished, fragrant smells. On his tongue, he felt the sweet, golden taste of childhood raspberries... the delightfully wet and slithery scent of oysters, cockles, and clams... the delicate, almost musical aroma of his favourite meal, his Dad's yoghurt and succulent lamb... just one note in an immense symphony of smells...

Then the blackness started to ripple, like a ruffled curtain, and he sensed something awesome was about to emerge.

Bleeding through the flimsy gauze of darkness, Jak saw an infinite wall of luminous colours drifting towards him.

But perhaps "wall" wasn't the right word. Although it appeared perfectly vertical, Jak's sensation was more like that of a midge being dwarfed by an unspeakably huge and curling wave. It simply seemed flat and upright to him, because he could perceive merely the tiniest fraction of it. Unimaginably far above

– higher than the sun, the moon, or the stars were to Earth – the tip of the wave was probably looming over his insignificant speck, ready to plunge down and engulf him.

Then, without any tsunamic violence, or even the sound of a splash, it had happened... and Jak was aware of floating inside a gargantuan cocoon of rainbow colours.

While from outside the wall had been an entity of perfect order, inside was a sort of dreamy chaos. Vibrant, vertical strips of purple, turquoise, red, and olive swam past him, some the length of two tribdwells, some, though infinitely tall, as thin as a hunting spear. Every colour in the entire spectrum was present, and Jak could feel the emotion seething off them. Together, they seemed to represent every human feeling possible. It was an emotionscape of colour.

A floating pool of warm yellow washed over him, triggering the memory of when he and Laura, as infants, played joyfully on a bright, sunlit day. The memory was so vivid, it felt like he'd been physically transported back through time. A soft, deep green brushed against him, and he heard a sound like insects, buzzing and clicking in the grass on a peaceful night. He reached out to the colour orange, and...

Suddenly, sharply, Jak pulled his mind back from the trance state he'd been in. What was happening to him? Buffeted by an overwhelming quantity of complex, multi-sensory data, he was hanging onto linear, coherent thought by a thread. He needed to *hold on.*

Some areas he passed seemed stable. Others were like thunderclouds crackling with lightning, the emotionscape seeming to fibrillate with volatile pockets of energy; areas of emotional upheaval and violence.

And there were other, much smaller pockets of activity. Pulses in the emotionscape, patches of colour with their own unique and recognisable identity. Jak perceived a small piece of violet nearby, like a puddle floating on its side. Its light continually glowed then faded, glowed then faded; exuding its feelings as if they were phero-mones. It seemed to drift through the emotionscape, as though in awe of its surroundings. Jak recognised who those feelings belonged to at once, as easily as if he were seeing her face. That patch of violet was, or at least represented, the emotions of Tessalli.

Amongst the deranging, disorientating swirl of the psychic environ-ment, Tessalli could sense Jakariah. Could pinpoint the locations of Martin, and her husband, and her two children, and anyone else she knew or cared to think of. Each had their own little pulsing island of colour, which blended in with – and contributed to – the overall emotionscape.

A word for those little islands of colour sprang into Tessalli's head, as if it had always lain dormant within her: luminances. It was a sign that her mind was starting to settle. That she was starting to get a handle on this experience.

The emotionscape seemed large enough to encompass every human still surviving on Earth. And yet, most of the minds she could detect felt familiar. They somehow had the day-to-day rhythms, the emotional make-up of Karthalians. But beyond them, skirting the periphery of her awareness, were faint impressions of alien cultures.

The shadows of minds belonging to nearby, different, unknown societies.

Jak tried to get a better grasp of those foreign minds, but to no avail. Maybe if he'd taken a stronger dose...

But those alien ways of being didn't feel much further away than the Karthalians. The emotionscape was like a gigantic, tightly interwoven hive mind, where everyone on the planet was within touching distance. It was just that the pulses from those beyond-the-World psychologies were weaker... their signals, fainter...

But where was he? Was this psychedelic trip happening within the confines of his own skull? Or had he mentally journeyed to some external, independent psychic space? He couldn't tell. But his sense of awe was calming down into something else... a serenity... a nascent sense of letting go...

With whatever currently passed for his eyes, Martin stared at a patch of bluish grey, entranced. It seemed to irrefutably be the exact colour of his Dad's tears on the evening Martin had seen him crying, a couple of days after Martin's Mum had passed away. It also captured the exact colour-tone of that memory.

The recollection should have stirred a sense of anguish in Martin. Instead, in the context of the grand emotionscape, it appeared reassuringly trivial. In a similar way, he felt like a much smaller being, but in no way diminished. He'd become more meaningful, part of a greater whole.

And with that interconnection and fresh, larger perspective, he felt all his guilt over Pavneet's almost certain death dropping away, like the scales of a sea-trapped fish fast-metamorphosing into a land mammal. His perception of that possible murder had shifted to another vantage entirely, and he'd been blown to that different spot, almost flown, on the winds of new emotions. It wasn't just him who was responsible for Pavneet's death. Everyone in Karthalia was – the Ragea, for actually doing it; everyone else, for not intervening. They all merited blame. They were all constituents in that society that had allowed Pavneet's death.

Distributed, the guilt shrank to a fraction of its former size, and became so much more bearable. And he began to see the whole picture in a bigger, more truthful way: saw all those people as links in the chain that had shackled Pavneet to his ultimate fate.

Everyone was culpable. The realisation was bliss. Martin no longer had to bear the load alone...

He wanted to surrender to the ecstasy of that knowledge... to relinquish his identity, and sink into the radiant, psychedelic swirl of a collective and unified ocean...

... in which Jak felt like he was gaining a greater sense of control. It was like awaking from a vivid dream, becoming aware that you're in your bedroom, and yet, for a little longer, the dream World in your head remains alive and operational, so that you have one foot firmly planted in the physical, and one floating in the oneiric.

That's what it felt like, when Jak realised that he'd entered a mode of split-perception. Half his mind was situated in the emotionscape: the other half was still active and absorbing sensory data, such as sight, sound, and smell, from the real World.

While floating in the emotionscape, Jak decided to try and move his hand.

At the same moment, Tessalli had also become aware of her split-perception. In the real World, she lifted her hand and in perfect unison, as if he were an angled reflection of her, Jakariah did the same. She looked at him. He was grinning at her.

Both of them rose to their feet uncertainly, as if slightly drunk. It felt a bit like relearning how to walk. Then, with a look of great carefulness and concentration, Jakariah walked slowly and cautiously over to the kitchen table.

With a slow, speculative movement, he picked up his empty cup. Raising it to his lips, he tipped it gently back – as if taking a sip of water – executing the move with great control. He placed the cup back on the table. Then, with slow, exact, and almost dreamlike progress, he walked over to the kitchen counter.

Once there, he wrapped his fingers around the handle of a long, serrated knife. A scattering of bread crumbs clung to its steel blade, from the school lunch Eli had made for his and Tessalli's children earlier that morning. Using his right hand, Jakariah lifted the knife and held it horizontally before him, with its sharp side pointing up towards the ceiling.

He let his left hand hover over the blade, with his palm facing towards the floor. Then he lowered the index finger of his left hand until it rested upon the blade's edge, a blade that could slice through objects with ease.

Tessalli stared as if she were witnessing some daring, fantastic public performance, as if it were a stunt from one of those old circuses which no longer existed, but which she'd briefly read about in the computer archives. In her dreamy and visual-rich mental state, she pictured a vivid rivulet of thick, dark blood seeping out of Jakariah's fingertip, and crawling down the polished steel.

But what she saw was different. With a slowness that was almost painful, Jakariah gently ran his finger along the blade's edge. It was a display of utter control. When he reached the end of the blade's length, he raised his index finger and showed it to Tessalli. The skin of his finger was intact, without even the smallest cut.

He grinned again, and she felt a smile break across her own face.

"I can do anything," he said. "Anything I want." His voice wasn't slurred or drawling, as it might have been on another drug. Tessalli felt her joy increase.

And she felt connected with Jakariah on two planes: the physical level, with smiles directed at one another; and on the plane of Oceanos, where she could feel the euphoric feedback loop of his joy radiating towards her luminance, and hers towards his.

Luxuriating in the warm feeling of pleasure coming from inside him, Jak cast a look across the room. He saw Martin's expression. It was blissful, trance-like. Jak could feel the waves of serene pleasure radiating out from him...

As he let his guilt slide off him, like slime, leaving him in a purer state... a state of total surrender...

As the experience soared even higher...

In the rushing stream of endorphins, a revelation struck Jak. Was this the answer? Did peace lie in the interconnectivity of a hive mind, like some insects had? In that sense, did humanity's salvation lie down the evolutionary ladder?

No one could rule over others, Tessalli thought, if they felt as interconnected as this...

And for Martin, there was almost no guilt left. Almost no thought. Just a sinking into blissful oneness. Then his endorphins spiked to the next level and suddenly...

... the experience...

... hit...

... its...

... peak...

... suddenly, the sublime lay within them.

The portion of Tessalli's mind which earlier had opened like a flower, now gently closed like one as well. Oceanos receded, and normality resumed.

As if waking from a peaceful sleep, she slowly opened her eyes.

"Wow," Jakariah said softly. Both his and Martin's eyes were also open. Judging from their expressions, the Oceanos trance state had evaporated from them as well.

"That was – that was *in-credible*," Martin said. "I've never felt this amazing in my life!"

The quiet, depressed man Tessalli had met earlier that evening had vanished. It was like Martin had been reborn.

With a huge and jubilant smile, Jakariah leaned over, and pulled Martin tightly towards him in a one-armed hug. And Jakariah wasn't a touchy-feely sort of person. It was as if he and Martin, both almost laughing for joy, had been reduced to ecstatic little kids.

"All that guilt," Martin whispered, in an awe-struck voice. "It just..."

"I know," Jakariah gasped, exhilarated. He flicked his gaze to Tessalli: "Is that how it felt to you?"

Tessalli hesitated, trying to make sense of a feeling inside her. "Definitely. It just..." She realised what it was.

The Oceanos experience had left a legacy. She felt connected to Jakariah and Martin on a much deeper level than she had before. It wasn't anything like years ago, when she'd almost dated Jakariah. Instead, it felt like when you meet a close friend who you haven't seen for a long time, and your relationship immediately clicks back into place, and you become aware of the deep bond that ties the two of you together. It felt like that.

Tessalli continued: "... yeah. C'était fantastique."

Then, with surprising speed, the old concerns of reality began crawling like millipedes back into her mind.

"But keep your voices down," she whispered, nodding at the wall opposite her. Behind it, her family lay sleeping.

"Sure sure," Martin beamed, his slightly chubby face still full of animation and exuberance. "But this is unbelievable. It could change everything. We've got to get the word out."

Jakariah's light green eyes maintained their somewhat spaced-out expression, as if he were still trying to soak up the wonder of the whole experience. "Yeah. You're right. That's the next step..."

Suddenly, the kitchen door creaked. Tessalli's heart skipped a beat, and she spun round.

"Oh," she said with relief. "Mnih enno hayde ente. You scared me for a second."

"Sorry," Laura whispered, closing the door behind her. "I heard you talking. So? Was it good?"

"Not to rub it in or anything," Martin said, "but... mind-blowing."

Jakariah nodded in silent agreement.

"And we could see each other," Tessalli said. "There were these things – I don't know why, I thought of them as luminances – and they were us, floating in this wall of colour. You could actually see what each of us was feeling."

"Luminances," Jakariah said. "Yeah. That's a good word for it."

"Sounds amazing," Laura smiled, as though she genuinely didn't mind missing out. "I'm so glad it worked."

Then she turned back to Tessalli. "So, did it change your mind? Do you think that we could permanently get rid of elites?"

The question brought Tessalli up short. The idea went against a conviction that she'd held for years, went against what she'd learnt on her job and everything she knew about past societies.

"Yes," she replied. "I can't see how there'd be any violence if everyone felt like that."

"Good," Laura said. She looked at the floor nervously, as if she wanted to say something. "And remember I gave up my place for you?"

A pregnant pause. "Yeah."

Laura looked up. "Well, how about you do me a favour in return?"

Chapter 26

In the Intel Tribe's main tribdwell, chairs lay thrown on the floor, papers covered in precious notes were scattered everywhere, and even some of the family mementoes on people's desks had been smashed.

What the hephus have I done? Tessalli thought. Her shocked, unblinking eyes took in the destruction as if it were the work of another person. *This is insane.*

Then she heard a noise, and looked sharply behind her.

Three figures stood in the room's doorway, the cowls of their coats concealing their faces. They were dressed in black from head to toe, reminiscent of the Ragea. It was the same outfit that Tessalli was wearing.

With the relief of people removing oppressively tight balaclavas, Jakariah, Laura, and Martin pulled the cowls from their faces. They'd arrived here later than Tessalli, as an added precaution. They couldn't afford to be caught.

"This look like a burglary enough to you?" Tessalli said, gesturing towards the room. The three of them looked at the wild and ruined scene, with expressions that were half impressed, half disturbed.

Oi, Tessalli thought. *Don't look at me like that. This was your idea.*

She was still partly in disbelief that she'd agreed to do this. Maybe riding the Oceanic wave of euphoria had swept her away from her senses.

"Right, c'mon. Let's get this done, and get out of here," Tessalli said, going to pick up one of the Intel Tribe's big, heavy-duty printers. It was one of the older ones, as evidenced by its surface, where the olive-green paint had cracked and come off in large pieces.

Jakariah, still hobbling slightly from his assault, came to help her lift it, while Martin grabbed the typewriter, and Laura picked up some fully charged solar cells and a stack of blank paper about three inches thick. The printer was also filled with paper that was ready for use.

But bending low to blow out the first of the room's several candles, Tessalli suddenly paused. Over the top of the candle's flame, she'd caught sight of Martin's face turned in profile: seen his acne-speckled cheek; his entire form bathed in the candle's soft and angelic radiance. He looked unearthly. Beautiful. And then, in the same moment, she noticed the back of his head, where the shaved section of his odd swirl-haircut had – over the last few harrowing days – grown out in a faintly silly-looking fashion. The divine and the comic, nestling against one another.

A flush of tender love, and amusement, and pity for him passed through her. Another result of that new, deep connection between them. That Oceanos after-effect.

The feeling made Tessalli all the more reluctant for what was to come later that night.

Blowing out the room's candles, the four of them left the Intel Tribe's HQ.

With haste, they transported the equipment through the darkness, the heavy printer, with its cold metal edges, digging into Tessalli's skin. And another pain that came with it: the knowledge that that month, everyone in her tribe would have to make a small sacrifice of food to pay for its replacement.

Above, the half-moon hovered high in a clear night sky, a slice of fortune that allowed them to better discern the way ahead. They didn't see anyone, nor did they become aware of anyone seeing them.

Then, mixing urgency and cautiousness, they gingerly carried the equipment down a steep slope of dry earth, at one point falling into a brisk, short-stepped run to prevent themselves from toppling over. Upon reaching the bottom – and after only a minor hesitation – they entered the deeper darkness of the under-repair sewage tunnel.

First, towards the faint noise of sewage water where it streamed along. Then, along an uneven and crudely built stone path that ran parallel to the effluence, they ploughed on in the opposite direction to the flow of dirty water, the patter of their footsteps echoing in the damp tunnel. They were like midwives, delivering something new and precious down a grimy birth canal.

In the pitch-darkness, they frequently bumped into an arched wall at the points where the tunnel's stony, serpentine body curved in its course. Tessalli wrinkled her nose at the smell. The tunnel felt like a mean and bitter place, too long cut off from sunlight.

"We're here," Martin finally announced, and Tessalli and Jakariah came to a halt just behind him and Laura. They set the printer down on the wet floor.

By now, Tessalli's eyes had adjusted to the darkness. She could just about make out that the tunnel had broadened into something like a huge room, with the stream of sewage running through its centre.

Jakariah struck a match against a coarse piece of card, both of which Tessalli had given him back at her tribdwell. The flare briefly illuminated his face. In his eyes, there was now a glimmer of renewed excitement and hope. But beneath them, his grimacing, shadowed expression was full of its usual intense focus and almost battle-worn stoicism, two qualities that had dominated his personality during all the years Tessalli had known him. They were like twin demons, constantly cracking their whips to make him strive further. She wondered: could someone that driven ever just stop and be happy? Would he ever settle down and have a family, like she had?

Jakariah lit the torch that he'd been standing in front of. It came to life reluctantly, as if it had been enjoying its sleep.

"I hate this place," he muttered. "Feels like I'm a rat scurrying back down its hole."

Laura eagerly inserted the solar cells into the printer, then connected the printer to the typewriter. After checking that the paper was fitted correctly, she started to quickly press at random some of the typewriter's chunky keys, sending out a series of heavy *clunk* noise into the gloom and darkness. She was smiling to herself, her eyes entranced, like a child absorbed in the glow of a newly opened present.

Staring at Laura, Tessalli felt a mixture of emotions, all of it clouded with uncertainty. She didn't have the Oceanic bond with Laura that she had with Martin and Jakariah. And Laura had turned out to be far more cunning than Tessalli had expected, smoothly playing Tessalli to get the printer she wanted. The fact was, Laura wasn't the sweet, naive woman Tessalli had first taken her for.

Or at least, she wasn't anymore. She seemed to have changed her personality in a very short space of time. And maybe, in the long term, that change wasn't for the best.

Reluctantly, Tessalli turned to Jakariah, who now stood before her: "Anyway... I better go."

"Are you sure you don't want to stay?"

With a wry expression, Tessalli glanced round at the cold, damp surroundings. "Thanks, but..."

A small, melancholic, yet understanding smile flickered across Jakariah's face.

"But really," Tessalli continued. "I would. It's just... I can't leave my family."

A tender moment lingered between them. Not knowing when she'd meet him again, Tessalli studied the details of Jakariah's features – the exact tone of his ashen skin, his high angular cheekbones, his short and untidy black hair, his serious expression – imprinting them upon her memory. Then Jakariah spoke:

"Well... thanks for everything. Now, at least we've got a chance to spread the word about Oceanos. And Pavneet's innocence. If all this amounts to anything, it's because of you."

Tessalli hugged Jakariah goodbye, knowing that – for her family's sake – she couldn't risk any more visits to see him.

She was in the middle of hugging Martin when Laura called out: "Hey, it works! Look!"

Laura hurried over, and held up a piece of paper. It was blank, except for a single image that had been printed in the top left corner

Part of the symbol was something that looked like a large 'O'. Tessalli recognised it as a currency symbol from before the Great Crash. This almost 'O' was filled with tildes that resembled little wavelets, so that the 'O' appeared to be something like a circular window looking out onto a black and white ocean.

Tessalli quickly understood what it meant. It was a subtle masterstroke, fusing two pre-existent characters into a fresh hybrid, into a distinctive and meaningful icon.

"I thought of it earlier," Laura said. "It's a symbol for Oceanos."

Chapter 27

"Done..." Laura sighed, her face lit up with wan satisfaction.

Exhausted, she turned round to share her triumph. But Jak and Martin's heavily shadowed forms still lay curled up, sound asleep, on the uncomfortably hard stone floor. She decided not to wake them. They needed all the rest they could get.

Rubbing her bleary, stinging, and no doubt bloodshot eyes, she dredged up the energy for her last task: to check her work. With the finally completed test copy in hand, she trudged towards the nearest torch to examine it in a better light.

Irritatingly, even though she'd proofread the typescript several times, she'd missed a spelling mistake. But otherwise, she was pleased. Printed out, her words seemed somehow stronger.

Plus, by using the variegated inks found within one of the printer's compartments, she'd crudely decorated the paper's border with intricate, swirling motifs composed of bright, joyful colours. It was to give the pamphlet a small, sincere, heartfelt, optimistic quality, to show others that Jak and Martin didn't fit the villainous character models that maybe was now expected of them. Maybe, if she could get that positive feeling across straightaway, then people would be more likely to listen to them.

Maybe...

Maybe it was a good idea, maybe it wasn't. She'd be able to tell better in the morning.

From behind her came the noise of rustling clothes. She turned, and saw Jak groggily walking towards her.

"You not slept?" he said.

"La'. Stayed up all night to complete it." She swallowed, her mouth, deprived of sleep and water, tasting dry and sickly. "'Least, I think it was all night. It's hard to tell down here."

While she'd been working, the darkness had neither paled nor deepened. It was as if they were living inside a grim, macabre graffiti painting. Frozen in a moment of time.

"Yeah," Jak said, glancing round. He peered over Laura's shoulder. "Can I have a look?"

"Bien-sûr."

She handed him the piece of paper, and he positioned himself under the torch's wavering light. The page read:

```
To all Karthalians,

    In the past week, news of a horrifying
event has sent shockwaves both through
the World and what we thought it stood
for.
    But I want to tell you that Jakariah
Marcy and Martin Fellash did not kill
a member of the Ragea Tribe. I know
this for a fact. And many of you know
them personally - in your heart, you
know they couldn't have done it either.
    I also want to tell you that Pavneet
Hansraj was not being hounded by the
Ragea because he'd done something wrong
```

– but because he'd discovered something that scared them.

I'm well aware this next bit will sound impossible, but Pavneet found a way to end <u>all</u> human-inflicted pain, to elevate everyone and make them truly equal. And not just for one day. His astounding breakthrough could change society for the better permanently.

It's been tested, and I know it works.

However, for the Ragea who have recently used threats and assaults to secretly enlarge their power, Pavneet's discovery made him into a dangerous enemy. This is the real reason they were after him.

I don't know if the Ragea have killed Pavneet, but if they have, it is unjust, and demands retribution. And many of you, unwittingly, will know someone else the Ragea have victimised. They've caused too much suffering already. So we're going to put an end to it.

Soon, we will release Pavneet's discovery, and make the World into a better place. Into a true utopia – the fulfilment of what our ancestors dreamed of when they built Karthalia.

But we need help, from those of you who are brave enough to defy the Ragea and improve both your own lives and the lives of your children. If we act together, they cannot stop us.

So let me prove to you that everything I've said is true (this is the information the Ragea will kill to keep secret):

Get a leaf from the lilaxe plant. There are plenty of them in Devil's Orchard, and as far as I know, this is the only spot in Karthalia where they grow.

Then take a leaf from the marvlene plant. Any flower is supposed to do, but I'm 100% sure this one works.

Put both plants in a container, light them, and inhale the fumes. Then you'll exprience Pavneet's discovery, something he called Oceanos - a state of incredible bliss and harmony. Then you'll understand the limitless possibilities that are open to us.

But again, if I'm telling the truth, the Ragea won't let you do this.

Pavneet died trying to spread this information. Jakariah Marcy and Martin Fellash are being hunted for believing it could bring us a better World. But for us, it means only one thing...

We have everything to gain.

Sincerely,

The Oceanos Movement

N.B. In future messages, I'll talk in
more detail about the Oceanos state,
and what we know of the Ragea's sickening and calculated violence.

Running her fingers nervously through her interwoven light and dark hair – partly just as a means to keep herself awake – Laura awaited Jak's verdict.

"You missed a spelling mistake," he said.

"*I know.*"

"I'm only teasing. It's brilliant." He gazed at the page enrapt, as if he could see the future written upon its lines. "And 'the Oceanos Movement'. I like that. I've got contacts who'll put their necks out for this. We can use them to spread these pamphlets throughout Karthalia."

From beneath the heavy weight of her exhaustion, Laura muttered: "Contacts? D'you mean friends?"

"Sort of. It's a network I put together, to keep me aware of everything that goes on in the World. Anyway, they'll do what I need them to do."

Laura felt a chill. He was talking about those people as if they were his pawns.

"Is Tessalli part of that *network*?"

Jak must have caught the coldness in her tone. He looked at her with concern. "Yeah. She is."

Then his frown transformed into a kindly, reassuring smile. "Come on. You're tired. You just need some sleep."

Maybe he's right... Laura wondered. Fatigue had rendered her thoughts vague, fragmented, and as slippery as fleeing eels.

... maybe I'm seeing things that aren't there...

Jak guided her to a relatively dry patch of stone where she could lie down. As she snuggled up on the hard, freezing floor, her eyes already shut, she murmured:

"So... I don't understand. Why did you put that network together?"

"I already told you. To keep me informed about things."

"But why?"

A slight pause.

"To make sure the World was on the right course.

"Get some rest. Tomorrow, we'll print off those pamphlets, and then I'll drop them off at my contacts' tribdwells. We can leave each one with a note, telling them what to do."

Laura barely heard him. The black jaws of sleep had almost swallowed her. But in a remote corner of her mind, a faint question nagged at her: what if she was just one of his pawns as well?

Chapter 28

Leo stood in a barricade of Ragea, all dressed in their long-sleeved black tops and black trousers. They were guarding the perimeter of Devil's Orchard, against a small crowd of people from various tribes who were clamouring to get in.

Two days ago, those pamphlets had come out of nowhere. At first, there had only been a few people trying to access Devil's Orchard. But now, those few had grown into a huge problem.

"Look – our apologies!" Leo shouted for what felt like the thousandth time. "But we can't let you in!"

The Ragea were incinerating each pamphlet they could find, but it wasn't enough. Word of mouth was winning out. But how had Jakariah and Martin even managed to steal a printer? And where was Corin in all this? What was he doing to stop the situation getting worse?

Looking over the head of a short man who stood in front of him, Leo could see a mural painted on the side of a distant tribdwell. The mural was an 'O', with little wavelets inside. The same type of 'O' that they'd found on the pamphlets.

Murals of that symbol had started popping up across Karthalia. And there were too many of them for it to be the work of Jakariah and Martin alone.

He wondered how much longer the Ragea could hold back the siege.

Laura's fingers clattered across the typewriter's keyboard. She felt dizzy. She'd barely slept, and she hadn't eaten for several hours, all because she was busy typing. Her posture was slumped, her back ached, her eyes were sore and bleary.

But at least it was a good way to pass the boring hours down in the sewer.

Click-clack click-clack click-clack.

She fidgeted with a wavy lock of hair at the side of her head, her exhausted mind groping blindly for the next sentence. She couldn't follow a train of thought. Couldn't track a single carriage of an idea for longer than a second, before it fizzled out of her consciousness. This was going nowhere.

"We got morrrre," came a jubilant voice, half-echoing down the tunnel. Laura turned. Martin and Jak were striding towards her through the trembling illumination of the gloom, each a little out of breath, each bearing a small wooden crate.

"You were out for a long time," she said, with a tone that hinted: *you shouldn't be taking unnecessary risks.*

"Gitem," Jak breathed, carefully lowering his crate down near the room's centre. "But there was more stuff this time."

"Yeah," Martin said, plonking his box next to Jak's and wiping the sweat from his forehead. "And we don't know how long these donations are gonna last."

On the lid of each crate was a small, crude painting, both done in different hands, but both depicting the same thing: a blue, slightly elongated 'O' with little wavelets inside. Within the packages' cool interiors, there were slices of cooked meat, several pieces of delicious-looking ka'ak bread that gleamed in the torchlight, and a mixture of strawberries and raspberries.

"And they were just randomly scattered about again?" Laura asked.

"Yeah," Martin replied. "We even saw another one, which we'll have to go back and get later. I still can't believe people are giving us their food. I mean, they must be going hungry, just to help us out."

"It is impressive," Jak said. "I mean, I don't think it's many people, but it's a definite start."

In spite of her tiredness, Laura couldn't repress a weak smile. These donations were the profits of her pamphlets. They meant all the effort was worth it.

"They must mostly be from people who already knew about the Ragea's savagery," Jak added. "Because with them guarding the lilaxes, I can't imagine anyone's tried Oceanos for themselves yet. But hopefully the fact the Ragea are stopping them is raising suspicions. Anyway, I like the idea of the Ragea's victims coming back to haunt them. It's like they've gifted us with our own private army."

"Our what?" Martin said.

"Our *army*. It's an old word. It means, a large group of believers who follow you into a conflict. It's a military term, for when they used to have wars."

With a fairly blank expression, Martin nodded and muttered: "Ah bon."

Then – obviously unable to resist anymore – he began tucking into the food, a big ravenous grin on his face.

There's the old Martin, Laura thought. *The epicurean. The lover of life in all its sensual pleasures.* For a second, her gaze lingered on him. The naive joy he found in simple things offered a welcome respite from the foreboding underWorld in which she was now trapped.

"Next time you go out," Laura said a few minutes later, as she was midway through eating a piece of ka'ak bread, "I think I need to come with you. Being in here all the time, I'm getting a bit... claustrophobic."

"Sure," Jak said. "You can go instead of me. Oh, and while we were out, Martin had an idea you could use in your next pamphlet."

"Yeah?" Laura said. Right now, writing another pamphlet was the last thing she wanted to think about.

"Uh, it wasn't anything big," Martin said. "I was just thinking, Oceanos is almost like the next stage of love. Because love is a really strong one-to-one connection, right? That's why some people can sense when a loved one passes away. It's like the bond between them's been broken. Well, maybe Oceanos is the next level of that. 'Cause instead of being closely connected with *one* person, you're connected with *everyone* simultaneously." He paused, and shrugged modestly. "I dunno. It's just kind of what it felt like."

"It's a weird idea though, isn't it?" Jak said. "That as humans, we haven't yet evolved the ability to love at the highest level. That there's a stage we're still waiting to reach."

Later that same night: Jak sat in a dark corner, thinking. Martin lay asleep, making a deep, nasal, and grating snoring noise. And Laura, listlessly – like an addict who couldn't let go – was applying the finishing touches to her second pamphlet.

He must go unconscious soon as he shuts his eyes, Laura thought jealously, as Martin's snoring kept butting into her already stuttering thought processes. It was even more impressive considering he lay on an unforgiving bed of stone, and that his one set of clothes – like Jak and Laura's – had, thanks to that same unforgiving bed, by now become cold, damp, and unpleasantly sticky.

She heard the soft noise of leather sandals on smooth stone: Jak was coming towards her, still moving gingerly on his injured legs. It reminded her of three nights ago: the same event of a sound signalling Jak's isolated approach, the same reality of Laura working on a pamphlet as he did so. Repetitions in the darkness.

"Vonts es?" Laura whispered, not wanting to wake Martin. She was glad to have some conversation to distract her.

"Yeah, fine," Jak replied, his pale face drifting into the torchlight's glow. In his serious expression, there was something secretive and faintly conspiratorial. Sitting down beside her, he whispered: "I've got an idea. From now on, I want you to put me in the pamphlets."

Laura felt her face twist into a frown. "How do you mean?"

"Portray me as someone persecuted. Someone who's fighting for the oppressed, for the betterment of everyone. Who's been cut off from his family, and been punished for doing what he believes is right, by having one of his friends captured and probably killed by his enemy. Paint me as what I am – but just do it on a grander scale."

"Why?"

Apart from Martin's snoring, their hushed, heartfelt voices were the only sounds that were audible.

"Because we need to step this up a gear. Get more support. And the way to do that is to give them a figurehead. Someone they can believe in."

"Sounds like you're trying to make yourself into a – a religious figure."

Jak's gaze didn't waver: "Exactly."

There was a silent moment, in which the two of them just stared at each other. Over the last few days, Jak's stubble had grown into the beginnings of a dark beard, and that only added to the rough, demanding intensity of his stare.

Then he dropped his gaze, and softened his voice:

"Look. It's just propaganda. We've told them how to try Oceanos, and that's about as much proof as we can give. But it's not enough. We need more recruits, and I think this could help. People need more than an abstract concept like peace if they're going to act. They need someone to rally behind."

Laura, hesitantly: "Okay."

"Also, I'll give you that description we talked about, of exactly how the Oceanos experience unfolded. That'll make it seem more real to those people who still don't believe us. All you have to do is write it up in the most inspiring way you can."

"Why me? If it's your experience, why don't you write it up?"

Jak looked genuinely, almost theatrically taken aback. "Because you're doing such an amazing job. Neither me or Martin could do it as well as you."

He smiled and soothingly rubbed her arm, but Laura couldn't tell if he was just manipulating her. And she'd never felt she had to question his actions like that before...

He leaned in towards her, the long shadows sliding over the angular bone structure of his long, thin face. His deep-set eyes were like jewels of dim green radiance in rivers of blackness.

"But this is very important," he said. "Soon, there's going to be a battle. Maybe just a small skirmish – the three of us against the Ragea. Or, if we get nearly everyone on our side, maybe we'll neutralise the Ragea with barely any violence. But probably, it's going to be somewhere between the two. A group of us versus a group of them. And there's only going be one winner. For it to be us – and Oceanos – we need all the people we can get.

"So let's give them someone to embody their best aspirations. Like you said, every religion has someone like that: Jesus, Mohammad, Krishna, Sangar. Make *me* into a symbol like them – something people would risk their lives to protect."

"Al-right," Laura murmured. But as she stared at her brother, all she felt were dark, frightened thoughts racing through her mind.

"Look," – Jak relaxed his posture and tone of voice – "I know I must sound a bit crazy. But it'll work, and that's what we *need*. It's just that living in this darkness, it plays with your mind. Makes everything seem ominous and uncertain. But when we get back into the light... when we've created that better World... it will feel like this was obviously the right thing to do. You'll see.

"But you're only going to write well if you *believe* it's the right thing to do. So... do you?"

In the fug of her mind, Laura wondered if he *was* right. After all, he was her brother, who had always looked out for her. And everyone said he was extremely intelligent. Surely she could trust him, despite her doubts...

"Yes," she said.

A smile broke across Jak's lips. "Perfect. Thank you."

He reached out again and touched her arm. "You'll be doing something meaningful. Giving them fresh energy. Putting courage in their hearts for when they need it."

He let his touch linger for a moment. Then, maintaining his smile, he rose to his feet.

"Right," he said. "I better leave you to it."

And walking back towards the chamber's deeper, more contemplative darkness, his feet padded softly across the floor.

"Jak," Laura called. "Do you really think there'll be a battle?"

"Yes." His expression was grim and stone-like, a living embodiment of Fate itself. Then he carried on walking away.

Laura turned back to the typewriter. Torchlight flickered and danced hypnotically over its black metal surface, visible beneath its cracked olive paint.

Put courage in their hearts... she told herself... *that's a good way to think about it...*

Chapter 29

"Why are you working so hard, Laura?"

The question echoed in her mind.

"Hmm? It's obvious," she replied. "To help the Movement."

There was a pause, as if the initial question was being rethought. "I heard you and Amik broke up. How d'you feel about that?"

In the darkness of the sewage chamber, Martin sat opposite her, awaiting her response. Jak had gone out to try and top up their food supply – the mission only requiring one person, he thought it safer if he went alone.

"Fine," Laura replied. "Just... fine."

"Really? I thought that you two were going to settle down and have kids. That must have been hard to give up."

"It was. But like I said, *I'm fine.*"

"Look, I'm not trying to upset you. I'm just worried about you."

"Why?"

"'Cause I think you're overworking yourself. You don't know how exhausted you look."

"Wow. *Thanks.*"

"Sorry. That's not what I meant. It's just... well, you know that my mum died a couple years after I was born," he said, a fragile tenderness entering his voice.

"Yeah," she muttered consolingly. "I know."

"Well... there was this period when I was younger... I kept getting upset, because I couldn't picture her face. I could imagine her body, and her clothes, but where her head should have been, there was just... a black emptiness. And it was horrible. I felt like I'd somehow betrayed her. Like I was letting her slip away."

The darkness of the chamber seemed to heighten Laura's imagination. It reminded her of evening theatre – where the darkness, the imagination-enabler, the nemesis of daylight and tangible reality, was drafted in as part of the performance.

"Anyway, my dad saw me crying one day. So I explained why. And he told me not to be silly – she wasn't gone. She was with me every day – *inside*. Yes, I was crying – but only because of her and what she meant. In that way, she was still with me. She was still shaping my life.

"I just wonder if you're still carrying your grief over Amik inside *you*. And all this work is you trying to pretend that you're not. That's how he's shaping your life – with you reacting against him."

Behind the hurt in Laura's eyes, a keen, searching, outraged sense of denial roared through her. She wanted to say something that would refute what he'd said. How could he talk to her like this? She'd even put more energy into the OM than him and Jak combined...

And with that realisation came a sharp inner pang. A painfully vivid picture of who she'd become.

"Anyway," Martin said, shifting uncomfortably. "Maybe I shouldn't have brought it up. I just... thought I should point it out. I'll leave you in peace."

He rose to his feet, smiled sympathetically at her, then walked over to the three crates huddled in the corner, leaving her with a sense of desolation.

Turning back to face her typewriter, she felt... nothing. For the first time since they'd gone underground, her compulsion to write had abated. Suddenly, it just didn't seem that important.

Slowly, as if moving through water, she stood up, and went to eat some food with Martin. Jak would be back soon. Then they could all just sit down and enjoy each other's company.

Tomorrow, she'd get back on with the writing. She knew she would.

But for now... maybe the best thing for her would be to have a little rest.

In the darkness, Jak lay on the stone floor, smiling. Or at least, it was something between a smile and a triumphant, intoxicated grin. He felt invincible.

Coming from near him, he could hear Martin and Laura's steady, quiet breathing. There was also the noise of dripping water... the faint sound of scurrying rodents... the putrid smell of faeces, urine, and other disgusting things – a smell that, before he'd gotten used to it, had made him physically gag – being washed along the sewage stream that passed through the chamber...

And yet, despite all the miserable impecunious grimness that penned him in, he felt like one of life's victors.

The thick darkness that enveloped him seemed somehow rich, almost tingling with its own strange, dark life-force... as if pregnant with a newfound potential for the World. Everything was coming together as he'd felt it should. As if, mentally, he'd tapped into the tiniest fraction of the universe's cosmic and controlling pulse... and now, he could sense its energy shifting... changing... operating to fulfil *him*.

Deep down, he knew the Ragea's secret agenda of terrorising Karthalians would be brought to an end. It was inevitable, like the arrival of the next full moon.

Smiling, he closed his eyes. And in the pitch-blackness behind his eyelids, saw dreamy, flickering images of his approaching better World.

Chapter 30

Leo scaled the stone staircase. In his massive, tightly clenched fist was another of Jakariah and Martin's pamphlets. He gripped it as though trying to throttle the life from it.

On his way to this building, he'd passed more of those sickening murals – those spray paintings of an ocean-blue 'O', filled with little ripples. But now, worryingly, variations had begun to spring up.

In one, the 'O' had been elongated, two curving lines added to its top so that it resembled a teardrop, as if the mural-maker were commiserating with Jakariah and Martin's position as fugitives. Another mural-maker had even turned the 'O' into a single link in a chain, a link dissolving into separate droplets of water – old shackles falling away.

The pamphlets were gaining more and more support.

He reached the top of the wide and winding staircase, the lilaxe-blood throbbing through his temples like a quickening drumbeat. On the landing, he took a frustrated glance out of the enormous triangular window inset into a cold, pale wall. It afforded a rare, aerial view over Karthalia and its sprawl of bungalow tribdwells.

In the whole World, only one other building – apart from the two that corresponded with this one – was tall enough to provide such a sight: the soulless stone monolith of the Cemetery Building.

Sanif...

In the distance, high above the horizon, Leo saw a flock of white tern crossing the sky. And five storeys below, at the building's base, orange trees swayed in the dying breaths of the sea breeze.

Unaware that this tranquil yet slightly troubled view had deepened his sense of personal disturbance, he turned to face the landing's only door. A huge arch of dark and glossy cedarwood, its two halves rose in a curve to meet at a single tipped point. Seizing the handle – a ring of black-painted steel – he pulled back the door with a shrill scraping groan.

The room beyond was as large as an entire tribdwell, and felt almost cavernous. Near its centre, Corin perched on the edge of a low stone wall, his runt physique hunched predatorily, his thin weak arms propping up his chin, and his eyes fixed on the floor. The position made him look even smaller than he was when standing. Like Leo, he was dressed in the Ragea's long-sleeved black clothing.

The low wall Corin sat on formed a circular pool, with a fountain gurgling softly at its centre. Behind him, at the room's far end, was another enormous triangular window. In its top half blazed a bank of sunset-orange clouds. In its lower half sat the distant yet immense statue of Sanif, its stone head jutting into the view's upper section, blocking out a small portion of the clouds' effulgence.

Striding forward, Leo headed towards the fountain's almost inaudible whispers.

This was a meditation chamber, its bareness and vastness designed to encourage undistracted and expansive thought. Above the fountain hung the room's only other ornament: an alabaster head, dangling from a rope, swaying and twisting in the soft breeze. It hovered off the ground at about the height of Leo's shoulder, like a decapitated hanged man. The visage had a full and beautifully carved beard. It was the lined and serious face of a wise man, and an orange sheen of sunlight skimmed slowly across its smooth, spinning surface.

Leo had no idea who it was. He didn't care.

He stopped a short distance before Corin, his imposing, powerful physique towering over that of his master. Corin hadn't reacted at all to Leo's approach, but simply kept his eyes fixed on the floor. Bowing his head deferentially, Leo waited to be acknowledged.

Finally, Corin shifted his searing, paranoid gaze upon Leo, his face an image of scorn.

"So?" Corin said, snarling out the word.

"We're still holding people back at Devil's Orchard. Telling them it's a sacred equinox, and we can't allow the lilaxe to be plucked right now. Most people still think Oceanos is too far-fetched to be true. Or they've written off Jakariah and Martin as murderers."

A pause. No response.

"But those murals," Leo continued, "are popping up everywhere, so it can't be just the two of them doing this. And more and more people are hearing about Oceanos. If the number of people at Devil's Orchard keeps growing... we won't be able to hold them off forever."

He raised the pamphlet and squeezed it even tighter.

"The printer. Any news?" Corin said, as if Leo's emotion or opinions didn't matter – only the bare facts that he conveyed.

"... No. And there's no sign that anyone at the Intel Tribe is friends with Jakariah or Martin."

You should have made sure they were dead when you had the chance, Leo thought.

"What about their families?"

"Still under watch. They can't have made any contact with them."

Do you even realise how bad things are getting?

"But they've got support now," Leo added. "This is getting out of hand."

Come on. Say something. You need to act.

Corin remained silent. But like the fierce grip of an eagle's talon, Leo wouldn't let the subject drop. He remembered how terrifying Oceanos had been. Remembered how he'd felt his sense of self, and all the certainties he'd built his life on, slipping away... hacked to pieces in that toxic whirlpool...

"If Oceanos spreads," Leo said, "then that's it. Everyone will know when anyone's in pain, and all our power – all our influence – will disappear. You *need* to stamp this out now—"

"*Don't*," Corin barked, baring his teeth like a growling jackal. "Don't ever push me."

And in Corin's ruthless glare, Leo could see that vicious animal savagery, could see the duel he lost to Corin for leadership of the Ragea, and all his own inadequacies and failings. Despite the armour of arrogant self-belief supplied by the lilaxe, those poisonous blades still cut through.

Averting his gaze, and swiping his shaggy ringletted hair away from his eyes, Leo bit his tongue and choked back his pride.

"Is that *all*?" Corin's harsh voice resounded through the cavernous room.

"Yes."

"Then go. Let me think."

Leo bowed, and in the silence, the silent alabaster head spun slowly in its tightening noose. Through the large window at the far end of the room, he caught sight of the statue of Sanif, the right side of its stern face burnished by the light of the dying sun.

Marching out of the meditation chamber, hearing only the steady gurgling of the fountain, his mind seethed. Nothing had come of that meeting. Nothing had changed.

Interlude

There was a mighty crash, the ground shuddered, and a thunderous noise reverberated throughout Karthalia.

Chapter 31

Corin stared ahead, his unblinking eyes burning with an impotent rage.

"When did it happen?" he said through gritted teeth, asking the male Ragea who had brought him there.

"Apparently, around 2 a.m. last night."

On the ground before Corin, the once-awesome statue of Sanif lay collapsed on its side. The morning light, already hot, showed fragments of splintered stone scattered around the fallen giant like drops of blood. The grey head, snapped off at the neck upon impact, gazed face-down into the grass, while its nose pressed into the dry earth beneath. The enshadowed ruby eyes, once imperious, now looked feeble and defeated.

Nearly all of the Ragea had been deployed to form a barricade around the lilaxes in Devil's Orchard, leaving the monument unguarded, and unwatched.

For Corin, the toppled statue wasn't simply a statue. It was a grand, hulking signal that he'd entered a horrid new reality.

Small knots of people had swarmed towards this scandal – towards the carcass of Corin's vision – and were now whispering. Rumouring. It was obvious what had happened. Support for the Oceanos Movement had grown. Blocked from answers about the lilaxe at Devil's Orchard, the protestors believed the Ragea were guilty of what Jakariah and Martin claimed, and so they'd done this in retaliation. Maybe the rebels even included some of the people the Ragea had terrorised. Maybe it had gone that far.

It didn't matter whether Jakariah had organised this act, or whether others had done it off their own initiative: it crystallised how dangerous the OM had become.

One of the onlookers sidled up to Corin. She was a woman with a stooped back, somewhere in her seventies. She put her arm on Corin's shoulder. Corin suppressed a flinch at the physical contact.

"I'm so sorry," she said.

Corin didn't reply. He didn't even look at her. The lady seemed to take that as a sign that he was stoically bottling up his grief.

"I live over there," she said, pointing across the grass to a nearby tribdwell over which the statue had loomed. "When the ground started shaking," the lady continued, "I thought it was the start of another earthquake, like the ones my dad told me about."

Corin barely heard her.

He was thinking of the risky plan that had been bubbling in his mind over the past few days – the one he'd been reluctant to put into action. But now, he didn't care what it would cost the Ragea. Their current approach, of secretly intimidating others and steadily growing their power, would have to be scrapped for the time being. They'd have to come out of the shadows, and put themselves at the centre of the stage.

The last earthenware cup was filled with arak.

"Khmenk," Martin smiled. He, Laura, and Jak raised their cups for a toast, lifting them out of the shadows of their bodies, and into the torchlight's lambent glow.

They'd found the small handleless wooden cups in another crate of donated goods, along with the latest edition of *The*

Web. Fittingly, the dramatic front-page news had been written by Tessalli. Reading it, the three of them had then hurried, with barely contained excitement, towards the agora and – from a distance – seen the proof of the story for themselves.

The crate of donated goods had also contained a flask of arak. It was as if their generous benefactor knew that they'd want to celebrate.

"A toast?" Martin said. Despite being in a cold, miserable sewer, he held the cheap arak as though it were the finest drink there was, fit only for the best occasions.

"Sounds good to me," Jak replied. Then, with a wry grin: "To the Ragea's downfall."

Laura and Martin chimed in: "To the Ragea's downfall!"

The three of them tapped their cups together, smiling.

"I'm sorry I didn't come last week. Things have got... busy."

Leo paused, thinking what to say next.

"I guess you know what's happened," he continued. "That statue of you... they've destroyed it."

The urn, its brown clay overlaid with elegant, gilded brush-strokes, sat on a bare stone shelf at the same height as Leo's head. Inside it were Sanif's ashes.

Whenever he visited this urn, Leo's life felt like a crap version of the one he used to have. Since his best friend's death, the World had been a dimmer, more wretched place to live. He came here religiously once a week.

I'm the only one that ever visits him, he thought, as the vigorous, insistent beat of his blood pulsed through his temples. He always dosed up on the lilaxe before seeing Sanif's urn. It was a mark of respect.

Along the length of the bare, deserted granite corridor that he stood in ran three shelves: one at chest height, one at waist height, and one at knee height. On each of them, spaced at regular, close intervals, was urn after urn after urn, as though unto eternity, each individualised with its own distinct painted design; a scene repeated endlessly throughout the corridors of that labyrinthine, towering edifice. This was where Karthalia housed the ashes of its dead; or at least cenotaphs to them, many choosing to sprinkle the ashes of their loved ones at sea.

The greatest physical achievement in the history of Karthalia, a land judged by its populace to be a utopia, was a monument to the dead.

"He's doing nothing," Leo muttered into the corridor's granite silence, thinking of Corin. "And I..."

He remembered that glare Corin had given him in the meditation chamber, and the dark memories stirred inside him once more: a bloodthirsty crowd of Ragea watching him fight that weakling. The certainty he was going to win. The defeat. Despite the lilaxe chemicals now coursing through his system, a riot of impotence, bitterness, and humiliation swept through him. On that day, in front of everyone in his tribe – nearly everyone he knew – he'd learnt, beneath all his muscle, how pathetic he really was.

Subconsciously, he touched his broken nose.

The noise of rapid yet restrained footsteps began echoing down the corridor. Leo turned his head, and saw one of his subordinates marching towards him.

"You need to come now," the man said promptly, as if he wanted to whip through any formalities. "Corin's called a meeting of all the Ragea."

"All of us?"

"Everyone apart from the people guarding Devil's Orchard."

Nothing like this had happened since Sanif's death. Hurriedly, Leo followed the messenger, and left the Cemetery Building.

Muttering anxiously to one another, the forty-or-so Ragea began to disperse. The assembly was over. The plan was set.

Chapter 32

The word had rapidly spread throughout Karthalia: the Ragea had an announcement to make about the murderers, and their pamphlets, and the stand-off at Devil's Orchard. An announcement that all Karthalia needed to hear.

Now, Corin stood concealed behind the slope of a small hill, with nearly everyone in Karthalia gathered on its other side. A sea of eager, excited chatter drifted over the verdant rise and swirled about him like a whirlpool, while – in the distance – a legion of dark, ominous clouds crawled across the sky towards Karthalia.

On his way there tonight, he'd passed several more murals. For one, the 'O' had been painted in green and subtly altered so that it resembled an elongated leaf, like the growth of a new movement. In another, the wavelets were shaped to resemble brain waves, intimating how Oceanos would transform people's minds.

The signs had been there all along. And he'd been too slow to react.

Consciously, he drew his shoulders together in a defensive, self-minimising posture. Twisted his expression into a fear-stricken, injured look, as though the World had bullied him into this moment. Then he turned, and ascended over the hill's crest.

Eight hundred Karthalians dropped their conversations, and fixed their gazes upon him.

For a frozen moment, he stared down at the thousand-eyed crowd, as if summoning the courage to speak. Then, in a quavering voice:

"A-as most of you know, my name's Corin. I-I'm from the Ragea tribe. In a little bit, I'll explain why I'm speaking on behalf of them. But first... I-I have something to tell you."

He cleared his throat.

"Many of you have heard about something called Oceanos. It's supposed to be a-a higher mental state, that will produce a better World. But to access it, you need a lilaxe.

"This is what we've been stopping several of you from getting. We said we did this because of our religion, and that's true. But it's not the main reason. We stopped you because one of our tribe had already inhaled the lilaxe fumes. He'd experienced Oceanos. And it was agony. That "miracle" – Oceanos – nearly destroyed his mind."

He gazed at the rapt crowd. Then, from his pocket, he pulled out a sheet of printed paper. With a trembling hand, he held it up like a piece of irrefutable evidence.

"This is one part of the Oceanos Movement's propaganda."

He began to read, his timid voice growing louder and more authoritative:

"*Soon, we will make the World into a better place. Maybe even into a utopia. But it can only happen if everyone experiences Oceanos together. To make that happen, we need the help of brave people. If we work together, nothing can stop us.*"

Slowly lowering the pamphlet, he let those last, ominous words hang in the air.

"Ignore their lies, and their ridiculous claim that somehow a plant will create an even better utopia than the one we have now.

This is the real truth: that they want to release the lilaxe fumes, with or without your consent. And if that happens, you'll all suffer the same pain that one of our tribesmen did. Then they can use that opportunity to escape justice for the murder they committed.

"If you fight for the Oceanos Movement, *that's* what you're fighting for. And our tribesman was lucky. His sanity was saved. But for many of you, if the OM do release a higher dosage like they want to... there might be no going back."

For a moment, an eerie, stifling silence pervaded the air. No one spoke. No one moved. It was as if Corin's words were still detonating in their heads, leaving them in a state of shock.

Then someone in the middle of the audience shouted out:

"He's lying! If that's true, why didn't they tell us this straight-away? Why all the secrecy?"

Fresh uncertainty flooded the crowd. But Corin had been waiting for this question. The man in the audience was a plant.

As if weighed down with a sombre truth, the secret leader of the Ragea bowed his head.

"Because," he said tremulously, gazing down uncomfortably at the grass, "the person who suffered Oceanos knew you wouldn't believe him. He knew that, to prove he was telling the truth, he'd have to go through it again. Right before your eyes."

From the side of the hill, a Ragea tribesman – dressed all in black – walked into view. He strode slowly towards Corin as if in a funeral procession, bearing in one hand a smoking flambeau, and in the other, an earthenware vase. The vase contained a lilaxe and one other plant.

"That person," Corin told his audience regretfully, "was me."

He sensed a ripple of alarmed surprise pass over the crowd. But no one intervened to stop what was about to happen.

"I d-didn't want to do this," Corin said, riveting his eyes upon the approaching lilaxe, filling them with a look of dread. "But when people destroyed Sanif's statue... I knew I had to make sure they learnt the truth."

The vase arrived before him. Dutifully, Corin tore all the leaves from the non-lilaxe plant, and dropped them back into the vase, as if performing some primordial ritual that Karthalia should long ago have turned its back on. From the lilaxe, he tore off only one leaf, then, only a small strip from that.

"I'm just taking a tiny, tiny dose," he told his audience, releasing the shred of the lilaxe into the vase's pitch-black maw. "That'll be enough for you to see."

With reluctant hands, he took the vase, and turned it so that it was horizontal. The flaming stick was inserted inside it, igniting its green contents with a faint hiss. Then, as soon as the leaves were sufficiently lit, and smoke had begun to pour out of the vase's open neck, the stick was yanked away, and immediately as if in a fearful rush, Corin buried his mouth and nostrils into the top of the vase, blocking with one hand any small spaces from which the fumes might rise past his face and escape.

Maybe the pressure from the vase digging against his face was impeding his blood flow and blocking out his senses, but to Corin, as soon as he put his head into that vase, the World went deathly silent.

Careful, he thought. *Not too soon.*

Apart from having to fight the urge to gag, the fumes didn't worry him. The lilaxe had been a fake, another flower meticulously painted in just the right shades of dark green and purple. From their distance, the audience hadn't been able to tell.

And... <u>now</u>.

Then, with his face still pressed against and hidden within the vase, he began to scream.

It was an ear-splitting, animal scream, a howl of primal agony. He started jerking his body sharply, as if he were convulsing.

Collapsing to the floor, he spilled the vase from his grip. He was on all fours, digging his fingers into the grassy dirt, his eyelids clenched shut in fierce, soul-wracking pain. Through gritted teeth and flaring nostrils, he grunted rapidly, as if hyperventilating.

"No... no..." he muttered. It was as if he were regressing into some sort of beast, unleashing the most primal part of himself in a struggle of brute willpower. As if he were trying to cling to something vital, a sense of himself that was slipping away.

"... *no*..."

He dug his nails into the side of his head, as though trying to claw the agony out of his mind.

"*Get! Out!*"

Rivulets of blood trickled down his fingers, pouring from the constellations of red, crescent-shaped cuts that now hovered above his temples.

"*Get!*"

He raised a fist...

"*Out!*"

And slammed it down upon the earthenware jar, shattering a section of its hard substance, the shards slicing his hand's flesh.

"Aaagh! Yes!" he screamed out, as if in sudden ecstasy, as if the pain had sharply and for a moment brought him back to himself. "Yes!"

His bleeding hand hunted blindly around the vase and inside it, before closing around one of the earthenware shards. He lifted it up, pulled down the top of his black shirt, and began to commit quick, diagonal slashes across his flesh.

"Yes!"

Slash.

"Get!"

Slash.

"Out!"

Even though he was making the cuts as superficial as possible, pain was darkening Corin's vision. By now, he'd lost all awareness of his audience. All he could do was make his performance... perfect.

Then he dropped his shard-holding hand to his side, and collapsed onto the ground, breathing raggedly, as though the experience were still continuing, but had moved to a remoter area of his mind.

A brief, stunned pause. Then he heard members of the audience hurrying towards him. Now that the violence had passed, they seemed to have remembered their responsibility to a human in serious danger.

Corin forced his eyes to stay open. He saw members of the Ragea holding at bay some of the concerned Karthalians who were trying to come forward to help him. A couple of Ragea nipped over to Corin's side. After checking he was okay, they hooked their arms underneath his, and slowly assisted him onto his feet. Once upright, Corin swayed giddily. His subordinates stayed by his side to support him.

With dazed eyes that couldn't focus properly, he looked at the people surrounding him. Their faces were anxious, horrified, and in most cases, awed – awed at the trauma he'd just gone through for their benefit. The dynamic of the performance had changed. There was a new level of intimacy between Corin and his audience.

Bloody and ragged from his ordeal, he spoke in a quiet, enervated voice. "That," he said, breathing heavily, "is what the OM wants to do to all of you."

On his right, a gap started to grow in the ring of watchers, the people shuffling aside to let something through.

"And," Corin said, "they'll kill to make it happen."

Through the gap in the crowd emerged four solemn Ragea, their heads bowed, their shoulders bearing a large rectangular wooden box. The noses of the crowd members began to wrinkle in disgust; the box leaked a pungent, putrid smell. Its dark cedarwood was covered in scuff marks of dry dirt. Fear dawned on many of the audience's faces. From the smell alone, they had a fateful premonition of what they were about to see.

The box was lowered onto the ground, and the lid removed. The deep, oppressive silence seemed to coil even tighter, like a snake constricting its prey.

Inside the box lay a human form, mummified in black cloth. The two Ragea nearest the head crouched down, and started to peel back the cloth from its face. It was evident, from the fabric's occasional, heavy movements, that parts of it were wet. However, the men's bodies and moving hands obscured what they were revealing. Then, finished, they stood back.

The face was human. Its pale white skin, long deprived of running blood, sagged heavily in drooping pouches upon its frail bone structure. Chunks of flesh had rotted away from the cheeks, and a section of the chin and lower lip had fallen off, baring the decayed yellow teeth that lay behind – leaving a face that looked like a gruesome, incomplete puzzle. Its jaw hung slackly open, as though frozen in a moment of dim, uncomprehending surprise. At first, its eyes seemed to have shrunk. Then it became clear that they had simply sunk back into their sockets, as if retreating forlornly into tunnels of darkness and departing from the bright World where their purpose had ended.

"His name was Adam," Corin explained to the crowd, wearily and yet with anger bubbling in his tired voice. "He was the man from our tribe that Jakariah and Martin killed."

The death had been referred to on the 'Wanted' posters for Jakariah and Martin, but no name had ever been given.

Corin had slain Adam, one of his own subordinates, shortly after the incident in the forest, when Jakariah and Martin had slipped through the Ragea's grip. Adam had done nothing particularly wrong – but some sort of insurance was needed, in case proof was ever required of the danger posed by the OM. After his death, the Ragea had buried Adam in the cool earth to slow his decay. That's why the box was covered in dirt marks.

People in the crowd peered over obstructing shoulders to get a look at the corpse, and then, repulsed, immediately averted their eyes. Some of them no doubt recognised him.

"Of course, normally, we cremate the dead immediately," Corin said. "But... and I know it's unpleasant... but we thought it might end up being necessary for you to see this."

Corin was acutely aware that people further back couldn't see the body. He had to let them know what others were witnessing. When he next spoke, he shouted his words for all to hear.

"This corpse is a warning. It proves Jakariah and Martin are willing to kill for the sake of their mission. This is what you need to protect yourselves from."

His head drooped forward, and he breathed for a moment, attempting to suppress the sharp pain in his chest. Then he looked towards the Ragea gathered round the box.

"Walk it through the crowd," he muttered to them. "Let everyone see."

The four Ragea hoisted the still-lidless box back onto their shoulders. Then, walking forward at a slow, sombre pace, they merged into the parting audience, beginning their procession through it.

"And don't worry," Corin shouted through heavy breaths. "As long as you don't touch it, there won't be any disease. And straight after this, we'll give him a proper funeral. But I thought it was vital that you all see this for yourselves... Because just by living in Karthalia, you're all part of this struggle. Whatever happens next will affect you as well."

A look of dark, righteous anger flashed across his face. Empowered by his passion, he gently pushed the two supporting Ragea away from him so that he could stand up by himself. Barely raising his exhausted arms, he began to emphasise his words with stiff, dramatic gestures.

"How could your children endure what I've just been through? And that was just a tiny dose. A larger exposure, and their minds would be ruined forever.

"We've given Jakariah and Martin a chance to do the right thing. To come forward," he gestured towards the corpse being borne through the crowd, "and face justice for what they've done. But rather than do that, they thought only of themselves, abandoning their friend, Pavneet, to die. That's the sort of people we're dealing with. Not people of honour, or people who practice the morals they claim to possess. Just cowards. Murderers. People trying to save themselves by hiding behind a false cause."

Burning with passion, Corin's voice was almost a roar.

"They have to be stopped. That includes anyone who helps them, whether they think they're doing good or not. The stakes are too high to do otherwise. The future of this utopia – that we've all built – depends on it.

"That why I believe anyone who supports the OM must be exiled. And if they resist," Corin scowled bitterly, "they leave us no choice. They'll have to be killed. I know that's a horrid thing even to imagine. But if it's the lives of everyone, versus the lives of a few, then that's the lesser evil we have to take.

"But let's not allow it to go that far. Let's make sure everyone who supports the OM surrenders *now!*"

Driven into a frenzy by Corin's words, the bulk of the crowd howled in agreement with him, pumping their fists in the air.

Following the speech, fights and accusations erupted between neighbouring tribes. In rare cases, people even denounced members of their own clan as secret supporters of the OM.

The utopia was over. The civil war began.

Act III

THE

FREE PEOPLE

THE

SCHISM

THE
OCEANOS
MOVEMENT

Prelude

Tribal allegiance was decided by a vote.

In some, the majority sided with the OM. But more tribes – far more – committed themselves to Corin and his mission.

Any dissenters to a group verdict had little choice: they had to abandon their tribal family, abandon the people they had lived amongst all their lives, and seek out the side that had just been branded as their tribe's enemy. Of these, OM supporters fled in fear for their lives, while Corin's supporters departed more slowly, filled with fury or heartbreaking remorse at their tribe's fateful error.

Past victims of the Ragea's intimidation and brutality – hoping to sway the vote – bravely, finally, and cathartically revealed their wounds to the public. But it was too late. A fever of fear gripped Corin's supporters, and they distrusted anything in defence of the OM. Some even accused the wounded of somehow injuring themselves, weeks or months in advance, just to trick others. The Ragea's victims had bared their pain for nothing.

The Free People, as Corin's followers became known, seized the west of Karthalia. The OM, still scattered and disorganised, did at least claim the east, where – luckily – Jak, Laura and Martin's sewage hideout was located.

And so the geography of Karthalia mutated, its sides splitting

195

apart, leaving a wide vertical strip of land at its centre – land filled by huge empty spaces, deserted tribdwells, and stifling, ghostly silences.

Some of the people who followed the OM's call were sold on the idea that Jakariah really was a prophet for a better World. Others came because they had grown suspicious of the Ragea, or had had their eyes opened by someone who personally knew of the Ragea's secret viciousness. They believed the Ragea were trying to kill Jakariah simply because he opposed them, and because with him gone, it would be easier for them to further their own power.

Now, in the east of Karthalia, Laura stood with Martin and Jak, the three of them anxiously waiting...

Chapter 33

Via covert word of mouth, Laura, Jak and Martin had bruited the time and place for all OM supporters to unite. Soon, they would know how strong they really were.

Currently, about one hundred people had joined them beneath the hot glare of the morning's utterly normal, Mediterranean-blue sky; potential proof that, if there were gods, then earthly affairs had little significance for them from the vantage of their celestial abode. Some of the new OM recruits were aimlessly milling about, or quietly talking in groups. Others sat on the grass in meditative, mournful silence. No one seemed sure what to expect next, and the hushed atmosphere only heightened the general sense of tension.

And all the while, Laura kept looking about in desperation, looking for the two people she *needed* to appear there... her Mum and Dad...

Then suddenly, her roving gaze fixed upon something, and she froze, staring in stunned amazement. It wasn't her parents. Instead, she thought she'd glimpsed someone familiar, just before they'd vanished behind a nearby tribdwell. Someone tall, with broad shoulders, a beard, and strong, chiselled features... Amik? Before he'd turned away, the man had seemed to be staring at her. But the moment was so fleeting – it could easily have been a trick of her imagination...

"Look! There they are!" Jak shouted at Laura. She spun round.

In the near distance, across a large and empty expanse of grass, a group of about sixty people were heading towards them. Laura recognised who they were at once, because she would have recognised every one of those sixty-odd faces. It was the Teachers' Tribe. And two people were leading the way...

"Mum! Dad!" Laura shouted, racing forward, with Jak following in her wake. Now her parents spotted them. Like everyone in the Teachers' Tribe, they were carrying possessions in the sort of wooden crates normally used for storing food. Practically dropping those crates to the ground, they hurried to meet Laura and Jak, and Laura saw her parents do something she hadn't seen them do for about twenty years, not since when they played with her as a little girl: run. In a lighter moment, their awkward movements could almost have been funny.

Finally reaching her Mum, Laura collided with her in an embrace. She hugged her fiercely, like someone hugging onto a boulder for safety against the dangerous pull of the sea.

Sniffling, Gemma whispered into Laura's ear, her voice cracking with emotion: "We were terrified we'd never see you again."

"Me too," Laura whispered back, her voice just as fragile. "I-I was worried the Ragea would do something to you, to get back at us."

Then, switching with Jak, she hugged her Dad, tears of relief brimming in her eyes.

After they all reluctantly let go of each other, Gemma glanced at both her kids. Behind the thin copper rims of her glasses, her wet eyes glistened with awe, as though she still couldn't believe that her children were standing in front of her. Gazing at her Mum's face, Laura noticed that the past week's stress had prematurely aged her.

"We brought some of your stuff. From your tribdwell," her Mum said, bashfully wiping away the tears from her eyes. She also quickly touched the edges of her bob of grey hair, to make sure it was still presentable.

"Yeah?" Laura replied indulgently. Still riding high on her wave of joy, she couldn't have cared less about material things.

"Yes. Just wait a sec. I'll get it for you," and she urgently tottered back the way she'd come. *Typical Mum*, Laura smiled fondly. *Always bustling to be useful.*

A moment later, Gemma returned with the crate she'd been carrying when Laura first spotted her. Laura recognised that particular crate because, somehow, long ago, it had gained a distinctive knife-mark down its side. Gemma removed the lid, and playing along for her Mum's sake, Laura peered inside.

A mishmash of souvenirs and sentimental objects, all belonging to either her or Jak, greeted her eyes: the miniature, stylised wood-carving Jak had kept on a bookshelf in his bedroom; some of Laura's necklaces and bracelets with their dim, multicoloured jewels; a small pile of Jak's esoteric books, each of which was now creased and bent, having obviously been crammed into the crate in a hurry; and, near the top of that pile, a notebook that Laura recognised immediately. A feeling of dawning alarm shot through her. She snatched the book out of the crate.

"Honey? What's wrong?" Gemma said, sounding panicked.

"Ma chi," Laura replied softly, her voiced tinged with a conflicted apprehension. "Where did you find this?"

"It was underneath your bed," her Dad said. "Isn't it yours?"

Laura stared down at the notebook, its right side fastened shut with two pins. A plain white sheet of paper formed its front cover. She turned it over slowly and uncertainly, as if testing the weight and feel of an unknown substance. Then in a dull, emotionless voice, she said: "It's Amik's diary."

Without looking, she detected her parents' surprise, followed by their sudden air of awkwardness.

"Ente mniha?" Gemma said, placing a consoling hand on Laura's arm. "Sasha told us about your break-up."

"Yeah..." Laura said, anxiously biting her lip. *Maybe the notebook could help her understand why Amik had seemed to get over their relationship so easily... maybe it could redeem him in her eyes...*

She had enough self-awareness to know that these were dangerous thoughts; thinking about Amik was an obsession she'd forced herself to suppress. But now, with the truth about him in her hands, the temptation to reopen that wound gnawed away at her...

"It's a better turnout than I expected," Kevin said, in the slightly strained voice of someone trying to change the subject. Beneath his receding black hair, his studious, thoughtful eyes glanced about at the day's arrivals.

With the Teachers' Tribe, the OM now totalled at about one-hundred-and-sixty supporters. And looking ahead, Laura could see other tiny specks journeying towards them.

Kevin added wistfully, as if in conclusion to something: "At least we might have a chance."

After another hour of waiting (during which Jak, Laura and Martin were reunited with Tessalli, who they hugged like one of their own tribe) they decided that everyone who was going to turn up was there. It amounted to roughly a third of Karthalia.

Gathering everyone around him, Jak began to speak:

"Firstly, to everyone who's come here today, I can't express how much that act means to me. You've come here completely on trust. You don't know what my plan is, or even if I have one. But you believe that Oceanos is the path to a much better World. Or at least, you realise how dangerous the Ragea are, and that they need to be stopped if we're going to have any meaningful World at all. Well, let me tell you right now: Oceanos is real. And it's not dangerous at all. Nothing like I've heard the Ragea made it out to be.

"So this is what we're *not* going to do. We're not going to sit back passively, waiting for them – "The Free People" – to come to us. And we're not going to rely on hope or fate for see us through. Instead, we're going to outsmart the TFP, overwhelm them, and *make* the better World happen.

"When we seize the lilaxes, it'll be in such a way that they won't be able to stop us."

Laura glanced around. Many of the people in the crowd, frightened and in need of assurance, began to smile tentatively with the first flickerings of optimism, belief, and a sense of trust born out of desperation.

"But before that happens," Jak said, "we need to set up a base. Somewhere we can all stay. I vote we head to the Yesod Tribe. I don't know why, but... deep down, it just feels like that's the place we're supposed to go."

Laura frowned, realising what a clever, manipulative move this was. The Yesod Tribe were clothing manufacturers, but the word 'Yesod' originally meant 'unity'. Everyone knew that. And Oceanos was about unity. Jak was deliberately tying together theme and reality, making it feel as if the OM's story was meant to be – and in doing so, reinforcing the sense that he really was some sort of preordained prophet.

In less polite speech: he was bullshitting them.

But in the faces around her, Laura saw a newfound conviction glowing and growing. Jak's deception had inspired them. His lie had done good.

After finishing his speech, everyone agreed with his suggestion, and so he started leading the OM towards the Yesod Tribe.

From high above, the long, stretched-out collection of marching OM members resembled an immense snake of human flesh crawling its way across the planet. But from a ground perspective, all that Laura saw were the determined, and determinedly hopeful, expressions of the people around her. Their mission to save and elevate Karthalia had begun.

Through the densely packed, moving crowd ahead of her, she caught sight of Martin walking with his dad. The two of them were catching up in animated fashion, both overcome with the same smiles she and her family had had when they found each other again.

Meanwhile, her own Dad was beside her, and – in typical style – was muttering away, talking to himself as much as anyone. It was funny – several days of nightmarish separation, a brief emotional reunion, and suddenly, it was like their relationship was back in its same old grooves.

"... and this split in Karthalia," he ploughed on absent-mindedly, shaking his head like some mournful philosopher. "How has it come to this?"

Then, from the waists of a couple of people not far ahead of her, Laura caught sight of something gleaming in the sun. Her eyes followed the light to its source, and saw objects sheathed in leather holsters, with wooden handles poking out the top. Beneath those handles, she glimpsed thin slivers of metal – the origin point of the gleams – and realised what the things were. Blades. Weapons for murder in the coming battle.

Confusion, like a horde of locusts, settled across her mind. It suddenly felt like a precious illusion was slipping away from her, and instinctively, desperately, she tried to claw it back.

"... The world has ended in violence once already," her Dad droned on, using 'world' in its archaic sense. "The people who founded Karthalia – they lived through that. I can't believe that now, after all that misery, we're letting it happen again..."

Staring at those sheathed blades, Laura imagined them stabbing into the enemy, into men and women from the "The Free People", with the blades then being ripped out of their flesh and drenched in gore, in the blood of people Laura had known all her life, had passed and said 'hello' to on her trips through Karthalia. Those people, those familiar faces – they were the enemy. And those blades would kill them.

"... Karthalians have lost their way..."

Why was this horror only hitting her now? A battle had almost always been inevitable. She'd known that. So what had changed? Maybe it was seeing the weapons snatched out of her vague, half-imagined notion of a battle, and turned into fact... maybe the reality of something was a lot more horrid than the idea...

Conflict and violence – this wasn't right. This was the opposite of what Oceanos stood for.

"Still," her Dad murmured, "this wasn't our choice. They've made it so we have to fight them."

Laura turned to look at him blankly, still half-stunned. She didn't agree. They still had a choice. Until a deed was committed to history, it was only a possibility. And a possibility wasn't something she had to commit to.

Now, all her old dread and anxiety had returned. The joyful reunion with her family was only a fleeting moment, a sliver of light between the darkness of her recent life as a fugitive, and the unknown terror of the looming battle which, like a monstrous whirlpool, was sucking every life in Karthalia towards its maw, toward the future which that maw represented. The pull felt inescapable.

The worst was yet to come.

Chapter 34

The urge to read Amik's diary nagged at Laura.

Sometimes, the temptation was so strong she couldn't think clearly about anything else. What if the diary could somehow absolve him in her eyes? What if it showed he'd still loved her, even as he made that devastatingly calm speech introducing his statue? Then there might be a chance for them to be together again – a chance for things to go back to the way they were, before she discovered what the Ragea were really like, and that knowledge split her and Amik apart.

But no. She couldn't look. He'd always made it strenuously clear that he wanted his diary to remain private, and if he meant anything to her, she should respect that.

At least, that's what she kept telling herself, as she sat within the shade of an olive tree, the afternoon gloom rendering her light and dark hair almost indistinguishable.

The secluded spot lay just beyond the Yesod Tribe's cluster of tribdwells. *It's good to get away,* she thought, *however briefly, from the oppressive atmosphere that pervades that place. There are too many people there, all burdened by the knowledge of just how precarious their futures are.*

Two days had passed since the OM's arrival there. They'd quickly established themselves in the Yesod Tribe's haphazard sprawl of tribdwells, piling crates of possessions everywhere, both inside buildings and out, transforming many previously beloved homes into mere storage facilities.

The area's ambience had also undergone a change. Initially hushed and deserted (the Yesod Tribe having sided with the Ragea) it was now drenched in a different type of quiet. Like the calm before a storm. It didn't help that there was a charged stillness in the humid air, as if a real thunderstorm were on the way.

And in the black clouds of Laura's mind, the image of those blades, gleaming with the sun's gold, still haunted her. So did the way Jak was manipulating people into thinking he was a prophet, even if it was for the greater good. She urgently wanted to talk to him about it. But that was the problem – for the last couple of days, he'd been impossible to get hold of.

Unlike her and everyone else, Jak didn't have to sleep on the floor in a tribdwell crammed full of OM members. Instead, as the OM's de facto leader, he'd been granted a tribdwell of his own. *He needed a private space to contemplate,* his supporters had said, *to think through what their plan would be and make it as effective as possible.* Embarrassed, he'd refused their demand several times, before eventually giving in.

Since then, Laura had knocked on his door on numerous occasions. And each time, as she stood before the enfoliaged doorway, bouncing on the balls of her feet in a mixture of nervousness and impatience, she'd received the same answer: "Uh, I'm working on something right now. Can you come back in a bit?"

At these moments, his voice had always sounded a little strained, a little hurried and frantic. It was as if he were buzzing with energy, immersed in some project that he couldn't bear to tear himself away from. Only once had she caught him when he was leaving the tribdwell:

"Jak, wait! Are you free for a minute? I need to have a quick chat about something." She'd spoken earnestly, trying not to let any trace of pleading slip into her voice. She didn't like this new side of him. He'd always made time for her in the past.

"Sorry," he replied, slowing down momentarily as he hurried away from her. "I've got to meet someone. It's about a plan for the OM. But you might be able to catch me later."

"What plan? Wait – what are you doing in there?" she pointed at his tribdwell.

"It's nothing to do with that. This is just some other stuff that needs to be worked out. Listen, I've got to go."

Exasperated and lost for words, Laura had watched him rush off. But as she did so, one detail from their encounter had begun to plague her mind: as Jak had gone off to prepare for a battle that would lead to the death of many people, he'd not only been full of that energy she'd been hearing in his voice – he'd also, and openly, been grinning.

For a while, the memory of that disturbing image kept popping into her thoughts, accompanied by a profound sense of unease. What secret task was he working on in there? And how could he be even slightly happy, given the terrifying weight of his responsibility, and the lethal days that lay ahead of them all?

Perhaps his idea – that he should present himself as some sort of saviour – had got out of hand, and now, he'd fallen for it himself. Perhaps he believed that he really was divinely blessed, and therefore, untouchable.

Yet Jak's apparently deranged euphoria was only one of Laura's worries. The other lay behind her.

Glancing over her shoulder, she saw Martin sitting cross-legged on the grass, before the small, squat building of an art wall. His hand, limp and lifeless, rested across his knee, holding one of the cans of spray paint that had been found within the Yesod Tribe.

From her vantage, she could only see the side of his face, in a sort of angled semi-profile. But it was enough. She noticed the way his slightly chubby, acne-speckled cheeks hung in a dolorous frown. Spotted the dead, resigned look in his brown eyes as he stared transfixed at the wall in front of him.

He'd been sat there for at least four hours. It was as if his depression, from before he'd tried Oceanos, had suddenly and inexplicably returned.

Part of Laura wanted to go over and find out what was wrong with him. But both his grief-stricken look of concentration, and the slow, rhythmic activity of his spray-painting, made it seem as if he'd entered a trance-like state. He was behaving as if the World around him didn't exist, and she didn't want to intrude upon an experience that might be private and precious.

Yet gazing at him, it felt like the man who had a zest for life – who had been Jak's closest friend for years – was a million vasters away. Even his distinctive haircut had changed, its shaven swirl pattern having grown out during the past two weeks into an odd and uneven mess. It only increased Laura's sense that the past was a wonderful place, from which very few things had survived.

Squinting, she tried to make out exactly what Martin was spray-painting. Whatever it was, it formed a very dark image, its black and grey tints blending together into a murky, almost impenetrable fog. And from the fog, someone made of the faintest silver lines was emerging... someone with a feminine shape...

Someone Laura didn't recognise at all.

Would she be waiting for him on the other side?

Utterly absorbed in his work, Martin sprayed another glittering silver streak onto his jet-black meditation exercise. At this stage, he was painting only half-consciously, letting his feelings flow through his body, his spray can, and onto the wall. His mind was elsewhere... wandering, ghostlike, through a series of dark thoughts.

He was thinking about the woman he was painting. Thinking about her death.

Her name was Abi. For a very short time, she'd been his Mum, having died when he was still a baby. He'd thought about her frequently over the years, but always in a dim, distant way. But now, he knew his own impending death was closing in upon him. And the more he thought about it, the more he found his thoughts turning towards her.

Would she be waiting for him on the other side? Martin didn't believe in any god, but he couldn't help imagining himself seeing – in death – her welcoming eyes.

He knew he couldn't survive the coming battle. He wasn't a quick runner, he wasn't strong, and he didn't know how to handle a weapon. The people in the Hunters' Tribe – they would know what they were doing. But not him.

The cruel truth was staring him in the face: he didn't have long left in this World.

And that's when his terror had begun. The nauseous, claustrophobic sense that his life was trapped in a sinister black room, where the walls were suddenly closing in and were only moments away from crushing him. What about all the things he still wanted to do? He'd taken it for granted that he still had plenty of time left – that he could do them at some point in the future. And now, all that possibility, all that potential, was being cut short.

He would only get to be half the person he thought he'd be.

The same might become true of the people close to him: his Dad... Jak... Laura... He pictured them in the battle, all impaled on the enemy's weapons, him utterly impotent to stop it.

And it was all down to something that he, Jak, and Laura had begun. Still, he knew they'd done the right thing. Even if he could take their fateful actions back, he wouldn't.

Besides, the revolution didn't really belong to him or Laura anymore. They'd both been swallowed into the relative obscurity of Jak's growing shadow. Frankly, Martin preferred it like that. He didn't want the responsibility for what was to come.

Pausing in his painting, he tried to soak in the details of what he'd accomplished so far. That's when, at the outermost edge of his consciousness, he registered the faint twittering of birds.

And like the cracking of a tree in the dull roar of a thunderstorm, revelation struck. He realised that, when he was gone, birds would still twitter... the sun would still rise... seasons would still pass... and people would carry on living, as people always had. So, in a very real sense, what did his life matter at all?

But, in a more logical region of his mind, he knew that was simply his depression speaking...

It was strange. On one level, he felt like he should just shake off his black mood, and make the most of what remaining time he had. After all, his depression wasn't real in the sense that you could touch it. In a way, it was a figment, something that existed only in his own head.

And yet, every human action in history stemmed from such figments of emotion. Without hate, love, boredom, curiosity, lust, and all the rest, there was no impetus to do anything. Even to think anything. Emotions were the subliminal forces that controlled all.

Shaking his spray can, and looking for some sort of solace, Martin continued to delineate a woman he'd never really known – venting the melancholy inside him, and capturing its realness in a painted reality.

Laura turned away from Martin and his painting. If his depression persisted, she would try to find out what was wrong.

But for now – and she was annoyed with herself for thinking so selfishly – she had enough problems of her own to worry about...

Chapter 35

Laura halted upon the threshold of the Yesod Tribe's main tribdwell. This is where she'd been told Jak was.

Scanning the large and busy room, she spotted his almost cadaverously thin figure at a table located just off the room's centre. As ever, he was sat perfectly upright. If Laura had known the word, she would have thought that his bearing, through some imperceptible shift, now verged on being 'regal'. But that adjective had drowned in the waves of history long before her birth.

Huddled before him were a group of five people, all elderly apart from one, including a dreadlock-haired woman with a severely hunched back, as if she were doubled up in pain. Stood front and centre of the group was its age exception, a small girl of about twelve years old. She held Jak's slender hand, staring at his palm intently.

Ducking under an overgrown piece of greenery that dangled in the entranceway, Laura nervously crossed the room towards her brother. She needed to get hold of him now, before he hurried away somewhere else. Needed to snap him out of the stupid, mindless optimism that could put his followers' lives at risk.

Having been gutted by the Yesod Tribe, the tribdwell Laura strode through was almost devoid of furniture, its few remaining long tables converted into makeshift dining areas. A heady aroma of fish, lemon juice, black pepper, and bay leaves scented the air: it came from a red mullet being grilled over a charcoal fire in the corner. And pinned to the building's sunbaked walls were large square cut-outs of richly dyed fabric; presumably, preliminary tests for clothing projects which the Yesod Tribe had been forced to abandon.

Slowing to a halt, Laura hovered near Jak, not wanting to interrupt whatever he and the girl were doing. She noticed that a black beard had begun to grow on her brother's untended cheeks, adding a dishevelled wildness to his already outlandish appearance. He glanced up at her from his dark, sleep-deprived eyes, then back at the girl.

"... is very significant," the girl said, tracing with a gentle finger one of the lines on Jak's palm.

The action made Laura realise where the five people were from: the Clairvoyants' Tribe. The clairvoyants believed that their youngest members, by virtue of being innocent and also the least corrupted by prejudice, were most in touch with divinity. This little girl must have been their current leader.

Glancing at a man nearby who was also watching the palm reading, Laura's eyes met his. A knowing, I-can't-believe-anyone-believes-this-stuff look passed between them.

But turning her attention back to the girl's large, hazelnut eyes, Laura saw – or at least thought she saw – tiny, separate pools of quivering white light glistening within them. It must have been an optical illusion – afternoon light streaming through the tribdwell's rectangular windows, and being reflected and caught in the girl's gaze. Yet those bottomless, childish eyes... they were mesmerising...

Brushing a loose strand of hair from her face, the girl spoke: "Your main palm line is strong. You will have a long life, filled with strength and power. We've also discussed your fate," she tilted her head towards her fellow tribe members, "and read the hidden signs of the universe..."

As they spoke, Laura noticed something through one of the tribdwell's windows...

"They say you'll be victorious. That you were born destined to triumph."

... people piling up a huge collection of logs, building a pyre for the coming night. Laura felt her anxiety spike, without knowing why...

"This is the premonition we've had." The white pools in the girl's eyes were now glowing brighter than ever, as if radiating out from inside her. "It's what has led us to join you."

... then it hit her. The pyre. Setting up something to burn. That's what this conversation with Jak was like.

And as Laura looked at him, she saw what she feared: Jak's mouth broadening into a confident grin, as though he were indomitable. The clairvoyants had done their usual trick – told someone exactly what they wanted to hear. And right now, that was the last thing her brother needed.

Thanking the clairvoyants for their insight, Jak rose to his feet.

"I would also thank you," he added, "for your bravery in joining the OM. But I suppose it's hard to be brave when you always know what the outcome's going to be."

Except for the girl, who didn't seem to understand, the clairvoyants smiled politely at his joke. Then Jak started to walk away, that self-satisfied grin still plastered across his face, before Laura strode forward boldly, half-lunged to reach him, and tapped his arm.

"Hey," she blurted, over-eagerly.

"Oh. Hi," Jak replied, as if mildly startled. For the briefest moment, a blank look crossed his eyes, as though he couldn't process what Laura was doing there with him. Then he blinked, and the look passed.

But almost immediately, he started heading for the tribdwell's exit again, compelling Laura to keep pace with him.

"Look, I'm really sorry," he said, "but I'm in a rush. There's something I need to do. But we'll talk later."

"La'!" Laura said in a low voice, grabbing his arm. He stared at her in surprise. Even she was a little shocked by her own forcefulness. "We need to talk now. Come over here."

She led him to the side of the room, where the two of them could have some privacy.

"Laura, what's wrong?" Jak said, that old brotherly instinct immediately rising to the surface. "Has something happened to you?"

"No. Jak, I'm worried about *you*. I've barely seen you for the past two days. And every time I have, you've had this big... *smile* on your face, as if the World couldn't be better. What's wrong with you? People here are going to die soon, and what they do next depends on what you tell them. So forget whatever the clairvoyants just said to you. You need to start taking this seriously, and *wake up*."

Her trembling fear for him had slipped into her voice, and a lump had formed in her throat. There was so much more she wanted to tell him: that the whole prophet charade had gone to his head, that too much was changing in their relationship, that she'd never felt so distant from him. Yet something choked those words back. Maybe they were too honest, revealed too much of her vulnerability. So, desperately, she tried to convey all those pent-up feelings through the sincere, unflinching look in her eyes.

But as she'd spoken, Jak's furrowed forehead had smoothed out. All trace of his anxiety had disappeared.

"Laura, don't worry. I'm on top of everything."

That disconcerting smile had spread over his face again, as though he were privy to distant knowledge. He pulled her close to him in a hug, and kissed her tenderly on her forehead.

213

"Trust me," he whispered. "Everything's going to work out for the best."

For Laura, pressed against her brother, the space between the two of them grew taut with a strained silence that screamed to be broken.

Then, belatedly, she became aware that the fraught tension wasn't confined to her and Jak. A sense of shock was rippling through the rest of the room, spreading from group to group, and leaving a frightened silence in its wake. Faces turned towards the tribdwell's doorway, then froze in horror. Laura followed their gaze.

A hulking, muscular man stood slumped in the doorway, propped up on either side by two smaller men. All three figures had their backs to the sun, casting their faces in shadow. But despite this, Laura could still see – on the central man's face – the smears of crimson blood that had recently seeped from his long, gaping lacerations. Could still see the fresh, bulging bruises that deformed his face around his cheeks and eyes. His head hung forward on his neck, lolling limply from exhaustion, while his bleary eyes looked up at the people in the room through fluttering, half-closed lids.

Laura recognised the two men on either side. They were from the OM. The man in the middle was a mystery. But he was dressed wholly in black.

"Is Jakariah here?" one of the men from the OM called out, his panicked eyes scanning the room.

A beat.

"Naam," Jak called back. Laura twisted round. Her brother's usually stern face was a mixture of uncertainty and wariness, and he was recoiling slightly from the sight of the bloodied man in the doorway.

The man propping up the draped figure continued: "This man's come here to speak to you. He says he's from the Ragea."

Laura looked at the pitiful stranger. His barely open eyes were now fixed upon Jak, as if pleading for help.

"What's his name?" Jak called back, starting to walk hesitantly towards the mute and battered new arrival.

The man to the side answered: "He said it's Leo."

Chapter 36

They manhandled Leo into a vacant tribdwell, into its kitchen and dining area.

Two large, muscular men – brought by Jak – shut the tribdwell's front door, and closed the window shutters that hung above the kitchen cauldron. Apart from the beams of light that penetrated through the angled slats of the shutters, falling upon the wooden floor in pale golden bars, the room was now saturated in a cool darkness. Jak didn't want any prying eyes for what was to come.

Leo – still standing where they'd left him, confused and disorientated – was physically ushered across the room by the two stern men, before being carefully lowered into one of the chairs set at the dining room table. Then, performing their new, impromptu roles with great professionalism, Jak's two accomplices took up positions on either side of the front door, quickly blending into the pervading gloom and silence.

Suddenly, it felt like Leo and Jak were all alone.

With his beady pale blue eyes, framed by his shoulder-length tangle of curly, Odysseine hair, Leo stared at Jak. He appeared wary and vulnerable. Yet after he'd arrived, he'd received a brief treatment for his injuries, and it had turned out his cuts were only superficial. He could still be dangerous.

Jak sat down opposite Leo, deliberately making sure that the table's short width would be all that separated them. But as he did so, he hesitated mid-movement. For the first time, he saw in Leo's battered face an echo of what he himself had been through. Touching his lip, still ever so slightly swollen from the Ragea's assault, he felt an unwanted note of sympathy being struck within him.

Banishing that sense of empathy from his mind, he faced his captive. They were about the same height, but Leo's broad-shouldered, athletic physique made him vastly more intimidating.

Jak leaned forward, in a way that he hoped exuded a mixture of calm relaxedness and undeniable authority.

"I'm sorry we had to bring you here," he said. "But I'm sure you understand. We can't take any chances."

"Of course," Leo nodded quickly, seemingly eager to please. The water applied to his wounds by caring OM members had perked him up, and although his body was still slumped with exhaustion, his eyes were alert and engaged. Words tumbled out of his mouth: "I can tell you anything. Whatever you want to know. Like Corin, he's now the leader of The Free People. It's because we—"

"Machkour," Jak cut him off. "But we can discuss that later."

Consciously trying to appear impassive, Jak fixed his keen eyes upon Leo's face, probing for any hint of deceit. He was visibly trying to put pressure on Leo, to see if he would crack. But Leo's fatigued posture was open and honest, like a man who knew he had nothing to hide. And through the blood and bruises of his square-jawed face, his willingness to help emanated powerfully, to the point where Jak found it suspicious.

"What I want to know," Jak said, "is why you're defecting now."

Leo turned his head ever so slightly away from his questioner. As he gazed at the floor, a bitter, defeated look crept over his face. "Because," he muttered, "when the battle happens, I don't think The Free People will win."

Jak frowned. "Why?"

"It's Corin. Like I said, he's the leader of The Free People. Well, before that, he was in charge of the Ragea. And he was... awful. Completely unsure of himself, unable to act. Not a leader at all." Leo seemed to almost sneer at that last line. "Under him, The Free People can't win. And I don't want to be on the losing side.

"I mean, you know how the whole Schism was his idea? Well, it's ruined the Ragea. There are too many eyes on us now. And even that speech he gave to Karthalia about experiencing Oceanos, even that wasn't true. It was me and two other Ragea that suffered that."

Worms of disgust crawled over Leo's face. "He's got nothing of substance. I can't fight for someone like him."

Leaning back in his chair, Jak glanced over his shoulder at one of the guards. There was no hint of surprise on the man's face. Presumably, what Leo had said about Corin's speech was true. Then, curious, Jak said:

"You experienced it?"

"... yes."

As Leo said that, did he wince? Through the darkness, Jak couldn't be sure.

"And what did you see?"

"Colours, everywhere. Spinning round me. Making me lose my sense of who I am..."

In this, at least, he was telling the truth.

"Anyway," Leo said, "I can't get rid of Corin. Even if I managed it, the other Ragea would kill me for it. But I can't serve him either. Which left me with only one option."

"Coming here."

Jak glanced over Leo's bloodied cuts and bruises once more, trying to puzzle the whole thing out. "And that's why they beat you? Because you left them?"

"Yeah."

"How did you get away?"

"For a moment, they stopped hitting me. I mean, a lot of them are my kin. They didn't *want* to hurt me. That's when I lashed out at them, and ran."

"But... why hurt you at all? You're one person. It's not like you're going to change the fate of the battle single-handedly."

"It's because they've got a secret. And they're terrified I'll reveal it."

Leo leaned across the table, as though about to say something he didn't want anyone else to hear. Jak craned forward to listen. It was as if the two of them were co-conspirators, and Leo had returned from a mission with vital information.

"You know how we said we worshipped the lilaxe?" he whispered. "Well, that's a lie. We didn't worship it. We *ate it*. Do that, and it boosts your strength. Gives you an adrenaline rush. Makes you feel invincible."

Still-raw memories – of a mob of Ragea attacking him as he lay helpless on the ground – flooded through Jak's mind. He remembered how phenomenally agonising those punches and kicks had been, how they'd been far more painful than he would ever have expected, and how each powerful blow felt like it was going to snap one of his bones. Now, for the first time, all that agony was starting to make sense.

Leo continued: "D'you see? Even without Oceanos, the lilaxe can change you. That's why the Ragea are protecting it. They *need* it. It's what gives them their self-belief and their power. They think that, with it, the coming battle's already won."

Leo leant back.

"But you don't?" Jak asked.

"No. Not with Corin. He's as good as cursed." As if he'd said all he had to say, Leo stared expectantly at Jak.

Jak glanced at the guards. They didn't seem to have heard what the enemy's traitor had revealed. And they never would. No one could know about it. That information was too dangerous.

In the ensuing tense, pregnant silence, Jak trained his judging gaze back upon Leo. Something still didn't feel right. It was too unlikely, this man from the Ragea just turning up out of the blue. He could put the lives of everyone in the OM in danger. Jak couldn't afford to miss a thing.

"You said," Jak persisted, "that Corin was the leader of the Ragea. So your tribe gave itself a hierarchy?"

"Yes."

"And how senior were you?"

For a split-second, Leo hesitated. Then...

"Very," he admitted. "I was Corin's right-hand man."

For a moment, Jak just stared at Leo, not altering his expression at all. Then he spoke:

"Wait here." He stood up and left the tribdwell, taking the two guards with him.

Striding round one of the tribdwell's corners, to a place where Leo definitely wouldn't be able to see them, Jak stopped by the green plant-wall. A couple of minutes passed with him whispering with the two guards.

At one point during their conversation, Jak snuck round to the tribdwell's rear, and surreptitiously peeked in through the slats of the kitchen's shuttered window. Leo still sat in his chair. Jak could only see him from behind, but Leo's head was tilted up towards the ceiling. Maybe he was gazing at it apprehensively, or maybe it was out of a mixture of exhaustion and boredom. Jak noticed that Leo's right hand was resting on the dining room table, and that his middle finger was constantly and quickly tapping on the wood, as if out of anxiety.

There was no breaking out of character. No sign that Leo's

defection, and his earnestness in front of Jak, had all been part of some grand deception.

Then Jak called over a nearby OM member, and asked him to spread a message around the camp: *There would be a disturbance. He wanted everyone to be aware of what was about to happen. There was no need to panic.*

Afterwards, Jak walked away from the window, and motioned for the guards to follow him. The three of them headed back into the tribdwell.

Once more: Jak opposite Leo, the guards either side of the doorway.

Jak spoke first: "We're going to have a Socratic dialogue, and you're just going to answer yes or no. D'accord?"

Leo nodded. He obviously didn't know what the term "Socratic dialogue" meant. His swollen face began to look apprehensive.

"I want you to imagine something," Jak said, adopting the voice of someone in perfect control, as though he were still a teacher talking to a child. "Imagine you're the leader of a large group. You've all been drawn together by a shared belief, and they're like a family to you.

"Then a stranger from an enemy group appears. He claims he's defected to your side, but there's no way you can be sure. And if you do let him into your group, he could potentially hurt the people within it. You'd have to be suspicious of him, wouldn't you?"

Uncertainty flickered across Leo's face, as though he feared he were being tricked, drawn towards some clever verbal trap. "I guess..."

"Yes or no?"

Jak waited patiently.

"... Yes."

"Then you learn that stranger was a very senior member in the enemy group. There's a *possibility* that he could be a spy, isn't there?"

Leo said nothing. The air suddenly had a charged quality, as if at the confrontation between a predator and its prey.

"Just answer the question honestly," Jak said. "That's all I'm asking."

"Yes, of course. But I'm no—"

"This isn't about *you*. It's just a hypothetical situation."

Leo exhaled heavily, as though expelling his nerves. A hint of anxious irritation seemed to be creeping into his small, blue eyes.

"And what's more," Jak continued, "you won't gain anything if you accept this stranger into your group. He's already told you the enemy's secret. But there are major risks. He could injure other members of your group, or even kill them. And chances are, you wouldn't have time to stop him. So if there's no benefit – nothing in it for you – then it's an unnecessary risk, isn't it?"

Leo replied through clenched teeth, almost hissing: "Yes."

He was now picking nervously at his lower lip, his earlier posture transformed into something hunched and defensive.

"But what about if you let him leave? He could go back to the enemy. You might have to face him in battle. In effect, you'd be *giving* him the chance to kill someone in your group. And remember, they're like your family. Their lives matter above everything else. So if you want to protect them – and that's the only question *you*, as their leader, have to answer – if you want to protect them, then the *safest thing* you can do – for their sake – is to get rid of this potential killer right now, while he's in your power. Isn't it?"

Leo had clammed up.

"Remember," Jak reassured him in that perfect, controlling voice, "this is only hypothetical. Nothing's going to happen to you."

"Well, then—*yes*," Leo snapped almost petulantly, as if he just wanted to get through this. Get it over and done with.

"So you agree?" Jak said. "You'd have to have that person killed."

From the wings of the doorway, the two huge guards strode towards Leo, their arms raised as if to seize him.

"What's going on?" Leo shouted, his battered, enervated body recoiling in its seat. "What are you doing?"

The two guards grabbed him, each clamping their big, strong hands around Leo's arms, pinning him into his chair.

"La'!" Leo struggled against them. He was an imposing, powerful man himself. That's why Jak had brought two such physically intimidating men with him. Only together could they handle Leo.

"Dzerkerd kashek!" Leo shouted. "Hellllp! Somebody help me!"

"No one's going to come," Jak muttered flatly, as if the screaming didn't faze him at all. "They know exactly what's happening."

He was walking towards the far end of the room, towards the kitchen drawer. He pulled out a large knife made for chopping meat.

Then, with the blade's shadowy tip pointing at the back of Leo's thick neck, he began returning towards the table. Still pinned in his chair, Leo twisted round, looking over his shoulder to see what Jak was doing. Then he turned pale, his eyes fixed upon the approaching knife.

For a moment, it was as if Leo couldn't move. As if he were caught in a bubble where time had ground to a halt. Then the bubble burst, and he began thrashing his body again, struggling twice as hard as before.

"Laa!" he raved, tossing his head wildly, with spit flying from his lips. It was as if he'd gone mad. "This isn't what you're meant to do! You're about peace! *You're not killers!*"

Bending down, Jak stared at his victim face-to-face: "No. But you are."

Standing back up, he towered over Leo's helpless figure. "After all... this is only what you promised to do to Pavneet."

Leo stopped writhing. The last rays of hope died in his eyes.

"That wasn't me," he muttered in a small, pleading voice.

"But of course, that's the problem with you," Jak said, deliberately twisting his lips into a cracked, psychotic grin. "We can never know if you're telling the truth."

Slowly – prolonging the moment – Jak strode past one of the guards, so that he stood directly behind Leo's chair. Leo started struggling again. He jerked his shoulders left and right, and it was as if his upper body was spasming from some sort of seizure. But this time, the resistance was half-hearted. Something he felt he *should* do, without any belief that it would actually work. The arms of his oppressors pinned him fast. He was like a fish: removed from its natural element, its flapping body held firmly down so that the killing blow could be easily delivered.

Jak brought his knife-wielding arm round to the front of Leo's head. Then he drew the blade back towards him, so that its extremely thin, extremely sharp edge pressed against the Adam's apple in Leo's throat.

"You know," Jak whispered into Leo's ear, "it's a shame Corin didn't send you. We'd let you live a bit longer. We'd still have some use for you."

"But he didn't." Leo's voice trembled pathetically, as if he was trying not to cry: "But I can still help you, I promise!"

Jak smiled wickedly. Although Leo couldn't see the smile, Jak hoped he could sense it. Hoped it sent a cold shiver through Leo's body, and made the hairs on the back of his neck tingle and prick up with fear.

Jak hissed: "Not good enough."

Then, in a motion almost quicker than the eye could follow, Jak thrust his arm forward, spinning the knife in his hand so the blade pointed at Leo's chest. He drove the knife in towards Leo's heart.

"NOOOOO—"

Leo's painfully loud scream abruptly stuttered out, as if cut short by a sudden, visceral shock. He looked down. The knife lay suspended in mid-air, frozen still in Jak's white-knuckled grip. Its steel tip touched the thin fabric of Leo's shirt, but nothing more.

"Okay," Jak muttered, letting the blade fall to his side. "Seems like you're not lying. You can stay with the OM."

He turned to the guards. "Look after him. Give him some bandages, and find a tribdwell where he can sleep."

Then, bending down, he whispered forcefully into Leo's ear: "And that secret you mentioned? That stays between us."

Leo nodded meekly, as if afraid of any more attacks. From behind his own cold, impassive gaze, Jak looked at him with sympathy. He didn't enjoy what he'd just done. But necessities were necessities.

Heading towards the tribdwell's exit, Jak paused mid-step. A question had dawned on him... but he was scared of its answer.

He turned to face Leo: "Did you go through with it?"

Jak wanted the intense, meaningful look in his eyes to convey what he was referring to. But Leo just sat there, a pitiful Ragea thug, looking dumb and frightened. So Jak asked a second time:

"Did you kill him?"

A glint of recognition flared up in Leo's small eyes. Immediately, Jak wished he hadn't asked the question.

"Yeah," Leo replied heavily. His eyes were completely hidden by dark, anguished shadows, and it sounded as if admitting this truth physically pained him. "We did." Then, as though under the weight of his guilt, Leo bowed his head.

Jak glared at him. He could feel an old fury, reawakened after a spell of dormancy, breathing with fresh life through the rising and falling of his chest. Part of him – a small part – couldn't believe the Ragea had actually done it. Unwittingly, he'd sheltered a glimmer of hope for Pavneet. Leo's words had extinguished it.

With an effort of will, Jak ripped his gaze away from Leo and strode out of the tribdwell. But just beyond the threshold, without knowing why, he glanced back over his shoulder.

Leo sat slumped in his chair, head still bowed, with the guards tending to him. Despite the speed of his look, Jak noticed Leo's trembling lips, and the tears sliding down his cheeks. He was in a state of shock, the aftermath of an unfair, terrifying ordeal.

Jak hurried on his way.

Chapter 37

Beneath an overcast sky that bathed the landscape in a dull, grey light, Jak was leading the OM out of Karthalia. He hadn't told anyone where they were going. He'd simply said that he had something to show them.

Although it was a risk to leave their Yesod base almost completely unguarded, The Free People were unlikely to attack in the short window of time that the OM would be gone. Instead, the real danger might be amongst them right now...

"I think it's a bad move," Martin muttered to Laura in the soft quiet as they walked along, referring to Leo. "We've had one traitor already – whoever told the Ragea that me, Jak and Pavneet were gonna be in that forest. I mean, that person might have infiltrated the OM, and we'd have no way of knowing. So why let one of the Ragea join us as well? They've already proven they're jackals that can't be trusted."

"Have you talked to Jak about it?" It felt like the issues surrounding Jak were drawing her and Martin closer together.

"Yeah. He just replied in his usual stubborn way: 'I've tested him. *He's fine.*'"

Laura gave a slight nod of her head, her expression tinged with concern. She had an emotionally transparent face: it didn't hide the feelings bubbling away beneath the surface.

At least, she thought, *Martin now seems merely serious and thoughtful, not depressed. Maybe his funereal mood was only brief and passing.*

The reverse was true of her brother's messiah complex. The clairvoyants' prediction that Jak was "destined to win" had wildfired throughout the tribe. Laura had overheard numerous people talking excitedly about it. Talking fervently, as if he really were some sort of religious saviour. But she knew her brother; knew he was only human.

Looking up from the ground and away from her thoughts, she spotted – up ahead in the throng – several large mahogany storage trunks, each so heavy that it was being carried by two people. She wondered what was inside them, and why they were being brought along...

The OM approached the border of Karthalia, the Wall towering above them. As Laura gazed up at it, its stone-grey immensity caused her to feel a sense of vertigo. It was one of the only features in Karthalia not to have at least a mask of Nature upon it. Nothing was allowed to grow over it, for fear that its stone-work – too gargantuan to be maintained – would become cracked and destabilised.

Staring at the Wall, vertigo trembling through her mind and senses, a new, alien conception of her homeland crawled into Laura's mind. Karthalia was like an enormous pit, where the inhabitants were sealed inside by the steep, unscalable heights of the Wall. A pit into which two warring sides had been dropped, like a snake and a jackal being placed into a hole in the ground. Fighting was inevitable. There was no room to hide, no room to retreat. All the two sides could do was clash, battle, and struggle, until one of them emerged triumphant.

Her homeland wasn't safe. It was a pit where slaughter was inevitable.

Bewitched by this frightening, truthful perspective, she nearly bumped into the person walking in front of her. The whole group was slowing down. She looked up: they'd reached the Iron Gate.

It was roughly twice as tall as Laura, and she had to tilt back her head to view the top of it. With the sun overhead and to the west, the Gate's latticework of horizontal and vertical bars were silhouetted menacingly, dripping blackness. Jagged horns of rust jutted out from all over the flat steel strips that formed its body, but despite that, the aged, ancient barrier still looked strong and sturdy.

An excited muttering started up. Most Karthalians almost never left the cosy, comfortable embrace of their homeland. Beyond the World – it was still something exotic, something largely unknown and which thus possessed a thrilling hint of danger.

Peering over the heads and shoulders of the people in front of her, Laura strained to get a look at what was happening. Fastened to the Wall – just to the right of the Gate – was a square piece of metal, a short length of steel that terminated in a ring projecting out from its centre. Hooked irremovably to this ring was a slender chain that dangled to just above ground level, with a long, tarnished, and weighty-looking steel key linked in at the end of it. Bending down, Jak picked up the key, inserted it into the Iron Gate, and twisted it.

A sharp clang resounded outwards, like the sound of a metal bar in the lock shooting back into its receptacle. Then, arm outstretched, Jak marched forward, driving the heavy Gate back.

Slowly, as if with a mounting sense of awe and apprehension, the OM trickled out through the opening in the Wall, leaving ten gatekeepers to defend the crossing point, and to allow them back into Karthalia in case of an attack. Then, weighted to fall back in on itself, the Gate slammed shut behind them, its metallic cry reverberating through the new, silent air.

Beyond the World, the planet was a dry and sickly grey-brown; a dead wasteland, untended and too far from the River Menignus' life-animating touch.

Karthalia's grass had given way to bland, silty ground that made a soft crunching noise beneath Laura's feet. There were no grape vines, no banana or apple trees here. None of Karthalia's signature violets springing from the soil – only withered, isolated plants were occasionally visible. And unlike those in Karthalia, there was no sign of movement or sentience from them.

An unsettling feeling wormed its way through Laura. Where was her sheltering Wall? The planet was so vast and intimidating. She felt exposed and vulnerable.

Compounding this feeling, she noticed on her right – in the distance and beyond some ruins – the encircling walls of other societies that lived near Karthalia... unknown places, where many Karthalian ancestors had been killed, and which everyone said were still dangerous. They were part of the reason why the OM's choice – if they lost to the TFP – wasn't between exile or death in battle. It was between a slow death (in a barren, hostile land) or a fast one.

Still following Jak's lead, Laura began walking up a fairly steep incline. Then she glimpsed over the ridge, and suddenly, out of nowhere, there it was, in all its awe and awfulness and awesomeness.

The sea. It rooted Laura to the ground through a sudden awareness of her own insignificance. Through a sky packed with thick rainclouds, a solitary cone of sunlight fell diagonally upon its rolling waves, transforming a circlet of its waters into bright, sparkling azure. The rest was mantled in a drab, stormy grey.

It was the single largest entity on Earth: something with a vast enough body to touch every continent simultaneously. Humans had shaped the land beneath their feet, flattening its terrain, chiselling its rock faces, and colonising its surfaces. But they couldn't shape the sea. An eternally flat and rippling super-entity, it was still exactly as it would have been if humanity had never existed.

Laura didn't believe in a god, but she believed in the sea and the elemental superpowers like it. They were the true gods – beings that were totally alien, supremely powerful, and whose scale made them almost incomprehensible to a human mind; species of a higher order, with no physical, psychological, or spiritual cognates to human beings.

All around Laura, OM members muttered quietly, their minds captured by that mind-expanding, terrifying, reverence-inducing wonder. It occurred to her how, on one level, it was strange that most Karthalians never bothered to come see it, especially considering it was so close. But then again, it lay beyond the World. And how many other natural beauties, like a sunset, were ignored or forgotten in day-to-day life?

"Lrutyun!" Jak shouted. "Everyone! Gather round!"

He stood a few feet from the cliff edge, his back to the sea. Beneath his leather sandals, the grey silt had disappeared, supplanted by a wide band of stubbly yellow grass that snaked along the contours of the coastline. Nearby were even a couple of monstrously gnarled, misshapen trees, their branches sprinkled with pallid and brittle-looking leaves that flittered in the cold sea breeze. Only the spray from gigantic, furious waves could have enabled this last-gasp re-emergence of Nature.

The OM huddled around Jak in a semi-circle. It was as if he were a small object with an incredible gravitational pull, bending the much larger mass of the group towards him with his sheer magnetic force.

As she shuffled into place, Laura noticed Leo's imposing, muscular figure on the opposite side of the group. The people around him were keeping their distance slightly, as if something nasty about him were contagious. For his part, he ignored them, his small eyes staring staunchly and defiantly ahead.

231

She wanted to feel sorry for him. His purple-bruised, half-pulped face... his nose, bent to the side, apparently broken long before his current injuries... like many people there, he was a victim of violence. But he was also from the tribe that had attacked her brother. So all he did was make her feel afraid.

"Right," Jak said, his deep voice ringing out across a silence so heavy and complete, even that was of a type not found in Karthalia. "First off, I want you to look behind you."

Along with everyone else, Laura turned round.

The sight of the distant Wall confronted her. Its perilously wavy structure, and the jutting irregularities of its stonework, ran along the coast before sweeping far inland. It was odd seeing it from the outside.

"Inside that Wall," Jak said, "is everything you love. Everything we're trying to save. And this is how we're going to do it.

"As you all know"—his audience faced him once more—"the lilaxes only grow in Devil's Orchard. So to get them, we'll have to break through the TFP's defences, and steal enough of them to envelop all of Karthalia in their fumes. Because if we don't... if anyone's left in a non-Oceanic state... then they'll still be able to attack us without feeling a thing, and we'll be vulnerable. You all understand that, right?"

Everyone nodded or muttered their assent. Then, with his slender arm, he gestured towards the people who had been carrying the storage trunks. They were clustered together, a smaller group positioned within the OM's mass.

"Here," he said, "are the weapons we'll be using in the battle..."

The people in the small group nodded, bent down, and removed the tops of the trunks, before each withdrawing one of the weapons concealed inside.

Out came axes. Kitchen knives. And long wooden torches that could be set ablaze with searing and deadly flames. Each weapon was held aloft for everyone to see, before being passed along so that others could inspect it more closely.

"We scoured the Yesod Tribe and those around it," Jak said. "This is everything we could find."

Laura frowned. She hadn't heard anything about that search party. When had that happened?

Nearly everyone on the opposite side of the group to her now held either a knife or an axe, testing its weight and looking at it with fascination, as if it revealed a sliver of their future.

The sight reminded her of an old religious story she'd heard when she was younger. It was about how time was already fixed. And how, in that sense, the prophesied moment of humanity's golden apotheosis had already happened, the force and magnitude of its significance sending shockwaves of divine revelation and divinely inspired action back through time, creating the very events that would allow it to be.

That's what this was like. The approaching battle was already fixed in time. And it was such an explosive event that it was sending shockwaves of itself back into her present, shockwaves powerful enough to disrupt the normal laws of everyday life, and which manifested as the weapons that these usually peaceful people were holding with a dark sense of fascination... weapons that symbolised an invasion, from the future, of a more brutish reality...

"But as you all know," Jak said, "the TFP outnumber us. That's why the Techno Tribe have been developing something that will give us an edge."

Courteously, he stepped aside, and a woman with long, wavy black hair strode confidently into the vacant space, accompanied by two of her tribal siblings. One of them held in his hand a black-grey machine.

"Merci," the woman said seriously, nodding her head appreciatively towards Jak. She didn't seem fazed by speaking in front of an audience. "Yes. As Jakariah said, we've been trying to innovate something that will help all of us. And now, we're ready to show you it."

The two other Techno Tribe members seemed to be giving the steel machine one last check. Above its thick handgrip, and inset into the metal, was a small square of dull amber-coloured glass. The machine reminded Laura of something she'd come across during her History lessons: a gun. A murderous, outlawed weapon.

One of the tribal siblings muttered something, and the other one nodded. Then the first one disappeared back into the audience, while the second strode off to the right, beyond the confines of the crowd's inwardly turned gaze.

With his arms fully outstretched and his legs spread in a wide and solid stance, the man raised the machine up, pointing it at a swollen, arthritically twisted tree that lay nearby. Everyone in the crowd swarmed up behind him, to see what he would do.

"This is what we've invented," the woman said, now standing somewhere to Laura's left, off beyond the tightly pressed crowd. "It's based on a design from centuries ago that we found in the computer archives. It's called a solar taser."

Her voice was dry and matter-of-fact.

"Okay Simon," she called to the man aiming the device. "Time to show off our hard work. Pull the trigger."

Laura frowned. Trigger – she vaguely knew that word. She felt its dark connotations spread through her mind, like the tentacles of a malevolent sea creature.

Around her, the crowd watched and waited in an eager, strained silence. Laura realised she was holding her breath. Then the man holding the machine clicked that switch... the "trigger"...

Something shot out the end of the device, flying so fast it was almost invisible. Laura snapped her head to the right, trying to follow the trajectory of whatever it was. Then a long and jagged bolt of blue lightning burst into existence on the tree, its tines fastened to the trunk, its electric spine writhing wildly like a snake in agony. With a roar, the trunk of the tree exploded into flame, and the earthbound lightning instantly disappeared. The pallid, brittle leaves began to crackle, blacken, and blow away as ash in the breeze.

Immediately, two members of the Techno Tribe rushed across the jaundiced grass, and began using blankets to douse the flames. Dimly, Laura noticed them yank two tiny objects out of the bark, which were positioned where the ends of the lightning had been; things attached by long and incredibly thin wires to the taser's barrel.

But although the flames were being extinguished, that's not what Laura saw. Instead, superimposed upon the tree, she imagined a woman screaming out, her face contorted by the claws of horror and agony, as the flames ate her alive.

"We have three tasers like this one," the woman from the Techno Tribe said, emerging back in front of her audience. "And don't worry. We only put them on maximum power so you could see what they're capable of. At normal level, they shouldn't produce any flames."

"We can use them," Jak said, still standing off to the left of the audience, "to fire at the TFP from a safe distance. But each taser takes about a day to recharge, so we'll only get one shot from each of them.

"However, that should be enough to take out several members of the TFP's frontline, and create a lot of confusion in their ranks. Then, en masse, we can charge into the new gaps in their defence and send them into disarray."

By now, he'd strode back in front of his audience.

"But first," he said, "we need to decide who's going to lead the various units of the attack. Obviously, I'll lead one of them. And I've talked it o—"

"Quoi?" someone in the crowd to Laura's right blurted out. It sounded like a man in his late teens. "But we can't put you in danger. You're our leader. You need to be protected."

Murmurs of assent rippled through the crowd, and people began nodding vigorously and with conviction.

"What?" Jak said, as if he couldn't believe what they were saying.

A gruffer voice in the crowd spoke up: "Yeah. And if you're in the battle, everyone in the TFP's gonna target you 'cause they're gonna know that, if they get you, then we'll be demoralised. So we'll probably have to spend a lot of energy defending you. Tactically, it doesn't make any sense."

The hint of an amused smile crept across Jak's face: "But... it doesn't matter whether I live or not."

"Of course it does," a voice in the crowd replied sharply, and everyone nodded defiantly in agreement.

The image of the burning tree still blazing in her imagination, it nonetheless struck Laura how odd the words were that Jak had just used. *It doesn't matter.* How could he say that? And why was he wearing that stupid smile again? What did he know – or at least think he knew – that other people didn't?

"Fine," Jak said, in a placating tone. It was as if he were talking to children, allowing them a silly little victory in an act of good humour and kindness because, from his more mature perspective, it really didn't matter. "I won't go."

"And I'm not going to fight either."

Along with everyone else, Laura looked round in surprise. The voice – a man's – had been completely unfamiliar to her.

"Why not?" Jak said sternly, a sharp edge of frustration in his voice.

"Because," Leo replied, "I'd have to attack my own tribesmen. People I've known my whole life. Just because I don't want to fight *for* the TFP, doesn't mean I want to fight against them."

From where she stood, now on tiptoe, Laura could just make out Leo's head through the forest of bodies that lay between him and her. Despite his mangled face, and all the vulnerability that spoke of, there was a conviction in his eyes.

"So?" Jak said. "Other people here have also had to leave the bulk of their tribe. They'll be fighting people they've known all their lives as well. What makes you exempt?"

"They'll be fighting for what they believe in. I just accept that this is the way the World is going to go. You guys will win, and we will live in an Oceanos society. I just don't want to be killed in the process.

"Besides, look at the way everyone's standing off from me. No one here trusts me. And that's the last thing you need in a fight: worrying if the person next to you is going to stab you in the back or not. So I think it would be best for everyone – including me – if I didn't go. Anyway, hayda khayare. Hayda ha'e el meenawi."

"What do you know about morals?" Jak muttered snarlingly. "It's your tribe that's trying to kill us."

For a moment, Jak's severe, burning eyes remained fixed upon Leo, as if daring him to break rank. Then something that had been boiling up inside Laura, even before that taser demonstration, spilled out.

"You can't make him go!" she blurted out.

Instantly, everyone turned round to look at her, as if she were an intruder in their midst.

"No one should be forced to fight," she said. Then, in a quieter voice: "And I'm not going either."

Jak simply stared at her, but Laura could imagine what was running through his mind. Three people, all well known throughout the OM, opting out of the battle in less than three minutes. It must have felt like the movement – everything they'd worked for – was teetering on a precipice. And of all the people to push it there, it was his own sister.

"I'm sorry," Laura said, restraining the tears in her eyes. "I know you've got to do this, to make the World better. But I-I can't. I can't kill someone."

"But you knew we'd have to," Jak said softly.

"I know. But... till now, I didn't really understand what that meant."

With her eyes, she pleaded with him to accept what she'd said, and to forgive her. For a moment, the crowd stared at Jak, waiting for his verdict so that they would know the correct way for them to respond to the situation. Laura bowed her head in shame. It felt like she was betraying everyone around her as well.

At last, Jak spoke:

"Fine."

And judging by the tone of his voice, all of the heavy thoughts that had been plaguing his mind for the past few moments had suddenly and inexplicably fallen away. Laura looked up. A subdued calmness covered Jak's face, as if he'd received whispers of mantic knowledge from a higher realm. Glancing between Laura and Leo, he said: "You can both do what you think is right."

Gazing at his audience, he raised his voice:

"We're not here to force people to fight. Anyone can opt out of this battle anytime they want. But you all know what the stakes are. And if we fail to win, it's *all* of us who will pay the consequences."

Laura's sense of shame grew.

"Let me show you why I brought you here," he said.

He turned and, with a sweeping gesture, indicated the grey sea behind him, where it shrugged restlessly against the shackles of gravity.

"I want you," he said, "to look at this sea, and perceive it as a metaphor for what we're going to do.

"If we release Oceanos, not only will it radically alter Karthalia. It could also be the starting point for transforming the whole planet.

When other societies hear about it... hear how it induces peace, and how it represents a higher stage of evolution... I believe they'll want it for themselves, and it'll be geographically dispersed across the globe. This is like the sea's breadth, curving across the planet.

"But imagine... once that's happened, Oceanos would never be abandoned. Every society would be knitted together, in one global web. And that would be a new dawn for the entire planet. A true Oceanic era. The future of all human life – every single person that came after us – would have been changed by what *we* did during the battle.

"Our victory would not only reverberate geographically across the globe – it would also echo down through the ages, like something echoing down through the sea's almost unimaginable depth.

"This is how significant and immense our triumph could be," he said, motioning towards the sea as though it were on display as an illustrative aid to his words. "This is the scale of the legacy we can leave. Never before in human history has there been an opportunity like this.

"And I know a lot of you are afraid. I was too," he said, beaming with serene self-assurance. "That's completely understandable, and nothing to be ashamed of. But there's no need to be. What we're doing... when it's done, all our lives will be improved. We'll all be happier. You'll never feel lonely again. The misinterpretation of other people's feelings, which has plagued all human relationships for so long, will be gone. Instead, you'll feel intimately connected to everyone, through a network of deep and sincere emotion.

"You will constantly be aware of how you exist in the grand scheme of things, and that you do truly matter. You'll feel your self-worth. And you'll know every other person around you matters equally and infinitely much.

"We're not fighting for bloodshed, or glory. We're not reverting to the barbarism of the past. We're fighting for a better, happier

World. Something meaningful and beautiful that we can pass on to our children.

"What's going to happen over the next couple of days will be the high point of our lives. So be passionate. Be fearless."

He was almost shouting now, his voice fuelled by raw, heartfelt emotion, his green eyes blazing.

"And let them hear," he declaimed, making a bold and dramatic gesture towards Karthalia, "how unafraid you are, and how you will fight for a better World!"

Throwing up his right arm, he started pumping his fist into the air.

"Fight!" he shouted. Then, with slow, rhythmic stress: "Fight! Fight!"

"Fight!" the many-headed crowd chanted back, pumping their fists in a perfectly synchronised reflection of Jak's movements. It was as if they were mirror versions of him, reproduced at various angles, on and on in a warped and grotesque pattern, until he was faced with a crowd of zealous imitators.

"Fight! Fight! Fight!"

Laura kept her hands by her side. She felt like she was the only one in the crowd not gripped in the pervasive, hot-blooded spell. Around her, faces lit up with dawning, hope-filled belief.

And then, a different sound started to muffle out through the crowd. At first, it was unintelligible, smothered in the dominant chant. But then it spread, growing louder, until it drowned out the word 'fight' in a confused noise, and a new chant rose up:

"Jak! Jak! Jak! Jak!"

Through the forest of pumping arms, Laura caught Jak's reaction. His rising arm slowed to a halt, before dropping to his side. The colour seemed to bleed out from his already pale face. Then, after a protracted and frozen moment, he smiled, as if everything was happening exactly as it should be.

To the rest of the OM, so desperate for any ray of hope, he had become that religious figure he'd wanted Laura to turn him into. It must have been that prophecy from the Clairvoyants' Tribe – it had tipped their faith in him up to the next level. They were chanting his name as if he were a superbeing, while her earlier outburst, her heartfelt pacifism, had been relegated to a footnote in the day's events.

The only other person she saw not joining in with the chant was Leo. She sensed her uncomfortable affinity with him. She hadn't wanted to defend him, but it had felt like the only thing her conscience would allow her to do.

Soon, at Jak's gentle bidding, the chanting faded into a confident, euphoric silence. Laura could tell by glancing at the people around her: everyone was buzzing.

"Uremn," Jak said. His poise and self-assurance were faultless. He was only half the brother Laura had known all her life. Somehow, and in a way she didn't like, he'd reached an apotheosis. "Here's my plan for the battle."

He explained to them what they would do.

"... those lilaxes," he said, speaking his final words, "they're meant to be harvested by our fire."

In the same moment as those last syllables died on his lips, the grey clouds overhead burst.

In small groups, the OM members took shelter, huddling under the pallid leaves of nearby trees. For a while, everyone watched the poetry of the landscape. Watched a layer of light mist rise like steam out of the dead, silty ground. Watched the rain patter upon the surface of the sea, on the back of that great leviathan, creating a ripple effect. A sense that everything was unstable.

Sombre thoughts filled Laura's mind. Whether the OM won or lost the coming battle, it felt like something important was doomed.

After much waiting, the OM members trekked back to Karthalia through the downpour.

Chapter 38

Throughout the rest of that day, the storm had grown worse.

Now, in the 2 a.m. blackness of the morning, its booming thunder could still be heard inside Jak's tribdwell – inside the study where he'd been working on his secret task.

Sheets of paper were strewn all over his desk, covered in cryptic diagrams and tiny, black-inked notes written with a frantic hand. Beside them, Jak lay flopped face-down on his bed, exhausted, his arms and legs sprawled out like a starfish.

Saturated with thoughts relating to his private toil, his mind was naturally slipping back through time... back to the moment when this project had really begun...

He's eight years old again. His Mum is taking him on one of her rare geo-historical field trips. It's the first time he'll set foot beyond the World.

Towering over his diminutive form, the Iron Gate screeches open with a deafening noise. Then timidly, his small pale hand clutching his Mum's, he steps outside.

A fresh universe greets him, brimming with novel experiences. He sees his first-ever mountains – snow-capped, and veiled by the haze of a vast distance... gawps, as he hurries to keep pace with his Mum along the coast, at a pod of monk seals, their fat gleaming bodies splashing happily in the waters... and notices flotsam dredged up from the ancient past: a sodden plastic bag and plastic bottle, washed up amongst a cluster of sea boulders like two nameless corpses from a crime committed centuries ago.

Now, he's playing with abandon across the tilted roof of a half-buried Roman temple, his short black hair tousled by an oceanic breeze. Nearby, there lie the remains of a collapsed 21st-century skyscraper, its endless metal and glass debris also half-devoured by the land's silty grey-brown maw. To him, there's little distinction between the two civilisations. They're both simply ones that failed.

Running across the roof, he suddenly slows to a halt, glimpsing something that – somehow, as if in a dream – he hasn't spotted till that moment.

It stands halfway between himself and the horizon, resembling – to a degree – Karthalia's Wall: an immense stone-grey edifice, arranged in a loose circular shape. But it's more like the bone-crown of some extinct giant that used to blot out the sun, with a ring of steep, narrow spires rising up from its base, tripling its height, and which appear as sharp as a predator's teeth. Positioned in the desolate wasteland, the whole monument possesses a deathly allure.

Jumping up and pulling at the hem of his Mum's shirt, he asks her what it is.

She tells him it's a place where people live.

People like us? he asks.

Probably not, she replies. *They're probably quite different.*

Turning, he stares at the edifice once more, his excited mind entranced. Before seeing that structure, he's only been vaguely aware of the presence of other societies, and his whole life and all his imaginings have, in one way or another, been bounded by the Wall within which he's spent his entire existence.

But now, his thoughts are breaking free.

Even as he stares at it, he feels the sight of the monument searing itself onto his memory, as if he instinctively knows that it will play an important role later in his life; as if some part of his mind exists outside of time, and everything is preordained.

Crouching down, he picks up a rough, jagged stone the same colour as the bone-crown, to help him remember it and what it means to him...

Then the dream ended, and Jak woke up, smiling.

He'd been inspired by that alternative society sixteen years ago... and now, he was on the verge of delivering a completely new type of society into being – a change more fundamental than any in human history. How could he not be superstitious? How could all of this not be meant to be?

The truth was clear: inklings of the future were buried in the past. It was as if each life were predetermined from beginning to end, with foreshadowings such as this elliptically and neatly tying it all together – as if each human life were a literary work of art composed by some higher-dimensional entity.

Guided by his sense of oneness with the cosmos, Jak pushed his thin silhouetted body up from the bed and opened the trib-dwell's front door. Rain pelted against his face. He walked out into the storm.

The sky thundered, its noise rolling, roaring, and crackling through the air, deafening like that Iron Gate in his dream. Its rain hammered the earth, drenching him within seconds.

He gazed upwards. The dense pack of pitch-black clouds, each the size of a leviathan, each the colour of a pure nightmare, hung suspended above him. They looked like they were about to descend and devour the World at any moment.

In his heart, Jak knew what the storm was: it was everything that stood in his way. Everything in the universe that wanted him to fail.

His smile widened.

It was everything that fate and destiny were crushing underfoot, in order to clear a path for his triumph.

The wind whipping through his sable hair, he spread his slender arms wide against the downpour, in a gesture mixing inner peacefulness with a sense of victory. Euphoric exhilaration rushed through him – the exultant feeling that everything was coming together as it should.

"It's happening!" he shouted at the storm, his voice almost lost in its monstrous roar. "And there's nothing you can do to stop it!"

Chapter 39

The bracelet clapped shut around Leo's wrist, his muscular arm dropping slightly, as if he'd underestimated the weight of the device. It was made of metal an inch and a half thick.

Leaning over it, the Techno Tribe woman – her eyes protected by a thick, tinted visor – began welding the bracelet's two halves together, sealing the joint. A cloud of blue vapour hissed into existence over her blowtorch, crackling with sparks of strobing white light.

"Sorry about this," Jak shouted over the noise, glancing up at Leo. Although Jak was unusually tall, Leo was still half a head taller. "But we have to take the precaution."

Laura stood beside her brother, uninterested in the dazzling light show before her. The two of them were positioned on the outskirts of the Yesod Tribe. It was the final day before the battle.

Through a gap between two greenery-covered tribdwells, she glimpsed OM members bustling with crates, distributing weapons to everyone in the camp. Others were transporting tables, chairs, and sundry pieces of wooden furniture towards a spot from which she could hear the cracking of axe blows and the ringing of hammers – more preparation for Jak's plan.

Otherwise, there wasn't much left to do. Mostly, people were spending time with their loved ones, trying to fill the remaining moments of their lives with as much meaning as possible.

At least, if this was to be your final full day, it was a beautiful one. Last night's storm had passed, leaving a clear blue sky and a sun of blazing silver fire. The air was humid, and the earth smelt fresh, pure, and cleansed, as if this were the first day of life. As if this day were fixed in eternity, beyond the reach of Time's decaying touch.

The crackling ceased, and the cloud of blue vapour disappeared, melting almost instantly into the air.

"Meshe el hal," the Techno Tribe woman said, standing back up. She lifted the visor from her face, revealing a serious, careworn expression. "That's done."

"You're certain it's secure?" Jak pointed at the bracelet on Leo's right wrist. The two halves were now fused together, merging in a small puddle of frozen, white, molten metal. The acrid smell of burning singed the air.

"'Long as all the heavy-duty weapons go to the Harvest," the woman replied, "there's no way he's getting out of that."

The Harvest – a new term for the battle, coined from Jak's speech. Yet another thing the OM had lapped up from him.

"Even if he got hold of something like a kitchen knife," the woman continued, "he'd be sawing that metal non-stop for years before he got through it."

Jak nodded, satisfied. But the woman had sounded distracted. She kept flicking her gaze back towards the heart of the Yesod Tribe, as if she were eager to return to her tribal family. The sense that time was running short, that the sundial of Life was by now almost completely devoured by the blackness of night, weighed heavily upon the air.

"Obviously, though," the woman added, addressing Leo, "after the Harvest, someone'll be able to get it off you. They can just crack it open with an axe or something."

"Oh," Leo muttered sardonically, as though he were being treated like an animal. *"Great."*

Ignoring the tone of his remark, the woman crouched down, reaching her slim and disproportionately long arms into the crate she'd brought with her. When she stood up, she held a thin, rectangular piece of metal, roughly the size of two books placed spine against spine. The device was clearly old, with the back (the side facing Laura) both scratched and marked with impurities.

"Alright," the woman said, tilting the machine so it was horizontal with the ground. Laura and Jak stared at its black screen. Encoded upon it was a grid of dark green lines, with – towards the edge of that grid – a luminous, dark green dot, pulsing steadily. The woman gestured at it.

"That's him," she said, indicating Leo. "And this map"—she ran her finger around the screen, through its field of blank, empty squares—"covers the radius of the Yesod Tribe, and a little bit further as well. Within that, you'll be able to track him wherever he goes. What distance are you aiming to keep him at?"

"Close enough," Jak said, "that he can't contact the TFP, and give them information that might help them."

"And far enough," Laura added, "that he can't hurt us or the children." Only those under thirteen years old, along with her, Leo, and Jak, would remain at the Yesod Tribe during the battle.

As she'd spoken, there had been a brittle sternness in Laura's voice – a quality that didn't come naturally to her. She was convinced that, ever since her pacifism had superficially allied her with Leo, people had been avoiding her. Looking at her as if she were somehow contaminated. What about the fact that she was one of the three people who founded the OM? Didn't that matter? Why was she shunned, while her brother was elevated beyond all belief?

So now, whenever she was in public, she wanted to distance herself from Leo as much as possible.

"Well," the woman said, "as you can see, when he's standing on the outskirts of the Yesod Tribe, he appears on the edge of the map. And here—"

—she pointed at the dead centre of the grid—

"—is the heart of the Yesod Tribe. So all you have to do is tell him what area you want him to stay in. Then, if he strays out of it in any way, you'll be able to tell immediately."

"Perfect," Jak muttered with a sense of awe, his eyes fixed raptly upon the screen. He didn't have a mind for technology, which is probably why it always fascinated him. In the twin black seas of his pupils, two tiny green dots pulsed their slow, hypnotic rhythm.

"So, you're both clear on that?" the woman said, sounding tired and keen to get away. "That's everything you wanted to know, yeah?"

"Um, yeah. Think so." Laura glanced at her brother for confirmation.

"Yeah, that's good," Jak said, before finally breaking his entranced eyes away from the screen. "Thanks."

"No problem," the woman sighed exhaustedly, picking up her crate. "Now, if you'll excuse me..."

And, bearing her crate in front of her stomach, she disappeared back into the tribe.

"I better head off as well," Jak said, before adding hastily: "But we will speak tonight, I promise. It's been too long."

By now, when Jak said this sort of thing to her, Laura just felt a mixture of resignation and disappointment.

"You're sure?" There was a note of fear in her voice. Even though she wouldn't be in the battle, it still terrified her. So many unthinkable things, all flitting horrifically through her imagination, could happen tomorrow.

"Definitely. Laura"—an extra layer of meaning crept into Jak's voice—"you know I've always been there for you when it counts."

She thought how that was true. Then she saw his confident, reassuring smile – the same smile he dished out to OM members whom he didn't personally know, to assuage their doubts, and convince them that they had joined the right side. A smile that could be for anyone.

She watched him leave.

Feeling aimless and alone, she glanced round, before a startled look flashed across her face. She'd forgotten Leo was still with her. Although he'd escaped the TFP with his life, he hadn't escaped with any spare clothes. And so, he wore a vaguely ill-fitting, light-coloured T-shirt and trousers, both given to him by the only other person in the OM who matched his tall height.

Facing away from the Yesod Tribe, he was looking down at his exposed forearm, his mop of thick, curly hair concealing his expression. He was running two fingers along his veins almost nostalgically...

"What you doing?" Laura asked. She knew no one was around to see them together, and yet, still uncertain of his character, she made her way towards him with a faintly childlike sense of caution.

"Nothing," Leo answered in his gruff voice. He dropped his arm to his side. "I just... don't have the same self-belief that I used to."

From behind his purple wounds, he stared sombrely, almost stoically, at the Cemetery Building in the distance. Behind its exterior of unvegetated stone and large wooden shutters, there hung a long, horizontal strip of luminous orange clouds, providing that memorial to the deceased with its own glorious backdrop. Although the setting sun was hidden behind those clouds, its blazing rays, striking the cumulus, gave them their fiery life. For many people, this would be their final sunset.

The building still reminded Laura of Amik.

She turned back to Leo. "Are you thinking of someone interred there?"

"Yeah," Leo said, his beady eyes still scrutinising that distant, towering edifice. The upper two-thirds of his squarish face, including his narrow, crooked nose, was bathed in the evening's orange glow. He looked like he was steeling himself for something.

He continued: "I often feel like, if I ask him for something, he'll hear me."

"Sure," Laura said, her light, high-pitched voice like a direct counterpart to his. She doubted that the dead did communicate with the living, but then again, what did she know? Maybe Leo wasn't like the other Ragea. Maybe he was more human than she'd thought.

"Are you asking for something right now?" she said.

"Yes."

"What?"

Leo hesitated, as if he wasn't sure whether to confess his feelings. "Strength. For what's to come."

Laura nodded, turning her gaze towards the Cemetery Building. "Yeah," she said understandingly. "I get that."

Chapter 40

Night – the final night.

A base part of Martin (this was probably true of everyone in the OM) had wanted to spend it sat alone somewhere, letting his mind go numb and blank, and trying to forget about the bleakness that lay waiting for him in the dark, obscure undergrowth of tomorrow.

But a higher, purer, more social drive had prevailed. At someone's instigation, the OM had ascended various ladders up onto the flat roofs of the Yesod Tribe's tribdwells, to gain strength in each other's company, and to savour the bittersweet, glimmering, and remarkably clear night sky.

Spread across the tops of the tribdwells, which were built close together in an erratic non-design, the members of the OM sat in small, softly speaking circles, six or seven to a group. A cold dampness from yesterday's storm seeped from the roof vegetation through Martin's trousers, while at the centre of each circle, a metal tripod with a long, upright wooden torch illuminated those gathered in stationary orbit around its light.

Feeling melancholic, Martin imagined those torches as a collection of giant, ephemeral fire-flowers, blazing despondently against the night.

Later, as the OM members dispersed, ambling back to their respective sleeping places, Martin felt someone touch his arm: Jak. He motioned for Martin to follow him into a secluded passage between two tribdwells. Without a word, Laura accompanied them. Before anyone spoke, Martin knew why they'd brought him here: to say goodbye.

In the alley's thick black shadows, he noticed the wet gleams in Jak's eyes. They were edged by faint traces of moonlight.

"You know," Jak said, "you have the same right as everyone else. You don't have to fight tomorrow."

"Che," Martin replied softly, suppressing tears. "Es piti krvem."

He imagined the painting of his Mum. "But it's okay. I've thought about this a lot. I'm alright dying for a good cause."

With great reluctance and pain, the three of them embraced in one large farewell hug. From the fierce passion with which they both clung to him, Martin sensed the truth: they both believed that during the Harvest he would die.

And in this awareness of the final moments of two dear friendships, in the surge of raw emotion that came with it, Martin experienced something he'd never felt before: his inner Wall of Time crumbled. Memories of Jak and Laura stormed through the breach, bearing all the vividness and visceral emotional power usually reserved for the present. They came from a time before Pavneet's death... when their involvement with Oceanos was just beginning...

He saw Laura's smiling excitable face, felt her joyous love for Amik radiating from her. Saw Jak, unwounded, grave, a lone ponderer on the fringes of normal thought, completely different from the elevated, widely hailed prophet he was today.

In Martin's mind, these memories stood side by side with the present in a painful crystal clarity. His willpower crumbled. Tears broke through. The three of them seemed so young back then... so naive and innocent and with futures filled with such hope.

Then the hug ended, and his sense of time resettled into its familiar frame; normal reality returned, and the extratemporal insight was evicted.

10 a.m. the next day: Martin marched towards the site where the Harvest would take place, a fierce wind whipping at his side, wildly blowing his long uneven brown hair and making the march that much more of a struggle. Apart from the Khamsin, he hadn't felt a gale this forceful and blustery in years.

Beside and behind him strode roughly two hundred people, all divided into large units, all dressed in clothing that was either manufactured orange or spray-painted so. An ad hoc uniform, allowing the OM to quickly differentiate between themselves and the TFP in the bedlam of battle.

Against the resistance of the wind, this orange wave – filled with a single purpose – rolled steadily across Karthalia's green landscape.

Or, as the TFP might have said, they swarmed like bees from the same hive, foreshadowing the mindlessness and absence of individuality that the OM wanted to impose on everyone in Karthalia.

Despite the fact he'd only got four hours of tormented sleep, Martin's senses felt alive. The early-morning World – its shapes and colours – appeared crisp, sharp, and vibrant. A pre-death gasp of vitality; adrenaline annihilating his fatigue. Judging by their eyes, the same was true of his Dad, Tessalli, Gemma, Kevin, and everyone else marching beside him.

Yet inside, Martin's stomach crawled with the idea of what, should he live long enough, he would have to do: murder someone. Perhaps murder many...

The terror of killing – had everyone always felt that? Presumably, Palaeolithic people hadn't. But millennia later, he did. Again, an emotion had changed somewhere along the line. And he'd been born and raised in a pacifist utopia. It felt like he'd have to quash his most core instincts to commit that awful deed.

Maybe he and his ancestors weren't much alike at all. And in the giant sweep of human history, he suddenly felt a bit more alone, vulnerable, and afraid.

Then Devil's Orchard came into view.

As he approached it, the small forest swelled in size, like an ugly green tumour growing out of the earth. But Martin remembered it hadn't always seemed like that. Before its own nature – its unique flora – had determined that it would be the site of a massacre, he'd been fond of that tranquil, earth-sprung haven. He remembered him and Jak sitting inside it, discussing how to contact Pavneet, while Ragea patrolled nearby. That had been the seed of the OM... and now, Devil's Orchard could be the site where the OM was terminated.

The closer he got to it, the more apocalyptic the setting became.

At first, he could only see – behind it and towards the horizon – the thin band of grey stone that was the Wall, and above everything, the overcast sky, its bushy-shaped clouds like a drab and immense reflection of the forest's bushy treetops.

Then, drawing nearer, he saw flecks of sea foam spraying up from behind the Wall, when from a distance they had been invisible against the dove-grey sky. This sea-spit exploded upwards with a certain regularity, as if to the rhythm of a mighty pulsebeat drowned out by the gale. Martin pictured what he knew must be happening: the sea crashing against itself tempestuously, its immense dark waves rolling, writhing, and thrashing as if with the violence of an agonised birth or a brutal death. Like a macro-symbolic rehearsal of the savage chaos he was about to plunge into.

Then, through the whistling lion-like roar of the wind, he heard a noise...

Bloodthirsty, primitive shouts. They broke out from Devil's Orchard, from trunks arranged like bared and rotten gapped teeth, as if the forest itself were crying out for battle.

Aaaaaagggghh! Aaaaaagggghh!

The screams of humans who had thrown off all inhibitions, all the shackles of being civilised. The animal screams of humans who wouldn't hesitate to kill.

Aaaaaagggghh! Aaaaaagggghh!

Martin felt his heart tighten with fear, and his breath go short. He halted in his march. But only for a moment. Then he strode on.

The OM strode with him, minutes from the start of the battle.

Chapter 41

Sat against the tribdwell's wall, her legs curled up beneath her, her head hanging forward limply, Laura stared at the floorboards with lifeless, shellshocked eyes.

In the grief-glazed periphery of her vision, she saw her brother stalking back and forth across the room, his slim, moon-white fists clenched so hard that his nails must have been digging tiny crescents into his flesh, his dark baggy eyes mad and glaring.

And in a numb, remote area of her consciousness, she remembered...

Remembered the bloated, uncomfortable silence between when the OM were ready for the battle, and yet before they were willing to set off. The dead surplus of minutes. At first, no one knew what to do, what to say.

Then, like a magical piece of clockwork machinery tinkling of its own accord into life, it began...

Gathered together on the grass in the centre of the Yesod Tribe, surrounded by a mass of weapons that would soon be used for murder, the people of the OM – without any prompt and in a perfectly concerted, as if pre-choreographed movement – started to hug each other. Along with everyone else, Laura felt herself drawn into this compassionate, dreamlike tide of activity.

She hugged Rosie, her childhood best friend, but someone she'd drifted away from since. Hugged Cass, a friend she'd performed guitar duets with at several Art Evenings. And she hugged Tessalli, the woman who had initiated her into a darker but more truthful understanding of life. Who had helped elevate her to a new level of maturity, and so made her into a richer human being. Without Tessalli, the OM might never have coalesced.

With Tessalli were her husband and two small children. Ultimately, she'd failed in her desire – as a mother and wife – to shield them from the growing violence of the World.

Then Laura had to confront the goodbye she'd deliberately left till last. How could she compress into a few words what their lifetime of love and kindness had meant to her? How could she let go of her parents knowing that soon, in all likelihood, they'd be walking straight to their dea—

Laura suppressed that last word – the last part of that thought – before it could fully take its monstrous shape.

Then, in the same manner in which it had begun, the painful and poignant procession had ended, the fairytale clockwork grinding to a halt with its own silent, jarring noise. The fighters of the OM had departed. And slowly, furtively, she and Jak had retreated into the nearest tribdwell, like two guilty people who didn't want to face the consequences of what they'd done.

Now, back in the present, the only noises were that of the rushing gale outside, and the beat of Jak's feet across the well-worn cedarwood floor. His hands, rigidly curved like an eagle's talons, were scratching at his temples in small circular movements, as if he were trying to claw out the demons that lay within his mind.

"This isn't right," he breathed in an agitated, frustrated voice. "I should be out there with them!"

As he said this, he lashed out, kicking a dining room table onto its side with the bottom of his foot. The heavy table hit the floor with a painfully loud *bang!* and Laura winced, jolted from her morbid stupor. Then Jak shoved the table onto its back and began stamping on its supporting struts. Splinters flew from his leather sandals like sparks.

For several seconds, Laura didn't move, remaining slumped against the wall. Although it was a very rare occurrence, she knew this was how her brother sometimes reacted in moments of extreme stress. Knew she was in no danger whatsoever.

But, with a wrenching feeling in her heart, she realised there was already too much violence in the World...

Pushing herself up from the floor, she walked towards him and, from behind, gently placed her olive-skinned hands on his narrow shoulders.

"Jak," she whispered in her distraught, trembling voice. *"Calme-toi."*

As her words and the sound of her particular voice struck his consciousness, his movements began to slow. Due to his exertion, his breath escaped in small, puffing snorts, while the features of his long and high-cheekboned face twisted, an inner struggle taking place as he tried to put his anger back on its leash.

"Even if you were there," she said, trying to assuage his guilt, "you couldn't change the outcome of the battle."

As if stung by her words, he turned sharply, looking down at her with the black rage in his bitter, impotent eyes. She met his gaze with her tearful and imploring one. Faced with this sight, his hard rage wavered, then melted.

"Sorry," he muttered. "I just... hate feeling this powerless."

To Laura, it felt like her brother was the one element in her life that she could still affect, still depend upon. She needed to help him be strong, and so create for herself a rock of stability within the tempest of her life.

"You need to remember," she said softly, trying to alleviate the unbearable pressure he was placing on himself. "You're not the superhuman everyone thinks you are."

Jak suddenly flicked his gaze on her, as though he couldn't believe that she would think that about him: "I never thought I was."

Then his dark eyebrows twitched slightly, as if something connected with what they'd just said had occurred to him:

"I've got something to show you." His eyes seemed to light up with a fresh excitement, and all the saturnine traces of suppressed fury disappeared from his face, like a black sky being turned into bright day by the impossible radiance of a single streaking comet.

And like a comet passing too close to the planet, there was a sense of danger to this light.

"Come on," he said, grabbing Laura's hand – an unusual move, as he wasn't a tactile person – and cocking his head towards the tribdwell's front door. "Follow me."

"Why? Where are we going?"

"Remember all those times you knocked on the door of my tribdwell, and I said I was busy? I want to show you what I was working on."

He tilted his head towards the front door again: "Come on."

A couple of days ago, Laura would have been desperate to find out the answer to that mystery, to learn what Jak had been slaving upon in secret. But now, she didn't care. People she knew – on both sides of the battle – were dying at this moment. How could whatever Jak had been doing possibly matter now?

But maybe showing it to her would distract him from his pain. That, at least, was worth something. A pinprick of goodness in a hell of darkness.

"Alright," she muttered.

Jak smiled, and headed towards the tribdwell's front door. Laura began to follow, before remembering the OM members' children. They were all sequestered together in one tribdwell, where they were being cared for by the few members of the OM who were too elderly or infirm to go to the Harvest. (Watching those kids being rent from their parents was the most heartbreaking thing Laura had ever seen.)

And as Laura thought of them – the elderly and the young, all unprotected – she wondered where Leo was.

Having almost forgotten the slim, handheld computer given to her by the Techno Tribe, she picked it up off the floor, wanting to see if it was still working. It was. The blip lay near the edge of the screen, which meant that Leo was still on the outskirts of the Yesod Tribe. The stationary light blinked rhythmically on and off, like a calm green heartbeat in the dark.

Pulse. Pulse. Pulse.

Laura followed Jak to wherever he was taking her.

Chapter 42

Only one thought filled Martin's mind, a barely audible, constant, droning frequency:

They're the enemy, they're the enemy, they're the enemy, they're...

On and on it went, while in the hectic chaos of battle, kitchen knives – their blades glinting green for a split-second in the forest sunlight – swiped by him... while long wooden spikes, usually used in sea fishing, raised their thin necks above the tumult, before diving back into the fray to commit a series of rapid forward-stabbing thrusts... and while jagged metal throwing weapons – lethal stars of death, dreamed up by the TFP – sliced through the air, so quick their victims didn't have time to react.

In his hyper-alert state, Martin's senses felt painfully raw, their doors open to the World's noisy barging crowd of impressions that inundated his mind with an overwhelming amount of information.

... the enemy, they're the enemy, they're the enemy, they're the...

In battle, you don't get to choose who you kill. His first had been a man he recognised. One stab, then a flash of revolting feeling in Martin's guts, then a sense that everything that made him who he was had just caved into a bottomless pit. The murdered man collapsed, disappearing from sight, and Martin's mind started withdrawing into itself, thoughts bleeding away, being pared down into that mindless numbing subliminal drone:

... enemy, they're the enemy, they're the enemy...

From then on, each subsequent kill became easier – horrifyingly so. He'd found the key to survival: block out mind and conscience. So he just kept thrashing, swinging his machete wildly and letting blind luck puppeteer his arms, not knowing how he could possibly still be alive.

Wherever he looked, there were always more Ragea, as if fresh ones kept materialising out of thin air to replace those just killed; an inexhaustible assault, their black clothes forming endless black marks in the churning, colourful sea of battle. They were berserkers: screaming, snarling, whirling their weapons with insane abandon, and almost frothing at the mouth.

In private, Jak had told Martin of how the Ragea ate the lilaxe, and what it did to them. Now, it looked like they'd gorged themselves on it, sending their bodies into savage overdrive.

Against this and the TFP's massive numerical dominance, the OM had only one thing in their favour: the Techno Tribe's more advanced weaponry, which they'd used to initiate the battle. Martin had stood in the OM's frontline with, opposite him, a densely packed wall of the enemy, built from a mixture of those who were almost paralysed with fear and – in the Ragea's case – those who were baying for blood.

The ranks of OM had stood in the morning light. The TFP, in the delicate, guarded shadows of Devil's Orchard.

There was silence, then...

Bzzzzzz!

The sound whistled through the air, the first taser having been fired. Martin glanced to his left, saw a man in the frontline of the TFP spasming as if he were having a seizure, his arms and legs jerking uncontrollably, before the OM charged forward in a loose wedge formation, driving into the TFP through that sudden chink in their defence, and all the apprehension and orderliness disintegrated into cacophony and chaos.

Now, in the deranging maelstrom of the battle, Martin became dimly aware of a new danger that, somehow, he sensed had been near him for several minutes: a faint crackling noise... the hint of an acrid smell...

Then, suddenly, a tangle of thin black wire engulfed him. What was it? A net? Another tool from the Fishers' Tribe? He hacked his way out of it.

BANG!

The noise erupted through the air, as if splitting it in two. In those dizzy, swirling, blood-pounding moments, Martin didn't have time to work out what it was. But it sounded like a noise he'd only ever heard from footage in the computer archives: a gunshot. But here? Had the TFP recreated that monstrous ghost from the past? Or had some Karthalian, peaceful and normal on the surface, secretly kept one of those outlawed weapons for years?

The question shot through Martin in a blast of cold, alarming fear; a half-thought, quickly swallowed back into his vital mindlessness. Drowned out in the ambient roar...

He heard primal shouts and screams, as would have been emitted by prehistoric man during his physical struggles; heard clanging blades, weapons which had been used since ancient times; and heard – perhaps – gunshots, a noise that characterised most of the warfare from the second millennium onwards; plus, earlier, the modern-day sound of a solar taser.

Together, they were like symbols of every battle ever waged, clustered here, in an event that might trigger a whole new era for humanity. It was as if time, one unbelievably vast line of it, were reaching its conclusion, and in summary of everything that had gone before, all of history's previous conflicts were being compressed – in symbolic form – into this single struggle. Into this grand finale.

Such a delicate thunderbolt of insight was beyond everyone embroiled in the mental white noise of the conflict. Their awareness didn't even extend to the oranges, lemons, and apples that dangled from the tree branches only a few feet above them; bright and pure spheres of colour untouched by the blood spatter below.

Still turning coevals into corpses, Martin became aware of something urgent to his right. Glancing to his side, he saw – towards the edge of Devil's Orchard – a gigantic, tree-immolating tower of fire. The low crackling noise that had continuously been on the threshold of his consciousness suddenly became a roar, and the faint acrid scent accompanying it burst into visceral, nauseating life. Martin had detected those sensations earlier... but only now, in a fuzzy flash of knowledge, did he understand. One of the tasers must have misfired—hit a tree—set it alight—

Now, the blaze was devouring trees left, right, and towards the forest's centre. Towards him.

"Agh!" Martin cried, as something heavy – stone-like – smashed into the right side of his forehead. He collapsed into the grass with a painful impact, darkness engulfing his mind...

... dark like the darkness in his spray painting of his Mum...

... while the fire ate its way towards his small body, instantly metabolising anything it ingested, incinerating it into ash. Martin's last thought, just before the light of his consciousness went out, was: *Of course... of course it was always going to end... like this...*

Then he was aware again, of a light black mist parting within the deep blackness of his mind. From within an abyssal silence, his eyelids snapped open, and colour, noise, and life poured back into him like a relentless and tormenting curse.

Then he saw his olive-skinned arm (most of it exposed, as he was wearing only a T-shirt) flopped heavily and limply across his chest. Two deep gory cuts had been sliced into it, and in one of them – the more grievous of the two – a lump of muscle the size of a child's fist had been gouged out. The gobbet dangled askew, still attached to his skin by the fleshy flap of the wound. And within the congealing darkness of that injury, Martin glimpsed the white of his own bone.

Recoiling from the arm, as if from a monster made from a part of himself, he wriggled frantically to get it off him, a mixture of horror and revulsion squirming through every cell in his body. But for some reason, he could barely move. Choking back an urge to retch, he pushed at the self-abomination with his free left hand, but still it resisted, its disgusting dead weight squatting stubbornly upon his chest. It felt cold and inhuman. His panic surged higher.

Then, still struggling, he experienced a tingle on his right side, beneath his shoulder. He looked, and saw that the sleeve above the dead arm was a pale green, whereas his had been orange...

Twisting his head, he faced the corpse lying shoulder-to-shoulder beside him. Its left arm had fallen palm-down across his chest, crossing over at his elbow to create the macabre and stomach-turning illusion. Craning forward to peer over that arm, he saw that his legs were pinned beneath the left one of the spread-eagled corpse. That's why he couldn't move.

Exhilaration and relief swept through Martin. In his explosion of panic upon awaking, his awareness had contracted to focus upon the horror. Now, it seemed absurd that he hadn't instantly perceived the truth for what it was.

Terror still trembling through his heart and muscles, he forced the lifeless Karthalian off him, scrambled to his feet and, for a brief moment, stared at that arm belonging to a dead member of the enemy.

It could have been his... even his own mind had confused his body with that of the stranger's... and his T-shirt was soaked with the man's blood. On some profound level, they were almost interchangeable.

And if that was true of him and this man... wasn't it true of everyone on the battlefield? Whether they were from the OM or the TFP? The living or the dead?

But that path led to dark thoughts. Thoughts he couldn't afford. Shutting down his mind, he began the dehumanising refrain once again.

They're the enemy. They're the enemy. They're the...

This time, though, the chant was weaker. Less convincing.

He snatched up his machete from nearby. His arms, his weapon, and the whole scene around him were now bathed in a fiery, poisonous, ghostly light, while the pack of shadows it conjured trembled mesmerically like something out of a dream. During his unconsciousness, the blaze had grown bigger, and the World seemed to have been remoulding itself into its own darker image, a scorching, ever-deepening nightmare.

But the battle itself – that is, the number of people fighting, and how they were spread out across the forest – was still much the same as when he'd last seen it. Not much time had passed.

Machete raised and ready to strike, Martin charged at the nearest member of the TFP, struggling to quell his insurrectionary conscience that told him he was rushing to kill people just like him.

Chapter 43

At a slower, more dismal pace, Laura trailed behind Jak as he strode towards the tribdwell that had recently formed a barrier between the two of them whenever she'd tried to talk to him.

Clutching her slender arms against the cold – the fierce sea wind barely moving the stiff, elongated waves of her parti-coloured hair – she traipsed through a pocket of open space. Yesod tribdwells reared up around her on all sides in a loose, higgledy-piggledy formation, their verdure a soft, muted green in the grey light.

And, closer still, were other presences: wood carvings of human figures that populated the enclosed scene. Just short of life-size, their designs were somewhere between that of detailed realism and abstract archetypes, their cedarwood having become a pale bright yellow through long exposure to sunlight. All were frozen in dramatic or dynamic postures; effigies of long-dead Karthalians who, during their lives, had performed a feat so great that they deserved to be enshrined in history. Laura weaved her way through a field of legends.

The atmosphere of profound history, combined with her already unhinged mental state, made it feel as if she were walking through a dream.

Arriving at his tribdwell, Jak opened the door to let her through.

Inside, small portions of the living room walls were spray-painted with colourful, childlike drawings. Presumably, the trib-dwell had once been the home of indulgent and loving parents.

Her brother closing the door behind her, Laura shivered, an after-effect from the cold outside.

"I'll light a fire in a second," Jak said, already making his way towards the next room. "What I want to show you's just through here."

Crossing the threshold after him, Laura stepped into a small study. A large, dark wooden, heavy-looking desk immediately caught her eye. Upon it, there lay six separate and neatly organised piles of notepaper, arranged in two rows of three.

"This is it," Jak said with the faint trace of a smile, as he stood beside the papers, gesturing at them.

Carefully placing the Techno Tribe's slim computer down on the desk, Laura – feeling a flicker of curiosity inside her – began inspecting the sheets more closely.

They were covered in rough, hasty, and poor sketches of strange objects (her brother had almost no aptitude for drawing); in brief, blue-inked annotations and in long, detailed paragraphs that were scattered about the page and crammed in at whatever angle they would fit. All of it was done in Jak's frenetic, chicken-scratch handwriting.

On one sheet, Laura spotted a diagram that appeared to be an aerial view of Karthalia, yet with the land divided into odd geometric segments, as if her brother were considering a way to reorganise the structure of the World. On another piece of paper, she saw a drawing of a vehicle that looked – like a bird, or an ancient machine – as if it were designed to fly. A panoply of images, ideas, and visions lay spread before her.

"What are they?" Laura asked, into a silence that had been deepening for some moments.

"Plans. Blueprints for what Karthalia should become, once Oceanos has been released."

Laura frowned in thought. Her brother had always had a taste for weird and unusual ideas. Bending forward, she peered at the sheet on top of the pile nearest to her, scanning the first note that caught her eye. She was only able to read it at a glance because she was familiar with Jak's writing.

It read:

The negative human emotions (fear, envy, hate, anger, anxiety, grief, etc) have long outnumbered the good (joy, happiness, contentment).

Above that note, and to its right, another longer stretch of scribbling ran diagonally across the page:

Everything meaningful can be boiled down to an emotion. If there's no emotion, then it's not meaningful. This applies to all the arts as well, where every element in a composition is organised to create meaning.

And Laura speed-read a third note, squeezed into the margin on the left-hand side of the page:

You can know that something is morally right. But until you <u>feel</u> that it's morally right, you probably won't care enough to change your usual habits. Emotion is the motive to action.

Each of the six pages that topped a pile was packed full of such notes. And each pile was several sheets thick. The tiny, inspiration-rapid scrawl of the jottings... the numerous rough sketches of disparate ideas... the pages reminded her of the notes of a great thinker, examples of which she'd briefly seen at school. Someone like Leonardo da Vinci or Marcus D'Almaud. The sort of high-up, far-reaching intellect that only comes around once in an Age.

She'd known her brother was smart, but she'd had no idea he was capable of anything like this.

"Have you shown these to anyone else?"

"La," Jak replied, crouched down in the room's corner and igniting the fire. "Only you."

A soft crackling started, and white smoke flowed up towards the room's chimney. Jak rose to his feet.

"It just hit me one day," he intoned in a distant, dreamy voice, as if his mind were drifting to a remote and private location. "And even though I tried to give an inspiring speech when we were all stood by the sea, I knew it didn't really matter. That the battle wasn't what was important."

Laura shot him a horrified stare, picturing the friends and family who were dying for the sake of that battle.

"No," Jak said apologetically, seeing Laura's face and snapping out of his trance. "That's not what I mean. Obviously the battle's important. But to us – not to history. We could win, and Oceanos will be released. Or we could lose. But even then, the *idea* of Oceanos will live on. It can't be put back in its box. Something as significant as this will be remembered and passed down from generation to generation. And eventually, either from curiosity, or from someone trying to break the shackles of their repression, it will be released. One way or another, it is going to triumph."

Behind the unkempt, bristly black hairs of his beard, Jak's lips curved into a small, proud, and grateful smile.

"All we needed to do," he said, "was spread the idea. Your pamphlets had won this battle for us, even before it had begun."

He glanced at his papers with a poignant, almost wistful look. "So I started planning for the next stage."

271

A chill of self-pity entered Laura, as if, long ago, she'd been lowered into a pool of icy water, and was only now realising just how cold it was. Stinging tears that had so far been restrained suddenly broke through:

"But... what am I doing now?"

"Chou?"

"Other people are out there... *dying* for the OM... you're building for the future... what am I doing? How am I still helping in any way?"

Tears glittered in her traumatised eyes.

"Are you... regretting staying behind?" Jak said.

"Y—" One letter into the word, Laura silenced herself. "... not exactly. I don't think I was wrong not to fight. It just... it doesn't feel right anymore, either."

Slowly, Jak stepped towards her, and wrapped his arms around her trembling body in a loving, soft, and sensitive hug.

"Well," he whispered down to her. "I'm glad you're here."

There was a fraction of a pause, then he said: "I wouldn't want to deal with this alone."

A tender silence rose up between them, cocooning Laura in its warmth. She didn't speak. Didn't want to break the delicate, precious emotion that she felt they were sharing between them – the first meaningful connection she'd experienced with him for some time.

"Do you know..." Jak said, looking down at her, his gentle, gently smiling face filling up most of her vision. "I admire you for your pacifism. You stood up for what you believed in, despite what everyone else thought. I always respect that."

Laura remembered his stunned gaze when, in front of everyone, she'd told him she wouldn't fight in the battle, and the guilt that had welled up inside her.

"You didn't look like you admired it."

"That's because I was worried that other people would copy you, and the whole plan of attack would fall apart."

"So," she sniffled, "what changed?"

"I remembered that Oceanos was public knowledge. That it would inevitably happen, as if the future had already been written."

He looked down at his pages.

"Oceanos... the idea's out there now. Shaping everything."

From amongst the ear-splitting tumult of shouts and screams, somewhere to Martin's left, a louder cry erupted. A cry from a group. Turning, he saw the source of the commotion.

A unit of OM were pressing forward, trying to break through a one-man-thick barricade of TFP fighters. Behind those TFP, there lay a large swathe of lush grass, thickly carpeted in the dark greens and purples of the lilaxe; enough of the flower – according to the OM's pre-battle calculations – to transform every person in Karthalia.

Through the tightly packed battlezone, Martin carved a slow, difficult path towards them, yelling to his fellow combatants, "This way!", having no idea if anyone would hear him or take notice.

He pushed deeper into the forest... through the crush of duelling fighters... through the thick, clogging reek of shit and gore from sliced-open, freshly dead bodies... forging ahead towards the lilaxes. The blaze's pale, spectral glow flickered over everything, blanching the blood-drenched wounds and the contorted bodies and the fierce expressions of the fighters, transforming them into elements of a scene where everyone's essential spiritual selves were revealed, and where it wasn't bodies that were being killed, but spirits that were being destroyed.

Reaching the TFP barricade, he only had to wait seconds before, somewhere further along the line, it was punctured. Storming through the opening, the OM dispersed the overwhelmed TFP and seized that small spot of land for themselves, forming a circular perimeter edged with their constantly slashing machetes. Now, from his new vantage, Martin could see the blaze itself, its stark light throwing into sharp relief the wave-after-wave of shadowy Ragea that were rushing headlong towards him.

Meanwhile, within the encompassing shield provided by their allies, OM members with linen sacks frantically harvested the lilaxes and other random flowers, stuffing the plants into each bag's wobbly curving maw – the shape of which was like a replica, in microcosm, of the wobbly shape of Karthalia's Wall.

And against blast after blast – second after second – of TFP ferocity, Martin endured.

Then, from behind, he caught a shout through the uproar. The lilaxe-bearers... they'd collected enough of the plant.

He saw others in the defensive line rearranging their positions. They were trying to create a passageway made from two lines of OM protectors, through which those carrying the sacks could make their escape from Devil's Orchard, towards the next site in the OM's plan.

Furiously, desperately, Martin cleaved a path towards that emerging escape route, that improvised avenue of flesh, before absorbing himself into its ranks.

A man and a woman stood shoulder-to-shoulder with him. He looked along his line: it was strong. And in his peripheral vision, he noticed that the OM members behind him – the two lines facing each other with their backs – had assembled as well. The passageway was ready.

Crouched down to protect themselves within this human barricade, the lilaxe-bearers began hurrying behind Martin's back in single file while carrying their loaded sacks. As they progressed towards the outskirts of Devil's Orchard, the organic tunnel would rearrange itself, contracting at the rear only to extend further forward at the front; a mobile defence unit that moved like an enormous groping slug, inching its way towards the forest edge, pulling its bulk towards open air and grey sunlight.

And as Martin shuffled sideways in fits and starts, maintaining his position, he fought back the barrage of TFP assailants who were desperate to stop the lilaxes' escape. Some of these TFP members were venomous, others seemed to be driven purely by a blind sense of panic. At one point, the woman to his left slashed across his vision, saving him at the last second from an enemy's lunging attack.

Then he spotted numerous other OM members – maybe about thirty of them – charging from the general battle towards his defensive line. Arriving, they span round, and with wild and fierce strokes of their blades, helped to fight back the constant assault of the enemy.

And he and his squad were luckier still. In the mayhem of the battle, they were attracting the wrath of only a small portion of the TFP. Perhaps, due to the deafening noise, the others hadn't been alerted to what was going on. Or perhaps they hadn't processed its significance. Whatever the case, the crucial event in the battle was apparently being overlooked by the majority of its combatants.

His unit peristalting towards the forest outskirts once more, Martin glanced backwards, to check that no lilaxe-bearers were being left behind. That's when he saw, in the protective tunnel and in its wake, the dead that littered the grass.

Some had been part of the defensive line, and now, collapsed upon each other in twos and threes, were bathing in a growing pool of mutual blood. Others lay further back, amongst the dense patch of flowers: lilaxe-bearers. Cranial blood dribbled from the deep wounds in their skulls; wounds wrought by missiles – rocks, sharp-edged metal throwing weapons, or other things – which had got through the OM's blockade. Those men and women had never even got beyond the stretch of lilaxes that they'd reaped, and their sacks sagged upon the grass as if in defeat, lying amongst the spilt green and purple detritus which they'd surrendered back to the earth.

Smothered under a growing pall of smoke, the light of the forest became dimmer, and shadows crawled like nether-worms over those fallen friends. At least the OM had brought more lilaxe-bearers than they needed. It had been assumed that some of them wouldn't make it out of Devil's Orchard alive.

A rough, hacking cough wrenched Martin's gaze away from his comrades. Thick, acrid-tasting smoke from the blaze was invading his lungs. Tears in his eyes, he swallowed back the dry and coarse irritation in his throat and fought on, his whole World enveloped within the clashing, screaming, fire-crackling din of the battle.

Fought on, while killing Karthalians who simply had a different idea of what was best for everyone.

Then he became aware of a problem to his left, towards the head of the twin defensive lines. The tunnel—it was disintegrating, people fleeing from it towards the forest edge, towards the untouched trees to the left of the spreading blaze. Probably trying to escape while they still could.

"Run!" someone shouted near Martin. And not knowing if there was some imminent danger, Martin – body bent low for extra protective cover – raced down the avenue formed by his allies that was falling apart even as he sped through it.

Whooosh! He froze mid-stride. Something heavy had just shot past his head. He glanced to his right, to where the projectile had come from.

Through a thin gap in the OM line, between two people who were standing side by side, Martin spotted one of the Ragea – his snarling mouth dripping with saliva and bloodlust – stamp his foot down, into the skull of an OM member who had collapsed face-down onto the grass.

In his head, Martin heard the noise of the skull cracking open.

Horror-struck, he glanced down at the victim. It looked like Tessalli.

But – no. He couldn't be sure. He was too far away, and most of the woman's face was hidden – the right half buried in the grass, the exposed left half still partially obscured behind the grass' upright stems. For his own safety, he couldn't leave the shielded passageway. But he needed to know...

Then someone, rushing by, grabbed his elbow and gave it a sharp yank in the direction they were fleeing.

"Come on!" the woman shouted.

With a blank and stunned mind, Martin blindly hurried after her, his body going through the motions necessary for his survival. But his mind was somewhere else completely, filled with that burning memory – that frozen image – of a brutally murdered woman who could potentially be a friend that he loved.

Still thinking about the idea of Oceanos, Jak muttered: "All we can do is let it play itself out."

Chapter 44

"Okay," Jak whispered to Laura in a soft, reassuring tone. Then he ended their warm embrace, sat down at his desk, and picking up his white-feathered quill, gazed at a piece of notepaper intently.

It took Laura a moment to realise what was happening.

"Wh-what are you doing?" she asked with a dawning sense of alarm. "You're not writing now?"

Jak glanced at her, before returning to his work. "I have to. Things need to be worked out, for what happens next."

"What do you mean, 'next'?"

"I mean what's going to happen after the battle, if we win."

Laura stared at him silently, all warmth and tenderness bleeding out of her, leaving her body cold. She wanted her gaze to pierce into her brother's heart, to make him feel the revolting incompassionate inhumanness of what he'd just said. How could he meditate upon the future, when their Mum and Dad, their closest friends, could be dying at that very moment? How could he focus on his work now, when she needed him more than ever?

He wasn't the brother she'd thought he was.

"Laura, *please,*" Jak said in a stern, strained voice, this time not taking his eyes off the page. There was almost a hint of begging in his tone. "I have to get on with this."

For a moment, Laura kept her gaze fixed upon him, giant waves of disbelief welling up inside her. For one of the first times in her life, she wanted to scream at him, to grab him and shake him and do anything that would turn him back into the brother she'd always known. But the words, the actions wouldn't come. She couldn't attack the last precious person that she definitely had in this World. Someone she'd looked up to and loved for so long.

Yet her disgust, and her now overwhelming sense of powerlessness, needed some sort of release. So she stared at her brother, drinking in every detail of what he looked like – the particular pale colour of his skin, the curve of his high cheekbones beneath his deep-set eyes, the almost emaciatedly thin frame of his body – drinking all of this in and everything he meant to her at that moment, she thought, in a tearful trembling tone: *I hate you.*

Then she stormed heartbrokenly over to the desk, snatched up the slim computer that she'd left there – Jak obviously didn't care enough about anyone else to make sure the kids were safe – and hurried out of the room. But just beyond its threshold, she halted, taking one last look back.

Framed in the crack of the half-open doorway, Jak sat with his perfectly upright posture: head bowed, quill poised above his notes, eyes utterly absorbed in whatever they were reading. As if Laura were a million miles away... as if she didn't matter.

She turned sharply away.

Striding out of the faint and growing warmness of the tribd-well, she had the remote sensation of cold, fresh air hitting her, of the indoor oppressiveness collapsing into a vast and hostile outside World. The wind should have shocked her and calmed her down, but it didn't. Her thoughts – hot and suffocating, like embers whirling in a choking black smog – burned all her clarity into ash.

She even thought she heard, within the wind, the impossible: a constant soft din of screaming. But Devil's Orchard was too far away to be audible.

She needed a distraction – something to take her mind away from Jak, and the battle, and her rampant thoughts of death. Then, with a startling inner glow, as of something inside her being vanquished, she realised she had exactly the thing.

Heading straight towards a nearby tribdwell, she shoved open its front door and raced into the building's living room, where wooden boxes – stuffed full of possessions belonging to OM members – were piled up everywhere in crooked towers, some of which were even taller than her. Blocking out most of the light from the two windows in the far left wall, they reduced the room into an ambience of silence, swirling dust motes, and deep shadows.

Guided by memory through the haze of her distress, Laura moved through the faint aroma of spiced food – a leftover from when this tribdwell was still a home – to an open-topped wooden box lying near the top-right corner of the room. Placing the slim computer on the floor, she pulled the container from its perch, put it on the ground, and crouched down in front of it.

The box's sides were sanded into a smooth and polished sheen. And on the side facing Laura, there was the crucial identifying mark she was looking for: a long and very thin cut in the wood, as if a knife had accidentally sliced into its surface.

Plunging her hands into the box, she fished about amongst the items that her parents had salvaged from the Teachers' Tribe. Her calloused fingers brushed against her first instrument, a recorder; against the rough, jagged stone that Jak, with unusual sentimentality, had kept from his childhood; and against a crumpled piece of music her dead aunt had written, to celebrate Laura's birth.

Then her hand found what it had been searching for, and she tore from the box Amik's diary.

She was desperate to start reading it, to finally learn the truth about who he really was. But even in her flushed, chaotic mind, she still remembered the vital duty she'd been given. Best to do it now, to stop her conscience nagging at her as she read.

Checking the screen of the slim computer, she saw that the green blip lay in exactly the same spot as earlier; perfectly stationary. With nothing to be concerned about, she put the computer back down.

Then, with quivering hands... as if she were opening an old wound... she opened Amik's diary.

Almost immediately, she flicked to its last recorded days. She wanted to know what had been going through Amik's head around the time they broke up. Had he been upset? Or felt guilty? Or had it been what it looked like: that he moved on straightaway, his work quickly filling the small space that she'd clearly occupied in his heart?

The right-hand page was empty, the left one containing the diary's last entry. She scanned it, fragments of private thoughts fluttering over her eyes:

... said he thought my statue was stunning...

Despite their split, Amik was obviously still obsessed with his work. Things that seemed to be ideas for future projects jumped out at her:

... tapestry-engravings running all around the Wall...

... stone giants scaling the Wall up to an arch??...

And there were snatches of writing that mentioned her in a pretty obvious code:

... guess it's really over between me and L...

... her her <u>her</u> in my head all the time...

She didn't care that he'd still thought about her. It just made her angry, because why then did he tear them apart? How could she still not have been enough for him? How could he have chosen his project over their relationship and the future they'd planned?

She wanted to feed her anger even more.

Flipping back a few pages, searching, she found the entries dated around the time they broke up. Almost instantly, she spotted a single-letter word: 'J'.

Jak?

Her eyes zoned in on that section of the page.

Near the 'J' was the word 'Ragea'. It was higher up the page, in an earlier entry. Immediately hooked in by it – by the inchoate sense that Amik had hidden something important from her – she began to read that log in the diary.

It only took her a few seconds to skim through it. But by the end, the blood had drained from her face.

More slowly, she read it a second time. (The 'L' clearly belonged to her, and the 'J' to Jak. The 'P' must have referred to Pavneet – or at least, that's all that made sense in the scrambled stunned silence of her mind):

17th – Found note by door at L's. Worked out that it must be from P, left during the night. Note said where J & P were meeting (tonight, glade in Grid 3). Memorised it, put it back by door, and told Ragea. I hope they really break J this time. He can't destroy me and L – smirking over it – and just get away with it.

Laura kept rereading the entry, feeling devastated and hollow inside. Feeling her blood pulsing loudly through her temples as if she were drowning. A flushed warmth filled her face, a result of shock and the sense of a cold, slowly unfolding fear.

"I hope they really break Jak this time." What did the "this time" mean?

She remembered Jak's drunken, anti-Ragea speech at her and Amik's party... and how, two days later, he'd been hauled out of his classroom by a mob of Ragea and savagely beaten. She'd assumed they'd heard about what Jak had said but... not through Amik. He couldn't have done that to Jak, to her... could he?

In her head, lines were being drawn between dots of memory and information, creating a perfectly clear picture that she couldn't bear to believe in. But behind the hot tears streaming from her eyes, her old cherished vision of the man she'd loved was slowly shattering, like a stained-glass image from a strasmag being crushed under an increasing amount of pressure. *Crack. Crack.*

Squashing her hands together, she scrunched up the diary as if trying to squeeze it out of existence. It couldn't be true, it couldn't. But she needed to know. There had to be some way she could...

Then she remembered the man standing near the outskirts of the Yesod Tribe. He'd been part of the Ragea when they attacked Jak. He must know if Amik had committed this sick betrayal of her brother – if he'd set up Jak to be murdered.

And yet, if he did know, maybe he'd deliberately kept it to himself. More deceit. The World was becoming uglier and more horrid with every moment.

She snatched up the slim computer from the floor. The blip was still beeping in the same spot. She hurried off to find Leo.

Chapter 45

Crashing through a wall of leaves and shrubbery, Martin burst out of Devil's Orchard. Half-running, half-staggering with a sort of delirious exhaustion, he looked around, saw his goal in the far distance, and charged towards it.

He raced past a demoralisingly long stretch of empty grass... past the south side of the deserted Engineers' Tribe... and on towards where the flat terrain bulged up into a low-lying hill.

Come on, they had to be there... they had to be waiting at the Wall...

Feet pounding against the ground, blood pounding through his temples, he drew closer towards the rising green, a sharp cold wind blowing almost directly into his face. Squinting through it, watery-eyed, he saw several of the lilaxe-bearers running ahead of him. Weighed down by their loaded sacks, they were sprinting clumsily, sometimes with two people carrying a single sack, while others were lugging their burden all on their own. All struggling onward through this, the final stretch of their mission.

But Martin only half-saw them. His mind, a much more vivid place, was imprinted with other scenes. He saw the woman who might be Tessalli lying slumped face-down in the grass, her skull caved open. Saw OM members dying selflessly to protect the escape of the lilaxe-bearers. He saw nobility and he saw horror, and all reality seemed to have been sucked into a swirling confusion of the two.

They'd given up so much for Oceanos. It had to be worth it. They had to make it happen.

Breathing hard, he ascended all the way to the hill's crest, then, pausing for a brief moment, took a fateful look into the distance below.

The ladders – hastily and crudely cobbled together from bits of wood cracked off Yesod Tribe furniture – were there. Tall as the towering Wall and propped against it, there were several of them, spaced roughly twenty paces apart from one another. At the base of each ladder were positioned two OM members, one on either side, with each person having a small pile of wooden sticks gathered together at their feet. Most of these allies were crouched down, setting a particular stick alight with a torch; the rest were standing and holding out a now-flaming piece of wood, urgently and desperately waiting for someone to take it. The OM members who had fled the forest ahead of Martin were rushing forward to grab them.

An immense sigh of relief swept through Martin. The TFP hadn't spotted what they were doing here, hadn't interfered with this vital part of the plan.

Dashing down the hill and over to one of the less occupied ladders on the left-hand side – a spot sheltered from the wind – Martin rushed into a dark cloud of wafting torch-smoke, accidentally inhaling its acrid smell. It tasted almost invigorating; a signal of approaching triumph. Knelt down, the tough-looking woman before him was pressing a thick, sturdy, and fairly straight branch into the flame of her torch, her impatient eyes willing it to catch light.

As he waited, Martin couldn't help but hear the deep, heavy reverberations resounding through the thick Wall in front of him; a noise like thunder trapped in stone; aftershocks of the sea pounding viciously against Karthalia's protective barrier. And glancing to his right – beyond the stretch of dull, withering gold formed by the Maize Tribe's crops – he glimpsed its source: giant tongues of spume lashing over the Wall, their vapour trails being disintegrated by the wind while still high in the sky.

But shifting his gaze upwards, he saw lilaxe-bearers scaling the various ladders at vertiginous heights, their sacks slung over their shoulders. Light showers of dark purple and green were spilling downwards in their wake, falling past the torch-bearers ascending from only a short distance below – the flowers swaying through the air with an almost poetic grace.

The woman thrust at Martin his flaming torch and, with his one free hand, he began to climb.

Between tribdwells, Laura strode rapidly towards the outskirts of the Yesod Tribe. Her mind seethed with anger, upset, and a sense of betrayal, a black trinity driving her on towards Leo.

Then suddenly, near the edge of the Yesod Tribe, she halted in the chill wind. Fear and anxiety erupted in her mind. Beneath the grey, tempestuous sky, the stretch of grass was empty.

She checked her slim computer. It confirmed her dread. Leo was supposed to be straight ahead of her.

In her head, the far-off din of the battle – the shouts, screams and cries – began to amplify. Her heart – like the heavy pounding of a drum – began to hammer against her chest, and her thoughts started spinning frantically, dizzyingly, as if it wasn't her thoughts that were spinning, but the World.

Then she spotted something poking out of the grass, where Leo was supposed to be. It was about the size and shape of a small, dead animal.

Cautiously, she approached it. And gradually, the green blades revealed what they were hiding...

A severed hand lying in a pool of blood, the tracking bracelet still attached to its wrist.

Sprinting along the top of the Wall – his body half-crouched and angled sideways to shield his torch against the howling, whipping wind – Martin pushed on, through the sea-born gale driving against his left-hand side – a gale so powerful it felt like, if he did stop, it would fling him off the Wall.

He dashed past lilaxe-bearer after lilaxe-bearer. They'd taken positions at regular intervals around the inner side of the Wall but, as the edifice was roughly the width of two men lying down end to end, Martin was able to run between them and the large solar panels bolted down, like vertebrae, along that epic lithic spine. These lilaxe-bearers were gripping their linen sacks fiercely, pressing them against the stone ground, sometimes even using one foot to help pin them down and stop the ravenous wind from snatching them away. The open, waiting mouths of the bags all pointed inwards, towards Karthalia.

At the same time, torch-bearers were scrambling to find a lilaxe-bearer that needed them or, having found one, had begun to set about their task.

Martin powered towards the lilaxe-bearer that stood furthest away along the curve of the Wall. Running past the non-Karthalian landscape that lay far below on his left – that wasteland beyond the World – past its pale ruins in the silt, he felt a dawning sense of joy. Before, history had always repeated itself, giving birth to civilisation and letting it grow, only to grab its head and drown it in war. The OM were about to break that vicious cycle.

Then, his path swerving right, he was pelted by spume that flew over the Wall. And in a flash, he thought of the sea spread out beside him, and of the scale of the change that they were unleashing. In the seemingly endless, immutable universe, one speck of a planet would never be the same again.

He couldn't believe it. They'd almost won, almost broken through all the tragedy into something fresh and meaningful.

He reached the sack he'd been racing towards. Immediately – his back to the sea – he shoved his torch through its opening, burying its flames in the lilaxes. Sheltered from the wind, they – and the other random flowers – began to catch fire. Soon, the black, heavy fumes started crawling out into the open.

Then Martin got a whiff of that familiar, electrifying smell, and a tingle coursed through his whole body. Green vitality burst onto his tongue. Golden passion on his palate. Profundity. Oneness. Greatness.

Having escaped the sack by a few inches, the fumes were now being scooped up by the gale and whooshed forward. Swept over the lip of the Wall and away from the brunt of the wind, they began to merge with other smoke-offerings, slowly descending as one great black cloud upon Karthalia. Sacks flew wildly across its darkness, cast off once their internal fires had eaten through their linen and were almost within singeing distance of their lilaxe-bearers' bodies.

Through gaps in the cloud's shape, Martin glimpsed the lush-green grass that covered Karthalia... glimpsed the curving blue of the River Menignus, which bisected the World on its course out towards the sea... and glimpsed a small patch of grey rubble, all that remained of the Ragea's fallen statue.

Swirling, the fumes devoured all those sights, and slowly, new gaps opened up. Then several of these absences conjoined, forming a familiar figure...

But this time, she wasn't graffitied on a wall, but drawn upon negative space. She had two small, parallel blots of fumes for eyes... a thin vertical trail of smoke for her nose... and below that, a horizontal streak of black vapour that could have been interpreted as either a frown or a smile, except that Martin felt an instinctive warmth inside him, and knew which of the two it was. Instead of the ghostly white of his graffiti portrait, her outline was defined by holes in the cloud, and by the shadowy contours of the World that lay visible beyond them. The image... it was identical to the one Martin had made, of a woman emerging out of the darkness. It was his Mum.

Then, as slowly as she'd appeared – almost peacefully – the vision began to disperse. And with it, quietly, went something that had been hanging over Martin for a long time: the sense that he was soon going to die. The image took it with her; a parting blessing, leaving Martin with a weird mixed feeling of longing and joyful fulfilment.

He watched the great cloud of fumes descend upon Karthalia.

Laura raced through the tribdwell towards Jak's study. Then, reaching its open door, she froze.

Standing just inside the doorway, his body angled halfway between being in profile and facing directly away from her, was Leo. His right arm was pressed to his chest, blood drooling out of its hacked-open wrist and dripping onto the floor, while his long ringletted hair obscured most of his face. He didn't react to her arrival. His eyes were fixed upon the ground.

In front of him, Jak lay collapsed upon his back, his body still, his eyes half closed. One pale, slender arm was draped limply over his torso, as though trying to seal the seven or eight deep gashes that punctured his chest and stomach. Large islands of blood drenched his T-shirt. And the reek of it... of so much of her brother's blood...

She felt a convulsive tightening of her throat, as though it were trying to stifle a surge of rising vomit. But the sensation seemed distant, as if her mind were no longer in her body, but sinking down into the gore below.

Slowly, she looked back up... and saw the crimson-soaked knife that Leo gripped in his left hand... before seeing his face, still angled away from her and staring at the floor. As if she wasn't there.

Then, as though his reactions were merely delayed, he raised his head, and – in a movement so drawn out it was almost unbearable – turned it round to meet Laura's gaze. Only then did she see – behind the short curls of his uneven beard – his insane, gloating grin, fixed in place like a madman's smile. Only then did she stare straight into his beady, unblinking, pearl-blue eyes... into unbridled horror... into his sadistic glee.

The fire crackled in the background. Nothing moved.

Suddenly, Leo threw back his head, spread his arms, and howled in triumph.

Then, out of nowhere, the fumes of Oceanos swept down the corridor and into the study.

Coda

Chapter 46

In the darkness, Laura lay half-collapsed against a wall, clutching her head and screaming.

Jak was dead – and thick, heavy fumes were swirling all around her, disappearing her brother's small study behind their black veils, crawling up her nose and down her throat, choking her with their pungent disgusting taste; their toxic heat pressing in upon her, turning her skin clammy with revulsion. It was too much. She could barely breathe. And at the same time, it felt like a vicious, excruciating migraine was tearing her mind apart. Like she was going insane, and all her thoughts were straining to crack open the bone-prison of her skull and break free.

Thump!

Something large and heavy crashed into her shoulder, twisting her body and slamming it back against the wall. Then the thing was gone, rushing away, and Laura heard the bestial shrieking howl of, "No!" before the noise of feet receded into the dense and smoky blackness.

Suddenly, her migraine blossomed into a new, more vivid level of pain. Colours erupted inside her skull, sinister dark blue streaks against the overwhelming pitch-black. The colours thrashed about, like a stormy chaotic sea of grief and agony.

Jak. Dead.

That thought was like a bomb going off in her mind, a white explosion that annihilated every other thought around it. She turned that white explosion into a rock—

And it was... Leo... Leo's fault...

—a rock which – with hate-filled, clawing fingers – she could use to cling on to the reality around her, against the fierce black tide in her mind that was trying to swallow her up.

That large shape that had hit her – it had been Leo. Escaping. Pushing herself off the wall and lurching drunkenly away from it, she stumbled after him.

Her movements were slow, heavy, unwieldy, her mind still trying to adjust to its new split-perception, where half its attention was focused on the raging dark sea that was crashing about in her head, while the other half strived to navigate its way, trudgingly, through the opaque miasma of fumes.

Then the darkness gave way to a lighter darkness, and Laura found herself staggering through the tribdwell's open front door.

Outside, she gasped in the little extra air there was, sending her lungs into a fit of hacking coughs. That's when, for the first time, she noticed the sweet, acrid smell that tinged the fumes. A visceral memory struck her: of her and Jak as little kids on an adventure, sat alone in one of the woods along Karthalia's perimeter, in front of a small fire they'd built, him talking to her and telling her stories that made her giggle and feel safe.

Laura forced this memory, with the searing heartbreak it now caused her, out of her mind.

As her coughing subsided, she became aware of her heart hammering against her chest – that it had been in that state for the last few minutes, almost as if she were having a panic attack. She clutched her chest, but even then, only one thought dominated her mind, pulsing like that green blip on the computer screen: *Leo.*

Although the fumes now had more room over which to spread themselves, Laura – if she'd fully extended one arm – would have been able to see nothing beyond her outstretched fingertips. So where was he?

She span about, seeing nothing. But in her head – unmistakably – she could sense his extreme fear nearby.

And only then – dimly, with absurd belatedness – did her frenzied, destabilised mind comprehend that Oceanos had been released. Against the horror of Jak's death, the meaning of the fumes – and of her incipient split-perception – had evaded her. Even now, it only made a faint impression. But Oceanos was nothing like Martin had described. He'd talked about a great rainbow wall of vibrant, luminous colours. But all that filled her head was a writhing, abyssal sea, screaming with bloodshed and despair. All those fathers, mothers, daughters and sons that Jak had sent to their death in Devil's Orchard... had it been for this? Had the whole Oceanos Movement been a horrible mistake?

It didn't matter. Nothing mattered anymore. Nothing except one thing.

Through the inferno in her skull, which blazed even more intensely as sudden, individual cries of lightning kept flashing into existence, Laura tried to pinpoint Leo's fear in relation to her. From the aura it gave off, if his fear had had a voice, it would have been the voice of a child. Or was that the memory of her and Jak at the campfire, still intruding on her thoughts and warping her perceptions?

For a brief moment, she almost had Leo's position. Then his fear slipped beyond her grasp, sinking into the general maelstrom of agony. *No! No!* She dropped into a crouch, bending her head close to the ground and squeezing it in torment. *There had to be a way, there had to...*

Suddenly she froze. Then her fingers scrabbled across the grass, as if something precious lay just beneath its surface. The movements cleared away a small patch of smoke, revealing that her hands were now wet with blood.

Blood. A memory, like the blow of an axe, crashed into her head: Jak lying limply on the padded bench in their living room, his lip swollen, discoloured, and split. He'd just been attacked by the Ragea outside his classroom, and she was standing over him. Everything was hyper-vivid: the sense of horror in the room; the way the sunlight slanted across the terracotta wall behind him; the smell of blood; Jak's face blurry due to the tears in her eyes. She knew she needed to speak to Amik...

With an effort that made her retch and almost vomit, Laura dragged her mind back to the present reality and, her jaw quivering, tried to block out the heartbreak that was flooding her mind. Revenge. That's what she needed. The hunger for it was the only thing holding her together, the only thing stopping her collapsing to the ground, curling up in a ball, and crying until all the tears were gone, and her body had given in to the loss and hollowness that was eating her alive from the inside.

The trail of blood had to be Leo's.

Groping ahead blindly, and crawling forward like something less than human, she followed the guiding wetness with her hands. Her body was feverishly hot, sweating from the fight to push onward. Her breathing leaden, ragged. But with every movement forward, the blood that stained her hands became fresher and fresher.

Sometimes, through the darkness and silence, she thought she heard footsteps (like the sound of Jak's fingers drumming on his desk as he studied some book or other) stumbling up ahead. Then they would disappear, and her doubt that she was on the right track would return, and everything in the World would once again feel unreal and treacherous.

After what felt like a couple of hours – but which could only have been about ten or fifteen minutes – the smoke began to thin. Laura hauled herself to her feet, rising slowly and sticking out her right hand to help her keep her balance. The World around her was hazy as if she were drunk, and it rocked from side to side, as though also writhing with the pain that was in her head.

Follow the blood.

From an open grassy area, she plunged totteringly into a tribe. It resembled a nightmarish vision of ruin. The fumes that coiled insidiously about the tribdwells looked like smoke from the burst husks of buildings. And onto the silhouettes of those tribdwells – pitch-black solidities amongst the black fumes – it was easy, in her current mental state, to project signs of devastation: walls collapsed inwards, roofs falling in, tribdwells sagging from their disrepair and leering at her with their bitterness. It cost her a moment of paralysing fear to realise this wasn't true.

Then she recognised where she was. Home. The Teachers' Tribe.

The place – through its strong associations – spewed memories of Jak upon her. As she laboured onwards, she remembered where they'd played as kids, and where they'd walked home together as adults. The memories even mangled the noise of her own footsteps, so that they sounded like a single repetitive refrain as she staggered through the pollutant mists: *Jak Jak Jak Jak Jak.*

She found herself passing the tribdwell that they'd shared, and couldn't help pausing for a moment, to stare at the place where they'd spent so many evenings together: where he'd kept her company, helping her unwind after work; where she'd laughed so many times with him, and where he'd made her feel important and special – without her ever really realising it – just by almost always being there when she needed him.

Now, their tribdwell was vacant, like every other tribdwell that she came across – their tribe like the remnant of some dark, abandoned, and dead civilisation, the delicate framework of a society that had taken centuries to build ripped apart in a few hours. She and Jak... they'd risked everything they loved in the hope of a better World. But the sacrifice had failed. And they were left with only the smoking carcass. The utopia that Karthalia had once been was utterly extinguished, and it was all their fault. *Her* fault. What had she done?

Yet although the tribdwells were deserted, she could still hear the voices that had once lived in them, could hear in her mind the wretched cries of everyone who was dying in Devil's Orchard... the cacophony was deafening and unbearable...

The faint grey smudges at the edge of her awareness – they were the only parts of her psyche that weren't inflamed with the searing sensations of grief and physical trauma; phantasmal emotions of distant people, in distant civilisations, coloured grey because those people felt emotionally neutral. Normal. Which was now an unreachable paradise.

Nothing like the fierce shrieking vortex seething through her mind: all the pain dished out by both sides during the battle, fused into one punishment for all. And every OM voice inside it now unanimously – and wordlessly – screaming one realisation with devastating force: *They'd made a mistake.*

The noise... it battered Laura's mind, almost sending her unconscious. How could there be so much pain in the World? *And the planet... was so much bigger... then how much pain was there alto—*

She couldn't even bear to finish the thought. The idea of it alone could be an obliterating force, could rob her of her willpower to live, even if she just *imagined* it comprehensively. How could she – how could anyone – ever have been so thoughtless as to add to the weight of human suffering?

She forced the thought out of her mind. Pushed on, standing and crawling as the smoke cleared and thickened, cleared and thickened.

Leo. Leo. Leo.

Occasionally, through the endless ear-splitting gale inside her mind – which was like the Khamsin wind, where each individual grief was like one grain of sand amongst the thousands carried by that desert fury – through that din, Laura heard – or thought she heard – Leo's low moans. An audio signal, giving her strength by giving her something to hang on to. Then, like the footsteps earlier, they would recede into nothing, and the silence would take over once more.

So she hunted Leo, clinging to the blood and sporadic moaning as if they were hope. Clinging to them against her delirium, and the black, grasping World of her unconsciousness that was always trying to pull her into its depths.

Follow the blood. Follow the blood.

From the Teachers' Tribe, the thin scarlet river led her through the Intel Tribe where she'd discovered Jak after he'd gone missing, and she'd feared he was dead... past the giant rubble of the Ragea's fallen statue, dim grey blocks through the fumes, spectral remnants of the collapse of her and Amik's relationship... through a patch of grass where, among many others, Jak had listened to her play her guitar... on and on, through a landscape of hallucinogenically vivid memories, mostly of Jak.

That's what Karthalia had become to her now. One big site for the ghost of her brother, the memory of his murdered prostrate body saturating everything she saw.

And surely time had stopped. No chase could go on for this long. Not when she was chasing a man bleeding to death. The World must have frozen still, with all the birds trapped in a death sleep in their nests, and all the dying in Devil's Orchard condemned to scream for eternity inside her head.

Follow the blood. Follow the blood.

In her delirious state, a thought that seemed to have a cold, icy logic to it ran through her mind: what if she was chasing herself?

Was Leo's fear hers? She could feel that chilling, petrifying terror flooding her mind, the desperate emotion of an animal on the run. The emotion of something bleeding and close to death, always staying just ahead of the shadow of the remorseless predator that was hunting it down.

Was that right? Did she kill Jak? Did she leave him dead on the floor, with the many gashes in his body that were like numerous tiny waterfalls, sources for the pool of dark blood in which he lay?

... blood... blood... all that blood... all her fault...

No! That wasn't her. She was getting confused. She had to think. Think through the pain.

Follow the blood... follow the blood...

The cries and wails of agony were no longer just in her head, but rang through the air as well. She must be close to Devil's Orchard. From the screams, it sounded like people were going mad with their pain, and she could imagine them all writhing, twisting, and whimpering pitifully and powerlessly. The air was thick with their voices of pleading, excruciation, desperation, and reluctant yieldings to insanity. With their screams for release.

How could each person carry such an endless abyss of pain within them? And how could there be so many people with these abysses, all adding their pain one on top of another? How could the universe bear to contain so much agony within it? No wonder so much of it was an icy black void, confining all its trauma to this speck of a planet.

Then Laura realised that the black sky she'd been looking at wasn't merely a product of the fumes, with the pale morning sunlight obscured behind a swirling pall of darkness. Because through the fumes, in the distance, she could see that the blackness was studded with numerous dim, tiny white jewels. Stars.

In the thunder and fire of her mind, it felt like she heard something small snap – a mental schism, ripped open by the pressures of facing an impossibility. How could it be night? That would mean she'd been chasing Leo for at least...ten hours?

That couldn't be. And yet she hadn't fallen asleep – she was almost certain of that. So what other explanation was there?

She tried to think of one, but was then distracted by the sight of something twitching on the distant, curving, and steeped masonic blackness of the Wall.

Faintly illuminated by a backdrop of faint stars, small human figures were writhing in agony, their helpless bodies contorting into sharp, ugly, rigid new shapes from moment to moment as they jerked and twisted about on the empyrean floor. It was like a piece of surreal, nightmarish theatre. And although they were too far away to hear, she knew their yowls were somewhere within the sinister blue-and-black cacophony roiling inside her head.

She'd heard the pain of others. But now, to see it crystallised there before her in physical form, was like a fresh dagger through her heart. Because it felt like, with each spasm of pain, they were tearing Jak's dream to pieces. Destroying a part of him that Leo's knife hadn't been able to touch. Warping him so that he'd be perceived as a dark force from here to eternity, if his name survived in any way after Karthalia's death.

Things had to be balanced out. She had to inflict some sort of justice upon the World.

Slowly, through the fug of her agony-riddled thoughts, she became aware that Leo was closer than she'd expected. In the emotionscape, she could feel the terrified tectonic stress in his mind, as it sent out deliciously black tidal waves of abject scuttling panic battering against her consciousness. His sense of fear had increased. He knew that she was near. That she was truly intent on killing him.

And her mind was strong enough to withstand his fierce, defensive waves. Her bloodlust too hard and bitter to be chipped at, broken apart, or washed away. It was like a pearl of pure white love, hardened into its shape as a perfect unbreakable orb by trauma and a voracity for vengeance, which could survive intact within the most miserable depths of someone else's darkest emotions. Pristine hatred. Unable to be split or softened by pity or conscience.

Instead, his prattling fear only increased her bloodlust. She knew she almost finally had what she craved. And her increased bloodlust only heightened his fear. It was like a vicious circle, and Laura found it grimly thrilling, as if on some level she was already squeezing the life out of Leo's body.

She pushed on, through the darkness... through minutes which seemed to have melted into a cauldron of eternity... and almost tripped over Leo.

She dodged his body at the last moment, her new Oceanic sense giving her just enough warning that he was there through his now shudderingly intense level of fear.

Halting, she looked down at him.

Through dark, translucent tendrils of fumes that crawled along just above ground level, she could see his imposing athletic physique lying supine on a bed of black smog, rocking from side to side while he whimpered, as if he were fighting an inner torment that was wracking every nerve in his body. He wasn't even clutching the gory open hole of his stump anymore, instead letting it palpitatingly flail with the rest of him.

He'd clearly collapsed from loss of blood. Even in the darkness, his square-jawed face looked pale, as if halfway on its journey towards its new state as white ashes. His lips were drawn back, his teeth bared in a silent, visceral expression of torment, his eyelids squeezed shut so hard it was as if he wanted to crush the eyes within them.

Oceanically, Laura again had the impression – more acute than before – that the fear before her was like a child's: lost, confused, frightened by the World around it, and scared to face the repercussions of what it had done.

She took in all of these details about Leo at a glance. Then she saw him, slowly, reluctantly – as if he could barely bear to witness what lay before him – open his beady eyes.

Revealed, his two pupils were shown to be filled with a sort of frozen, quivering horror. As if his body, from the neck down, was gripped and practically mummified by the talons of Fate, and the pointed beak of Death was leering down upon him, ready to rip his life from him in one sharp bite.

As if he were clinging to life by a thread, and silently begging Laura – in a painful, degrading show of dependence – not to cut it in two. Pure vulnerability.

She kicked him viciously in the stomach, then screamed out in pain and grabbed hers, but continued her deliberate movement with conviction – so that as Leo rolled onto his side and curled up into a foetal position, she stamped down on his gaping stump.

They both screamed at the same time. His was the most powerless, pathetic scream you could imagine, an explosive strangled bellow that descended into a pitiful whine, cruelly satisfying. Hers ripped through the air, a shrill, piercing, prolonged scream, joining the bleak chorus of agonised moans, wails, and cries that had become the single voice of Karthalia.

These two screams, male and female, intertwined in the air, spiralling upwards like a piece of DNA.

The instant the sharp pain shot through her head, Laura had jumped backwards, yanking her foot off Leo's stump. She barely managed to stay on her feet, seizing her head and digging her fingers through her dishevelled light and dark hair, as she staggered and swayed about like someone who had been stabbed (*Jak!*) who was bleeding to death, and who was trying to stay on their feet.

But clenching her teeth, punishing herself, she forced herself to keep going, as if in some sort of penance for her brother. As if it was the least she could do to show how much he meant to her; a heartbreaking, abysmally small tribute on her part.

So she fashioned her hate. Made it into her crutches, to stop her falling down. Into her source of strength. Into her savage ally, who alone could see her through the pain of what had to be done.

Still swaying slightly, but regaining a decent measure of balance, she looked down at Leo. He remained curled up on his side, eyes squeezed shut, body shaking with the effort not to let the excruciating spasms overwhelm him.

He – this hulking, powerful murderer – was weak and at her mercy. She was like his creator, and he the trembling and frightened creation, aware that – at any moment – the clay of his being could be crushed back into mulch.

Then, as though her adrenaline had made her hyper-aware, she caught sight of something strange up ahead.

Peering through shifting tentacles of smoke, she saw it. The thing lay just a few inches beyond Leo's head: a large, pitch-black rectangle of ground which stood out against even the darkness of the fumes, its edges uneven and jagged.

At first, Laura had the chilling thought that it was the evil force which the winemakers spoke of: a black hole, stuck fast to the planet, slowly devouring everything nearby.

Then she recognised what it was: the gaping hole in the earth which she, Jak, and Martin had used to enter Karthalia's sewage system. The repair site, leading down to the tunnels where the Oceanos Movement had really been born.

And even as she gripped her head with the searing agony inside her mind, Laura realised – in a strange moment of dark poetry – how fitting it was. The Oceanos Movement had begun in a wound in the earth. It was only right that it should end on the same spot, but above ground and in the open, exposed for the miserable mistake it had been.

This is right, she thought. *This, as Jak said about the lilaxes, is all meant to be.*

Then she kicked Leo again, and again, and again, and the pain spiked through her head in deafening thunderclaps, and she could hear Leo retching and the wet noise of him hacking up blood, and the spiteful bestial rage in her was torrenting out, and she could feel Leo heading towards death and dragging her with him through their shared bond of pain, and she was so close to getting the revenge she craved more than anything in the World, and then and then and then she was screaming for it all to stop.

She stumbled, reeling, barely able to stay on her feet, her vision going black at the edges. Why did Leo's pain have to hurt her so badly, when so many others that she could feel through the emotionscape were close to death as well? It must be because of Leo's proximity. The closer someone was, the more intensely she felt their suffering.

She grabbed her nose, expecting blood to be pouring out of it. She clutched her stomach, and it felt like her insides should be wrecked with internal bleeding.

Then she glanced at Leo, and saw that blood was streaming out of his crooked, broken nose. That, from his fluttering eyelids, he was barely hanging on to consciousness. And she knew that, from the way he way he was curled up with his arms clutching his stomach, and from the number of vicious kicks that she'd hit him with, that he must be bleeding internally. He was her pain, captured and reflected back at her.

And on top of that, all the other pain in Karthalia was still surging into her skull, ripping her mind apart like a flock of birds tearing to shreds the fresh corpse of a wild boar. It pushed her torment up to an almost unbearable level, where Laura wanted to die rather than live a minute more like this. As though an axe – so hot it gave off red light – was halfway through splitting apart her brain, but had somehow become stuck, and was constantly pressing its sharp blade further downwards to finish the job.

But the biggest, most aching pain of all was that Leo still lived. And Jak was dead.

Tears trickled down her sorrow-wracked face, cleaving a clear path through the sootiness that the fumes had left on her cheek. Why did this thing that she *needed* have to be such a struggle, when it was so insignificant compared to everything she'd lost? Why couldn't she even get this small dose of relief, which on some level she already knew was futile, and wouldn't do anything to heal her pain?

Summoning her feeble reserves of strength, she forced her body to stand still for a moment. And in that moment, it felt as if the future were balanced on a knife-edge, and could fall either way. As if the World were frozen in a tableau of grief, somehow preserved in order to edify every generation that was to come.

Then – with intent – she staggered towards Leo's head and stood beside it, staring her desire directly in the face. Pain throbbed remorselessly in her head, banging loudly and rapidly like the drumbeat of some initiation ceremony.

One more blow. That's all it would take. Stamp down on his skull, cracking it open.

One heavy step. That's all that stood between her and justice.

Quaking, with terror in his eyes, Leo stared back at her. His face was hideously misshapen, swollen with lumpy, fresh, purple-black bruises. And in many places, cuts – both those new and those reopened – split apart the flesh around his cheeks and nose, exposing narrow ravines of blood.

Then suddenly, Laura saw something in his eyes change, and she sensed the same alteration occurring within the chaos of her mind. His childlike fear disappeared, a look of rash, wild defiance irrupting upwards to take its place. Through his broken teeth, and out of his blood-drooling mouth, he screamed:

"It's not my fault! I was *meant* to kill him!"

Because of the swelling around his lips, his words came out slurred, but still intelligible. The ugly distortion in his voice only made reality feel more twisted.

"There was even that... white smoke from the chimney... guiding me straight to him..."

Into his now-softer tone, there had crept the sense of a nasty jubilance and triumph. As if he was glad that destiny, or the universe, or whatever, had singled him out for this task.

And that – although it felt like it should have been impossible – only increased Laura's hatred for him, pushing it up to a still more intolerable level. She screamed at herself to kill him – to end this. A scream so fierce, it was almost as loud as the mingled shrieking and roaring of Oceanos in her head, which was like the noise of enough shrieking bats to blot out the sun, combined with, below that, the cacophony of a black and bellowing sea.

Yet even then... it was so difficult to push through that mental barrier of pain. She already felt physically battered. And she had the sense that one more blow – as heavy as the one that she wanted to deliver – would kill her as well.

Leo continued, the glee emerging even more fully on his now snarling, self-satisfied face. He could sense her weakness. And from his eyes, Laura could tell that he was lost in the past, reliving a memory that – judging from his thrilled expression – could have belonged to pure fantasy.

"And there he was," he said. "The all-powerful prophet... lying dead before *me*. And... I stared into all those red gashes that I'd made..."

His face still crumpled up in a tense, agonised position, his small shadowed eyes gazed off intently into the distance, as if he were seeing that wounded body before him once more.

"And it was..."

His snarl broke into a faint smile.

"... perfect."

Die, Laura thought. She lifted her shoe over Leo's head, and tried to stamp down on it. He deserved to die... he *needed* to die...

But there was so much resistance to that last, fatal movement, all coming from inside her head. It felt like she'd already pushed herself to the highest, trembling threshold of pain, and now, every cell in her body was screaming for her to stop, to not go any further. And at the same time, they were using her terror of death to lock up the muscles in her leg, so that she couldn't push it down.

But more than that, she also had to fight against the awareness that Oceanos had given her. There was already so much pain and bleakness in the World. So many tears, so many moans, so many cries, so much wailing, so much grief, so much sobbing, so much heartbreak, so much anger, so much loneliness, so much spite, so much guilt, so much remorse, and so many feelings of being insignificant.

That was the World as it was. And on some level, as it always had been. How could she take something so precious to her, and scar it even more?

How could she deliver this blow that might kill her, and which, in the process, would exacerbate the agony of everyone she loved who might still be alive?

"AAAAAAAAAAAAAAAAAGH!"

Her scream ripped through the air. It was the loudest, most heart-rending scream that had ever been uttered in Karthalia. The scream of a broken human being.

She collapsed onto her hands and knees beside Leo in an abject image of defeat.

Chapter 47

Falling...

Falling from a lofty, god-like height, the perspective of the birds... down, beyond the panoramic view of the sparkling sea... into Karthalia... into its rising hum of everyday noise... and then plunging through the roof of a tribdwell, through its beams and plaster...

Only then did Laura's bedroom become visible.

She lay supine beneath the beige, rough woollen blanket of her bed, seemingly in a peaceful sleep. But on closer inspection, it was clear that her closed eyelids were flickering wildly. Then, suddenly, they snapped wide open, and her body froze in a rigid position.

Into the blackness of her slowly waking mind had flashed the image of Jak's gash-riddled body... his clothes saturated with vivid dark stains... his mouth hanging open, paralysed in a look of muted shock... his long pale face, now a sort of empty white, tipped lifelessly back on the floor.

Mentally, she'd just relived that horror, except this time, it was injected with its own special dreamlike intensity.

She'd endured the same awakening for many mornings, and yet still, it always caught her by surprise. Moving back in with her Mum, to escape the tribdwell she'd shared with Jak and the now-excruciating memories it contained, hadn't helped. He was still with her.

Several long moments passed, time spent simply lying there while climbing out of an inner abyss. But giving her the support she needed – and without which she felt certain she couldn't have gone on – was the larger world that Oceanos had opened up inside her. Every emotion, of everyone in Karthalia, now pulsed within her, and this new, bigger context made her own grief seem smaller and more manageable. She knew everyone was suffering their own heart-rending sense of loss, that it was just as painful as hers, and that they were pulling through it. And so she knew she wasn't alone.

Strengthened by this feeling of blissful togetherness that always gleamed within her, she summoned just enough energy to drag herself out of bed.

She ate breakfast... got dressed... then ambled slowly – almost reluctantly – outside, double-checking the hour on the nearby stonework of a sundial, before heading onwards.

The world she walked through had changed more in the last sixteen days since Oceanos was unleashed, than it had in the whole of her life. And yet, the eternal elements of it remained the same: the gentle radiance of the sun on her face; the chirpy twittering of unseen birds; the sense of optimism expressed in the soft pristine blue of the sky, which itself was artfully decorated with a smattering of clouds, their white and stirred-up appearance reminiscent of whipped cream.

In the first days of Oceanos, all of these impressions would have triggered strong emotional associations within Laura that would have been beyond her control. But, now that Oceanos had normalised in her body, those kind of jarring and involuntary reactions no longer occurred.

However, the emotionscape within her was still vibrantly vivid, its rainbow wall of colour almost thrumming with life. Although it seemed to lie far in the distance, its unspeakably vast scale nonetheless filled the entire vision of her mental eye.

With dreamlike slowness and weightlessness, she sent her mind drifting towards it, even as her feet traversed the earth.

In the enlarging picture of Karthalia's current emotional make-up, two colours dominated: a faint green of growing hope, its pale hue echoing the general hushed, subdued atmosphere in Karthalia; and, in amongst this sea of pale green, tiny black whirlpools continually blossomed, each belonging to one person in Karthalia, each representing individual attacks of depression and pain. Despite the fact that these whirlpools kept flaring into existence, they always shrunk up and died within a few hours, overwhelmed and uprooted by the green and harmonious touch from the majority of minds in Karthalia.

To Laura, the emotionscape was like a glowing, psychedelic collage made up of everyone's luminances... like a great piece of art, combining a beautiful appearance with a beautiful meaning. In this case, that meaning was human interconnection and empathy. And this life-affirming art was something she always had with her, carrying it around inside her head.

More than that, her Oceanic sense had become her most far-ranging sense of all, able to home in on the emotions – or luminance – of any person in Karthalia. And there was one luminance she began to home in on right now...

It lay nearby, and so she could discern its feelings strongly and clearly. Its quiet, thoughtful mood reflected her own. And its unique emotional register – a quality that all luminances had, but which was hard to define – made the source of the emotions as easy to identify as if he'd been standing right in front of her.

"Marhaba," Laura said somewhat weakly, raising her slender arm in greeting as she made her way across the grass. Leaning against the last tribdwell at the easternmost edge of the Teachers' Tribe, waiting for her, was Martin.

Dark bags hung under his brown eyes. He looked like he'd been up for a while – like the day, still in its early phase, had already drained him.

Laura stopped in front of him, and the two of them exchanged affectionate, comforting, and faintly melancholic smiles. They both looked a bit more gaunt, in face and body, than they had three weeks ago, as if their grief had physically eroded them away.

Without another word, they began to walk, talking intermittently, but mostly were quiet and thoughtful, content in each other's silence, and happy in each other's company.

The people they passed, as if unable to do otherwise, gave them lingering looks of solemn, quiet, and grateful respect. But more than her, they stared at Martin. Referring to this, Laura asked softly, as if not wanting to disturb the general hushed atmosphere:

"You nervous about tomorrow?"

Martin's verbal response was wry, possessing a subdued good humour while it evaded answering the question. Nonetheless, the faint tremors in his luminance told Laura everything she needed to know.

Further up ahead, along the dirt path they were walking, a grand arch loomed steadily closer. It was like nothing that had been built in Karthalia before.

Several architects (some of whom Laura knew from her visits to Amik) were fastened insect-like to its surface, most lying on the arch's flat top and craning their heads down over its edge, the rest perching on ladders at its side. All were chiselling away.

Once, those members of the Architects' Tribe had belonged to the TFP. Now they, like everyone else in Karthalia, thought of themselves as part of the OM.

As for the arch, its design had been reverentially lifted from one of the drawings found in Jak's copious reams of notes, which he'd left in his study in the Yesod Tribe. Until a few days ago, Laura had forgotten all about those papers. Then, remembering, she'd fetched them, and word of their existence had spread through Karthalia like the flames of a lightning bolt through a desiccated tree.

Erected from a kind of sandy-orange stone, the arch was roughly three times as tall as Laura, its presence heavy and imposing. It was intended as a huge monument, and running around it – just below its top – was a long frieze, carved into the stone. Although only partially complete (the members of the Architects' Tribe were adding more detail to the frieze now) there was enough there for Laura to work out what it depicted: it showed constellations, and rainfall, and figures of labour and love.

In the throb and flicker of the emotionscape, Laura could sense arches such as this being constructed all over Karthalia – could sense the toil out of which they were being formed. They offered meaningful, proactive distractions for those with devastated hearts.

And they weren't the only progressions inspired by Jak's notes...

Wandering beneath the edifice, Laura felt its shadow fall upon her. She looked up, and saw, all across its underside, the sole feature that hadn't been in her brother's diagrams: names, elegantly and sedulously engraved into the sunset-coloured stone. These incisions had then been perfused with a thick black spray paint, to make their meaning clearer and more prominent.

They were the names of people who had died in the Battle, set in stone so that their bravery, and the tragedy of their end, would never be forgotten.

A chill ran through Laura. With vivid sharpness, she remembered collapsing on her knees beside Leo, screaming, and then tumbling forward onto the grass and blacking out, drowning in the sea of pain's dark shrieking depths.

Then she remembered waking up, and now, in the present, the smell of rotting human flesh once again filled her nostrils, like musical notes of the past drifting back through her mind...

When Laura eventually awoke after collapsing beside Leo, she felt like she must have been unconscious for a week. In reality, it had only been about seventeen hours.

She didn't know it till much later, but because no one else had struggled against the black storm of Oceanos for as long as her, every other survivor left in Karthalia had already regained consciousness by the time her heavy eyelids fluttered open. Yet, as she lay there in the fume-stained grass, without the energy or willpower to move, she saw no one. As if no one had risen to their feet: as if no one had realised they weren't among the dead.

All she heard – the only external sign of human life – was the occasional sound of whimpering, from those who were nearby but out of sight.

Like her, everyone else in Karthalia was emotionally wrecked, not only by their own grief, but by the grief of everybody else, which came torrenting into their minds through the emotional connections that Oceanos had opened them up to. This psychological pain overwhelmed the anguish of any physical wound suffered during the Battle, by stripping that conflict down to its harrowing essentials: it was the loss of loved ones, and killings that the murderers – now wracked upon the heartache they'd unleashed – now wished had never happened.

And so every Karthalian lay broken upon the ground, a society self-shattered by the full gravity of what it had done; lay amidst the stench of hundreds of corpses which, rotting in the sunlight, choked the air.

To Laura, this reek felt like a manifestation of the nauseating grief that seemed to smother everything in her homeland. But perhaps this reading was merely a by-product of Oceanos, as it infused the elements of the world around her – through synaesthesia – with intense emotional associations.

However, against this monstrous and devouring despair, an odd new sensation emerged in Laura's head, like a tiny pocket of light tucked away amid all the darkness. Like the soothing presence of a loved one, constantly by her side.

Obscurely connected to this first change in her psyche was another one. Her mind now felt like it was suspended in a higher, somehow more airy plane. As if, until then, her thoughts and feelings had existed in an earthbound fog, but now they'd risen above it, to a height that afforded a clearer and much larger perspective on things.

But this vantage only revealed to her the bleak, never-ending landscape of grief spread out before her, which seemed to stretch from the here and now way into the future, beyond the distant horizon.

This was the view that everyone in Karthalia had, the sight further bleeding them of their strength and willpower. And so they remained slumped across the grass, grimly fantasising about ending the misery of their lives, and yet trapped by their abulia, with barely enough energy to turn their heads, let alone get up and commit the deed.

A few valiant OM members were the exceptions to this rule. Compelled to stop Oceanos simply fading out of the collective consciousness – and thereby undoing all their bitter, hard-won sacrifices – they staggered up onto their feet... lit bunches of lilaxes... and spread the fumes to every Karthalian they could find. No one rejected Oceanos now: not even members of the TFP. Instead, against their overwhelming despair, they hungered for the sense of comfort and love provided by that new, unknown, and much vaster state of mind.

Time and again, such noble OM members rose up to feed this appetite, before collapsing through exhaustion back into unconsciousness.

And still no one in Karthalia had drunk, eaten, or talked since Oceanos had been released. To most people, it felt like there was no point, just as there was no point left in life.

But after a couple of days like this, weak flickers of happiness, now so rare and precious, began to appear in the tenebrousness of the emotionscape. Perhaps they were caused by some feeble but kind-hearted joke, told by one prostrate person to another to alleviate their horrible situation. Or perhaps they sprang from the endearing memory of a loved one, a memory forgotten but unexpectedly rekindled in the private sphere of someone's mind.

Whatever triggered those weak flickers, everyone was connected to the emotionscape, and so everyone benefitted from them. They were like sparks of pale sunlight, finally falling on the dark landscape of everybody's minds.

And they illuminated what that soothing presence, that light-tucked-in-the-darkness, was. What till then had gone unnoticed but which, in hindsight, had clearly been there since Oceanos enveloped them: a new, interconnected feeling of love. The sort of intense, protective love you normally only feel towards those closest to you, but applied to everyone.

Slowly, slowly emerging from their cocoons of grief, people began to talk to each other; to, with parched mouths, open up about their pain. Their depression weakened: the landscape in their head grew brighter. And because everyone was connected to the emotionscape, everyone began to feed off this growing light. And so the emotionscape improved even more, leaving no one behind, making its strength available to all.

Eventually, throughout Karthalia, heads lifted... arms pushed...

and people rose to their feet. Time, the enemy of depression, had pushed back the darkness.

And Laura had realised that happiness is in no way frivolous: it is a vital strength, a rock and virtue that protects you against the dangerous tides of nihilism.

The birth of Oceanos had taken place in a sea of death, agony, fear, and adrenaline – undoubtedly the most intense storm of emotions in the history of Karthalia.

To Martin, that day felt both like it had happened yesterday, because his memories of the Battle and the eruption of Oceanos were still so raw and vivid: and like it had happened a couple of years ago, because so much had changed since then...

His and Laura's stroll was now taking them through the Teachers' Tribe, through the rich, creamy cooking smells of yoghurt and sizzling fried meat.

As he walked, Martin noticed – in front of the green and flower-decked facade of a nearby tribdwell – a small group of five-or-six-year-old boys. They were huddled close together, adventure gleaming in their eyes, clearly imagining themselves as intrepid heroes voyaging through mysterious lands.

And Martin considered how even they had changed. How, according to parents, all teasing, all squabbling amongst children had vanished. It was another effect of the Oceanic feedback loop – no one, including kids, wanted to feel the pain or upset of another.

To think, Martin reflected as he gazed at the playing children, *this is near the spot where, only about three weeks ago, Jak was viciously beaten up by the Ragea. Now, little kids don't even have playfights here.*

But it went further than that. People had begun to offer help and support to those in distress when – before Oceanos – they wouldn't even have registered that there was a problem. This empathy extended so far that Martin had heard something amazing: if a person had belonged to the TFP, and they knew they had killed a loved one of someone in the OM, then they were confessing their responsibility for that murder to the OM member, and vice versa. It was a way of giving some sense of closure to the mourners, by showing genuine contrition for what had happened, and by giving them a better understanding of their loved one's demise. And although it was a painful gesture for all involved, it did visibly help heal the emotional wound that – now that everyone was interconnected – hurt both of them.

Empathy, Martin thought. *Empathy had changed everything.*

Better still, with each new dose of the lilaxe fumes, the Oceanos effect was taking longer to wear off. It looked like Pavneet had been right: Oceanos would become a permanent part of their brains, and soon, they would be able to dispense with the fumes altogether.

Ambling out of the Teachers' Tribe and onwards, he and Laura eventually came to the collapsed and shattered statue of the Ragea. Near to it stood a small, new, placidly trickling fountain, the design of which – like the arches – had also been taken from Jak's notes.

Staring at the statue, Martin let his mind sink into the colourful radiance of the emotionscape, allowing its bliss to tingle across his skin in a light, pleasurable shiver. He saw that a dry, bristly moss was already clinging to the bases of some of the colossal stone shards: the first small step towards lifeless grey being swamped by fertile green.

Time and Nature – they would make the statue disappear, just as they would take all the pain caused by the Ragea, and make it fade into the background of people's lives. Hope and renewal, slowly devouring the past.

Then the emotionscape would be far brighter than it was now, the transcendent awe of its colours no longer tarnished by numerous tiny black pockets of individual turmoil.

Yes, Martin thought. *All the pain would go.*

And, remembering a phrase spoken by some famous, dead Karthalian, he found comfort:

In our hearts, we all live through seasons of emotions. The one thing that all of them have in common is that they pass.

When the Ragea-spawned grief had melted away, then Jak's brighter world would have dawned in full.

Martin smiled to himself. He was convinced that that day was inevitable, and not far away.

But for now, there were still remnants of the old world that had to be dealt with...

He turned to face Laura and, in a solemn tone, said: "Shall we go and see him?"

Pre-Oceanos, he would have asked if, emotionally, she was ready for such an ordeal. But the emotionscape told him that the answer was 'yes'.

Guards patrolled the tribdwells ahead of Martin. He and Laura were entering the Hunters' Tribe.

The two of them began walking down a wide avenue of grass, the two rows of tribdwells on either side of them forming the path ahead. Somewhere nearby was the person they'd come to see.

Waves of emotion battered against Martin's mind, like tidal waves spewed forth after a meteor strike. And their force grew fiercer the deeper he progressed into the tribe. He recognised the luminance that was their source. He'd met the man before. But this would be the first time that Laura had seen him.

And the closer they got to him, the more agitated she became. Her eyes darted about nervously. Her anxiety – which had been a flickering across her luminance – developing into a quivering electric stranglehold upon all her thoughts.

Her mind was like a taut fishing line, hooked into some unknown beast that lay concealed beneath the waves, and dragging her body towards it. Under the strain of the encounter, Martin wondered, was that line going to suddenly snap? Or was it going to endure, allowing her to turn the monster into something that was useful for her?

"Corin est-il toujours au même endroit?" Martin asked a nearby guard.

"Yeah," the guard replied. "Same lock-up."

The trace of disdain in the guard's voice echoed the tributaries of disdain that coursed towards Corin from everyone in Karthalia. The TFP now knew that he had lied to them about Oceanos. That he was the reason so many of their loved ones were dead.

But this disgust was more checked than it might have been. First, because the Oceanic bliss that suffused everyone's being quelled any such feelings of hatred. Second, because – with the larger worldview that Oceanos had bestowed upon them – people couldn't help being aware that they weren't blameless either. Corin may have engineered the battle and its killings, but they were the ones who executed them.

And third, because they felt the emotional state Corin was in right now...

These three wellsprings of peace were what were tormenting Laura. She desperately wanted to hate Corin... to do what felt natural and *right*... but living in Jak's Oceanic utopia made that almost impossible. There was too much sympathy. And yet, by not hating Corin, she felt like she was betraying Jak's memory. Revealing her love for her brother as weak and worthless.

She'd confided to Martin tearfully about it.

Now, the two of them traipsed further along the avenue of tribdwells, past wooden window shutters that had been thrown open, exposing – against the day's blue sky and pale sunshine – squares of cool gloom. And half-obscured within these patches of darkness, people stood – arms pinioned behind their backs – watching him and Laura.

Murdering a murderer as a sort of retributive justice, although it had never been practiced in Karthalia before, was now certainly out of the question. The extreme scenario of Laura trying and failing to kill Leo had pretty much proven that.

And so the Ragea had been imprisoned here, their legs and arms tied together with strips of linen to prevent any sudden escape. But, as everyone knew from the emotionscape, it was an empty precaution. The Ragea didn't want to escape. Oceanos had changed them too, like a knife dipped in a hallucinogen of truth.

Now, they only wanted to repent... make the collective pain, *their* pain, go away... and savour the unadulterated Oceanic bliss.

This, in turn, had established a strange new dynamic between the prisoners and guards. For their part, the prisoners looked upon the guards kindly, knowing that they really were trying to do their best for them, as – because of the emotionscape – it would be best for all.

Equally, the guards treated the Ragea with exceptional generosity, giving them regular filling meals, making sure they were bound securely but with a minimum of discomfort, along with numerous other acts of thoughtfulness. Again, this was due to Oceanos: any pain the Ragea suffered, the guards would suffer as well.

In his previous visits, Martin had even seen prisoners and guards talking to each other not as if they were prisoners and guards, but as if they were simply two sets of human beings trying to get their world to a better place. Historically, it was a more understanding relationship between detainees and their captors than Martin had ever heard of.

But for the moment, the Ragea were content – like admiring onlookers – to follow Martin and Laura with their gaze. They knew what was going to happen to him tomorrow. He tried to ignore their stares.

"This is it," Martin said to Laura.

They'd reached the edge of the tribe, on the opposite side to where they'd entered it. Just beyond where the tribdwells ended, there stood a single, solitary building.

Roughly the size of a large living room, it resembled the tribdwells in that it was covered in vegetation. However, unlike the tribdwells, its doorway was much bigger, as if to allow multiple people to enter or exit at once. And the door was locked on the outside. It was for locking people *in*.

That was because, before the Battle, the building had been a place unruly drunks were thrown into, and from which they couldn't leave until they'd sobered up. A place for maintaining the peace.

But not like this.

Leading Laura towards the door, Martin felt her luminance begin to blaze and crackle, scintillating like ball lightning.

The guard before the door put out his hand.

"Beetezer," he said with a courteous smile, full of gratitude towards Martin and Laura. "But I have to check."

He turned to solely address Laura. Martin already knew the rules.

"Are you carrying anything on you?" the guard said. "Anything he could possibly use as a weapon?"

"N-no," Laura said, fishing in her pockets to double-check. "Why? You think he might try and kill us?"

Martin understood Laura's confusion. With Oceanos, that shouldn't have been a danger.

The guard replied: "It's not you we're worried he'll use them on. But," he emphasised, "it is just a precaution."

Turning round, the guard slid the timber from the lock. Martin sensed a cool wind play across his skin.

Because of Oceanos, he felt as he had the last two times he'd faced the man who ordered the murder of his best friend: a mixture of sternness, calm, and a grudging sense of pity.

As for Laura, without looking, he knew she was bracing herself. The door began to be drawn back...

And Martin remembered what other people had told him Corin was like before Oceanos. That he revelled in sadism, and that in his rages, he had frequently hurt himself just to make a point. That he was a psychopath, unable to feel guilt or the pain of others. That it was in his DNA.

The door opened fully, revealing the black maw of shadow within. Martin squinted, and after a brief moment, his eyes adjusted, and he saw...

Saw Corin sat hunched against a wall in the darkness, his arms bound behind his back. Short, dark hair had started to grow across his formerly clean-shaven scalp. His face looked drawn and haggard, as if he'd suffered through a series of sleepless, torturous nights. And, staring searingly out of the shadows, his eyes... his eyes were stricken by a savage doubt, as if he'd gazed inside himself, and what he'd seen had traumatised him to his soul.

Laura stood, entranced by the sight before her.

It was a balmy, deep blue night. Stars shone brightly in the sky. And below them, an enormous fleet of fairy lights hovered above the grass, one set wrapped around the roof of each tribdwell in Karthalia, their soft, solar-powered light dressing the buildings in haloes that seemed to be mounted upon plinths of darkness.

The effect was beautiful. Staring at them across the river, her arms resting on the wooden railings of the bridge, Laura felt calm but somewhat sad. She was thinking about her meeting with Corin...

Her visit to him had been brief. He'd barely spoken, like someone locked up inside their own head with no key to get out. But somehow, seeing how pitiful he'd become – and *feeling* his inner torment up close – she'd realised he wasn't worth her hatred.

Not that she didn't still want to hate him, but it didn't seem worth fighting Oceanos anymore. And so she'd decided, for the time being, to simply push Corin from her mind, her guilt over not loving Jak enough having surprisingly receded with it. It was as if her brain had accepted that her emotions were too complicated to deal with right now, and so, for the moment, had given up the struggle of trying.

In their wake, those emotions had left a feeling of melancholy, which the quiet, still darkness only magnified.

Beside her, Martin gazed down into the River Menignus as it flowed by beneath them. Fairy lights were also twined around the bridge's railings, their small orbs reflected in the blackness of the water like submerged suns. Occasionally, ripples would disturb this cosmos, but the shattered parts of it always reformed, blue fish with gleaming scales swimming through this alternate galaxy.

All was silent, save for the whispering of the water, and the faint chirping of distant crickets.

"It's a nice night," Martin said peacefully. And there was the hint of a smile on his face, like the Martin he'd been before the whole Oceanos thing began.

"Mm," Laura agreed. Then, taking a lingering glance back at the illuminated Karthalia, she said: "It's amazing how different it all feels, isn't it?"

"You mean with the new lights and arches and everything?"

"Yeah. I know it's not much, but... it's a *lot* of change to happen in a couple of weeks."

"Irok. I guess people are just keen to bury the old world... and get the memory of all that bloodshed out of their minds. Also, it's a kind of tribute to Jak, isn't it? All of this came from his notebooks."

He pointed at the fairy lights on the bridge's railing:

"Seems like he was obsessed with lighting. And stonework. But, for the life of me, I can't think why. He was always so... *practically minded.* But these things" – he gestured towards Karthalia, at all the ideas that had sprouted from Jak's notebooks – "they don't serve any practical purpose. It just, chgitem... doesn't seem like him."

Laura turned to look at Karthalia as well. Simply talking about Jak had evoked warm memories inside her, their heat driving away her melancholy. Again, she stared at the faraway fairy lights and, in her delicate growing happiness, thought she understood them.

"Ana mech m'akkade," she said hesitantly. "But the fairy lights... they make everything feel kind of magical, don't they? And the arches and the fountains, and all that other stuff, there's a... a kind of a pleasing intricacy in their design. Like sometimes, when I look at them, they put me into this more delicate, more beautiful frame of mind. Do you know what I mean? Maybe that's what he wanted. To make the environment so it makes people feel happier. De toute manière... that's how it sometimes feels to me."

Martin smiled at her: "Ouais. Sounds like the sort of loopy, ambitious thing he'd try."

Then he added: "And I'll tell you something else that's weird. It's not just the look of Karthalia that's been changed by Jak's ideas. It's also people's minds, their behaviour... all stemming from Oceanos, which is down to him. All of this, it's what *he* wanted. As if we're just... living inside his mind, with his ideas still reshaping the world."

"Yeah," Laura smiled, half in disbelief. She gazed at Karthalia with fresh eyes. "I've never thought of it like that."

She stared at those dark tribdwells with their haloes of light, and in the pitch-black passages between them, she pictured the flow of a spectral, blue-tinged force which, with its invisible limbs, was silently reconstructing the world. It was the force that had hung up the fairy lights. The force that had erected the monuments. It was the intangible energy of Jak's ideas, a part of his life-force still alive and active even after he himself had passed away.

Laura knew this visual figment probably had little connection with reality. Still, it comforted her, and felt meaningful. Made it feel as if, on some level, Jak was still with them.

And it wasn't the first time she'd had that feeling...

She didn't believe in spirits, or ghosts, or anything like that. But in her dreams, she'd imagined Jak as one, invisible and flying at a lofty, god-like height... surveying the sparkling sea... before plunging down, into Karthalia... returning home...

And at other times, when she was awake, he'd felt... *close...*

A shiver ran through her body.

"You cold?" Martin asked, looking confused. The night was still warm.

"Nope," Laura smiled, but her voice came out sounding unsettled. "Just a shiver."

Martin looked at her, half amused, as if he didn't quite believe her. Then he said: "Well, I better head back. Gotta be ready for the big day tomorrow."

Beyond Karthalia, Laura could sense the shifting of other societies and, faintly, even other continents. The people in those other societies didn't scare her anymore, like they used to, because Laura could now sense what they were like. They felt very similar to Karthalians. The main difference was that, compared to Karthalia's newborn and growing bliss, those places felt emotionally like they were covered in a drab, pitiful grey.

"I'll head back as well," Laura said.

But before she left, she gave that view of Karthalia from the bridge one last look, thinking how those continents of grey might soon be gone, and how tomorrow might be the start of that new era.

Sometimes, the memory of waking up into their new world still haunted her...

Shortly after collapsing onto her knees in the lilaxe smog, Laura had collapsed into unconsciousness. Then, opening her eyes, she'd seen – lying beside her – Leo's decaying, fly-ridden corpse. In the heat, it had only just begun to putrefy, so the wounds she'd inflicted were still visible: ugly yellow bruises that left his powerful arms swollen and misshapen; dried blood, smeared across his lips and one bearded cheek, which he'd hacked up as she'd kicked him in the stomach; and, of course, the gory flaccid hole of his stump, its circle of flesh crushed and crumpled against the earth from when she'd stamped down hard on it.

She'd never have believed she could do that to someone else. She'd always thought of herself as a sweet person, someone who avoided violence at any cost. But there he lay.

And yet, little guilt broke upon her. He would have bled to death from his stump, whether she'd attacked him or not. What she'd done hadn't changed the end result.

Nonetheless, it had meant that – at the dawn of the new Oceanic era – she'd woken to a world of death.

From there, the endless funerals had begun. Now, that dark prelude was almost at an end. It was time for the final ceremony...

A huge gathering of Karthalians stood in Devil's Orchard, arranged in a semi-circle; their heads bowed; their mournful grey clothes contrasting with the deep greens of the forest around them. Above, an optimistic white sunlight filtered down through the trees, through the air's fresh and earthy fragrance, before illuminating grass still wet from the thunderstorm that had erupted late last night.

The early morning silence felt somehow sacred, and as if it had grown heavier and more significant with the silence of the assembled Karthalians.

Laura stood at the front of the semi-circle and near its centre, her Mum beside her. Everyone was packed close together, and it made her feel uncomfortable, as if reality were pressing in upon her. But everyone wanted to see what was about to happen just ahead...

Before the crescent of people, Martin was knelt down on one knee, his head also bowed. It could easily have been Laura in that position, but she'd made sure she hadn't been asked.

All eyes were on him. Everyone who had survived the Battle – every living Karthalian – was there.

For the last few days, Laura had questioned how strong her love for her brother really was if she was unable to hate the man who had ordered his murder, and the guilt from that had tormented her. Now, that painful ache in her chest – made from all the grief and anguish of the past two-and-a-half weeks – was growing inside her again.

Then, emerging from the forest's vegetation, the urn was brought out.

Jak's gash-riddled body, lying on the floor of his study, flashed into her mind once more.

Looking at that urn, she thought about the hundreds of cremations that had taken place since the Battle. All those incinerating fires lighting up the day and night, as Karthalians tried to prevent the rotting vestiges of someone's loved one from spreading a disease that would kill them. As the flaming skin disintegrated, it had revealed the bones beneath. Some of those skeletons had been only thirteen years old...

A woman carried the urn. She stopped beside Martin, and there was a soft rustle as she laid it down upon the grass. Martin didn't move his head to look at it.

Laura remembered the tears that had been in his eyes when, speaking about his dad – while around them towers of smoke poured up into the sky – he'd said, "He's with my mum now."

The woman withdrew a small wooden capsule from her pocket, opened it, and dipped her finger inside. Then, using that finger, she traced a diadem of honey around Martin's forehead. His head remained bowed, but his eyes were now squeezed shut. And, in the shadows beneath them, Laura thought she saw a single tear slide down his face.

The woman picked up the urn and removed its lid. Then, with an air of careful ceremony, she started lightly sprinkling its contents over Martin's head. Like a miniature Khamsin wind, Jak's ashes tumbled through the air, some of it falling in the honey; some, at the edges of Martin's hair; and some, as it streamed downwards, seeming to disappear into thin air.

Like a shriek of vile music, the pain in Laura's chest grew sharper, that aching knot – which was like a clenched, impotent fist – becoming bigger and heavier.

In her mind's eye, she tried to retreat into the comfort of the emotionscape. Its familiar pattern of vibrant rainbow colours had mostly disappeared, replaced for the moment by large dark spots of grief – like the spots upon a ladybird's wings – and by the shining whiteness of pure hope and belief. And the white far outweighed the black.

But beneath both of these emotions, there lay a strong under-current of solemnity and respect. Laura let this sentiment flow into her. It solaced her to know, on a profound level, how much Jak meant to everyone. How special he really was.

All of these things helped, a bit. But a stronger force was rising up inside her...

As the woman scattered the ashes, she had begun to give a sombre and dignified speech, the words of which she'd clearly memorised. But, in her tense, overwrought state, Laura only caught bits of it:

"... myth that ancient kings of this land were cremated..."

"... sprinkled on the crown of honey, the ashes..."

"... as a way of passing wisdom down the generations..."

Laura scrunched up her eyes. She was *not* going to cry. Not here, in front of everyone.

An arm wrapped itself around her shoulders, and in a tender, protective embrace, Gemma pulled Laura close to her. Burrowed in the warmth of her Mum's body, Laura thought about how it was only the two of them now. Jak... her Dad... the whole male side of their family had been wiped out, their luminances ripped from the emotionscape. And it didn't matter how beautiful the emotionscape might look – it would never have them in it again...

The woman's voice died away. Her speech had ended. Martin rose to his feet. He hadn't been invested with power over anyone else, but it was official: he would guide Jak's vision to its ultimate fulfilment. The ceremony was over.

But for one person, that end had come too late...

Unable to bear any more pressure, the thunderclouds of Laura's grief had broken, their tears streaming down her cheeks. And as she sobbed, the whole world was reduced to the blackness behind her eyelids.

The ache in her chest had swollen, filled with a terrible, utterly adoring, desperately longing pain. Proof that she did love Jak completely. The only question was, how? How could she ever have doubted it? She never would again.

Everything else in her life – her ideas, her memories, her thoughts, her beliefs, the things she thought were facts... all of that could be wrong. The one thing in the whole universe she could *know*, without a shadow of a doubt, was what she felt at a particular moment. No one could tell her that wasn't true.

She loved him.

*

A small contingent of mourners had broken away from the main group. They were departing purposefully from the site of the ceremony, with everyone else following in their wake, their sandals treading across the wet morning grass.

Tears still in her eyes, Laura had a small, half-wincing smile on her face. The searing pain in her chest was pleasurable, almost joyful. It felt as if all the doubt and anxiety over her love for Jak – which had been building up inside her like the secret pressure that triggers earthquakes and tsunamis – was finally being released. An overwhelming sense of relief, and love, and almost a sense of salvation coursed through her, as if she'd been rescued at the last moment from her own condemnatory judgement of herself.

Not far behind her, Martin ambled slowly at the tail end of the group, the honey and ashes wiped clean off his forehead, his luminance the pale blue of deep inner contemplation.

Soon, the hundreds of mourners stepped through the last screen of vegetation, and out of Devil's Orchard. The light of the sunrise greeted Laura's eyes, gleaming off her olive skin, her blonde-streaked dark hair, and briefly making her squint.

The sky looked gorgeous: in the far distance, a herd of young white clouds roamed, serenading the day with their presence... while, due to the sunrise, the sky itself was draped in bands of radiant colour – each one shading almost imperceptibly into the next – as if a rainbow had been stretched out over the world.

Laura and the other Karthalians were now in an open stretch of grassland, just beyond Devil's Orchard, where, before them, a strasmag had been left waiting. Its twenty-five muscle-bound horses scuffed their hooves impatiently, while behind them, the large carriage – a three-dimensional mosaic of windows and rich, stained glass, with each tessellating pane the shape of a giant teardrop – shone calmly in the sunlight. Each teardrop depicted a glycon, a pictorial symbol of an individual tribe.

For a long time, these glycons, all of which were shown on every strasmag, had captured a truth – that the tribes of Karthalia were unified as one. Then the Schism had happened... Now, Laura was glad that those glycons, gathered together, told the truth once more.

Everyone strode over to the strasmag, but only the smaller contingent of mourners opened its door and began to board the vehicle. And as they entered, and as the light knocking noise of their footsteps against the strasmag's wooden base rang through the still, quiet air, Laura remembered the excitement that had rippled through Karthalia shortly after Jak's notes had been revealed...

The notes contained a scale of thinking that no one had expected. They talked about expanding Devil's Orchard, and so increasing the supply of lilaxes dramatically. They included designs for a new type of boat, heavier and more durable than the ones currently deployed by Karthalians, and which could be used to traverse the world and visit other continents. And they also featured eloquent speeches, written out in full, which were crafted to persuade foreign, wary societies – if they spoke a language similar to the Karthalians' – to try the lilaxe fumes for themselves.

The notes made everyone realise that, for Jak, Karthalia had been only the first step. His mission wouldn't be over until the mind of everyone on the planet had been elevated and united by Oceanos.

And from his notes, it was clear what his plan would have been: *start with the societies nearest Karthalia, and fan outwards from there...*

With a light bang, the door of the strasmag shut, the sound drawing Laura's mind back to the present. Inside the carriage, the volunteers who had offered to try to spread Oceanos to the populations nearest Karthalia were seating themselves for the journey ahead.

The driver took the reins. The horses snorted and stamped their feet in expectation. And Laura squeezed her way forward, through the densely packed throng of onlookers. Before the vehicle drove off, there was something she needed to see again...

She reached the front of the crowd, standing directly behind the strasmag. And on its rear side, facing her, was a new addition to the pantheon of glycons, fashioned from stained glass like the rest, but which didn't symbolise any individual tribe...

It showed Jak sitting cross-legged, back straight, his hands resting on his knees in a posture of meditation... his face seemingly lit up not by sunlight, but by a gentle, beatific smile. Before him, two perfectly cut planks of wood lay diagonally on top of each other (reminding Laura of the shorter wooden crosses used by puppeteers to manipulate their creations). From the four ends of these two overlapping planks, curving flames of stained glass rose up, glowing with the colour of rubies.

But this wasn't an ordinary fire – it was a fire of ideas. Wreaths of dark, vitreous smoke emanated from the blazes, filling up the space on either side of Jak's smiling face. And hovering in these wreaths were symbols of her brother's ideas: the purple and green of a single lilaxe; a sheet of paper, its script too tiny to be legible, so that it could simultaneously represent Jak's notes and the pamphlets that Laura had helped him to make; and a circle of radiant white light, a symbol of his vision for the world.

The fire of ideas was meant to show that Jak had illuminated a new era for the planet, igniting an evolutionary fire – the first sparks of which had begun in Karthalia – but whose flames would soon embrace the world. Laura couldn't help thinking that it was this same fire which had also ultimately devoured him.

The glycon was intended as both a tribute to Jak, and as a sort of good-luck charm for the strasmag and its passengers. *A bit of superstition,* Laura thought with tearful affection, *but a nice idea.*

Then, suddenly, the glycon of Jak started to recede... the strasmag pulling away, its wooden wheels grinding across the small stones and mostly dry mud of a long dirt path that stretched straight off into the distance.

The vehicle carried far less than its full capacity of passengers, to make room for all the food, water, and lilaxes that those Oceanic missionaries needed. Plus, there were no weapons weighing the strasmag down. That's because there would be no imperialistic imposing of Oceanos upon foreign communities. The emotionscape – its interconnectivity – had made that notion ridiculous and out of the question. Instead, they would simply offer Oceanos, presenting it to those unknown peoples in the best light that they could.

One of those grey memorial arches, the design of which had been extracted from Jak's notes, towered over the dirt path in the middle distance. The strasmag rolled towards it, and just before it passed into the archway's shadow – which began slightly inside the arch, and which leaned far out of the monument's opposite side – *just before reaching this,* the strasmag's right-hand wheels dipped, one after another, into a small hollow, splashing through a sort of rainbow puddle that reflected all the colours of the sunrise-painted sky.

While, far above – on the arch's underside – the black spray-painted names of many who had died in the Battle were incised into the stonework, looking down.

A second after the wheel and the splash, the surface of the puddle began to reform, becoming a still and flat mirror once again. But in the meantime, the ripples had ruffled its colours: whereas in the sky the chromas graduated from one to the next in relatively neat bands, in the puddle they had coalesced into a psychedelic swirl, the calm blue, optimistic green, furious red, passionate orange, and more, all mixing and mingling together like hues upon the palette of a frenzied and inspired artist.

And then, as the puddle began to settle, black-lettered names emerged into view, seeming to float on the surface of those psychedelic hues. As on the arch above, they were arranged in an orderly, curving manner. And each of those names belonged to someone who had once had all those colours of the emotion-scape, and more, living inside them. Whole worlds of emotion that were now gone.

Of course, Laura couldn't see that spectacle. It was too far away. Instead, she saw the strasmag slip through the shadow of the arch, before following the dirt path as it curled to the right. Now in the far distance, the vehicle travelled parallel to the horizon, heading across the stretch of land between the arch and a hillock... passing behind the hillock... then, seconds later, returning to view, cantering forward only to pause in front of the Wall.

A tiny chink in the grey appeared; and, pulled back thus, the Iron Gate dimly revealed the faint blue sky that lay beyond Karthalia's bounds.

For centuries, Karthalia had been a bubble society, closing off its borders to the rest of the world, its inhabitants turning their eyes inward, breeding an ignorance over the problems and potential of the rest of the planet. This even manifested in their language, where Karthalia came to be referred to as the 'World', as though all of existence that mattered was contained within its Wall.

But Oceanos had brought an end to that belief. Through empathy, it forced Karthalians to be aware of the wider world. And with their consciousnesses expanded, they could no longer block out or ignore the truth: the world was a long way from being the utopia that Karthalia had almost achieved. It needed help – help that they could provide.

Jak's mission wasn't over...

The strasmag rolled out through the open gateway, towards unknown societies. And with that action, the old idea of Karthalia as a single 'World' finally crumbled down. They were now living in a much vaster, more encompassing 'world' – and they were heading out to improve it.

THE END

Acknowledgements

The bit that's tedious for anyone whose name isn't included here.

Special thanks to these people for their assistance and support in the production of this book:

To my translators Jeannette Issa (Lebanese Arabic & French) and Nata Voskanyan (Armenian), who have both been almost faultlessly brilliant, quickly and kindly answering even my follow-up requests.

To my sedulous proofreaders Julia Margetts, Donna Bond, and Helen Fazal, whose valiant efforts have saved me from manifold blushes and nagging regrets.

To Georgina Aldridge at *Clays Indie Publishing*, for taking the time to explain to me – face-to-face – how you actually design and publish a book, and for always sending swift and courteous replies to my emails. They made things at my end a lot easier. And to Julie Woon and Mathieu Triay, without whom I probably wouldn't have found Georgina in the first place.

To Charlotte Bunce and Dave Swindells of SKB fame, for their advice on book design, and for supporting the novel in a variety of ways.

To Lawrence Hunt, for stepping up with his video-skills when I needed to get the word out there.

To Niámh Keenan and Alan Ashworth Muñoz, for their artistic camaraderie, as they selflessly lent their talents to help me crowd-fund this book.

To Greg Shipp, for his excellent maps of Karthalia, and for making our collaboration a pleasure.

To Joe Tabrizi, for his superb Splendour Publishing logo design, and for being a typographical hero at the eleventh hour.

To Jon Fazal, for his part in providing me with rent-free accommodation when I first came to London (which set me up with a financial cushion), and for subsequently helping me get a job in a bookshop. In unplanned fashion, both came in very handy during the novel's development.

To Chris Zacharia, for years of literary and life DMCs.

To mage and sage Alan Moore, for his advice after I nervously approached him at the Cheltenham Science Festival.

To China Miéville, for his invaluable guidance on how to plan a novel, which I'm sure saved the story from being condemned to a knotty limbo of interminable continuity problems.

To CtrlF. I couldn't have done it without you.

Deepest gratitude of all to John Bebbington, whose staggering and casual generosity – seven years on – I still find mind-blowing. Without him, this novel almost certainly wouldn't exist.

& lastly, to Mum, for everything. You're the best.

THE WONDERFUL PEOPLE WHO FUNDED THE DESIGN AND PRINTING OF THIS BOOK

Omar Al-Khayatt
Chris Bailey
Michelle La Belle
Jon Bennallick
Morwenna Bennallick
John Bentley
Simon Bentley
Sylvia Bentley
Rev. Terry Broomhall
Will Brown
Dr Chancellor
Ian Chung
Tom Clarke
Carole Clayton
Alex Connaughton
Alex Crosby
Gaby Docherty
Sonny Drake
Danny Drucker
Isaac Ehrlich
Dave Evans
Ryan Evans
Jon Fazal
Matt Fazal
The Fedashes
Jess Fowler

Helen Gad
Amy Geoghegan
Lisa Gill
Emma Goode
Marta Grabowska
Will Grave
David Greaves
James Greenwood
Chloe J Hall
Tom Hardaker
Mike Hatfield
Chris Hill
Katie Hill
James Hinks
Nick Holtom
Sam Holtom
Lawrence Hunt
Reece Jackson
Ben Jones
Tim Kirby
Katherine Leach
Kristian Lundager
Oliver Lyu
James Macgregor
Jamie Mackay
Phillip Maira

Julia Margetts
Rei Melbardis
Christiane Mellak
Anne Mintoff
John Mintoff
Janet Morgan
Emily Murdoch
Sarah Murphy
Maria Neidhold
Nadine Passley
Kayleigh Petrie
Rossella Di Pietro
Andrew Pitkeathly
Sara Pitkeathly
Vicci Porton
The Prada's (Chris & Paula)
Emporium Purgatorio
Katie Quinn
Oli Rahman
Sarah Ross
V Shadow
Dave Simmons
Michael Skazick
Francis Slingsby
Rhys Mancell Smith
Ann Spiller
Gail Spiller
Mike Spiller
Mina Mae Spiller
Phil Spiller
Terry Spiller
Joe Tabrizi

Armand Tamzarian
Cate Taylor
David Taylor
Adam Thompson
Katie Tyler
Michael Walkden
Yoshe Watson
Lizzie Whittington
Julie Woon
Jo Yeomans
Chris Zacharia